THE LANGLEY PROTOCOL

THE
LANGLEY
PROTOCOL

RAY CHRISTIE

For my wife Yuliana

*Sancte Michael Archangele, defende nos in
proelio, contra nequitiam et insidias
diaboli esto praesidium*

ONE
Washington, D.C.—USA

The officer observed a car approaching the exit. He checked the license plate, made a note, then flicked a switch that activated the security gate. Danny Mercer held up his pass, bearing a different name, and eased his blacked-out Cadillac Escalade out of the secure area and onto the George Washington Memorial Parkway. The officer watched as the gate clicked shut before removing a cell phone from his pocket.

Mercer checked the fuel gauge, flicked the interior light switch, making sure it was deactivated, then reclined his seat slightly. He shot a quick glimpse in the rearview mirror, then checked out his new ID. *Fucking bureaucrats.* Despite the longer hair, a fresh beard, deep blue eyes, and a few unhealed grazes on his face, the CIA had done a good job of making him look like an average middle-aged American.

He had returned from the mountain regions bordering Afghanistan and Pakistan, where he'd spent most of his time hunting high-value targets, conducting covert reconnaissance and leading precision raids on insurgent strongholds. Before that, it was intel gathering on arms smuggling in Eastern Europe, some VIP escorts, and training local forces in Africa and South America. His Delta Force background made him invaluable—a skill set now vital to the CIA's Special Operations Group (SOG).

The wind picked up, rain began to fall, and darkness crept in fast. Mercer checked his watch, his side mirror, and the rearview once again. He flicked on his blinker and moved into a gap, then looked ahead for the next one. Washington's evening traffic was a slow-moving line of cars, with drivers stuck in gridlock, but Mercer forced his way through the congestion. He kept scanning the vehicles behind him, part habit, part necessity. The city projected power, but Mercer saw the truth. It was a hunting ground, crawling with foreign intelligence agents.

His mind snapped back to the mission that went wrong. The explosion slammed into him, hurling him backward as fire ripped through the compound. Screams cut through the crackling flames. He staggered forward to reach the others, searing heat burning his throat. He fought to pull them free, but the thick smoke took them away, and he crawled out just as the building collapsed on his team.

That night left him with permanent scars. All operations after that were paused until the intelligence officers involved produced their reports detailing what went wrong. Mercer knew what went wrong. Outsourcing reconnaissance to their allies, locals, who had been infiltrated by the enemy. From now on, Mercer would run his own operations. Though mentally unstable, he was capable of producing results, the kind that the White House required to settle unsolvable problems.

Focus. He shoved the memories aside, letting his thoughts drift to better times—the adrenaline rush of jumping out of a plane at 30,000 feet, the cold bite of the wind at high altitude, high opening jumps. Those days were pure; it was just him, his brothers, and the mission. Now they were gone.

The CIA was supposed to be a war-fighting machine, not a bureaucratic swamp. Men who had rarely set foot in the field dictated policy, initiating missions produced by intelligence from an AI program he didn't understand. And worse, some played for the other side. Mercer wasn't naïve. He had more enemies inside Langley than outside it.

His boss in the Special Operations Group,

Jeff Connor, was a prime example of the type of careerist bureaucrat he despised. A former field operative, he'd traded in his boots for a desk and now seemed more interested in climbing the CIA ladder than getting his hands dirty. Connor was a pain in the ass, always pushing him to follow the procedures and fall in line, but Mercer had never been one to play by the rules. Recalling their first meeting three months ago, Connor said, '*Mercer, you need to learn to play the game. It's not just about being the best on the field anymore.*' He had little respect for him, and the feeling was mutual. The man was simply another bureaucrat playing his own game.

Mercer turned his focus back to the road. He reached down to a compartment under the seat and removed a SIG Sauer P365. The weight was solid, reassuring. He holstered it and checked the rearview mirror.

Suddenly, a Dodge Durango shot across lanes, tearing past Mercer's Escalade. The police cruiser, its lights flashing a blinding red and blue, and its sirens wailing, was in pursuit of another vehicle—a red sedan that began to weave erratically through traffic.

Mercer watched on with amusement. *Likely a drug dealer or a carjacker.* He flicked on the police scanner, hoping to listen in on the conversation between the cops and dispatch.

The cruiser passed the sedan on the inside, then braked hard, attempting to stop the sedan. The suspect accelerated and jerked on the steering, trying to go around. The cop reacted quickly and clipped the front of the sedan. The impact sent the sedan spinning across the freeway before slamming into another car.

Mercer swerved, narrowly dodging the scattered debris. His pulse remained steady, instincts overriding any need for panic. A normal driver would slow down, rubberneck. Mercer didn't. He flicked another glance at the rearview mirror, watching the wreckage fade behind him. Other cars pulled over, drivers already whipping out their phones. He switched off the police radio, uninterested.

He exhaled through his nose and reached for the glove compartment, pulling out a cigar. He'd been saving this one for after the meeting. The flame flickered in the dark interior as he lit it. He cracked the window open an inch to keep the smoke from building up. The rain hammered against the windshield as the cool, wet air seeped in.

Mercer took a slow drag, exhaling as the smoke was pulled out into the night. The tension in his muscles unwound slightly. The police chase had been an unexpected jolt but nothing worth dwelling on. Just another night in downtown D.C.

It had been a hell of a day in Langley. Answering questions about the failed operation, then being made to sit through outdated intelligence briefings. If that wasn't enough, the legal and technical training on the new software had almost tipped him over the edge.

With soft strains of jazz filling the cabin, his mind began to unwind, finally—until a movement in the rearview mirror caught his attention. An unmarked black sedan, five cars back. It had been there earlier, taking the off-ramp when he did, maintaining distance. Not amateurish, but not standard surveillance either. He killed the music.

His instincts screamed at him not to dismiss this anomaly. Mercer's mind raced, plotting and planning as he decided to divert from his original route, steering toward a known safe house. He wanted to check if this was real, then gain the upper hand. He threw the cigar out the window and grabbed his burner phone. His fingers tapped the phone's screen, dialing the last voice he wanted to hear tonight, Jeff Connor. Mercer's voice broke through the silence of the car.

'Is there a team out tonight, shadowing me?' he asked.

Connor's response crackled through the phone. 'Nothing happening in D.C. that I know of. Better to check with the ops desk.

Listen, I am walking into a meeting and can't talk. Speak to them, and I'll call you when I'm done here.'

'Don't worry about it. It's probably nothing.' Mercer cut the call short, sliding the phone back into his jacket pocket. If Connor was lying, it wouldn't be the first time. He was on his own, isolated and without backup from the hierarchy. Something he got used to when operating in Karachi or Kabul, but the rules were different on American soil. Despite the risks, it was his nature to strike first rather than allow the enemy to return another day.

Mercer's eyes never strayed far from the rearview mirror, watching as the black sedan maintained its distance. The urban landscape transformed around Mercer as he continued, buildings becoming denser, their polished facades giving way to cracked brickwork and graffiti tags covering the walls. The vehicle behind him closed in slightly—a sleek, black Audi with tinted windows. The driver maintained a discreet but noticeable distance. Mercer made a series of turns; if they kept coming after him, in his mind, they were a threat—and a threat meant only one thing.

As he drove into a narrow alleyway, he watched the Audi hesitate for just a split second before following behind. *Perfect. Keep coming, you bastards.* In this area, no one would be in a rush to call the police if they heard gunshots or screams.

Mercer pulled into the alley and waited. A hundred yards back, headlights flicked off.

Mercer killed the engine, his hand resting on the door handle. He allowed himself time to think. *Legally, this checks all the boxes of a threat. Fuck them.* He slipped out of the car to get a better view instead of peering through the wet glass.

He dropped between two trash cans. The stench was putrid, and rats darted out before scurrying off. Further down the alleyway, he could see the faint glimmer of a car door reflecting light as it opened slowly. Two men jumped out; their movements looked organized. The first man drew a handgun, his drills precise as he swept the area, scanning for threats. Then he darted away from the streetlights, disappearing behind a row of run-down houses. The other figure remained near the car, covering the alleyway before moving into a concealed position.

Mercer weighed his options before rushing out from behind the trash and backing up beside a beat-up old car that prostitutes used to shoot up in. He moved and closed the gap on the man with the firearm to get a clearer picture of the situation. The rain got heavier, muffling his steps.

About fifty yards away, the other man nipped

into the back of a house and eased back a weather-beaten board, which replaced the entrance where a door used to be. Mercer watched as the guy ducked inside the crack house.

Drug addicts inhabited the decrepit interior, resembling zombies lost in their drug-induced state. Gaunt figures, surrounded by dirty spoons and syringes, avoiding eye contact with others, their incoherent mumbling a harsh chant through the mold-covered rooms. The sickening stench of feces, urine, and rotten food hung heavy in the air.

The gunman coughed up some phlegm and spat it out. He listened for a moment, then flicked a button on a small flashlight attached to his Glock, the light casting a direct beam along the corridor. After a quick sweep of the corridor, he pressed on, moving deeper into the house.

He climbed the stairs to the second floor, the weapon paired with his line of sight. The boards creaked under his weight. Ignoring the annoying sound of prostitutes and punters panting and arguing in the distance, he reached the top and swept the area. Once he cleared the landing, he searched for a window with a clear line of sight on the street outside. The intelligence picture of his target was highly accurate. The CIA assassin, named Mercer, code name Wrench, would easily spot the surveillance team.

A pattern in Mercer's behavior was recognized; he would close in to identify those tracking him. Days or weeks later, Mercer was known to come after those involved. *Not tonight,* thought the armed man. His goal was to lure Mercer into a trap and kill him in cold blood. The payment was worth the risk. He moved quietly into a room and made his way to the window, which overlooked the back entrance. A shabby curtain hung loosely from the rail, just enough to provide him some cover as he peered down, watching for his prize. He switched off the light from his Glock and waited.

Mercer crept along the alleyway. Something didn't feel right. Several minutes had passed, and the man still hadn't reappeared. *If these men are feds, an assault team would already be in place. The streets would be locked down. They must be contractors. Hired by who?* He didn't want to miss an opportunity and let them slip through his hands, but he had other, more important plans for the night.

Mercer sneaked back to the car with his head low and climbed in behind the wheel. The engine sparked to life, and he made his way down the alley toward the main street. Killing targets in the U.S. was hard to justify; there was too much heat after every death. *It's their lucky day.* There would be repercussions for their act, and that time would come.

Up ahead, he noticed a garbage truck backing into the alley. *Way too early for collection.* He checked his watch to confirm. *This is what they were waiting on; it's the trap.* Mercer removed his Sig and tucked it between his seat and his thigh. He slammed on the brakes and did a quick turn, then raced back down the alley. As he got closer to the Audi, he increased his speed.

A shot rang out—his driver-side window exploded. Glass sprayed across his face. His body twisted sideways, the force almost yanking the wheel from his grip. Searing heat tore through his shoulder like a white-hot blade. His vision blurred for half a second. Through the pain, he heard more gunshots ringing out.

He gritted his teeth, forcing a deep breath. Warm blood soaked into his sleeve. He clenched his fist—he still had control. The round had missed the important bits.

He pushed down on the accelerator and tore out of the alley. The car zipped around the corner, clipping a parked car and sending shattered glass flying. Mercer skidded to a stop in front of the house from which the shot must have been taken. Anger surged through him, a relentless fire that fueled his desire for revenge. This anger was what his special forces instructors had warned him about countless times: the inability to control his rage.

As his breathing increased, Mercer quickly

assessed his flesh wound. There was no time for hesitation. He grabbed the documents and stuffed them securely inside his jacket. Exiting the car, he sprinted toward the crack house, his Sig leading the way.

With a forceful kick, Mercer burst through the front door, shattering its flimsy lock. The interior was illuminated by the glow of a single light bulb. The inhabitants, consumed by a mixture of fentanyl and heroin, barely registered his entrance.

One of them, who had yet to take his fix, lashed out with a syringe in blind panic. Mercer ducked, sidestepped, and fired a round into the man's stomach, dropping him. Mercer drove his boot down hard on the man's neck. A sickening crack of the collarbone finished the job.

Stepping over the body, Mercer charged up the rickety staircase. At the top, he noticed movement in the darkness. Then a hail of bullets ripped through the air. Rounds smashed through wood and shattered the plaster all around him.

Mercer crouched down and returned fire. Six rapid rounds echoed in the narrow hallway, followed by a moment of silence. He sprinted up the last steps and charged into the first room to his right. Inside the room, he found his target, a masked figure climbing out of the window. Mercer squeezed the trigger. The bullet struck the gunman on the hip; his legs buckled, causing him to stumble. Mercer fired again. The round hit the man in the side of the head.

Mercer's shoulder throbbed with pain, but he fought through it. He dragged the body into the center of the room and removed the man's weapon. His hands worked fast, searching for identification. A black leather flip wallet came into view. He flipped it open. Mercer stared at the ID in his hands. FBI. Not just some contract hitter. *Fuck. This changes things.*

Mercer raced around the room, setting it up as a firetrap, then he hurried downstairs and grabbed the junkie he had shot moments earlier. The man was half-conscious but still alive as Mercer dragged him up the stairs and left him near the dead FBI agent. He lifted the man's limp hand, pressing it against the gun to transfer prints. A quick smear of blood onto the pistol grip. Messy, chaotic, maybe believable. Then he angled the body, making sure the entry wound faced the right direction. On his way out, he dragged furniture into a heap in the center of the room. Flames licked at the edges as he torched everything within reach, feeding the blaze until it roared, swallowing the space behind him.

Mercer bolted from the crack house and threw himself into his car. The house burned behind him, smoke rising in a thick column against the night sky. Curtains twitched in neighboring windows, but no one came out to help.

The second gunman is around here somewhere. Mercer twisted the ignition, and the engine roared to life, tires biting into the asphalt.

I've screwed up—badly. 'Fuck,' he muttered, yanking the SIM card from his phone. He flicked his lighter and held the sim card over the flame before rolling down the window and tossing the card onto the road.

No loose ends. Mercer checked the rearview mirror, scanning for any trailing headlights. Nothing. Still, he gave it a second look—paranoia kept him alive.

Several blocks away, Mercer's mind jumped to what he needed to get. He had to be quick. His house was classified as a secure location, but he wasn't about to linger. Just grab the bag—the one with his travel documents—check the wound, change clothes, and get out.

He pressed down on the gas. This was a pit stop, nothing more.

The sooner I'm out of D.C., the better.

Mercer's jaw tightened, ears straining against the distant wail of sirens.

The house—where he'd put down two men— sat deep in one of D.C.'s forgotten corners, a place the government had long abandoned. Here, people kept their mouths shut. Nobody called the cops. Nobody wanted them. The only regular visitors were ambulances, weaving through the streets on their nightly rounds, picking up overdoses or reviving the half-dead.

Between calls, the paramedics killed time at the 24-hour McDonald's, nursing bad coffee and swapping stories with the few cops who bothered to show up.

Mercer had heard rumors of an internal power struggle within the Bureau—an unsanctioned task force operating out of a warehouse in Washington's outer suburbs, its true allegiance unknown. The official reason was flimsy: an 'off-the-books' counterintelligence probe into CIA operatives suspected of going rogue. But Mercer knew better. The Bureau didn't waste manpower on casual suspicions, and they sure as hell didn't send agents into crack houses alone. Something about his movements had triggered the wrong kind of interest. Maybe it was the intelligence he'd been gathering, or maybe someone inside Langley had flagged him as a threat. Either way, the men following him weren't just FBI. They were something else—watchdogs for a game being played far above his pay grade. And that made them dangerous.

As Mercer rounded the corner, he eased off the gas, matching the speed limit. Flashing lights approached. He was hoping to see an ambulance tearing past. Instead, it was the police. Mercer kept his eyes on the road, in front and behind, and drove on. No brake lights. *Good. Keep going, boys*, he thought before stepping on the gas once again.

A few minutes later, he pulled his car into the garage, the automatic door shutting behind him. He bolted from the car and hurried inside. Striping off his clothes, he quickly inspected his shoulder. *The round missed my bone.* He grabbed an antiseptic, doused the wound, then slid a syringe into a vial of Cefazolin. After drawing the liquid, he injected it straight into the muscle. Next came a tetanus shot. He slapped on a bandage, swallowed a couple of acetaminophen and ciprofloxacin pills, then got dressed.

Mercer shoved the couch aside, then dragged a thick rug with it, revealing a safe crudely built into the floorboards. He unlocked it, chucked in his new CIA pass, and pulled out a passport, identity documents, credit cards under the same name, and a wad of cash. Last came a couple of burner phones and SIM cards.

Changing swiftly, he headed to the garage and fired up his motorbike, letting the engine warm. On a shelf, three pre-packed bug-out bags sat ready—each tailored for a different escape. One held cold-weather gear. Another, formal attire for cities like London or New York. The third, packed for the tropics.

Mercer grabbed the third one, slung it over his back, adjusted the straps, and pulled on a helmet and gloves.

He carved through the back roads on his black Suzuki Hayabusa before merging onto the Dulles Access Road. Minutes later, Mercer pulled into the parking lot on Saarinen Circle, near the main terminal.

He swung off the bike, yanked off his helmet, and instinctively patted his jacket—checking for the documents. Satisfied, he secured the bike, but his mind drifted. *The FBI agent. Dead. I shot him in the neck. Then burned him to death in a crack house.*

Mercer hoped the FBI would spin a story about a junkie killing their agent during a routine investigation gone wrong. They needed a cover for the media while their bosses scrambled to figure out the truth. A leak about corrupt FBI agents would be a disaster, too much for Washington to manage in an election year.

Were they up to something? Corrupt bastards. Mercer pictured the war room, the ones leading the investigation scrambling to contain the fallout, figuring out how to bury this before it spiraled out of control. *Connor would have given me a heads-up.* The doubt was creeping in.

There was nothing he could do about the deaths, or at least nothing he should do. It wasn't his problem anymore. He pushed the thought aside and rubbed his shoulder, working some life back into it before checking once more for any leakage. Satisfied, he strode toward the departure terminal with quiet authority.

A new passport. A fresh name. His past scrubbed clean, at least on paper. By the time the Bureau pieced together their version of events, Mercer would be someone else, somewhere else.

He adjusted the strap of his bag and stepped inside.

TWO

Four men sat around a heavy mahogany table. An unopened humidor full of Cuban cigars sat next to several bottles of expensive whiskey, while a pile of documents was neatly stacked in the middle. In bookcases that smelled of aged paper and tanned leather, old classics stood shoulder to shoulder with volumes on modern warfare, economic strategy, and the craft of clandestine operations. The men's custom-made leather shoes sank deep into the thick rugs beneath them while an antique grandfather clock ticked irritatingly. A map of the world hung at the back of the large room; a number of pins were inserted in various locations around the world.

No one spoke while they waited for the Director. The mood was not caused by the horrendous rain lashing the panes of glass on the Georgian-style windows, nor was it due to the urgent text messages they all received a couple of hours ago demanding their attendance at the old mansion on the banks of the Potomac River.

The tension was caused by a screw-up. Someone, someone possibly in the room, spoke to the wrong person. Tonight was the first time classified information made its way to the other side, from the CIA, directly or indirectly, to the FBI. For the men controlling the strings within the U.S. government, there was no way possible for that to happen. The FBI, the *other team, the unwashed,* as the Director often referred to them in close quarters, had access to something the men all worked hard to conceal.

As the men avoided eye contact, they were sure that the Director and the owner of the mansion, Georg Wilhelm Schelling, would not do anything rash. Not until a thorough investigation had been completed. Which would involve each of the agencies, the CIA, FBI, NSA and the ODNI. The depth that Schelling and the Black Orchestra had reached within the United States intelligence agencies was unprecedented, and it was Schelling who, at the top of the clandestine organization, was responsible for their success. Despite their mild confidence, the Director wouldn't act' recklessly; their minds were racing at the possibility their identities would be linked to the greatest scandal in the history of the United States.

Charles Clark shifted uncomfortably in his chair, his gaze darting around the room. The ticking of the grandfather clock grated on his nerves. As a shipping magnate, he was accustomed to control and precision, but here, in this opulent room, he felt out of his element. The weight of the situation was not lost on him; a leak from the CIA to the FBI was catastrophic. Clark's mind raced, pondering the consequences, fearing for the empire he had built. He twisted his large frame around in his chair to observe the clock, mumbling incoherently to himself before sitting back and letting out a sigh from the effort.

To his right sat a thin man, rigid and pale, wearing an immaculate black suit and a neat gold ring encasing a single diamond. A pair of thin gold-framed glasses perched loosely on his pointed nose. Thin black hair with flecks of gray was receding badly, normal for a man in his mid-fifties.

In contrast to Clark, John Elder sat still, his expression unreadable. The attorney was an expert at concealing his thoughts, his mind working like a chess player's, calculating moves and countermoves. His clients were mostly from New York or Washington, D.C. Those who could afford him were themselves high-powered, influential individuals. With such deep access to his client's inner secrets, business dealings, and alleged crimes, Elder had built up over the years dirt on the most powerful men and women the country had ever witnessed.

He sat perfectly silent and looked composed despite his mind calculating at high speed the number of people in his world who would pay millions of dollars to frame him and put him out of business. He made a lot of enemies over the years, yet he had also built up a huge list of friends. Mostly corrupt government officials, mafiosos, and foreign investors who were subjected to U.S. sanctions. He really did have a mixed bag of people in his circle. This was one reason for being part of the Black Orchestra: insurance. If he was going to be brought down someday by the highest court in the land, Elder knew that he needed so much power and so many dirty secrets that the risk of exposure to the public would be counterproductive. Therefore, he, like the three others in the room, all had their reasons to put their power together to become an indestructible force.

Together, the men had been sitting for thirty minutes. The Director always made people wait for him. It was the power that he had over them all that made it possible. As the minute hand completed its rotation, the grandfather chimed three times.

'Three O'clock in the bloody morning.' The third man spoke quietly, showing his discomfort at the situation unfolding. Kenneth Decker turned to face the men across the table from him. His weather-beaten face made him look much older than fifty-two, thirty of which was spent serving his country. First in special operations as an officer, a stint at Langley before moving into the Office of the DNI. The time of the morning didn't really bother him. The reason he was anxious was due to a lack of intelligence at his fingertips. When a law enforcement agent has been murdered by a suspected terrorist, he would be in a war room, all intel would be available, and his support staff would be collecting further information from the agencies based on his demands.

Decker's role in such critical situations was to rapidly assimilate and analyze data, drawing on the vast intelligence network spanning domestic and international sources. He hated being out of the loop, especially if it concerned something as significant as a high-risk tactic poised to change global affairs forever. Decker knew that coordination and dissemination of intelligence were crucial, particularly in the first critical hours following an incident.

The Directorate of Strategic Operational Planning would soon spring into action, formulating strategies and coordinating the national counterterrorism response. Decker was aware that the response to this incident would involve multiple agencies and departments. The FBI would likely lead the domestic investigation, supported by intelligence from the NCTC, CIA, NSA, and other members of the intelligence community. Abroad, the CIA and U.S. military forces might be called upon for operations against foreign elements of the terrorist network. This is what gave Decker the shits, sitting here in a holding pattern impatiently waiting for the Director to get his ass behind the table, while just across town, agents were actively chasing down leads on the very network in question. He should be in the thick of it, ensuring that none of the Black Orchestra's machinations were caught in the crossfire of the investigations.

'How much longer are we meant to sit here with our thumbs up our asses? There is a shitload of work to do out there.' Decker's patience had reached its limit. A man driven by action, he found it unbearable to be sidelined while a terror network operated on U.S. soil, potentially entangling his clandestine endeavors. Rising abruptly, he moved toward the humidor.

'Pass me one, young man. It's never too early for a Cuban,' Senator Rick Sanderson said. He had been dozing on and off for the past twenty minutes, unaccustomed to being awake at this hour unless it involved lines of cocaine and high-class escorts in his favorite private men's club. The Senator had good reason to be sitting around this table as part of the Black Orchestra. He was instrumental in bringing in new talent. The politicians, lobbyists, or business owners who were corruptible or in a valuable position of power made them a natural target of his. And Sanderson had perfected the art of entrapment. Usually, it involved attractive women in a hotel and a covert surveillance camera, or documenting the transfer of federal contracting information used for insider trading.

Sanderson was a prominent investor within the military-industrial complex and artificial intelligence start-up companies. It was crucial to keep in close contact with individuals who knew where the government planned to allocate contracts worth millions of dollars. The Black Orchestra, bolstered by revenues from their shell companies, held a powerful position to bankroll a large team of specialists both in the U.S. and in Europe to protect their interests. This gave the men a sense of bravado, protection from all angles.

Although Sanderson knew his place in the group and felt shielded, he appeared almost detached from the gravity of the situation. His mind wandered, not fully grasping the potential fallout of the leak. Used to the political games of Washington, he underestimated the seriousness of their predicament. His thoughts drifted to his usual distractions, power plays, and personal indulgences. Sanderson's involvement in the Black Orchestra was driven more by financial gains and power than true loyalty or comprehension of the covert world he had entered.

In the brief lull before the meeting commenced, Charles Clark's mind veered back to darker days, the foundation of his hardened persona. He recalled the stormy night on a remote Indonesian dock, where his first true test of ruthlessness had taken place. As a young entrepreneur, he'd found himself working with a local crime syndicate—a necessary evil to protect his burgeoning shipping enterprise. That night, under a relentless downpour, he'd made a decision that altered his path forever. Facing a betrayal that threatened to unravel his business, Charles had coldly orchestrated a decisive, brutal retaliation. It was the moment he realized that true power came from not just controlling the physical flow of goods but from manipulating human greed and fear. His actions that night had sent a clear message, cementing his untouchable status in the underworld of international trade. Ever since then, he formulated the idea that Indonesia was a perfect testing ground for new recruits to prove their value to the organization.

Those formative experiences had shaped Charles into the man who now sat in the opulent room, far removed from those lawless docks yet still playing a high-stakes game. His entry into the Black Orchestra wasn't just about business expansion; it was a natural progression of his insatiable hunger for power and control. The Black Orchestra provided a broader stage, a more complex game where global dominance was the prize. Charles's steely gaze reflected a mind well-versed in the art of treachery and intrigue, his ruthless nature concealed behind the facade of a successful businessman. This meeting was just another step toward a world shaped by his design.

The heavy doors of the room swung open with a creak, drawing all eyes toward the entrance. Georg Wilhelm Schelling, the Director of the Black Orchestra, stepped into the room, his presence commanding immediate attention. The air seemed to shift, the stress that had been simmering now underscored by a deep sense of respect and anticipation.

Schelling was a man of imposing stature with sharp, calculating eyes that missed nothing. His hair, silver and meticulously groomed, complemented the deep lines etched on his face, each one telling a story of the many battles—both literal and figurative—he had fought and won. His suit, tailored to perfection, spoke of power and an unwavering confidence in his own authority.

As Schelling walked toward the table, the four men stood up almost in unison, a reflexive show of respect for the man who not only led them but had also masterminded the complex network of intelligence and influence that they were all a part of. One by one, they extended their hands, each handshake firm, a silent testament to the dangerous alliance they shared.

Schelling nodded curtly to each man, measuring their expressions as if deciphering thoughts and gauging loyalties with a mere look. When he reached the head of the table, he didn't sit immediately. He waited until the room was quiet and for the men to stop fidgeting.

'Gentlemen, thank you for coming here on short notice. We have a situation that needs our immediate attention.' With that, he took his seat at the head of the table, signaling the others to do the same. The mood in the room shifted from tense anticipation to focused attention, each man preparing to delve into the heart of the crisis that had brought them together in the early hours of the morning.

As the men settled back into the soft leather chairs, Schelling skimmed his eyes over his notepad, flicking through the pages before setting it to one side.

'I've just had a call from a friend inside the CIA. It was one of their operatives, not a terror network, who shot the FBI agent.'

Charles Clark's brow furrowed. 'Why the hell was the FBI tailing a CIA agent?' he demanded, confusion evident in his tone.

Schelling studied Clark for a moment before answering. 'It was anticipated. They were after the documents I requested. Now the CIA has a lead to follow. This might slam some doors on us, so we need to be careful.'

Kenneth Decker's posture tightened, his face flushed with anger. 'Those sons of bitches! What kind of amateurs were used? Were these guys combat experienced? Think about this: we need to pull in our assets and find out who knows what within both the CIA and FBI, and settle this mess before someone drags our names into it.'

Sanderson, who had been swirling his whiskey in contemplation, cursed under his breath before speaking. 'Disastrous. We can't have people on our payroll so incompetent.'

John Elder, who had been silent, adjusted his glasses. 'Legally speaking, what are our options? We can't just sweep this under the rug. It could lead to an internal war between agencies.'

Schelling nodded, acknowledging Elder's concern. 'We need to be strategic and precise. Our first step is to safeguard this investigation and contain any press attention. We can't allow this to become political.'

The men nodded in agreement, each lost in

thought about the personal stakes involved. Clark worried about his shipping empire, entwined with the covert operations that could now face exposure. Elder considered the legal ramifications, his mind racing through possible scenarios to protect their clandestine group. Decker was already considering tactical responses to neutralize the threat. Sanderson, though appearing nonchalant, knew his political career hung in the balance.

Schelling cleared his throat before continuing. 'Our priority is identifying who's leading this investigation. The pressure on government heads will be immense. Even with media misdirection, certain factions won't let this be resolved quietly. Don't limit your inquiries to our investigative bodies here; we need to look at their partner agencies overseas. I need all of you to get hold of your trusted assets, offer them a decent sum if they front up with the following.' Schelling opened his notepad. 'We need to know every suspect, every lead they're pursuing. Track witness statements, their sources. Uncover any linked investigations and what's driving them.'

He turned a page. 'Secure all reports, surveillance data, evidence. As this unfolds, I want copies of subpoenas, search warrants, FISA applications. Monitor for any revival of COINTELPRO-style operations. Watch for whistleblowers, leaks in our network. Track unusual financial investigations, foreign intelligence interest. Keep tabs on congressional inquiries, oversight committees, any special task forces forming, as this investigation may spread further. We need to be tracking everything.'

He snapped the notepad shut. 'And remember, leave no digital traces. We need to stay ahead of this at all costs. Now, before you go, I want to address John's point about potential inter-agency conflict. If we can exploit the friction between the FBI, CIA, and others, it could expose their vulnerabilities. I'll explore this further and let you know how it develops.'

He glanced at his notepad briefly, then moved his attention back to the men. 'Those instructions were quite tardy; however, I trust you all know what to do within your capabilities. Gentlemen, it's early, and many senior investigators will be arriving at their desks in a few hours. You need to be ready.' With no further words, Schelling got up and left the room.

Elder removed his glasses and rubbed the lenses with a soft cloth, watching the others finish off their drinks. He made a mental note to clear his diary for the next few days. As he pocketed the cloth, he wondered which of his influential clients would be the first to break under pressure.

THREE

Bangkok—Thailand

anny Mercer's trip to Bangkok began with a pre-dawn flight from Dulles International Airport. He boarded a Qatar Airways flight, the quickest one-way ticket to the other side of the world. The flight, a lengthy seventeen hours with a brief stopover in Doha, provided Mercer with ample time to read through the documents before handing them to a CIA colleague. He took time to consider the implications of these new protocols from Langley. A world of possibilities opened up with these developments in technology. Advancements that made his job tougher and required delicate adjustments to eliminate threats. Modifications never interested Mercer. He preferred the bullet or the bomb.

Although sleep eluded him, he managed to drift off for a minute or two. Every time he closed his eyes, flashes of the previous night's screw-up haunted him. His shoulder, bandaged but still throbbing from the gunshot wound, served as a constant reminder of the threats and violence he was part of. All he could do was swallow a couple more pills and avoid the coffee.

Landing in Bangkok's bustling Suvarnabhumi Airport, Mercer felt the humid air cling to his skin as he made his way through arrivals. He flagged down a taxi, and within minutes, the city's vibrant colors and sounds blurred past him as he headed downtown. His mind buzzed with thoughts, but the training and objective kept him sharp.

In a move to cover his tracks, Mercer booked three different hotels under three different aliases. He knew the importance of staying off the grid, especially with the suspicion that he could be under surveillance.

Once he checked into his room, he grabbed a quick shower, then set about organizing the essentials for his journey north. The burner phone, which was charging on the bedside table, began buzzing. He checked the screen before answering. Jeff Connor, his boss. 'Mercer, about last night's call. Is everything alright?'

Mercer's gut told him they knew he was the one who shot the FBI agent. 'All good, just a minor hiccup,' he replied. Connor fished for details, as usual, but Mercer deflected the conversation.

After the call, Mercer headed out from the more expensive hotel that he booked to meet with a CIA contact in an alleyway behind a Thai karaoke bar, which doubled as a brothel.

The alleyway behind it was a stark contrast to Bangkok's opulent tourist areas. It was a narrow, dimly lit corridor sandwiched between aging buildings, their paint peeling off in large, untidy swathes. The pungent aroma of onions, garlic, and chilies wafted from the kitchen windows above, mingling with the less appetizing odors of decay and refuse.

Mercer tried to avoid the puddles as he walked down the alley. The noise of the city faded, muffled by the buildings on both sides. A man dressed in a cook's uniform opened a door and tipped out a pan of dirty water; he shot a glance at Mercer, dropped his head, and backed inside, slamming the door behind him. The alley came with its own localized noise, the constant shouts in Thai from windows higher up, the distant horns from taxis and tuk-tuks, and the persistent calls of street vendors trying to lure customers to their stalls. A homeless man shuffled through the trash cans, his movements slow and purposeful, while squealing rats scurried along the open drains.

Mercer's back grazed the alley's coarse wall, his pupils dilating in the dim light. A feline shape darted past, barely visible in the gloom.

He surveyed both ends of the narrow passage, his ears prickling for the rumble of an engine. Without warning, his contact appeared at his side. No footsteps, no rustle of clothing—just a presence where moments before there had been empty space. The man's sudden appearance spoke volumes about his field experience.

He was average height, lean, with eyes that were constantly moving, taking in every detail. He wasn't a field officer nor a trigger-puller. He was logistics—a fixer from the CIA's Directorate of Support, the kind of man who made sure assets had weapons, transport, and clean identities before disappearing into the background. They exchanged only a password phrase, then silence; the mission parameters required absolute professionalism.

The handover was swift. Each man looked over the other's shoulder as they conducted their business. The bag was exchanged quickly, as were the documents that Mercer handed to the contact.

When he turned to leave, Mercer's eyes caught a brief glimmer of something metallic in the shadows. His hand instinctively went to the concealed 9mm, but the moment passed, false alarm. He was glad to get rid of the paperwork. Encrypted messages worked best, but when it came to physical items, it was usual for them to be carried in diplomatic pouches. Not these ones; the CIA wanted to bypass the normal procedures, and Mercer didn't ask questions.

He left the alleyway with a renewed sense of urgency. With the handover complete, there was still a constant reminder of the dangers of working in Bangkok, and tomorrow's challenge loomed—the delicate task of moving across the northern border from Chiang Rai state into Myanmar. The mission was a black operation. No CIA assets, no backup. Once inside Myanmar, the agency would turn their backs on him. Right now, all he needed was a long, hot shower and to clean and dress his wound.

The smoky aroma of sizzling street food drifted through the humid air and cut through the smog. Pad Thai, grilled fish—his stomach tightened at the thought. He stopped at a stall, exchanging cash for a quick meal, then grabbed a handful of beers and a pack of cigarettes before heading out. Useful currency for the road ahead.

As Mercer made his way back to the hotel, the feeling of being watched gnawed at him. When he neared the second hotel he'd booked, he spotted two Chinese men with close-cropped hair and earpieces. These weren't ordinary tourists—they were trained operatives, and they were tailing him. Their movements subtle—but not subtle enough.

Without breaking stride, he walked directly

to the entrance and didn't look back. Once inside, he made a beeline through the hotel lobby and straight into the restaurant. He slipped into the kitchen and out the emergency exit into the alleyway, circling back toward the front of the hotel.

From his vantage point, standing in a darkened doorway, Mercer watched as one of the men argued with the reception staff, his frustration boiling over as he snatched a book from the guest register and scanned the names. Their rigid posture, controlled movements—everything about them screamed military. They weren't just looking for someone. They were looking for him. Mercer backed away, then moved along with the crowd, keeping to the busy streets with his head down until he reached the end of the block. 'Welcome to Bangkok,' he muttered. 'The third hotel it is.'

The next morning came fast. Mercer had been up most of the night tending to his shoulder, working out his route on a map, and preparing his equipment. A car was to be parked at the edge of the city. That way, he could be sure to lose any followers by utilizing several cabs. The time was just before six, and he could hear someone on the balcony opposite him hacking up their lungs and spitting. The occupants of the hotel room on the level above had woken, and the sounds of a local news program on their television were blaring. Down on the street, the tuk-tuk drivers were revving their engines while the hotel's staff for the morning shift arrived and began smoking cigarettes in the street below.

Mercer waited impatiently for breakfast to be delivered to his room. He ordered double of everything from the limited menu. What he couldn't eat would be taken with him, as he wasn't sure when he would have time to stop and eat again. He peered out the window from behind the thin curtains at the street below. He watched the patterns of movement, looking for something that didn't fit. Mercer's strength was his attention to detail. His life depended on it. Everything down in the busy street below had to be assessed.

The city contained specialist gunmen, men who navigated and operated on behalf of the gray areas of politics. Hired by those in power who could afford to execute him, no different from Washington or Berlin. All cities have assassins bought and paid for, standing by, waiting for the order. That is something Mercer knew more about than many others. As he was, and still is, an assassin.

The journey by cabs to the north of Bangkok went smoothly, the normal hectic chaos found in any Asian city complete with the high humidity and a complete disregard for road rules. Mercer was dropped off a few blocks from the Thammasat University Rangsit Campus, and from there he walked to the parking lot adjoining the Faculty of Science and education building where an old silver Honda Civic was parked.

Mercer checked the car over before starting it up and making his way north toward Thailand-Myanmar border. A full twelve-hour drive of over five hundred miles. Tachileik was circled neatly on his map with a red biro. The first destination where he could change vehicles before pushing on toward Mong La.

Mong La—Myanmar

Danny Mercer's first steps into Mong La felt like stepping into an alternate reality. The town, a notorious 5,000-square-kilometer fiefdom in the Golden Triangle, seemed to operate under its own set of rules, where lawlessness and opulence coexisted in a perverse balance.

As Mercer walked along the red-light district, he couldn't help but be struck by the surreal contrast of the town's blatant sex industries against the backdrop of everyday life. Garish hotels, seedy gambling halls, and nightclubs lined the streets, their gaudy neon signs illuminating the night in a mixture of colors. Further out, flashy casinos, catering to the throngs of Chinese visitors, stood as monuments to excess and vice.

Everywhere Mercer looked, signs of Mong La's decadence and corruption were evident. The town operated almost entirely in Mandarin, a testament to its Chinese influence. The currency, phone networks, and even the clocks were set to Beijing time, underscoring the town's detachment from Myanmar's control.

As he navigated through the bustling streets, Mercer noticed the omnipresent soldiers, garbed in green uniforms and armed with AK-47 assault rifles. They were the private police force of Lin Mingxian, the region's leader and a notorious drug trafficker, maintaining an appearance of order in this unruly enclave.

Mong La's economic power was highlighted on the roads. Luxury vehicles like Range Rovers, BMWs, and G-Wagons, rarities in much of Myanmar, were commonplace here, reflecting the newfound fortunes fueled by the influx of Chinese money. The construction boom, with hotels and apartments rising hastily, hinted at a town rapidly transforming under foreign influence.

Beneath this veneer of prosperity lay a darker truth. As Mercer delved deeper into the heart of Mong La, the seedy underbelly of the town revealed itself. Prostitutes, some alarmingly young, were openly advertised, and gambling was directed at all levels of society, with locals and Chinese alike pouring their fortunes hoping to catch a win.

The town's descent into vice was most apparent in its rampant wildlife trafficking. Restaurants and shops brazenly displayed exotic animals and their parts. Tigers soaked in baijiu for virility, pangolins curled up in death, ivory ornaments, and tiger skins laid bare the grim reality of Mong La's trade in endangered species. Smuggling routes for drugs, human trafficking, and endangered animals intersected here, with the lawlessness providing a safe haven for such operations.

The central Burmese government's absence had allowed Mong La to flourish in criminal enterprises, but China's expanding crackdown on cross-border cybercrime and trafficking syndicates was reshaping the landscape. Beijing's efforts had gained momentum, with authorities charging suspects with serious crimes, including murder and telecoms fraud.

China's involvement extended beyond law enforcement to diplomatic interventions, as Chinese officials facilitated meetings between the Myanmar regime and ethnic armed organizations. While this approach aimed to curb support for opposition forces, it also demonstrated China's commitment to stabilizing the border regions. The recent fall of mafia families in

Laukkaing, accelerated by China-backed insurgent attacks, further illustrated Beijing's resolve to dismantle entrenched criminal networks along its border with Myanmar.

Despite China's efforts, drug manufacturing continued, organized and protected by corrupt members of the military in both countries. The ethnic groups carrying out much of the illicit work were trained, funded, and manipulated by powerful figures within the hierarchy.

The CIA mission in Mong La was twofold: gather intelligence and assess the feasibility of a false flag operation. Though time was short. Mercer had only hours left to position himself, get what he needed, and get out. Otherwise, his continued presence would raise suspicion.

Mercer closed the door and checked his watch before stepping out into the dark streets once again. The journey to gather intel led him along the rugged Mong Lah Road. His target destination: a new industrial complex, strategically located less than three hundred meters from the Myanmar-China border.

The journey was arduous, taking Mercer through a dense jungle that clung to a small mountain range. As he trekked, mosquitos swarmed around him, and leeches found their way onto his skin, making the journey as much a battle against nature as it was against the elements of his mission. After a couple of hours in the dark, he reached his vantage point, southeast of the majestic Dwenagara Golden Pagoda. It was a spot carefully chosen for its clear line of sight to the industrial complex.

Exhausted but focused, Mercer wiped the sweat from his brow and settled into position. He pulled out his binoculars, the lenses sweeping across the landscape to the bright lights of the complex below. A newly paved road snaked its way from the complex across the border. It led toward the Daluo Port and the Agricultural Bank of China, a symbol of the growing economic ties between the regions. The road was an impressive feat, cutting through the rugged terrain to connect Mong La to the wider economic network of Southwest China.

The buildings operated all night long, twenty-four hours, seven days a week. Mercer thought about a meeting he had in Washington, D.C. a few weeks ago with the Drug Enforcement Administration. They produced a series of satellite photos showing many new buildings built over the past two years. A set of mugshots had been pinned to the office wall. Many of those men had already been arrested, only to be quickly replaced with fresh faces, possibly those now organizing the production and transportation of methamphetamine. Business was definitely booming in this part of town, and there was no shortage of workers.

He checked his watch once again and resumed his surveillance in complete silence, observing the night crew moving around below him, carting boxes from one warehouse and loading them into trucks. Other men with clipboards walked around barking orders while soldiers maintained security on the guard posts. With a sweaty hand, he wiped a black ant off his face before adjusting the dial on his binoculars. The industrial complex came into sharp focus. The place was a stark contrast to the surrounding wilderness, with its modern architecture, high-tech security cameras, and well-maintained facilities.

As the clock ticked past, the sun finally appeared on the horizon. *It won't be long now,* Mercer thought. Just then, he could see commotion out the front of the main warehouse. His eyes narrowed as he observed three black cars arriving quickly. They pulled up in front of the warehouse and were immediately met by the man with the clipboard. Three men emerged from the vehicles in suits, surrounded by their bodyguards armed with QTS-11 assault rifles, looking conspicuously out of place in this remote setting. Heavily armed Myanmar soldiers appeared from various buildings and took up positions along the outer fence lines, a clear sign of the importance of their visit.

Amidst the group of suited men, Mercer's

attention was drawn to one individual in particular—a Caucasian man who stood out in the crowd. He was engaged in what seemed like an animated discussion with his Chinese counterparts. The man looked vaguely familiar to Mercer, but the distance and the limitations of his binoculars made it impossible to confirm his identity.

Mercer watched intently, his mind racing with questions. *Who's this guy?* And more importantly, *how does he fit into Black Orchestra's operation?* As Mercer continued his surveillance, he took detailed notes on the pattern of life, capturing every movement, every interaction. The presence of heavily armed soldiers was a clear sign that whatever was happening at the complex was of significant importance.

The men disappeared into the building. Mercer scanned nearby roads, buildings, and the bordering Chinese hillside for counter-surveillance teams. There was nothing. When the men returned twenty minutes later and got into their cars, Mercer watched their every move. The short drive meant they crossed the border back to Daluozhen within a couple of minutes, their business completed.

Mercer was stuck in position; he couldn't move during the day. Reports of a white man emerging from the jungle onto the road would cause suspicion. The day was long and hot before the sun set, casting long shadows across the valley. The observations had been invaluable. He now had a clearer picture of the operations in Mong La and a new lead to follow—the Caucasian among the Chinese officials. In time, he would establish how to sabotage the operation, to cause distrust between the groups, which, hopefully, would lead to a war between them. All without both sides knowing the U.S. was involved.

As night fell, Mercer retreated from his position, disappearing back into the jungle. The methamphetamine trade he had spotted was not just a local scourge but a key part of the global drug trade. Despite having clear satellite reconnaissance images, it was important to get eyes on intelligence at the ground level. Now he had the knowledge of the area to prepare and launch his own attack.

Mercer moved slowly through the vegetation, trying not to leave a telltale sign of broken branches and flattened plants. Suddenly, he had a feeling he wasn't alone. He stopped for a moment to listen. Then he moved off, taking an indirect route, doubling back at intervals, eyes scanning the dense undergrowth for any sign of his pursuer. The silence in the jungle was occasionally broken by the distant crackle of branches, confirming his suspicion.

Once he found a patch of cleared vegetation,

he sprinted along the edge and ducked in the darkness; he changed direction and ran hard, keeping his head low. Mercer kept this up for a hundred meters, then changed direction and found the edge of the jungle, which opened up near a row of buildings. He moved behind them, keeping within the fields, and continued another kilometer, finding a concealed area where he could look back along the road.

He sat for ten minutes, checking the road before emerging and walking back into Mong La. For a moment, the thought crossed his mind about conducting an operation over the border in China to track down the Western guy. *Bad move.* The border region in China was crawling with the People's Liberation Army (PLA). It would be impossible to kill a player in the drug trade and make it out alive. *Fuck it,* Mercer thought, *I need to work this from a different angle.*

FOUR

Paris—France

Nestled in the heart of Paris's 7th Arrondissement, Mercer's safe house was a world away from the chaotic streets of Mong La. The tranquil ambiance of the upscale neighborhood, with its elegant Haussmann buildings and tree-lined avenues, provided a stark contrast to the gritty underworld he left behind.

Seated at an antique oak desk, Mercer methodically examined the documents Connor had dispatched from the CIA's Paris field office. The suspects' photos, each with a detailed narcotics involvement summary, unfolded a vast Black Orchestra network. Mercer's gaze fixed on each face, memorizing every detail.

The mission brief, crisp and freshly printed, lay before him. The intelligence was comprehensive. As Mercer flicked through it, he was impressed by how the CIA had collected much more information than he had seen over at the DEA's office in Arlington County. It was a familiar routine for Mercer: read, memorize, destroy. He appreciated the necessity for such caution, even if the agency's obsession with protocol often pissed him off. He was a man of action, and the confines of bureaucracy were constraints he had little patience for.

As he delved into the brief, some of which was heavily redacted, the dimly lit room was filled with the soft rustle of pages turning. The information was extensive, covering the Black Orchestra's operations from Asia to Europe, their ties to corrupt officials in the U.S., the Chinese Communist Party officials, and the level of detail on their drug trafficking routes via the Silk Road. Mercer noted the key locations and names, mentally mapping out his next moves. He studied the names and locations of the New Silk Road's crime routes sprawled across his table. The map of the greater Mekong sub-region was a stark reminder of the network's dark transformation from an ancient trade route to a conduit for modern crimes, drug trafficking, arms smuggling, and human trafficking.

Focusing on the details, Mercer considered the potential links between these routes and the FBI team that had pursued him. It wasn't just about narcotics or the Black Orchestra's operations; it involved controlling critical paths that connected different parts of the world. This control extended beyond criminal profits; it was about power and influence in a global context.

His fingers traced lines connecting Asia to Myanmar, identifying key locations along the way. Understanding the Black Orchestra's involvement in these routes was essential, potentially revealing connections to corrupt elements in international agencies, including those in the FBI targeting him. His approach was methodical, focused on gathering evidence and piecing together the operational landscape. The information collected was more than mere data points; it offered insight into a vast, intricate operation. Mercer realized the scope of this investigation was unlike any he had previously undertaken. Never before had he witnessed a trail of corruption that extended back to the halls of power in the United States.

As Mercer realized the unprecedented scope of this investigation, a sharp pang from his shoulder jolted him back to the present. The wound, a stark reminder of his recent encounter, required proper ongoing care. Under the bright lights of his kitchen, he cleaned the area with isopropyl alcohol, enduring the familiar sting of the routine. Next, he applied a thin layer of Neosporin to prevent infection. He selected a sterile adhesive bandage, which was designed for mobility and durability. This was wrapped tightly enough to secure the dressing but not so tight as to hinder blood flow. To manage the pain, he took two ibuprofen tablets, a necessary measure to maintain his focus.

With the documents reviewed and his shoulder tended to, Mercer leaned back in his chair and lit a cigar. His thoughts were torn between the shooter, who almost screwed up his shoulder, and the task ahead. Restlessly, he took a drag from his cigar, the smoke curling away as he approached the large window. Peering cautiously outside, he scrutinized the street below. From his vantage point, the upscale cars and polished facades of Saint-Thomas d'Aquin presented a veneer of elegance. But Mercer's gaze was analytical. He scanned the area for any sign of trouble. Paris might have been a city of lights, but for Mercer, it was another urban landscape, filled with hitmen fueled by money and the thrill of the hunt. Just then, the phone buzzed, its ringtone piercing the silence. Mercer moved to the table and picked up the cell phone. It was Connor.

'Mercer, update me.' Connor's voice was terse.

'I'm still working on it,' Mercer replied. 'The connections are confusing, those behind this have covered their tracks well. This isn't about new drug routes; it's about influence and control from some of our own agencies. How they are doing this is out of my skill set. I can concentrate on disrupting what I can, but the investigations will remain your problem.'

Connor was silent for a moment. 'Well, that's why you have been given the taskings. We don't trust the DEA over there, neither do we trust the FBI. Speaking of which, I've just had a run-in with the FBI. Their SAC came to my office.' Connor's voice was edged with frustration. The Special Agent in Charge's involvement indicated the seriousness of the situation.

Mercer felt a chill at the mention of the FBI. His pulse quickened as he weighed up the ramifications of taking out their agent. He glanced at his watch, calculating the time difference. Paris was six hours ahead. 'What did he want?'

Connor hesitated. 'This isn't a conversation for the phone. I'm catching a flight to Paris tonight. We'll talk after I land.' There was a pause before he added, 'I'm bringing someone who might help.'

Mercer walked back to the window and once again peered out from behind the thick curtains. 'Help? With what, exactly? You know I prefer to run my own affairs.'

'It's about that night you left Langley.' Connor's voice grew heavy. 'The FBI's digging for answers, and it seems I'm to play middle-man. I'll meet you at Le Faubourg Café on Rue d'Anjou, post-lunch.' Without another word, Connor ended the call.

Mercer returned to the window, another check of the street below. The conversation had stirred a nest of worries. *FBI involvement, fuck this,* he thought, his annoyance mounting as he braced for the looming consequences. The game was getting messier, and the stakes were rising.

Shifting away from the window, he gave the phone one last glance before sliding it into a Faraday bag, effectively severing its digital footprint. The soft rustling whisper of the bag was the sound of going dark.

He powered up a mini drone no larger than a sparrow, activating it with a subtle motion before sending it into the night. From his balcony, Mercer controlled the device as it flew around the entry of the building and its rear exit, the parking areas and laneways, its camera sending live images to a small tablet. The drone's feed showed nothing out of the ordinary. He guided the drone back, its mission providing a small assurance of safety. Every precaution was a step toward staying ahead.

With the drone stowed and his digital trace wiped, Mercer's mind returned to the planned meeting at Le Faubourg Café.

. . .

Rain had drenched Paris all morning. Now, as the sun pierced through fading clouds, the air turned humid. Mercer adjusted his shirt, unbuttoning it slightly to let the breeze cool his skin. The sidewalks along the Champs-Élysées buzzed with people venturing out for lunch in the quaint brasseries. Mercer's purpose differed as he strode a few blocks north toward Le Faubourg Café, intent on his mission.

This wasn't his first visit to the area that day. Earlier, under the guise of a casual breakfast, he had scouted the café's layout, marked fire exits and other potential escape routes. Before leaving, he had discreetly stashed a small Glock 26 in the men's restroom, a precaution ingrained in his meticulous planning.

As he made his way back, Mercer scanned the street. He checked his watch, timing his approach. With one last surveying glance, he turned left off Rue de Surène and onto Rue d'Anjou. He stopped at the CIC Iberbanco bank and pulled out a cigarette. There was a quick glance over his shoulder before lighting his cigarette. Then he stood back for a moment to smoke and casually observe the café.

Two men were seated outside. Americans. Noticed due to their larger stature, accents, and style of suits. From his position about thirty meters away, he could hear them discuss their food orders. Mercer focused on one of the men and couldn't believe what he was seeing. A face from many years ago: Decker. Kenneth Decker, ex-special forces and CIA, now employed with the ODNI. Next to him, holding a menu and looking somewhat confused by the language, was another tall and well-built man. Mercer was unsure about the man; however, he was intrigued by him and their presence.

Connor mentioned someone would come to help ease things out. Although the thought of surprises annoyed Mercer. He crossed the narrow street and approached the café. The American Embassy was a ten-minute walk away. He hoped it was a coincidence and the men weren't there to meet him. *Perhaps they've strayed*, Mercer thought as he checked out the few small European cars parked along the one-way street. Nothing unusual here, only suspicions of his own countrymen.

Once outside the café, he peered through the window and saw Connor inside chatting with another man. Connor locked eyes with Mercer and displayed no emotion. He nodded discreetly to the tables outside. Mercer turned around and noticed the two Americans rising to their feet.

'Nathan Harrow, and you must be Danny Mercer, yes?' The man who offered his hand was lean and muscular, clean-shaven, with short, cropped hair and piercing green eyes. Mercer shook his hand and said nothing.

Decker walked around Harrow to greet him. A smile flickered on his weather-beaten face as he grabbed Mercer's hand. 'It's been a long time, Danny. What is it, about seven or eight years now? Al-Bukama. What a beautiful city.'

Mercer remembered the operation Decker was referring to. Their small mission unit was surveilling a bridge over the Euphrates River in Eastern Syria, near the border with Iraq. A high-value target was due to arrive, and it was Mercer's job to capture and take him to a safe house for interrogation. Mercer was in no mood for talking. This wasn't about Syria or Iraq. That war has finished for him, and he isn't one to reminisce about what he did in the past. 'To what do I owe the pleasure, guys? These streets are a long way from, well...where are you men from? The Pentagon? Fort Bragg? Langley?' Mercer said.

Decker's smile faded, replaced by a more serious look. 'Where we are from is not important. The reason we are here is to work something out. I need you to work with us.'

Mercer's eyes flicked between Decker and Harrow, gauging their intentions. 'Let's talk, then,' Mercer said, his voice calm but firm as he leaned against the wall of the café, eyes still scanning the street.

Decker exchanged a wary glance with Harrow before addressing Mercer again. 'This is sensitive, Mercer. Not a conversation for public ears.'

Harrow stepped closer, his voice low. 'It's about that night in D.C. before you left for Asia. The FBI has questions, Mercer. Questions leading to some uncomfortable truths.'

At the mention of the FBI, Mercer's eyes narrowed with irritation. 'Uncomfortable for whom?' he asked sarcastically. He was all too familiar with the bureaucratic and political maneuvering back home, games he had long tried to distance himself from. The two men, alert and cautious, subtly surveyed the street, their movements betraying an intent to avoid attracting attention.

Mercer made his decision. 'Here's what we'll do. I'll talk to Connor, see what he advises,' he said, settling into his chair. As he contemplated his next move, his hand subconsciously drifted to the ankle holster, a reassuring weight against his leg. The small revolver hidden there and the other strategically placed in the bathroom were his only defenses against the men currently encroaching on his safety and any backup they might call upon.

Mercer understood the stakes; if any agency

wanted a trophy, they wouldn't think twice about taking him down. Detained, he'd lose any chance to expose the corruption he'd uncovered. As he sat, analyzing his options, and scrutinized his compatriots, torn between trust and suspicion.

The two men, their tension palpable, awkwardly maneuvered their stools closer, sitting nervously beside Mercer. Their discomfort was evident, a clear response to his notorious reputation for ruthless violence and unpredictability.

Decker took a seat beside Mercer. 'We need to keep this discreet, Danny. The walls have ears, and we can't afford any part of our conversations being picked up and relayed to the world.'

Mercer's gaze shifted from Decker to Harrow, his expression unreadable. 'I don't give a fuck; let's cut to the chase. What's the FBI's angle in all this? And more importantly, why involve me now?' There was a hint of skepticism in his tone, reflecting his wariness of cross-agency politics.

Harrow shifted his chair a bit closer. His voice barely above a whisper, he said, 'The night you left D.C., there was a fallout, not just the shooting. The FBI thinks you're involved in something bigger, something that goes beyond just your typical field operations. They're digging deep, and it's leading them to some places they, and we, didn't expect. Don't provide any statements without going through Connor.'

Mercer's brow furrowed slightly at the mention of the FBI's suspicions. He had always been cautious, but that his actions might have stirred up something larger was both intriguing and alarming.

Decker interjected. 'That's why we need you to work with him, Mercer. We can't let this spiral out of control. You have connections and insights that could be invaluable right now. If you are suspended, then your operation will collapse until new people are brought in. Which exposes intel to less capable officers.'

Mercer considered their words, his mind rapidly assessing the implications. Aligning with these men could either be a strategic move or a trap, but Mercer knew that staying ahead meant playing every angle.

'Alright,' Mercer said. 'I'll hear you out, but I'm doing things my way. Any move I make, I make it alone.'

Decker and Harrow exchanged a glance, an unspoken agreement passing between them. They both knew the value of having Mercer on their side, even if it meant accommodating his lone-wolf approach.

Just as Connor stepped out of the café and

made his way to their table, Mercer's attention shifted. 'Afternoon, Danny,' Connor greeted. 'This is William Baxter. Apologies for the surprise. Things are moving fast, and his presence was as unexpected for me as it is for you.'

Mercer studied Baxter before standing to shake his hand. At over fifty, Baxter had a presence that commanded attention. His tall and robust frame, combined with his deep-set eyes and neatly trimmed graying hair, marked him as a figure of authority. As the Director of the Counterterrorism Division, he played a pivotal role in the FBI's fight against both domestic and international terrorist threats. His responsibilities spanned not only operational oversight but also strategic policymaking, interagency collaboration, and advising top government figures.

Baxter's technical acumen and strategic insight were indispensable in the scope of modern terrorism. On a European trip that included stops in London, Paris, and Berlin to confer with counterparts, Baxter seized the opportunity to meet Mercer, a man the CIA had been keen to shield. Baxter quickly understood that higher-ups in the FBI had been influenced to sideline Mercer from any inquiries linked to the suspicious incident in D.C.

'What do I owe the pleasure?' Mercer asked flatly.

'The pleasure is mine,' Baxter said. 'I had the chance to review your field reports during my flight. You've had a rather remarkable career, Mr. Mercer.'

Mercer didn't like the thought of these suits reading up on him. Baxter could just as easily be threatening him as trying to soften him. 'How about we go somewhere more private so I can get a better understanding of why I have suddenly become of interest to your department.'

Mercer set his cigarette in the ashtray, stood, and walked off, leading the group to a secluded spot in the Jardin des Champs-Élysées, away from prying eyes. The park's serene atmosphere, with its lush greenery and tranquil ponds, stood in stark contrast to the tension brewing within the group.

'You see, Mercer,' Baxter began, trying to maintain a diplomatic tone, 'the FBI's involvement is crucial to ensuring national security...'

Mercer cut him off, his voice rising. 'National security? My work has nothing to do with your jurisdiction, Baxter. This is not the place for you to throw your weight around. I deal with physical threats, those that cause real damage to people and properties, not about your reputation or career path...'

Connor cut in, trying to diffuse the situation. 'Danny, let's keep this professional. We all have the same goal here.'

'I don't need babysitters, especially not from the FBI,' Mercer said in a low growl. 'I've been in this game long enough to know when I'm being sidelined. So, why don't you just stay in your lane and let me do my job?'

Baxter and Harrow exchanged uneasy glances, the former's attempt at control visibly faltering. 'Mercer, this isn't about overstepping bounds. It's about cooperation.'

'Cooperation?' Mercer scoffed. 'Or is it about control? You want to keep tabs on me because I know too much. Well, guess what? I don't play well with others when they're trying to tie my hands.'

Decker, who had been silent until now, finally spoke up. 'Mercer, regardless of our agencies' differences, we need to find common ground. We can't afford a rogue element in this situation.'

'Rogue element? Is that what you think I am, Decker?'

Decker squared his shoulders, stepping into his space. 'I think you're a valuable asset, Mercer. One that could tip the scales. But we need to ensure you're aligned with the bigger picture.'

Connor stepped in. 'Alright, that's enough. Mercer, go home. Cool off. We'll handle things from here.'

Mercer glared at the group. Without another

word, he turned and strode away, leaving the four men in uneasy silence.

Baxter rubbed his temple, the stress obvious in his demeanor. 'Is he always this volatile?'

Connor sighed, watching Mercer's retreating figure. 'Mercer's good at what he does, but he's a wildcard. Let me deal with him. I understand him better than anyone.'

Harrow nodded in agreement. 'He might be unstable, but he's right about one thing: he's not someone to underestimate.'

As Mercer faded into the city's backdrop, Decker turned back to the group. 'We need to keep a close eye on Mercer. His knowledge and connections could be pivotal. We should ensure he's looped into our efforts, at least superficially. It's crucial we stay abreast of what he uncovers. Make sure we are all dialed in on his movements, Connor. Okay!'

With a unanimous nod of understanding, the group dispersed from the gardens, each man disappearing down a separate path. Alone, Decker's stride along the gravel walkway grew brisk, his thoughts racing. *Mercer is a wild card, a dangerous element to our goals. If he cannot be steered in our favor...his elimination becomes necessary.* His fingers deftly adjusted his tie, a symbol of readiness. With every step, his determination hardened. Time was of the essence to safeguard the Black Orchestra's operations.

FIVE

Beijing—China

The conference room, deep within the Ministry of State Security's headquarters, embodied controlled austerity. Situated in the Yidongyuan compound in Beijing's Haidian district, this extensive building provided the Second Bureau men a secluded haven for their clandestine affairs. Dominating the room was a polished mahogany table, set against a backdrop of thick red carpet and windowless walls. The starkness was interrupted only by a solitary state emblem, underscoring the room's purpose for decisive action rather than prolonged discussions.

Charged with an unspoken authority and palpable undercurrents of tension, the air was a constant in these high-level meetings. The light in the room was muted, casting long shadows across the cold, unyielding faces of the officials gathered there. As the hushed conversations began, General Liu Xiang's fingers traced the grain of the mahogany table, a silent testament to the weight of the decisions made within these walls.

In the corner of the room, Liang Guang sat with an almost statuesque stillness, his presence as discreet as it was formidable. Positioned strategically where he could observe every nuance of the meeting, his intense dark brown eyes moved subtly, tracking the ebb and flow of the conversation. Despite his significant role in directing European operations, he remained silent, embodying the role of an observer, one who listens, learns, and acts without unnecessary words. His quiet demeanor belied the critical nature of his work with the kill teams, a stark contrast to the animated discussion around the table. Liang's role was to watch, wait, and execute without question.

General Liu sat at the head of the table, his presence dominating the room. Peppered with gray, Liu's hair was meticulously combed back, his dark suit freshly pressed, and a gold watch peeked out from under his sleeve. He cleared his throat subtly, commanding attention more effectively than words could.

'Recent events in the West,' Liu began, 'present us with both challenges and opportunities. It is imperative we evaluate our stance and adapt our strategies accordingly.' Liu paused briefly, his gaze fixating on the emblem on the wall, seemingly drawing silent strength from this potent symbol of state power.

To his right, Zhang Wei shifted slightly in his seat, fingers interlaced on the table. His eyes, always analyzing, flickered with a hint of impatience. 'We cannot overlook the advancements in Western technology, particularly in cyber and artificial intelligence sectors,' he stated. 'Our response should be aggressive in acquisition, yet subtle in implementation.' Zhang Wei's statement hung in the air, followed by a pregnant pause as all eyes turned to Liu, awaiting his strategic guidance.

Liu nodded, his expression unreadable. 'Indeed, subtlety is key,' he concurred. 'Yet we must carefully weigh our technological pursuits against the broader geopolitical landscape. A direct confrontation is not in our interest.'

Zhao Ming, with his seasoned diplomatic acumen, interjected with a hint of concealed ambition. 'Our international strategies require a nuanced approach. I suggest we leverage our ties with Senator Rick Sanderson. My years of cultivating him could prove beneficial in foreseeing and maneuvering around potential obstacles.'

The mention of Sanderson sent a ripple through the room. The officials shifted in their seats, recognizing the weight of Zhao's suggestion. Their eyes settled on Liu, awaiting his response.

Liu's expression turned steely, reflecting deeply on Zhao's words. 'Sanderson could indeed play a pivotal role in our operation,' he acknowledged. 'But let us not forget the broader picture. The conflict in Ukraine, the unrest in the Middle East, and the simmering tensions in Africa all serve as unwanted distractions for the EU and the USA. We can exploit these conflicts, prolong them through proxies, and weaken our adversaries without direct engagement.'

A murmur of agreement flowed around the table. Each official, an expert in their respective fields, understood the weight of their decisions. The MSS was not just an intelligence agency; it was a key player in a global game of power and influence where every move had far-reaching consequences.

Liu shifted slightly, his hand reaching for a crystal decanter of whiskey, pouring a measure into his glass. He offered the decanter around before continuing.

'Our actions,' he said, swirling the whiskey, 'must be like the currents beneath a calm ocean, unseen yet powerful. We are not merely reacting to global changes; we are coordinating them.' Liu set his glass down and leaned forward, his voice taking on a grave tone. 'Our strategic vision extends beyond mere reactions. For instance, we are mobilizing our brightest minds in a global initiative. We plan to send 5,000 of our top university students to major tech conferences, CES in Las Vegas, Mobile World Congress in Barcelona, Web Summit in Lisbon, DEF CON, and others. Their task is to gather intelligence on the latest in AI and other emerging technologies.'

Zhao Ming nodded in agreement. 'Our operatives, disguised as corporate sponsors, will shadow these students. They will extract real-time data, enabling us to offer speaking opportunities in China to these Western technology leaders, furthering our grasp on their innovations.' Zhao's knee bounced under the table, his energy getting the better of him. 'Indeed, the West's preoccupation with these wars opens avenues for us in cyber warfare and intelligence. It's time we intensified our efforts,' he stated.

Zhang Wei, cautious in his approach, followed up. 'Our actions overseas could stir unrest within our borders. We must consider the internal implications. Maintaining control, both at home and abroad, is essential.'

Liu made a couple of notes before asking Zhang Wei to continue. 'Our next move involves hosting international conferences in Beijing and Shanghai. Under the guise of collaboration, we will draw in Western researchers. This is our time for technology acquisition, allowing us to absorb their advancements and integrate them into our own.'

'This extends beyond technology,' Liu said. 'We must not overlook our geopolitical plays. While we maintain a cautious stance with Russia, we will engage North Korea to discreetly supply arms to the Russian front. This indirect support furthers our agenda in distracting Europe, without exposing our hand.'

'And let's not forget the importance of propaganda, especially in American elections. Our digital warfare units are primed to amplify divisions, creating a distracted and weakened adversary.' Zhao said.

Liu nodded. 'Indeed, every move we make, whether in technology, politics, or global influence, must serve our ultimate goal, to position ourselves and what we are building as the unchallenged superpower. The Western world and the CCP, preoccupied with international relations, will be blindsided by our ascent and takeover of our current government.'

Liu lifted a finger and pointed at each of the men, his eyes narrowing with resolve.

'Control,' he said. 'That has always been our prerogative. We must navigate these global changes with the same precision and efficiency that the Western intelligence agencies are known for. Our response will be multifaceted, technological, diplomatic, covert and, if necessary, with violence.' Liu's words shifted the atmosphere, steering the conversation toward the broader geopolitical strategy.

He paused, allowing his words to sink in. Liu's expression remained inscrutable, yet a subtle tightening of his jaw revealed the intense resolve fueling his strategic vision. 'Gentlemen, we are at a pivotal moment. The world is undergoing a profound transformation, and we must adapt accordingly. Our actions in the coming weeks will shape not only our future but that of our nation. Friends within our government may become enemies, yet we will remain focused. Sacrifices come at a cost to some. Let us be on the winning side. Never falter or question, for the future will hold great power and control over our people and the West.'

Zhao raised his glass slightly. 'To manipulation and control.'

The others echoed the toast, their glasses clinking softly, a sound that seemed to seal their sinister pact. The MSS, guided by the steely determination of Liu, was poised for action. Amidst the clinking of glasses, a hint of concern flickered in Liu's eyes.

Liu harbored a lingering unease about Zhao. Despite his simple words, there was an air of increasing boldness about him. Liu's attention lingered on him. Something about Zhao eluded him, a hidden agenda perhaps. It unsettled him. In this high-stakes game, every player needed to be predictable, and Liu knew the importance of keeping his allies close. Too much was at stake, and in the world of espionage, unseen threats were the most dangerous.

Liu's voice resonated with finality as the meeting neared its conclusion. 'Let us be unequivocal in our understanding,' he began. 'Our ongoing actions must remain shrouded from the Politburo, and especially from the President. He is preoccupied with forging international alliances and maintaining a facade of global harmony. Our operations, deeply rooted in black ops, cannot afford the slightest exposure. Remember, any breach of this confidentiality will be met with the most severe consequence, the death penalty, and the murder of your families.'

He surveyed the room, ensuring his words had sunk in. 'We are the architects of a new era, one where we will reign supreme, unbound by the constraints of the CCP. Once we seize control, any internal opposition within the Party will be systematically eliminated. Our objective is clear: to establish unchallenged power.'

His gaze hardened, reflecting an unwavering determination. 'Should anyone dare to obstruct our path, we will strike with relentless force. We possess the means and the will to do so.'

Liu's eyes then shifted to the corner where Liang Guang sat, an unspoken acknowledgment of his crucial role in their plans. 'With operatives like Liang at our disposal, we are more than equipped to deal with any threat.'

The room fell into a hushed silence, each attendee acutely aware of the gravity of their mission and the perilous road ahead. They were the unseen hand, poised to shape the future of their nation and the world.

Geneva—Switzerland

A black van was parked along the Rue des Pâquis, its windows blacked out and the engine running. In the front seat sat a woman, strikingly beautiful with long dark hair neatly tied in a bun, her sunglasses concealing her oriental eyes. Her task: to monitor the back streets encircling Hotel President Wilson, perched elegantly along Lake Geneva's shore. She relayed instructions through her collar mic to the members of her team, two of which were drinking coffee in the lobby. The others were seated in the back of the van. Inside, four Chinese mercenaries waited, ready. Their ears tuned for the command that would send them bursting from the van to execute their orders. Clad in black and gripping QBZ-191 assault rifles, these men were veterans of the Leishen Commando Airborne Force, now employed as hitmen in the lucrative, covert world of a transnational crime syndicate.

Using hand signals and hushed words, the mercenary leader reminded his team of their plan and the rules of engagement on Geneva's streets. In Switzerland, their bosses' influence waned, leaving them to navigate the murky waters beyond the Chinese Communist Party's reach. Their ex-fil plan was straightforward. Their mission: to seize their target and reach the Port of Genoa, where he would be concealed in a specialized shipping container for covert transport to Shenzhen. While some fidgeted with their equipment and others focused intently, a burst of static crackled through their earpieces, breaking the silence with a faint directive: *Target in the lobby. Cream suit, white shirt, no tie. Flanked by two guards.*

The men waited nervously, a mix of anticipation and apprehension tangible in the air. This mission, a staple in their playbook, had been often rehearsed within China, yet executing it on Western soil was an unprecedented leap. The moment the van door swung open, they would etch their names in history. Their edge lay in swift execution, the stunning impact of sudden violence, and the boldness of striking in a neutral country. Once their deed echoed through the streets, every Western law enforcement and the world's elite intelligence agencies would commence a relentless pursuit.

In the So Bar of Hotel President Wilson, Geneva, the atmosphere was one of discreet luxury. Philippe Dubois, a high-ranking DGSE operative, sat in a corner, his posture relaxed but alert. He had chosen this spot for its strategic advantage, offering a clear view of the entire room without drawing attention to himself. The air was filled with the soft hum of hushed conversations, the clink of glasses, and the faint notes of a piano playing somewhere in the background.

Philippe watched as Arnold Becker, a senior official from the United States Department of Justice, entered the bar. Becker's arrival was anything but subtle; his confident stride carried an air of arrogance, and the fleeting shadow of a smirk hinted at hidden agendas. Becker's gaze briefly lingered on a distant figure at the bar, a flash of recognition crossing his features before he turned his attention to Philippe.

'Ah, Philippe, always the man of mystery,' Becker greeted as he took a seat across from the Frenchman. 'You French have a flair for the dramatic, don't you?'

Philippe smiled thinly, unfazed by Becker's brash demeanor. 'Drama, Arnold, is merely the cloak we wear. It's the substance beneath that counts.' He gestured to the bartender for another drink.

Becker inhaled deeply, his tone taking on a more serious note. 'Let's cut to the chase, shall we? I hear things are getting heated in your neck of the woods. The EU's not too happy with the recent moves in the South China Sea, huh?'

Philippe's expression remained unreadable. 'The world is a complex stage, Arnold. Europe's concerns extend beyond simple territorial disputes. There's a broader narrative at play. Why don't you bring this up with your counterparts in the *Garde des Sceaux?*'

Becker scoffed. 'Come on, Philippe. We both know that your Ministry of Justice is run by the socialists. They won't talk sense to us. Forget them. Tell me, what is this about? China's making moves, and you guys are feeling the heat. What's the DGSE's take on this?'

'The DGSE,' Philippe replied carefully, 'is concerned with stability. What we're witnessing is a recalibration of global power. And it's not just about China. The ripples are being felt everywhere.'

Becker snorted. 'Ripples, recalibrations... all fancy words. What about taking steps,

Philippe? That's where we come in. You guys might prefer the background, but we're ready to step up.'

Philippe's gaze was steady, but he noticed Becker's occasional glances at his watch, a sense of anticipation in his eyes. 'Initiative without foresight, Arnold, leads to anarchy. Europe's strategy is more...nuanced. We believe in understanding the currents before diving in.'

The American's demeanor hardened. 'Nuanced, my ass. You're just afraid to get your hands dirty. Look, Philippe, we've got intel on the Black Orchestra. They're planning something big. We need to act and do so quickly. It's important we share intelligence on this.'

Philippe sighed, a flicker of irritation crossing his features. 'The Black Orchestra is a symptom of a larger disease, Arnold. Acting rashly will only worsen the situation. And your intel...let's just say it lacks certain...subtleties. Or perhaps there's more you're not sharing?'

Becker slammed his glass down. 'Damn it, Philippe! This isn't some wine tasting where you swirl around looking for undertones. These are dangerous times. We need to be on the same page.'

Philippe's response was calm but firm. 'Dangerous times require careful thought, not brash action. Europe has a long history, Arnold. We've learned the value of patience.'

'Look, Philippe, Europe's patience might be your downfall. The Black Orchestra's making their move. And what are you doing? Waiting for the perfect moment?' Becker said.

'Arnold, sometimes the most powerful move is the one you don't make. We're monitoring the situation closely. The Service isn't blind to the threat.'

'But are you willing to act?' Becker pressed. 'Or will you let the Americans do the heavy lifting while you sit back and watch?'

Before Philippe could respond, a waiter arrived at their table, his presence momentarily pausing their intense exchange. They watched as the drinks were set down, their conversation pausing as the waiter lingered. Once he departed, Philippe resumed, his tone laced with a hint of criticism.

'Your *heavy lifting* often leaves a trail of chaos, Arnold. We, in Europe, favor a more calculated, surgical approach. Like in Brussels, where we've seen a rise in Chinese espionage efforts. It's not just about gathering information; it's about influence and control.'

Becker waved his hand dismissively. 'Espionage, influence...we deal with it all the time. The real question is, can Europe handle the heat when it's turned up? China's not just playing spy games; they're making geopolitical moves.'

Philippe's demeanor remained unflappable.

'And Europe is not merely a spectator. We have our methods, more discreet perhaps, but no less effective. Your blunt approach might work for America, but we prefer the finesse of diplomacy mixed with intelligence.'

Becker settled deeper into the chair, a smirk playing on his lips. 'Diplomacy, huh? Is that what you call it? From where I'm sitting, it looks a lot like indecision.'

'The difference between indecision and strategic patience is something you Americans often cannot grasp,' Philippe countered. 'Europe has a deeper history, a longer perspective. We see the patterns, the long-term implications of these power plays.'

'Long-term implications don't mean shit if you're not around to see them. The Black Orchestra's planning something big, Philippe. And we need to be ready,' Becker said.

Philippe took a slow sip of his drink before responding. 'And what exactly do you propose, Arnold? A full-frontal assault? We need a plan, not a brawl.'

'The plan is simple. We take them down before they get any further. And we need Europe on board, not just watching from the sidelines.'

Philippe nodded. 'Europe will act when the time is right. But we'll do it our way, with precision. And we'll need more than just muscle; we require strategic insights.'

'Strategic insights, huh? Let's hope Europe's got enough of those to know which side to choose when the time comes. Your tactics are too sluggish. Immediate action is crucial, not continual waiting and observing.'

'Arnold, as we say in France, *Petit à petit, l'oiseau fait son nid.* In your rush for action, you risk overlooking the importance of building carefully, piece by piece. It is the meticulous and steady effort that lays the foundation for lasting success.'

Becker exhaled sharply, then stood to leave. Philippe remained seated, his mind already analyzing the layers of their conversation, aware of the game's complexity and the roles each player had to perform.

After uttering a brief farewell, Becker left the bar. His flight to Washington, D.C., was imminent, affording him no further opportunity to interact with the French. Frustration gripped him; he firmly believed Dubois had withheld crucial intelligence. This, he thought, was a serious mistake.

As he strode through the lobby, his heartbeat increased, reflecting the gravity of his next move. Casually, he brushed his fingers through his hair, a subtle yet intentional signal to the observers stationed discreetly around him. In Becker's estimation, Dubois had outlived his usefulness.

•   •   •

The van parked on Rue des Pâquis remained in position. Inside, the atmosphere was tense, each mercenary poised for action. The woman in the driver's seat glanced repeatedly at the rearview mirror. Her breath came in short, uneven bursts as she focused on the crackling voice in her earpiece.

'Target identified. Cream suit. Three minutes. Our orders are to capture him unharmed.'

Her voice, calm yet authoritative despite her growing anxiety, relayed the message to the team in the back. 'Weapons are last resort. We take him alive.'

Within the van's cramped confines, each man echoed the orders before making their final preparations. One man, his throat dry with anticipation, took a sip of water. Another, unable to ignore nature's call any longer, discreetly urinated into an empty bottle. Tension mounted as another team member meticulously arranged zip ties on his tactical vest, the sound of the plastic clicking against his gear breaking the heavy silence.

Outside, the quiet street offered no threats. A few cars went past, a cat ran past the van, and a food delivery rider made his way up the street. As he got closer, he crossed over and came to a stop alongside the van. The glow from his mobile phone and the rustle of food bags briefly captured the woman's attention. She sized up the rider, confused.

Inside the van, the mercenaries exchanged glances. Each man knew his role.

The woman's hand moved to her earpiece.

The rider's hand shot up, and in a heartbeat, he fired twice. The sharp reports ruined the night's stillness. The woman's head snapped back, blood spraying across the van's black leather interior. Inside, the mercenaries reacted, their boots scuffing against the floor as they swung their weapons toward the window. The rider didn't hesitate. He hurled a grenade through the window, the device tumbling past the woman's lifeless body and landing in the rear of the van. Panic set in as the men fumbled with the back door, hands clumsily grasping for the handle in a desperate attempt to escape.

A deafening boom rocked the street. The van's back doors blew off, slamming onto the pavement with a metallic crash. Smoke poured out in thick plumes, carrying the acrid stench of burned metal and flesh. Inside, what had been a carefully laid plan was reduced to fragments—shattered equipment, torn upholstery, and motionless bodies strewn amid the wreckage.

Car alarms blared in response to the shockwaves while residents peeked out from behind their curtains, drawn by the commotion. Police sirens echoed in the distance. Traffic, initially light, began to back up as drivers avoided the wrecked van, unsure of what had happened. At the Hotel President Wilson, security staff quickly initiated a lockdown, concerned about a possible terrorist attack.

Philippe Dubois picked up his whiskey and watched as hotel security rushed through the lobby. Their voices crackled over radios, sharp and urgent. He remained calm, his face showing a mix of satisfaction and cold resolve. In his thoughts lay information from the reports and briefings, evidence of a meticulously planned counterstrike.

He checked his cell phone. A message had appeared, the last image of the van before it was destroyed. Dubois knew the Black Orchestra had been closing in, their intentions clear. But what they hadn't counted on was his foresight, his connections within the DGSE, and their willingness to resort to extreme measures.

A man crossed the thick carpet and stood before Dubois, interrupting his thoughts. He glanced up as his contact from the DGSE entered, a grim expression etched on his face.

'We've confirmed it, Philippe,' the agent said.

'The hit was successful; the team sent to abduct you have been neutralized.'

Dubois nodded, setting his cell phone down. 'What about the contractor?' Dubois inquired.

'Vanished like a ghost,' the agent replied. 'Not a trace left behind. As agreed, we're officially unaware of his involvement. The hit appears like an act of random violence, unconnected to us or to you.'

Dubois rested an elbow on the chair's arm. *Random violence,* he thought. *A convenient cover for a necessary evil.*

The agent shuffled uncomfortably. 'It was a risky move, Philippe. Using a contractor, someone outside our usual channels...'

'Sometimes, risk is the only path to safety,' Dubois interrupted. 'The Black Orchestra is no ordinary adversary. We needed to send a message. One they'll understand. Fear is a language they speak fluently.'

The agent nodded, though the tension in his eyes remained. 'And what about the aftermath? The police, the media?'

Dubois' expression hardened. 'Let them investigate. Like you said, they'll find nothing that leads back to us. As far as anyone knows, it was a random act of violence on a quiet Geneva street. A tragedy, nothing more.'

When the agent left, Dubois turned back to his phone. The screen displayed a stark image of the wreckage. Twisted metal strewn across Rue des Pâquis. Brutal, but necessary. A reminder of what it took to win.

He pondered the potential fallout, the diplomatic uproar that could ensue if the DGSE's involvement surfaced, not to mention the strain it could place on Franco-Swiss relations. French politicians would be clamoring for answers, seeking a scapegoat for this act on foreign soil. But for Dubois, these were mere ripples in a larger pond. His primary concern wasn't diplomacy or political backlashes; it was the intricate play of strategy and counterstrategy he was engaged in against the Black Orchestra, a game far more significant than any temporary diplomatic scuffle.

Dubois noticed his glass trembling slightly as he took a sip of his whiskey. A cold shiver ran down his spine. The alcohol would help to steady his nerves; if not, he would have another one. The destruction in Geneva was a necessary sacrifice, a calculated risk in the grand scheme. He was well aware that his actions could ignite a storm of controversy, but the stakes were too high to play it safe.

The night's events were just the beginning of a dirty battle ahead. As he looked out the large window into the night, he pocketed his phone with a sense of finality. Thoughts were not on the havoc he had wrought but on the next phase of his strategy. The Black Orchestra had yet to realize the true extent of Dubois's reach and cunning. No matter what happened next, there was no turning back.

SIX
Washington, D.C.—USA

The heavy door of Connor's office clicked shut, sealing the room in a tense silence broken only by the occasional clink of ice against glass. In the dim light, Connor, a seasoned CIA officer, sat rigidly behind his desk, his fingers wrapped tightly around a glass of Bushmills whiskey. Across from him, two operatives from the Special Activities Division's Ground Branch, still marked by the sweat and fatigue of their recent, disastrous operation, mirrored his posture. The air hung thick with unspoken recriminations and the heavy scent of whiskey.

In the corner of the room, their travel bags lay discarded, a jumble of hastily packed gear and the remnants of plans gone wrong. An unlit cigar perched on the edge of an ashtray. The men's eyes shifted to each other. Nervous coughs punctuated the silence as each man grappled with the weight of their situation.

Above Connor's head, a small replica of the Windwalker was mounted on the wall. The bronze eagle, with its wings spread wide, seemed to watch over the room with a vigilance they all felt acutely in that moment. Its presence was a stark reminder of the values they were sworn to uphold: alertness, strength, courage, freedom. Qualities that felt strained under the current circumstances.

On the wall behind Connor's desk, the CIA seal dominated the space. The eagle at its center, the national bird of the U.S., symbolized the strength and alertness that were the backbone of their profession. Below it, the sixteen-point compass star spread its reach, representing the global expanse of their intelligence network, all roads leading back to this very room. And the shield, the traditional emblem of defense, stood as a testament to their fundamental mission: to protect and defend.

The room was a microcosm of the agency itself, a place where the responsibility of national security rested on the shoulders of those who entered. Connor took a slow sip of his whiskey, the smooth burn of the alcohol doing little to ease the tightness in his chest. The mission had been compromised, and now they were left with the shards of their best-laid plans.

'This can't happen again,' Connor finally said, his voice low and steady. The statement hung in the air, an unspoken vow that reverberated through the room. The others nodded, their expressions grim. They knew the stakes, and they knew the cost.

The clock on the wall ticked annoyingly as Connor shuffled paper and tried to look busy while they waited. The wait wasn't long. The door swung open, and Gregory Faulkner, the CIA Deputy Director, strode in. Faulkner carried himself with the authority of a man who believed he truly ran the agency, each mistake by others another opportunity to assert his influence. He was driven by ambition, constantly watching for weaknesses, ready to capitalize on any misstep that could solidify his position.

His eyes swept the room, taking in the slumped shoulders of the operatives, the whiskey glasses, and the unlit cigars. His gaze finally settled on Connor, like a hawk zeroing in on its prey.

'We pour resources into Operation Mong La, based on Mercer's intel, and this is what I get? Guys sent in with no knowledge of the area or the consequences of failure. Why the fuck did you not use Mercer on this?' Faulkner's voice was firm, each word laced with accusation. 'I want a full debrief, now,' he demanded. 'And someone better start explaining why I wasn't fully informed about every facet of this operation.'

Connor sat still, his expression unchanging. 'It's under control,' he said smoothly, attempting to diffuse the man's anger. But his reassurance seemed to have the opposite effect.

'Under control? You call this a success?' Faulkner slammed a fist on Connor's desk, making the whiskey glasses rattle. 'We've wasted valuable resources on a botched operation that I wasn't even fully aware of.'

The operatives glanced at Connor, eyebrows raised, a silent question in their eyes. They had assumed full authorization, and Connor's poker face gave nothing away. Connor's face remained impassive, but there was a subtle glint of satisfaction in his eyes. The operation's failure was a part of his hidden agenda, a detail no one else in the room was privy to.

Connor folded his arms across his chest. 'Questioning my call on Mercer?' he shot back. 'He's my man, not just another foot soldier of yours. Mong La can wait; Mercer has other taskings.'

Faulkner's voice was a low growl. 'Mercer is one of our best. If we can't deploy him where we need him most, what's the point?'

Connor leaned forward, his forearms resting on the table. 'Putting Mercer back in Mong La would have raised suspicions. His street work... can be too conspicuous for an operation that demands subtlety.'

'And since when do we prioritize subtlety over results, Connor?' Faulkner's nostrils flared. 'We needed results. I've been told that these two,' Faulkner stabbed a finger at the men, 'were captured driving around Mong La in an unlicensed taxi. How fucking discreet is that?'

'That is being investigated. We don't know how the cops got on to them so quickly. For now, we are pulling back. The best results come from restraint. We can't afford to act until the time is right. We need some more intel on the Western guy, once I get that we can resume the operation. End of story.'

'A war...might be preferable to this screw up,' Faulkner said. 'No results, no leads—nothing.'

Connor rose from his seat. 'I stand by my decision, Gregory. Mercer is a weapon, but not every problem is solved by starting a conflict.'

The Deputy Director finally broke the silence. 'This isn't over, Connor. We need to review our strategies and reassess our assets. Mercer included.'

'We believe the target had prior warning of our arrival in Thailand,' one of the operatives cut in, his voice tight with frustration. 'They must have been tipped off.'

The conversation was spiraling, the room heavy with accusations and defensiveness. Connor saw his opportunity to steer the narrative. 'Let's focus on your operational security. How did you ensure the integrity of the mission?'

The question hit a nerve. The two men, seasoned field agents, bristled at the insinuation of incompetence. 'Our opsec is not up for debate,' one snapped, his professionalism slipping. 'We don't need to be questioned about our methods, especially not in front of others.'

The other operative shifted forward, his eyes locked on Connor's. 'Don't disrespect our allegiance,' he said. 'We've been in this game long enough to know when we've been set up.'

Connor met their gaze evenly, unflinching. He needed to end this conversation. The suspicion and anger presented a volatile mix that threatened to blow up in his face at any moment.

Faulkner stepped in. 'Enough,' he said sharply. 'We'll conduct a thorough investigation into the leak. For now, everyone is to report their actions in detail. We need to sort this out, and fast.'

Faulkner's words carried the weight of a warning—careers were on the line. The operatives, still visibly tense, nodded curtly and stood, their chairs scraping against the floor as they prepared to leave.

'Gentlemen, ensure your reports are detailed. No stone unturned. We're only as strong as our weakest link. Send them directly to myself,' Connor said as he watched them leave, their steps heavy and their shoulders hunched. He knew he had played a dangerous game, manipulating the operation for his own ends. As the door closed behind them, leaving Connor and Faulkner alone, the room seemed to contract.

Faulkner studied Connor before speaking, his tone less fiery but more calculating. 'You've always kept your cards close to your chest, Connor. Sometimes too close. Your methods may have kept us safe, but they've also kept us in the dark.'

'In our line of work, Gregory, truth often becomes a liability.'

Faulkner let out a humorless chuckle. 'Poetic, but we're analysts, not philosophers. I need facts, Connor. Hard, cold facts.'

A heavy silence descended. Outside, the faint sounds of footsteps on the tiled floor filtered through, a distant reminder of those working to uncover what others try so hard to hide.

'I'll provide what I think is best,' Connor said, 'but understand this: some paths, once taken, don't allow for a return journey. We tread a fine line between law and order.'

Faulkner stood. 'Just make sure nothing comes back on us.'

With those parting words, Faulkner left the room, his departure as abrupt as his entrance. Connor, alone in his office, turned his attention to the CIA emblem on the wall. The eagle's unblinking eyes seemed to stare back at him. His expression remained unreadable as he contemplated the emblem, symbolizing the complex operations conducted under the guise of national security. His focus then shifted to a sealed envelope tucked away in his desk drawer. The faintest hint of a smirk crossed his face as he eyed the envelope, silently acknowledging how he would stay one step ahead.

The air in the FBI's Pennsylvania Avenue headquarters crackled with tension. Special Agent Mat Donovan, a figure of authority and determination, paced the room. He drummed his fingers against his thigh, impatient as he watched the agents settle in, preparing for an urgent briefing. The walls were adorned with charts and maps, the evidence collected from days of tireless investigation into the death of their fellow agent.

Donovan paused in front of a detailed timeline chart, his pen tracing the events of that fateful night. 'Look at this. The night our agent was killed, surveillance cameras around D.C. conveniently went dark. Too convenient.' Murmurs of agreement rippled through the room.

Agent Sullivan raised his hand. 'We also have inconsistencies at the crime scene. It's as if someone knew exactly how to cover their tracks.'

Donovan turned to face the team. 'And let's not forget the forensic fiasco. Contaminated DNA samples? That doesn't just happen. We've hit wall after wall,' he continued. 'And every turn we've taken has led us to more dead ends.'

An agent, her expression a mix of anger and fear, stood up. 'Sir, with this level of obstruction, it's like we're being shut down from higher up. What if this goes beyond the usual suspects?'

Donovan nodded. 'That's precisely what we need to consider. There's a possibility that this isn't just about criminal networks. We might be dealing with something...or someone within our own government.'

Agent Miller, a seasoned field operative, stood next. 'Are we suggesting a cover-up? Because if so, who are we implying is behind this?'

Donovan's eyes met Miller's. 'It's a possibility we can't ignore. And every lead brings us back to one entity. The CIA. It is possible they have good friends in the White House, which has authority over the executive branch.'

As Donovan mentioned the possibility of CIA and White House involvement, a moment of tense silence followed. Agent Sullivan's eyebrows furrowed in concern, his eyes scanning the room as if assessing potential threats.

The implication was clear to everyone in the room. 'You can't be serious. The fucking White House?' another agent questioned.

'Possibly,' Donovan replied.

Agent Martinez, a fiery presence, threw her notepad down on the table. 'So, we're saying this could be an inside job? That's a serious accusation.'

'Well, we don't know for sure, but we can't rule it out. The Black Orchestra's involvement could imply connections to many agencies, and if that's the case, we're not just pursuing justice for our colleague; we're uncovering a conspiracy that could shake the very foundations of our intelligence community.'

Agent Jensen, a younger agent known for her analytical prowess, raised her hand. 'Sir, if this leads us to the White House doorstep, what are the implications for our safety, our careers?'

'Yeah, going against them? That's a whole different ball game. They can use the CIA against us,' another agent interjected.

Agent Jensen's question resonated with the team. All the faces now turned to Donovan for reassurance. He understood their fears and waved his hand toward the documents adorning his desk and stapled to the walls. 'Look here,' he said, picking up a memo titled *Authorization for Inter-Agency Investigation* from the DOJ. 'We have legal backing. If this is a rogue operation, and sanctioned at the highest levels, then we have protection.'

Donovan moved to the next document,

Guidelines for Collaboration Between the FBI and CIA, outlining their cooperative framework. 'We're not adversaries in this. We're uncovering a potential threat within our ranks.'

Agent Martinez checked her watch, then sighed, unimpressed.

Donovan ignored her by moving on to the next document. The OIG's *Oversight Approval Notice*. 'Oversight is key. We're not in this alone.'

He took a sip of water to allow everyone to process the documents before addressing their legal standing. He held up a FISA Court Order and a *Memorandum of Understanding for Joint Task Force Operation* folder, highlighting their surveillance authority and joint operational guidelines.

Donovan's tone became more somber as he touched on *Protocols for Evidence Collection and Sharing*. 'This is about preserving integrity, ensuring that every piece of evidence is untainted.'

He addressed their Congressional oversight with a brief summary, emphasizing the gravity and breadth of their mandate. 'We're accountable, not just to ourselves, but to the nation.'

As Donovan moved around the room, he passed around copies of the *Legal Precedents in Inter-Agency Investigations*, stressing the historical significance of their work. 'We're part of a larger narrative, one that shapes the future of inter-agency cooperation.'

The agents absorbed Donovan's words, their initial trepidation giving way to a sense of purpose. Donovan, sensing their shifting mood, squared his shoulders and held up his finger. 'This isn't just another case. It's a pivotal moment in our careers, in the history of this agency. We're uncovering a potential conspiracy that could reach the highest echelons of power. We stick with the powers given to us, keep investigating, and stay one foot in front. That's how we keep ourselves safe.'

The mention of a conspiracy stirred the room, agents exchanging glances of both concern and determination. 'But sir,' interjected Agent Thompson, 'what about this man Danny Mercer's involvement? His name keeps surfacing.'

Donovan paused, carefully choosing his words. 'Mercer is a variable we're yet to fully understand. But rest assured, we'll follow every lead.'

As the meeting drew to a close, Donovan's final words resonated with authority. 'We stand at the frontier of truth and justice. Our resolve will be tested, but our commitment must remain unwavering.'

Agent Martinez flicked through the documents before standing abruptly, her frustration evident to everyone in the room. She walked to the wall next to Donovan, scrutinizing the documents closely. 'This is us legally protected, yes. But where or what protection was afforded to the agent killed in the drug house? Where is our physical protection? Legal documents don't stop a 9mm at point-blank range, sir. I didn't sign up to get assassinated by my own government.'

Donovan murmured something under his breath before taking a seat. 'I understand your concerns. I am fully aware that this set of circumstances may be closer to home than you all would appreciate. Therefore, I am giving you the opportunity to step aside and work on other matters. However, make that decision carefully. This is the job you all signed up for, and you all understood that when you took your oath to support and defend the Constitution of the United States against all enemies, foreign and domestic.'

Donovan's voice held a tone of controlled rage, and the agents could see a vein pulsating in his neck. As he locked eyes with Agent Martinez, he continued his speech. 'This is crunch time. Either leave my office and get back to your own cases or stay and show allegiance to your badge.'

Agent Martinez stormed across the floor, collected her notepad and cell phone, and left the office. After Agent Martinez's abrupt departure, a ripple of quiet laughter swept through the room. The remaining agents stayed in their seats.

'Okay, team. We are in this together. Agent Sullivan, control all access passes to this room. No one goes in or out without my approval. This investigation must be locked down tight. There can be no discussions of any sort outside of these walls. There is no limit to the reach of the CIA.'

Agent Sam Sullivan, one of the most loyal to Donovan, took some notes and nodded his approval to Donovan. A crisp smile was drawn across his face as he remembered the look on Agent Martinez's face when she left the room. Sullivan was an old-school FBI Agent and ex-Navy Seal who, for years, had been looking for something more exciting.

After a few minutes of issuing orders to each agent, Donovan stood and thanked everyone for coming. The agents all filed out, each one mentally preparing for the task ahead. Donovan remained in his leather chair, waiting for the door to close so he could pour himself a drink. As the commotion died down, his thoughts lingered on the chart, and he was aware that the path they were about to embark on was fraught with challenges and uncertainties. In the dangerous world of espionage, the pursuit of truth was a daunting path few dared to tread. Yet for Donovan, it was more than a path; it was a solemn duty he embraced without hesitation. He glanced at the closed door before reaching for his cell phone, his fingers hovering over the screen.

He knew he needed outside help, someone off the books, someone not caught in the trappings of bureaucracy and jurisdictional limits. His mind raced to a contact in Europe, an old ally who had proven invaluable in past off-the-record operations. Picking up the phone, Donovan contemplated the risks of making this call, knowing it could either break the case wide open or plunge him deeper into uncharted territory.

With a deep breath, he dialed the number. As the phone rang, Donovan's expression hardened with resolve. This call, unauthorized and risky, was a step into the unknown, but he was ready to take it for the sake of uncovering the truth.

SEVEN

Seated at a small table in the corner of Tabac de la République, Mercer waited with a simmering impatience as François Rousseau ordered a pack of Gauloises cigarettes. Rousseau, an old acquaintance from a long-ago mission in Morocco, exuded the quiet confidence of a seasoned spy. With two decades under his belt at the *Direction Générale de la Sécurité Extérieure* (DGSE), he had mastered the art of blending in. He was of average height, with sharp, observant eyes set in a weathered face that hinted at years spent in the field. His hair, peppered with gray, was neatly combed back, and his attire, though simple, a dark jacket and trousers, was immaculately tailored, befitting a Parisian. His appearance was unassuming, indistinguishable from the other Parisian café-goers; well-groomed, lean, and seemingly at ease, lost in a cloud of cigarette smoke and the leisurely enjoyment of an espresso.

Mercer shifted in his chair, angling for a better view of the street. The café's lights were glaring, uncomfortably bright. Before entering, he had employed a surveillance detection route, varying his path and making unexpected turns to flush out potential tails. The recent events raised threat levels and, with that, his paranoia. Confident no one had followed, he now casually observed the area, watching for anyone who might have transitioned from mobile to static surveillance.

Mairie de Clichy, off the beaten path of Parisian tourism, offered Mercer a rare sense of ease. His own safe house, a hidden gem acquired twelve years prior, was a welcome escape from the CIA's extensive network of shelters. Despite the agency's resources, Mercer often chose the solitude of his own arrangements, especially now, when his instincts screamed caution after the recent meeting.

Evening descended on Bd du Général Leclerc, cloaking the café in the rich aroma of café noir. The street, under the functional glow of the streetlamps, transformed into a hub of covert activity, its Haussmannian façades casting a stark, contrasting silhouette against the evening sky. The gentle clink of porcelain and the soft murmur of conversation in the café offered a soothing respite from the world of clandestine meetings and covert operations.

As he watched the other patrons of the café, Mercer cast his mind back to the meeting with Connor. The uninvited guests, particularly Kenneth Decker, infuriated him. Connor's decision to bring along not only the FBI but also Decker, from the Office of the Director of National Intelligence, was an unwelcome surprise. As Mercer contemplated their potential involvement, he subconsciously extracted his cell phone from his pocket. He carefully slid the SIM card out and tucked it into his shirt pocket, then neatly removed the battery and placed it on the table. *These men would never meet so openly,* he thought. *Senior officials from different agencies coming together is no mere coincidence. And despite the DNI overseeing the U.S. Intelligence Community, there's no logical reason for Decker to be inquiring on the streets.*

Mercer's mind drifted back to a stiflingly hot and humid night in Tangier. Decker was embedded with a CIA unit tasked with tracking the Moroccan mafia, intercepting their communications, and gathering intelligence on their financial maneuvers, all to be shared with the Direction Générale de Surveillance du Territoire. At the helm of the DGST was Salaheddine Boufal. Mercer, assigned to an over-watch detail, was responsible for security during the clandestine rendezvous between Decker and Boufal. The meeting was held in a nondescript office, barely a kilometer from the bustling Tangier-Med port.

As Mercer recalled that night, a twinge of discomfort gripped him. He had been surveying the meeting through his rifle scope, meticulously scanning each window, when suddenly, the audio in his earpiece cut out, just as Decker stepped into the building. He shifted his focus from one window to the next, trying to catch a glimpse of the two men, when a sudden flash from a window caught his attention. Outside, Boufal's guards, taken aback, scrambled toward the building. Mercer, positioned four hundred yards away, had no choice but to act, his M110 sniper rifle methodically engaging the targets.

Now, sitting in the relative calm of the Tabac de la République café, Mercer shook his head, the memory vivid in his mind. He remembered Decker's expression as he left the office, a chilling calmness. Decker had eliminated Boufal, fully aware that Mercer and his team would be left to handle the fallout. No official explanation was ever provided for Decker's actions, a fact that gnawed at Mercer. *This is no fucking coincidence,* he reaffirmed silently, feeling a surge of anger.

'*Désolé d'avoir tardé.*' Rousseau's voice was tinged with a strong Parisian accent as he approached Mercer's table, his apology fluid in his native French. Pulling out a chair, he settled into it discreetly, positioning himself for an unobstructed view of the street.

Mercer offered a small, understanding smile. 'No need to apologize, François. After all, I'm the one asking for a favor.'

Rousseau's hand sliced through the air, dismissing the formality with the grace of a man accustomed to favors and information. 'It's always good to see you, Danny. Our last venture was quite the escapade, *n'est-ce pas?*' His eyes held a glint of reminiscence, quickly replaced by the sharp focus of the present. 'Now, let's clarify your request, so I'm not misinterpreting anything. *Ah, un moment, s'il vous plaît.*'

Rousseau's sharp eyes drifted to Mercer's dismantled phone on the table. With a nod of understanding, he smoothly extracted his own phone from his pocket. His fingers deftly switched it off, sliding out the SIM card in a single, fluid motion. He tucked the tiny chip into his pocket, then retrieved a device, no larger than his pack of Gauloises, from another pocket. The small gadget hummed to life with a subtle click, and he set it on the table, effectively creating a bubble where all cell phone signals were nullified. 'This should keep Echelon at bay,' he remarked casually, a hint of a wry smile playing on his lips.

'Okay, I presume you need intel on someone. That, I can manage,' Rousseau said, just as the waitress approached with two steaming cups of espresso. He thanked her with a polite nod. 'Merci, madame.' He slid one cup toward Mercer and took a sip from his own.

After a brief pause, he folded his hands together and spoke. 'If it's Europol you're after, c'est faisable. Give me until tomorrow morning, and I'll have everything you need.'

Mercer's expression tightened. 'Afraid it's not that straightforward, François. I need your expertise in surveillance.'

Rousseau's eyebrows raised slightly. 'A French national?' he inquired.

Mercer shook his head. 'No, he's one of ours, from the U.S. intelligence community. And it's complicated. I can't overstate the sensitivity of this situation. This needs to be kept off the books. I'm not going rogue, but it's crucial to understand that there are...let's say, concerning elements within our ranks.' He paused, gauging Rousseau's reaction. Mercer was wary of diving too deep into the specifics; there was no need to overwhelm the one man capable of providing the essential and professional support he needed.

Rousseau took a moment, his eyes narrowing as he processed the implications. The café's ambient noise seemed to fade into the background as he mulled over Mercer's request.

'D'accord, I can assist. Although I must

provide a warning, given the recent events in Geneva, security in Paris is tighter than usual. It's going to be challenging. Everyone is on high alert, or as you Americans say, on their toes.'

Mercer nodded. He was grateful for Rousseau's help and was well aware Decker would surround himself with a ring of steel. He took a sip of coffee and casually moved his attention around the café before continuing. 'The target is Kenneth Decker, ex-CIA and now working within the Office of the Director of National Intelligence. It's puzzling why he's here in Paris, closely involved with the FBI and CIA. Decker is a D.C. figure, known for pulling strings from above. My hunch: Decker might be acting on a personal agenda outside DNI approval, or worse, he could be compromised. I'm leaning toward the former. Using my team is too risky with so many uncertainties involved, and that's where your help comes in.'

Mercer reached into his jacket, pulling out a small, inconspicuous SD card. He slid it across the table to Rousseau. 'This has everything you need to know about Decker,' he said quietly. 'Photos, personal details, his current living arrangements in Paris.'

Rousseau pocketed the SD card with a nod, his expression turning more serious. 'Understood. I'll start surveillance immediately.'

'I need updates on his movements every hour. If he meets anyone, I want profiles, background, everything you can dig up on them,' Mercer instructed with an intensity that matched the seriousness of their task. 'Decker won't be in Paris for long, another day at most. He's scheduled to fly back to the States. A man like him doesn't leave D.C. without a damn good reason.'

Rousseau's brow furrowed as he nodded. 'You'll have your updates. I'll ensure we don't lose sight of him.'

Mercer discreetly left an envelope on his seat as he stood up, the contents rustling slightly. It contained twenty thousand euros, expenses for the operation. 'This should cover any costs you incur. And François,' he paused, 'be careful. We're not dealing with ordinary targets here.'

Their hands met in a firm, brief handshake, a silent acknowledgment of the dangers and the trust between them. Mercer turned and left the café.

Outside, a worrying thought crept into Mercer's mind. He hoped Rousseau truly understood the gravity of the situation and the power that men like Decker welded. These were players who operated deeper than most could fathom. The risks were substantial, and Mercer knew the cost of failure or exposure could be immense. Shaking off the unease, Mercer quickened his pace along Bd du Général Leclerc before veering into the narrower streets toward the Mairie de Clichy Métro station on Rue Martre.

The underground ride to Champs-Élysées Clemenceau was quick. After alighting, he chose an indirect route, circling around an art museum to ensure he wasn't being followed. Kenneth Decker had covertly established himself at the Hôtel de Crillon, utilizing an alias for cover. Rousseau would have surveillance up and running within the hour, and Mercer wanted to cover the gap.

Kenneth Decker paced the confines of his opulent room at the Hôtel de Crillon, his mind overwhelmed by a mess of conflicts and conspiracies. The rich Parisian decor around him felt incongruous with the dark churn of his thoughts. The Black Orchestra's operations, once a well-oiled machine of subterfuge and influence, were now threading into risky terrain, especially with the Chinese faction's growing impatience and demands.

The evening lights of Paris cast a muted glow through the window, illuminating Decker's weathered features. Years of operations in war-torn countries had etched lines of tension and wariness on his face. He moved to his phone, a burner, the only kind he dared use for conversations like the one he was about to have.

The call connected with a soft tone, and a voice on the other end answered in Mandarin, terse and expectant. Decker, though not fluent, understood enough. He responded in English, laced with a firmness that belied his internal turmoil. The conversation quickly escalated. General Liu Xiang, the high-ranking official from the breakaway faction of the Communist Party, was infuriated over the botched operation involving Arnold Becker.

Decker's tone hardened as he argued, 'Becker's inclusion was required, despite the outcome. He needs to be seen to be working tightly with the French to gain what intel other agencies are withholding. You don't understand how we work in the U.S. Some fragments of the FBI are investigating us. We need to invent some Black Orchestra ghosts around Europe. However, the fact that Becker somehow drew attention to the kidnap attempt was... problematic. Those strong security precautions taken by the French were unprecedented.' His words were calculated, masking the fear of what the Chinese faction held over him, the intelligence leaks, shared drug routes through Central America, and corrupt deals would be used as leverage if he didn't deliver strong results.

Liu's reply was cold, a veiled threat, reminding Decker of the incriminating intelligence they possessed. 'Your personal indiscretions are of no concern to us, at this stage. Our focus is the failure in Geneva and the elimination of the team. You need to rectify this, Decker. You are unimportant to us if you cannot control this. It is your job to understand threats to your homeland, and that also relates to our relationship.'

Decker moved across the room and stood at the door. He listened for sounds out in the corridor before replying. 'I already have people in place to take care of things at our end.'

'The meeting tomorrow is crucial,' Liu stated. 'Ensure all arrangements are in place. Forget Becker; the FBI's internal turmoil is your opportunity. We need further infiltration into their intelligence and research sectors. You're playing a poor game, Decker. Keep your agency in tune, or you'll face the consequences from both ends.'

Decker's hand trembled slightly as he ended the call. Part worry, part anger at listening to this man. The enormity of his situation was suffocating. He stared out at the Parisian skyline, a city of lights and shadows. His eyes scanned while his mind raced as he contemplated his next move. *It's time*, he thought as he grabbed the phone once again. He made another call, this time to Georg Wilhelm Schelling, the leader of the Black Orchestra. 'Everything is set for tomorrow,' he reported, his voice steady, betraying no sign of internal turmoil. 'We will have the goods as planned.'

Georg preferred fewer words on the line. 'Very well. We will catch up when you return.'

Decker hung up, and his mind tossed through scenarios and contingencies. Tomorrow's meeting would be pivotal, a convergence of dirty agendas and power plays. He glanced around the lavish room, a gilded cage of his own making. Decker knew he was a cog in a vast and intricate mechanism, but he also knew the art of survival. Moving quickly across the room, he peeked out the window to the street below, more out of habit than actually conducting a proper inspection of the area. Decker felt safe here, always trusting the cities of Paris, Berlin, and London. It was the Eastern European ones that worried him.

Getting his head down and grabbing some sleep was necessary, but another matter required his attention. As Decker worked on decrypting and downloading the classified files, he couldn't shake off the feeling of unease. The clock hands showed it was a few minutes to midnight, and he knew he had to hurry. Suddenly, his computer screen flickered, and a message appeared: *Access granted. Files received.* Decker let out a sigh of relief, knowing that the files were now safely in his possession. A faint noise attracted his attention. It came from the corridor. Quickly saving the files onto an encrypted USB drive, he placed it on the bedside table next to his cell phone and rose from his desk.

He walked over to the door and peered outside, catching a glimpse of a hotel staff member carrying a bundle of bedsheets, disappearing into another room. Decker grinned to himself as he locked his door, reminded that he was no longer in the dingy alleyways of Karachi. Turning back into his room, his eyes settled on the fully stocked bar fridge, his grin evolving into a smile. *A whiskey nightcap will erase the bloody horrors of the past,* he thought, pouring a tumbler of Aberlour whiskey. With each sip, the tension in his head and the room dissipated.

He lowered himself into a leather armchair next to the tall windows and inched the curtains open just a fraction, allowing for a soothing view over the Parisian rooftops. *By this time tomorrow night, the hard work will be done,* he mused. Decker was finally at peace. As he drank down the remaining liquor, he noted how beautiful Paris looked at night despite its lurking threats. His eyes grew heavy as the alcohol took effect. With a final effort, Decker switched off the lamps and slid the curtains open a bit further, choosing to enjoy the city view as he drifted into sleep.

•　　　•　　　•

As darkness covered the city, Mercer got to work. His task was straightforward: to assess Decker's security measures at the Hôtel de Crillon. Drawing upon years of experience and an innate understanding of intelligence trade-craft, Mercer initiated a thorough reconnaissance of the area. Strolling casually a few blocks away on Rue du Faubourg Saint-Honoré, hands in his pockets, his demeanor was relaxed, but his senses remained razor sharp. Aware of the U.S. embassy's proximity, he dared not linger or appear suspicious. Mercer's eyes discreetly swept over the streets and parks, alert for subtle signs of surveillance. *Multi-layer surveillance teams would set up from around here*, he thought as he turned onto Rue Royale.

His training allowed him to spot anomalies, a strategically parked vehicle, a bystander whose gaze followed a pattern, too attentive for a casual observer. These were potential markers of a Stealth Team, professionals who blended seamlessly into the environment, observing without being observed.

As he continued, Mercer mapped the security layers in his mind, careful to maintain a normal pace, keeping his observations covert. His reconnaissance was not just about gathering information; it was about understanding

Decker's mindset. By analyzing the security setup, he could infer Decker's level of caution, his possible fears, and how seriously he took potential threats. This knowledge was crucial, forming the basis of Mercer's subsequent actions and strategies, and informing Rousseau without alerting those who might be watching.

Mercer's focus then shifted to uncovering the Stealth Team, the real threat. This required keen observation of minute details: a slight irregularity in pedestrian flow, an out-of-place reflection in a shop window, a car that turned just one too many times. These signs, invisible to an untrained eye, spoke volumes to Mercer, revealing the hidden layer of security that truly guarded Decker.

To get a view of the front of the hotel, the Place de la Concorde offered him no real protection. *The stealth team should be maintaining around-the-clock watch for threats,* Mercer thought, surveying the huge plaza before circling around toward the Terrasse de l'Orangerie, where he took position next to the museum. The landscaping provided some cover from security cameras and potential counter-surveillance operators. As he continued his observations, Mercer mentally mapped out the security layers, noting potential weak points, escape routes, and the likely positions of hidden surveillance cameras. He was aware that someone of

Decker's caliber would employ not only counter-surveillance measures but possibly advanced electronic surveillance equipment as well.

Mercer adjusted the range dial on his night vision binoculars, then held them steady as he focused on the surveillance camera perched above the hotel entrance, recognizing its capabilities and limitations. He examined the balcony above the entrance, looking for additional hardware, which would indicate Decker was using his own surveillance equipment. Below the balcony, a group lingering around the entrance, trying too hard to seem nonchalant, caught his attention. *That's the decoy team,* Mercer suspected, positioned to distract from the more critical security elements. His keen eyes scanned for less obvious signs: the presence of pavement artists, undercover agents adept at blending into the urban environment, their casual demeanor belying their sharp surveillance skills.

As the night deepened, Mercer concluded his initial surveillance. He had gathered valuable insights into Decker's security arrangement, enough to give François Rousseau a clear intelligence picture. This intel was not just about what he saw but also what he didn't see—the gaps and blind spots in the security that he could potentially exploit. Mercer checked his watch, then immediately made his way to the Metro. With each step, Mercer focused more and more on the potential for violence tomorrow, questioning whether his past actions had set a dangerous precedent he wasn't ready to face again.

Dawn broke over Paris, casting a warm glow across the rooftops. In the early morning bustle, a taxi cut through the congested traffic. Kenneth Decker, in its back seat, watched the city wake up, his mind on the day's critical agenda. He arrived early at a nondescript café in the Marais, a spot chosen for its obscurity rather than its ambiance. Today, he was without his usual security detail, a risky move dictated by the sensitive nature of the meeting. He felt vulnerable, a sensation he despised.

As he waited, he surveyed the space around him, noting every exit, every patron, every potential threat. His meeting with General Liu was crucial, and despite the apparent solitude, Decker played the part of a man backed by unseen forces.

Liu arrived promptly, his entrance unassuming yet deliberate. To the casual observer, he might have appeared as just another unremarkable visitor from the Far East, lost in the anonymous bustle of the city. Yet, there was an air of arrogance about him, a subtle assertion of his importance, noticeable only to those who understood the nuances of power. The two men exchanged nods, foregoing formalities.

Decker's opening remarks were direct. 'Mr. Liu, I appreciate you meeting me under these circumstances. Today's discussion requires discretion of the highest order,' he stated, his tone firm, betraying none of his underlying tension.

Liu's eyes flickered with annoyance. 'Mr. Decker, this is...an unusual setting for such a meeting. I must admit, being without my men in unfamiliar territory is not where I prefer to conduct business.'

'I understand your concerns, but discretion is paramount for what we're discussing.' Decker picked up his espresso and took a sip while allowing for a moment of silence.

Liu glanced around the small café, then slid his chair closer to Decker and sat down. 'Yes, discretion. But remember, errors in our line of work can be...costly. I do not trust the French, their methods, or their motives. We are both vulnerable here.'

Decker set his glass down next to a copy of *Le Monde*, and stared off into the distance for a moment.

The silence angered the General, a man used to others bowing to his presence. 'Mr. Decker, if anything goes awry, if there is even a hint of betrayal or incompetence...the consequences will be dire. For both of us.'

Decker nodded slightly. With the General on edge, it was time to conduct business. Decker signaled for the waiter to bring down two espressos before turning his attention back to the trade.

'Let's crack on with what we both need and keep things professional.' Decker glanced around the café before removing the thumb drive from a packet of cigarettes. 'I think you will find the information within to be really helpful, Xiang.'

Liu's eyes widened when Decker referred to him by his first name. With a furrowed brow, Liu contemplated storming out of the café; momentarily, he was caught in a brain fog.

'*Messieurs, voici vos cafés, profitez-en s'il vous plait.*' The waiter set down two coffees, then turned and left. Liu snapped back to life. He lifted his glass and took a sip. Immediately, he regretted the action. The deep flavor disgusted him, adding to his anger.

He set the coffee down and felt the need to get this handover completed quickly so he could leave. Without subtlety, he removed a thumb drive from his jacket pocket and purposefully dropped it onto the table. His dark eyes fixed on Deckers. 'This is all the information on your greedy leaders. Ensure you back them into a corner and leave them with no option but to obey your organization. I am not the man you want to mess with, Kenneth. Am I clear?'

'I will do what needs to be done. My years of experience within the intelligence community and dealing with politicians allow me to read their next move. They will dance only to my tune, Xiang.'

'Very well, Kenneth. I will look forward to seeing those friendly to, let's say, East Asian interests taking their seats within Congress and the Senate, then continuing to all levels of state and federal intelligence. There is no time to waste.' The General didn't wait for a response. He gave a firm handshake, then stood up and walked out of the café.

Decker watched the man leave as he flipped the thumb drive between his fingers before concealing it in a specially tailored pocket in his black leather jacket. He understood its monumental significance. This drive harbored a trove of intelligence gathered by Chinese cyber units, documenting the clandestine business dealings, market-rigging schemes, and insider trading of influential figures across the U.S. political and intelligence community landscape. The meticulous Chinese surveillance had capitalized on America's focus elsewhere, amassing data that could see numerous powerful individuals behind bars.

The Chinese intelligence agency, through their vast cyber warfare units based in Shanghai, had spent decades meticulously tracking high-value targets across the political spectrum, extending from New York to California. This comprehensive surveillance operation spanned influential figures in states like Florida and Texas. Simultaneously, the U.S. Defense Department's focus was predominantly on pursuing high-value targets (HVTs) through the streets, deserts, valleys, and mountains of the Middle East and Afghanistan, illustrating a significant divergence in strategic focus between the two powers.

Outside the café, Liu walked briskly down the street to his limousine. His operation was the linchpin in a grander strategy by his rogue Chinese actors. Led by himself, they operated from various defense and intelligence units across China, manipulating Western democracies from afar. Their goal was to upend the American dream, showcasing it as a flawed system and elevating the Communist ideology to a pedestal of global admiration. This was not mere intelligence warfare; it was a calculated maneuver to realign the world's power structures.

The American political and intelligence community, unbeknownst to them, was teetering on the edge of becoming puppets dancing to Liu's tunes. The thumb drive he handed over was the key to bending the will of America's decision-makers, a means to infiltrate and manipulate from within, a weapon to ensure that no force could oppose his ascent to global supremacy. With the Black Orchestra as the conduit, Liu's vision of a world under his command was edging closer to reality.

Liu's ambitions were clear in his mind. There was no turning back. His heartbeat rose as he settled into the back of a stretched Mercedes. The exchange with the Americans was complete. He removed the thumb drive, which Decker had given him, from his pocket and stared at it with curiosity. Intelligence collected by the U.S. government on influential Chinese bankers, businessmen, and scientists in the U.S. and Europe. Those who had wealth, power, and a good reason to fear coercion and blackmail by him and his network. Liu, with the backing of a few rogue agents in the Communist Party, aimed to dismantle their own President's power, positioning themselves at the helm of one of the world's most powerful nations. With the American intelligence community and politicians unknowingly serving the Black Orchestra's agenda, now the puppets of Liu, his path to global domination seemed unobstructed.

•   •   •

As Liu's car eased into the city's traffic, a lone bike rider pulled out and shadowed it discreetly. Unbeknownst to Liu, the French surveillance team had picked up both men as they entered and exited the café.

François Rousseau had relaxed a great deal after listening to Decker's phone calls the previous night. The ability to hack into the hotel via a security breach in the HVAC system allowed Rousseau to grab the details of each guest and their movements throughout the hotel. With a simple cross-check, the DGSE established who was accompanying Decker on the trip to Europe. Earlier in the morning, the surveillance team forwarded some good news to Rousseau: Decker was alone when he left the hotel, seated in the back of a taxi. The French cyber team breached the company's systems, sifting through logs to pinpoint Decker's final destination: Café La Perle, Marais. Rousseau swiftly deployed a second unit to monitor Decker's arrival while the initial unit stayed at the hotel, keeping an eye on Decker's personal security to ensure they didn't follow.

For François Rousseau, this was just another operation. As he scrutinized the surveillance footage, a thought crossed his mind. The task Mercer had set had unfolded more smoothly than he had expected in their line of work. He mused with a hint of skepticism, *C'était trop facile aujourd'hui*, reflecting on the unexpected ease of their operation amidst the gritty reality of their clandestine world. Rousseau couldn't shake off a nagging curiosity: *Why was Mercer so deeply concerned for his own safety when today had proven to be almost routine?* Rousseau, ever pragmatic, pushed aside his lingering doubts and issued orders for his teams to withdraw. Once the video footage and audio of Decker's conversations were securely dispatched to Mercer, he returned to his regular duties. In the complex realm they operated in, Rousseau found a moment to wish Mercer luck, an unspoken gesture of camaraderie in their line of work.

Liang Guang, the seasoned leader of the European kill team, had come out of retirement to settle old scores. Entrusted with Liu's safety, his expertise surpassed that of any other operative. Liang sat in a rented Citroën on Rue Vieille-du-Temple, his gaze fixed on Café le Perle. His hand casually resting on the concealed QSZ-92 9mm pistol under his jacket. As he focused on the mission, Zhao Ming's cautions against recklessness echoed in his mind. Consumed by a vengeful desire against the

French, blamed for decimating his team in Geneva, Liang wrestled with the urgency to retaliate and Ming's advice for strategic patience. Ming, adept in international politics and espionage, emphasized timing and discretion. *Patience*, Liang whispered to himself. *Revenge at the right moment.* His attention sharpened as Decker left the café. But Decker was not his target.

After a tense ten minutes, Liang's eyes narrowed on a new figure emerging from a blacked-out van, followed by another. *DGSE, found you, you dirty thieves*, he muttered under his breath. Quickly, he lifted a small camera, capturing a few shots before smoothly backing the Citroën out onto the street. *They'll regret their actions*, he grumbled as he eyed the traffic behind. The warm Parisian morning silently shared his tightly kept secrets.

EIGHT

Danny Mercer stared out the taxi window. The relentless rain turned Washington, D.C.'s streets into a scene of smeared lights and unfocused faces. He watched as the droplets assaulted the glass, each one distorting the reality outside a little more. Mercer sat forward and wiped away the condensation from the window with a deliberate swipe, a clear line of vision that allowed him to recalibrate his mind.

The car crept along Constitution Avenue, the usual buzz of the capital muted by the downpour. Mercer's mind churned, replaying the conversation with Rousseau. The information on General Liu had only deepened his unease. Sleep didn't come easy during the eight-hour, early morning flight from Paris. The only person on his mind was the high-ranking military official of the Chinese Communist Party.

Mercer grappled with the stakes at hand. *What could these men, such powerful men, be willing to do? What secrets or trades are they conspiring on? How far does the rot of our intelligence community go?* As the car neared 14th St, Mercer refocused and reined in his anger. The headache had reappeared, compelling him to exit the taxi and face the relentless weather bearing down on D.C. Instinctively, he reached for the door and instructed the driver to pull over.

He paid his fare and stepped out into the night. The change was drastic. From the warm taxi to the cold streets, the rain instantly lashed at his face and quickly soaked through his clothes. Embracing the downpour, Mercer was indifferent to the discomfort. The wild weather matched his mood. His stride was purposeful as he walked away from the taxi, keeping his head down but his eyes scanning all around. He navigated the soaked sidewalk, the thoughts of what lay ahead clear in his mind. The Herbert C. Hoover federal building loomed large as he walked past the imposing and secure structure. The building brought his mind back to the meeting with Rousseau. It had unsettled him more than he cared to admit. The intel on Liu wasn't just a piece of the puzzle; it was a warning sign of a much larger threat, one that could have ramifications far beyond the intelligence community. The questions that haunted him on the flight were more than just hypotheticals; they were a clarion call to action.

Mercer's footsteps splashed on the wet pavement, but rain didn't bother him; it was a cleansing force, washing away the stains of the commercial flight, if only for a moment. Up ahead, the Willard InterContinental Hotel, near Capitol Hill, bustled with politicians and lobbyists. All vying for the attention of those in power. With promises of donations and favors, the men and women were the real controllers of Washington. *There must be a simpler way to attract attention than...well...* Mercer trailed off, his plan unfinished. *There is only one thing these scheming bastards know,* he thought before turning onto Pennsylvania Avenue.

Mercer entered the lobby of the Marriott Hotel and collected his keycard for the hastily booked room. The only booking available was the king room with a view of the monument. He cared little for the view; his sole purpose was to shower, change his clothes, and prepare his tools for the night ahead. As the elevator climbed the floors, Mercer checked his watch. Forty minutes and counting before the Federal Policy Conference & Lobby Day's black-tie event commenced.

Once in the room, Mercer quickly showered and shaved off a few days' stubble with the provided toiletries. As he dried off, his attention was drawn to a soft knock at the door. Upon opening it, an unassuming man handed Mercer a black holdall, then turned and walked away. Mercer locked the door and returned to the bedroom.

The rich and powerful attendees of the Federal Policy Conference & Lobby Day in Washington, D.C. dressed and carried themselves in a manner befitting their status. Their impeccable style exuded confidence and authority, with tailored suits and gowns reflecting their wealth and influence. They moved with purpose and poise, their actions reinforcing their dominance in political and business circles.

Conversations brimmed with strategic discussions and high-level negotiations, each participant striving to shape the future of their industries and the world at large. The atmosphere was tense, with every attendee vying for an edge over the others. Constantly on guard, they knew that a single misstep could lead to their downfall. The stakes were high, and they were willing to do whatever it took to come out on top.

Mercer dressed neatly in the required black-tie attire and slipped into the grand room. As he reached for a glass of champagne, his dark eyes swept over the crowd, searching for the target amid a sea of influential figures. His mind remained fixed on the mission—focus and vigilance were paramount.

A few people locked eyes with him, their expressions laced with suspicion and calculation, each assessing the motives of those around them. The room was a goldmine of power and wealth, packed with lobbyists backed by millions, all eager to wield their resources to shape policy to their advantage.

Unseen beneath his impeccably tailored suit, Mercer's hand brushed against the concealed SIG Sauer handgun at his waist, a silent reminder of the high stakes of the game he was about to play. He knew that he had to plan his hit and escape carefully, considering every possible scenario and contingency.

As more guests took their seats, Mercer gained a better view across the room. His pulse quickened as he finally locked onto the target. Alexander West was engrossed in conversation with a group of old men at the center of the room. West cut through the crowd, shoulders squared against the murmur of voices, his polished Oxfords clicking against marble with the precision of a metronome.

Upon reaching the group, he picked up a canapé, using the brief pause to gauge the flow of conversation. He chewed slowly, eyes on West, listening for an opening. The men spoke in measured tones, their words careful, deliberate. Politics. Finance. A passing mention of defense contracts.

Mercer shifted his stance, angling himself closer. A polite nod at the man beside him, a slight lift of his glass. An outsider testing the waters. He caught West's eye and offered a subtle, knowing smile—just enough to suggest familiarity without presumption. A handshake might be too forward. A well-placed remark? Better. He waited, weighing his options, prepared to speak the moment the chance presented itself.

Mercer edged forward, his hand slipping into his pocket. He flicked a switch on a small device. Instantly, the lights cut out, and the grand room went into darkness. The music from the speakers died mid-note, giving way to sounds of nervous chuckles and murmuring. Mercer made a snap decision to forgo the gun, instead withdrawing a small carving knife, and stepped quickly toward Alexander.

The young entrepreneur, on the verge of making his first billion through AI research, didn't stand a chance. His Chinese handlers couldn't save him now.

With one hand, Mercer grabbed Alexander by the hair. With the other, he drove the blade neatly into the man's neck, slicing the carotid artery before severing the spinal cord in one swift motion. He let go, stepping back as the body slumped to the floor. Without hesitation, he turned and moved quickly toward the exit via the kitchens.

Less than a minute remained before the backup generator would kick in. He had to be clear of the security cameras before the lights came back on.

Mercer jostled through the bewildered cooks, brushing past them as he made for the rear of the prep area. He booted the emergency doors open, triggering an alarm, then bolted into the downpour. His heart pounded as the heavy rain washed the blood from his sleeve.

As Mercer sprinted eastbound on Pennsylvania Avenue, he kept his head down to avoid the surveillance cameras. To passing motorists, he was just another pedestrian caught in the downpour.

The distant wail of emergency vehicles echoed as he approached the parking lot on East St NW. Ducking inside, he moved quickly to the rear, scanning for a black Chevrolet Malibu.

He found the car and retrieved the key fob from its magnetic hide under the front fender. Thoughts racing, he unlocked the doors and slipped into the driver's seat.

Let's see who has my back, Mercer thought as he ignited the engine.

The CIA would be notified the moment one of their spare cars was activated. Internal cameras equipped with facial recognition software would alert the correct department that an operative was using the vehicle. Mercer knew that if state or federal law enforcement were actively searching for a suspect, the car he was in would effectively become invisible. A CIA liaison would coordinate with the police to ensure its passage remained unimpeded.

Before pulling out of the parking garage, Mercer traced the road in his mind, familiarizing himself with the primary and secondary roads before setting off.

The rear of the FBI Headquarters reflected in his mirror as he traveled westbound. Within a minute, he passed the White House on Constitution Avenue. He slowed slightly and lowered the passenger window. Through the rain, he spotted a helicopter hovering near the South Lawn, about three hundred feet from the Oval Office.

Reports of Alexander West's death will have spread across town quickly, Mercer thought. He was tempted to pull over and observe the fallout, but that would only attract attention he didn't want. The news anchors would be swarming soon.

From a hidden panel beneath the dash, he pulled out an LCD remote and switched it on. The police radios buzzed to life through the car speakers. Some units were setting up roadblocks, while officers on the scene were ordered to stop all vehicles and their occupants from leaving.

Mercer exhaled slowly. The police would meticulously cordon off the area to preserve the crime scene, and the CIA would step in quickly to protect him.

Unless they want to screw me over. The ball's in your court, Connor.

It was time to test Jeff Connor's true colors.

Mercer drove on. He had seen enough and could already piece together what would unfold across D.C. tonight. As he cruised along the George Washington Memorial Parkway, he watched the Potomac River flow steadily to his right. The rising waters were black as tar, the floodwaters furiously pulling soil from the eroding riverbanks.

His cell phone beeped, snapping him back to the task at hand. He scanned for a place to pull over and read the message.

It was from an old friend—someone he had worked with years ago in Africa. An Englishman now with MI6, once a warrior in the British Special Air Service. An operator Mercer could trust. Someone he turned to when he needed more than the CIA would provide. Sometimes, it paid off. Other times, it led to dead ends and cover-ups.

In the past twenty-four hours, Edward Hobbs had been tracking a man MI6 had suspected for years. One of many. These investigations usually trailed off when American intelligence agencies thanked the British for their intel and assured them they would handle the matter.

Frustration had grown within MI6's hierarchy as the same men remained entrenched in their circles of influence, corrupting politics through lobbying and backroom deals. When Mercer needed a clear, unbiased picture, he went directly to Hobbs.

His cell phone displayed an address and several photos of a man with bright, silvery hair. Surveillance images, taken from a distance—*perhaps Milan*, Mercer guessed.

His destination was a weathered mansion hidden behind towering oaks and a tangle of wildflowers, its brick chimneys just visible through the trees along the Potomac riverbank. After navigating the dark roads, Mercer pulled off and backed into a quiet lane, retrieving several items from the trunk. Despite his formal attire, he chose to approach the property silently through the surrounding fields. Before getting too close, he took a knee and pulled out his phone, needing further clarification on his target.

Mercer's voice was low, nearly lost in the wind moving through the tall grass as he dialed Hobbs. The encrypted signal buzzed briefly before connecting. 'Hobbs, I can't talk too much. Can you give me a quick rundown on Georg Wilhelm Schelling? What's his profile?'

'Mercer, yeah, I understand,' Hobbs's voice crackled through, the British accent crisp against the backdrop of static. 'OK, listen to this. Schelling is deeply involved with corrupt Chinese elites from the Communist Party. A bunch of high-profile men who are working outside party lines and have gone rogue. He seems to instigate deals between Western Universities, research departments, and all levels of government. Schelling himself is the head honcho within this criminal organization known as The Black Orchestra. Last month, he hosted a gathering in Saint Barthélemy. Notable attendees included some key figures from the Chinese faction. Seems they're not just casual acquaintances.'

Mercer listened intently, waiting for his moment to add something. 'What is in it for Schelling? What does he get out of it?'

'Power and influence. The higher up he goes, the more he has to trade with. Their organization is looking at billions of dollars. Much of it comes through various banks in Europe and the Caribbean. The problem we are dealing with is locating the origins of this money. The Communist Party's meticulous accounting makes it clear the CCP isn't funding this, reinforcing the likelihood that these Chinese operatives are acting independently of their government.'

'Risky for them. If their President finds out,

it will be the death penalty for them all,' added Mercer. 'Those photos from the party. Can you send them over?'

'Certainly. Where to?' Hobbs was all business, the professionalism of an MI6 operative clear in his tone.

'Secure drop. I'll text you the address. Keep this between us.'

'Copy that. You'll have them within the hour.' Hobbs's assurance was firm.

'Appreciate it, Hobbs.' Mercer ended the call. He didn't want to be on an open call for too long, with or without encryption. He quickly typed out the secure address in a message. The screen, dimmed to the lowest level to prevent illumination, made the task slightly slower. Mercer looked up at the mansion in the distance. It was roughly two thousand feet away, yet appeared imposing at this range. He remained there for several minutes, ears straining in the silence, before moving. Birds roosting on tree branches peered down into the darkness as Mercer treaded softly across the wet grass toward his target.

Mat Donovan's evening was cut short by the frantic call. Seeing her husband's stunned expression, She took his half-eaten dinner and stored it in the fridge—a ritual repeated too many times over the years. Donovan's wife hated nights like this, never knowing where he was going or when he'd be back. Donovan had no time for reassurance. He grabbed his jacket and keys and rushed out of the house.

Less than an hour later, he stood at the head of a long, sterile conference table in FBI headquarters. The room buzzed with low, intense discussion, punctuated by the shuffling of papers and the click of laptop keys. Around him, his investigative team was deep in analysis, piecing together the brutal murder that had occurred an hour ago, a few blocks east.

At the scene, police were busy taking witness statements, while FBI agents examined the evidence as heavily armed specialist officers secured the outer perimeter. Though the crime fell under the Metropolitan Police Department's (MPD) jurisdiction, the method of execution, location, and the victim's identity had drawn multiple agencies, each seeking insight into the motive and a possible suspect.

On Pennsylvania Avenue, officers from the United States Pentagon Police, Park Police, and Capitol Police hovered around, eager to pull whatever intel they could. Their presence only added to the MPD's frustration, especially when the lead investigator learned the hotel's surveillance cameras had captured nothing.

'Alright, let's bring it in,' Donovan said, his voice cutting through the ambient noise with authority. The room fell silent, all eyes turning toward him.

'Do we have any leads on known or suspected individuals or groups involved in the incident? And before anyone raises their hands, are there any immediate threats or related activities that require our attention?' asked Donovan.

Nathan Harrow was the first to respond. The ex-Navy Seal and CIA operative, now an FBI Agent, was determined to provide what little he could and be done with the investigation. 'I just came off a call with William Baxter. For those in the room who don't know Will, he works within the FBI's counterterrorism division. His specialty is cyber terrorism and digital forensics. Initial investigations suggest that the suspect, or suspects, were able to switch off the power. That's widely known, but interestingly, footage from the hotel's hard drives and cloud servers has been deleted or scrambled, leaving us effectively blind.'

Harrow leaned back in the high-backed leather chair, clasping his fingers together, hoping his work was finished. He exhaled slowly as if releasing the tension of the past few weeks, but a quick twitch in his left eye betrayed him.

His mind drifted to the meeting at Le

Faubourg Café on Rue d'Anjou in Paris—the deal that should have set everything straight. He and Will Baxter had met Danny Mercer to discuss black operations, a rendezvous made possible by Jeff Connor and Kenneth Decker. They had approached Mercer carefully, knowing the impulsive paramilitary officer wouldn't trust anyone easily, least of all two men tied to Connor and Decker.

Harrow shifted uncomfortably as the agents around the room made notes or tapped briefly into their laptops. *Something is not adding up,* Harrow thought. *This was the second killing in D.C. in as many weeks, and both times, forensics had been tampered with.*

He had once been willing to root out problems within the intelligence community, but not anymore. The dirty politics behind these operations were becoming too murky, the maneuvering too reckless. If someone didn't put a stop to it, the consequences would be far worse than another body in the morgue.

Harrow recalled it was Decker who had requested the meeting with Mercer. It was his attempt to settle the tension between the FBI and the CIA. Everything about that off-the-record day in Paris was unprecedented, causing Nathan Harrow many sleepless nights. A power play seemed to unfold between Connor and Decker, a battle of minds for control over the actual intelligence, not just the sanitized versions presented to the White House. Decker was a wildcard, and Harrow wondered if he was involved in the recent killings. His eyes moved across the room, analyzing faces for signs of betrayal.

Time felt like it had stopped as Donovan considered the implications of advanced digital blackouts, which Nathan Harrow mentioned, but he needed information about the suspect. His eyes lingered on Harrow for a moment longer than they should have before he spoke again. 'Agent Miller, what do you have regarding the victim?'

Agent Miller opened a folder and cleared his throat. 'Early reports coming in from the Metropolitan Police Department confirm that the victim, Alexander West, was the intended target. Preliminary examination shows that the victim suffered a lethal assault, resulting in two critical injuries: a deep laceration to the left carotid artery, followed by a precise severance of the spinal cord in the cervical region. The attack appears to have been executed with a sharp object, indicative of a professional or highly skilled assailant. Of course, the nature of the attack suggests premeditation and a specific target rather than a random act of violence. The precision of the wounds indicates the attacker possesses advanced knowledge in anatomy or combat techniques, possibly pointing to military or specialized training.'

Miller set the folder down before shifting his attention to Donovan. 'This was the most brazen attack we have ever seen. There is no doubt the attacker was sending the message that he can reach anyone, no matter the location.'

Some agents in the room made notes while others looked around nervously at each other, seeking reassurance. Donovan noticed how the mood in the room was wavering, so he walked over to a large board and picked up a marker pen.

'Yes, I am fully aware, Agent Miller. What I am asking you is about the victim.' Donovan flicked his eyes toward his desk before writing on the board: *Alexander West, AI research entrepreneur*. 'I want to know everything about this guy. Starting with a dive deep into West's AI research. What was he working on that could have led to his death? National security implications, international tensions, or foreign involvement. Are there any rumors of surveillance or attempts to recruit Alexander or infiltrate his life? Our enemies are always watching, always waiting. Start with Alexander's inner circle, his professional ties, personal relationships—we need to know who stood to gain or lose from his death. Enemies, competitors, even foreign agents posing as friends.'

Agent Sam Sullivan, a trusted friend of Donovan, set a bunch of paperwork to the side and removed his reading glasses before speaking. 'Are the security protocols at his lab and home fortress-tight, or are they full of holes? Any recent breaches, anomalies? Communication is key. Cyber activity, emails, texts, encrypted chats, anything that smells of coercion, threats, or desperation. Was Mr. West being watched, hacked, or was his information scrubbed? If he had secrets in his personal life: lovers, quarrels, debts, then we need to explore these. I want to know what this man was about and how he lived his life.'

Donovan finished writing some bullet points on the board before speaking. 'Thank you, Agent Sullivan. I also need Alexander's passport details, credit card statements, investment portfolios, betting accounts, subscription services, and international banking accounts.' Donovan frowned as he checked his watch. 'Let's talk about methodology. This wasn't a random act. It was professional, calculated. Any parallels with other tech figure assassinations? Patterns, signatures? That's a lead I need someone to start working on ASAP.'

Donovan drew an arrow on the board. 'Underground networks, black markets in tech or information, and the bigger picture: how does West's murder impact the AI community and the tech sector? We're not just solving a crime; we're safeguarding the future. Team, listen up; no one is going home until I receive assessments on my desk.'

Donovan's orders were final. The agents sprang into action, each focused on their own lines of inquiry. Donovan took a seat and ordered Nathan Harrow to remain behind. There was something Harrow was withholding, and it was time to make the man speak.

Mercer edged closer to the mansion, which was illuminated by the glow of security lights and a neat row of iron lamp posts lining each side of the gravel road. A large fountain sat proudly in front of the Georgian Revival-style property, partially obscuring a Rolls-Royce Phantom. Nestled in the elite outskirts of Washington, D.C., the mansion stood as a bastion of affluence and power. Stark red bricks formed its formidable facade, while white accents starkly contrasted the sprawling, untamed grounds. The large, wide windows revealed nothing but the faintest glimmer of light seeping through heavy drapes.

Internally, Mercer assessed his options, considering every angle and exit strategy. Lacking specialist gear, his approach relied on leveraging the environment and the element of surprise. *The front is covered. The service door is my best option. Timing, precision, and controlled aggression,* he reminded himself.

Mercer circled the property slowly, staying several meters deep into the surrounding vegetation until he reached the building's rear. The ground level, where a recently added wing stretched toward the horse stables, had a door left ajar. As Mercer allowed his eyes to adjust, he checked each window for movement.

Suddenly, a yard light flicked on, illuminating the space between the wing and the stables. *A sensor.* He watched as a cat darted from the door toward the property's darkened edges. He dropped to his stomach, waiting for someone to investigate the light. No one came to check. The pet's innocent actions had made security complacent, ignoring the frequent triggering of the sensor. He sprang up and sprinted across the grounds to the rear wall. Once in position, he crept to the rear door and peeked inside. The room served as a mudroom for removing boots and jackets, keeping stable dirt from tracking into the mansion.

Before stepping inside, he fastened a silencer to his FNX-45 Tactical, the muted click signaling the shift to covert engagement. The sounds of cooking—pots scraping across a stovetop, water running, vegetables being chopped—

reminded Mercer of the innocent civilians caught between him and his target. The back door had been left slightly ajar, likely by a cook slipping out for a cigarette or by house staff trying to clear the kitchen air of heavy cooking smells.

Mercer took a slow measured breath, centered himself, and shouldered the door open, bursting inside as a man in a chef's uniform let out a startled shout. With a swift motion, Mercer struck the man's temple with the butt of his gun, knocking him unconscious before he hit the ground.

Panic erupted among the remaining two cooks. One grabbed a large meat cleaver and hurled it across the room. Mercer ducked left, then fired a round into the man's shoulder, dropping him to the floor.

The third man bolted, bursting through the double swinging doors. Hot on his trail, Mercer raced down the hallway, rapidly closing the distance as the man fumbled with the door leading into the formal dining room. Mercer wrapped an arm around his neck, cutting off his oxygen supply. Within seconds, the man's struggles weakened, then ceased. Mercer eased him to the ground with a controlled grip. The scent of gunpowder lingered as Mercer searched the area, his senses on high alert for the next threat.

•　　•　　•

Georg Wilhelm Schelling sat undisturbed in his library. He was basking in the warmth of a large fireplace, surrounded by the comfort of dark-wood paneling and intricately carved bookcases. Oblivious to the drama unfolding just rooms away. Schelling's fingers traced the aged edges of Machiavelli's *The Prince* as he leaned closer to the fire's glow. Each turn of the page brushed against the stillness of the library, a quiet reminder of the dark counsel within. His eyes, alight with intensity, absorbed the text, nodding occasionally as if finding an old truth in the words.

A familiar creak on the old hinges caught Schelling's attention. As he lifted his gaze from the pages, a brief moment of confusion immediately vanished. His cunning eyes lost their glow at the sight of a figure standing in the doorway. The silhouette was unmistakable, even shrouded in darkness—a presence he had not anticipated but recognized all too well.

'Mercer,' Schelling whispered to himself, the name tasting like poison on his lips. The fire crackled as Mercer stepped into the light. His face showed signs of fatigue, his dark eyes fixed on the silver-haired man seated before him. Schelling closed the book with a soft thud.

'To what do I owe the pleasure of this

unexpected visit, Mr. Mercer?' His voice was calm, betraying none of the alarm he felt in the pit of his stomach. Mercer didn't respond immediately to the mention of his name. Instead, he surveyed the room, the grandeur of the library a stark contrast to the mess he had left in his wake.

'I'm here for answers,' Mercer finally said, his tone firm, leaving no room for the usual pleasantries. 'And believe me, Schelling, I will get them.'

'Answers, yes. We all want answers, Danny. May I call you Danny? I heard a lot about you. Busy man, running around, trying to clean up Washington and unwilling to cooperate with us.'

Mercer crossed the room and sat down on an old cloister chair, his weapon pointing at the door. 'Tell me, Schelling: who is *us*? The Black Orchestra?'

Schelling let out a nervous laugh. 'The Black Orchestra, what a strange name. My boy, you are welcome to come along. Be part of something. Kenneth Decker filled me in on your background. We need someone with your talents. Who would say no to twenty million dollars split into different accounts in Switzerland and the Cayman Islands? Huh? I can have this set up within forty-eight hours. No more working in the gray zone, for what? Three hundred, four hundred thousand per year? Fucking peanuts, if you pardon my French. The CIA is taking advantage of you. Especially when half the intelligence community is on the take.'

An uncomfortable feeling swept across Mercer. He couldn't work out how much truth was mixed into the lies he had just heard. As a sign that he was willing to listen, Mercer lowered his weapon and rested it across his lap. He needed a bit more information, another lead. 'Who would I be working with? At least tell me how I might gain trust in what you are saying. You can't expect me to walk out of here without guarantees.'

Schelling finally felt his pulse coming down. He praised his vision, his manipulative and unflappable manner, which had taken him from a victim to the controller once again. An air of power entered his lungs, allowing him to declare truths, just enough to bring Mercer into the fold. 'Your old colleague Kenneth Decker spoke highly of you, yes. Someone you don't know, Arnold Becker, from the Justice Department. Then we have John Elder, a fabulous attorney from New York, and Senator Rick Sanderson, to name just a few. These men are the backbone of our organization, Danny. You can see from the talent that our goals and ambitions are not dreams; they are real. With our contacts and high-powered friends in China, there is no limit to our success.

'The Middle East's oil fields are no longer relevant. The Far East is where the money and power are. You can stay and do the hard graft and risk your life. For what? A Flag? Or you can come with us and taste actual power.'

Mercer let his eyes float around the room. Far down the hall, he could hear the cries coming from the injured cook. A distressed phone call or silent alarm would soon attract the cops. Mercer didn't have much time left. He hadn't counted on such an opportunity. A flood of considerations crashed through his mind as Schelling laid out the offer. Power and wealth were laid out like bait, but Mercer kept his expression neutral, feigning interest. Internally, he was analyzing, calculating.

Twenty million dollars, he thought, *a fortune that could fund countless operations. Or a neat retirement package, yet here it serves as bait.* Mercer was aware that accepting Schelling's offer would mean playing a game on two fronts: to maintain his facade with the CIA while burrowing deeper into the Black Orchestra's business. The notion of walking away crossed his mind, a fleeting temptation to reject the offer and confront the immediate threat by delivering two rounds into the man's forehead. But Mercer was a spymaster, a strategist at heart. He recognized the value of the information Schelling dangled before him—names, locations, plans.

Each piece could be a steppingstone toward his ultimate goal: the eradication of the Black Orchestra.

Schelling's eyes narrowed in the silence that stretched between them, a glimmer of satisfaction—or was it anticipation flashing through? 'It's more than just money,' he pushed, his tone smooth as silk yet with an edge sharp enough to cut. 'It's freedom. Power. Everything you've been fighting for, but on your terms.'

Mercer's hand rested casually on his lap, tightening around the weapon. A gesture unnoticed yet full of intent. 'And what's the price?' he asked.

Schelling leaned forward. 'Trust,' he said simply. 'Complete allegiance to our cause. Your talents, undivided,' he added, his voice carrying the weight of an ultimatum.

Mercer stood, the chair's noise a subtle break in their standoff. 'I'll think about it,' he said, his decision hidden. 'But I need reassurance. Objectives, partnerships.'

Schelling's response was a confident smile. 'You'll get it.' Before Mercer could leave, Schelling reached for a pen and a notepad. He quickly scribbled down some information and handed it to Mercer. 'Jakarta, on the eleventh. Yes!'

Mercer took the piece of paper and stuffed it into his jacket pocket. His dark eyes zeroed in on the silver-haired billionaire. 'I came here tonight with one purpose. If you screw with me, Georg, I will hunt you down and easily finish what I started.'

Schelling's confidence didn't waver. 'I am not in the business of screwing partners, Danny. You will realize that soon enough.'

As Mercer left, the door shut with a solid click behind him. The distant sound of sirens floated through the Virginian woods, and red and blue lights flickered against the wet trees. Mercer jogged back to his vehicle, taking a slightly different path. Rain pounded, turning the ground to mud that clung to his shoes. In the solitude of his car, with the rain drumming on the roof, he allowed himself a moment to consider the gravity of what lay ahead. Jakarta wasn't just a destination; it was a test, one he had to pass, and not just for the mission. Failure meant being locked out. Success got him a seat at the table—then he could pull it apart from the inside.

NINE

Seated across the table, Jeff Connor's wife was busy discussing something about their young child's football practice or music lessons. Connor couldn't be sure. He hadn't listened to a word she said.

His head throbbed from a lack of sleep and the anxiety of the day ahead. A text message he had received a few hours earlier alarmed him. An assassination of a young entrepreneur. Deputy Director Faulkner had asked for a meeting later in the morning.

Jeff's mind switched back to Mercer, again. Mercer worked outside the scope of professional boundaries, and keeping him in check had fallen to Connor, bypassing Faulkner. Despite Faulkner's lower position, he held great power and had tight connections within the agency. Connor knew he needed to play this right. Faulkner was a man who needed to be managed—intelligent, manipulative, but not violently dangerous. Mercer, on the other hand, was a different animal altogether.

Connor viewed Mercer as an untamed draft horse; the ex-Delta Force operator became unpredictable once he caught a scent of something that piqued his interest. For Mercer, it was revenge. *Against whom?* Connor asked himself. *Against those that rose up stronger each time the head of a cartel was eliminated. Or his distrust in the CIA hierarchy and other intel agencies?* No different from previous operations in Mexico, fighting cartels.

Every time Mercer took out leaders from the Sinaloa Cartel in Culiacán, a new boss would run the show within hours. Mercer believed these gangs were never meant to be eliminated. Repeatedly, he would quiz Connor on their agenda. *Why are we cutting the head of these snakes and not going after the suppliers of fentanyl and other precursors coming in from Asia to Mexico?* Connor had run out of excuses, and Mercer was gaining too much respect within the agency to be ignored.

'Are you listening to what I am saying, Jeff?'

'Yes, of course. I am sorry, love. I didn't sleep well.' Connor smiled and filled her glass with freshly brewed coffee. He had made a promise years ago that breakfast would be the one time when he would function as a normal husband

and father by keeping the television off and leaving his phone, along with his car keys and jacket, at the front of the house. Today, this irritated Connor more than usual. From the kitchen, he could hear the phone vibrating with each text received. Faulkner was still after answers about the botched Mong La operation and Mercer's exclusion from the team. He had requested a report, which Connor hoped would be delayed; there was no chance in hell he could justify his actions. *Mercer is too involved, too calculated. The Black Orchestra is growing, and I can't be caught holding the bag. Things have to change,* he thought.

After breakfast, Connor quickly kissed everyone, grabbed his phone and keys, and left the house. His cell phone rang as he reached his car—*Deputy Director Faulkner.* Connor ignored the call again.

Instead, he opened his messages and scrolled through the list, dismissing updates on Alexander West's murder, threat warnings, surveillance activities, and the usual complaints from field agents. Then, a name he couldn't ignore appeared on the screen, sending a jolt through him.

Georg Wilhelm Schelling.

Schelling, often referred to as a shadow broker within the intersecting worlds of American politics and global finance, commanded a level of influence that stretched far beyond the typical reach of a lobbyist. His network, meticulously constructed over decades, comprised key figures in strategic positions across both political and corporate spheres. Schelling's modus operandi involved leveraging this network to subtly shift policy decisions and market dynamics in favor of the interests of his clandestine group, the Black Orchestra.

For Jeff Connor, an experienced operative within the CIA, the sudden, direct outreach from Schelling was a clear signal of an unprecedented situation. In the realm of international relations and espionage, Schelling's well-documented preference was for indirect manipulation through his extensive contacts. A direct approach from him was not just unusual—it was a red flag. This suggested Connor was caught in a critically important scenario, surpassing typical intelligence operations.

Connor's worry was real, cut from the hard facts of his dealings with the Black Orchestra. Yet, there was an aspect of this relationship he found less concerning, even beneficial. Connor viewed himself not as an informant but as a conduit, channeling crucial insights to those in higher power than his own agency. In his view, he was merely facilitating the flow of information to the upper echelons, aiding in decisions that stretched beyond the CIA's reach.

To Connor, the exchange was a mere perk of navigating the murky waters of intelligence, a way to secure his financial future post-service. He rationalized his actions by the company he kept; these men were influential patriots, deeply embedded within the nation's fabric, from the historic halls of the White House to the classified corridors of the Pentagon. Their recommendations—be it a burgeoning tech firm on the verge of a breakthrough contract, making it a hot commodity on the NYSE, or a biotech company in the S&P 500 about to announce a groundbreaking medical discovery—seemed like safe bets. Connor saw himself as part of an elite circle, safeguarding national interests while securing personal gain, oblivious to the broader ramifications of his actions.

Upon arriving at the office, Connor's first task was to confront the message from Georg Wilhelm Schelling. He opened his secure communication app and found not only the message but also a photo—a snapshot of him passing documents to Senator Rick Sanderson. A damning piece of evidence in the wrong hands. This image served as a silent threat, a reminder of the close surveillance and control Schelling had over him.

Georg's message was concise, a directive that chilled him despite its simple content: *Monitor Mercer from a distance. He is valuable to us.*

Ensure he is not hindered in his work. The implications were clear—Connor was to act as a guardian over Mercer's activities, regardless of his reckless behavior or the potential fallout within the agency.

As he processed this, Connor readied himself for the upcoming meeting with Faulkner. He knew Faulkner would seek explanations for numerous issues, especially Mercer's use of a CIA safe car the previous night. He skimmed over reports of the assassination in the Willard InterContinental Hotel, a violent act that bore the unmistakable hallmarks of Mercer's handiwork, searching for anything that might hinder the investigation.

Could Mercer be acting under someone else's direction, perhaps even Georg's? The thought only added to the stress of the meeting ahead.

Connor needed to choose his words wisely to both satisfy Faulkner's inquiries and protect Mercer. The possibility that Mercer had taken extreme actions the night before—actions that now demanded Connor's tacit support—was difficult to accept. Yet he knew he had to cover for Mercer, hoping to deflect further scrutiny.

Georg's demands hit too close to home. Doubts about the morality of his actions, along with concerns for his safety and autonomy, plagued him. The threat in Georg's message and the accompanying photo was unmistakable: Connor was under Georg's control, expected to comply or face career-ending consequences—if not worse.

A sudden knock on the door prompted Connor to flinch. Faulkner barged in, followed by his assistant. 'You can wait outside,' he commanded, his stare fixed on Connor. The brief silence was broken only by the click of the door shutting firmly behind Faulkner.

'Good morning, Gregory. Can I get you a glass of water or something? You look flustered,' Connor greeted, his tone even.

'Cut the crap, Jeff,' Faulkner snapped, slamming a file onto the desk. 'Where was Mercer last night? What was he involved in?'

Connor leaned back, unflustered. 'Mercer was doing what he does best—surveillance. He could have been in the area, but honestly, it's better if we don't know the specifics.'

Faulkner's jaw clenched. 'And the surveillance cameras? What have they picked up? Who's leading the investigation into the murder?'

Connor shrugged. 'The usual—nothing. Cameras capture shadows, reflections from headlights, heavy rain. As for the investigation, let's just say it's being handled. We need to keep our agency out of the limelight, under the guise of national security. We are not a domestic agency. Our focus is overseas.'

Faulkner's eyes narrowed. 'Well, explain the FBI agent's murder. This requires the same level of discretion, Jeff. We can't afford another screw-up.'

'We sidestepped that situation for a reason, and we'll do the same here until we fully grasp what's happening,' Connor said.

Faulkner stabbed the desk with his finger. 'Jeff, you need to be on this! Mong La was a disaster, and now D.C. is rife with rumors of political assassinations. This is on both of us!'

Connor's expression hardened. 'I'm well aware, Gregory. But as you know, we play on the edge for a reason. Our role in world affairs is not exactly dinner table conversation. We'll manage our position, like we always do. But panicking? That's not how we operate.'

Faulkner leaned in. 'Listen, Jeff, if the FBI catches wind of this, we're in serious trouble. It's one thing for the CIA and NSA to play supporting roles, but the last goddamn scenario we need is the FBI on our case, complicating every move we make. And let me make one thing crystal clear.'

He paused, ensuring he had Connor's undivided attention.

'If there's even a hint that you've directed illegal assassinations on U.S. soil, I won't hesitate to take action. The Intelligence Identities Protection Act isn't just for show. A quick call to the Department of Justice's Criminal Division would end your career, if not land you in a federal prison. So, you better make sure we're clean on this.'

Connor leaned back, arms crossed. 'Don't forget who you're talking to, Gregory. If you make threats like that again, I'll pull your file and go through it carefully. I'm sure there are skeletons in there somewhere. Listen to me—I understand the big picture here. Let me make some calls. I'll pull Mercer in, then ship him overseas on some wild goose chase until I set this right. Yes, this looks bad, and undoubtedly, the FBI and the White House will demand answers. If word gets out, the press won't be far behind. Let the FBI do their thing. We can keep tabs on them, so don't worry.'

Faulkner exhaled deeply. 'Make sure you do, Jeff. Because if this blows back on us, it's not just your head on the line. Resolve this and keep me informed.'

Without another word, Faulkner turned and left the office, leaving Connor alone with his thoughts. The gravity of the situation was undeniable. He had sidestepped the deputy's probing, but at what cost?

Mercer, you bastard, Connor mumbled under his breath as he reached for his phone.

•   •   •

In the Ministry of State Security's starkly lit conference room, General Liu Xiang stood with quiet authority, his presence commanding the room. He held a thumb drive, an object unremarkable in appearance but monumental in significance, received from Kenneth Decker. It contained intelligence on influential Chinese bankers, businessmen, and scientists across the U.S. and Europe. The data exposed men of wealth, power, and connections—now vulnerable to coercion and blackmail by Liu and his team.

Zhang Wei inserted the drive into a computer terminal, tapped a few commands into the keyboard, and moments later, the screen on the wall flickered to life, displaying a list of names.

'As you can see,' Liu began, 'we have individuals who have strayed from our collective path. They live in Berlin, London, Monaco, Oslo, Jakarta, and Florida, controlling properties in many other places. Driven by profit, they've turned their backs on China.'

Murmurs of discontent stirred among the attendees.

'This is permitted. There is no issue with that. What are we actually here for, General? We are the government, and we seek to expand our business interests overseas. It is natural for our businessmen and women to be based all over the world.'

Others in the room murmured in agreement.

'We are not triads,' one official objected, his voice edged with unease.

Liu banged his fist on the table. 'You have objections? Yes? Maybe some of you have secrets we should uncover. I will dissect every financial transaction if that's what you prefer! If you claim there is no problem, fine—I'll hand your personal business dealings over to the MSS and let the forensic accountants assess your honesty.'

Liu's voice was cold as he scanned the nervous faces in front of him. His next words carried a direct threat.

'Our mission transcends individual moralities. This is about the greater good of our nation. I, for one, will not stand by while our power is stripped from us. Those who steal from our country will beg for forgiveness.'

As his words settled, General Liu poured himself a glass of baijiu and took a slow sip.

No one dared to speak.

'Let me show you some people the Americans have been working with to weaken our power.'

Liu turned back to the PowerPoint presentation. Each slide was meticulously detailed, profiling men whose allegiance to China was now in question. Their faces glowed on the screen, accompanied by satellite maps pinpointing their locations, business graphs charting their financial ascents, and snippets of intercepted emails highlighting their refusal to heed the MSS's call to return to China for compulsory meetings.

As he continued, exposing their financial contributions to various European and Indonesian political parties, the room seemed to shrink, faces hardening, breaths holding, as if every word were a weight adding to an unspoken burden. 'Look closely,' Liu demanded, pointing to the screen. 'Donations to the Social Democratic Party of Germany, Irish Sinn Féin, Norway's Sosialistisk Venstreparti, La France Insoumise, Italy's Partito Democratico, Indonesian Democratic Party of Struggle.'

One official, attempting to diffuse the tension, ventured, 'This is merely international business etiquette, General. Supporting parties in countries we operate within secures our interests. It's standard practice globally.'

This interruption only fueled Liu's anger. Without missing a beat or appearing frustrated, he dispatched a terse message from his phone, then resumed the display. This time, he focused on financial transfers exiting China, funneling into accounts across Miami, London, Liechtenstein, and Stockholm, unraveling a network of shell companies siphoning money from Chinese markets.

'Their actions,' Liu barked, 'undermine our economic sovereignty. Our universities, too, are complicit, prioritizing collaboration over protecting our intellectual legacy. This one-way transfer of knowledge ends now.'

Suddenly, the conference room's large double doors swung open, and a group of heavily built men filed in. Liu pointed to a nervous-looking man seated, his arms folded, beads of sweat forming on his head. Liu's bodyguard team swiftly grabbed the dissenting official, a silent message to all present. The man's protests faded as he was dragged out, leaving a chilling reminder of the stakes involved.

Soft voices of conflict hummed beneath the surface, quickly stifled by the realization of Liu's unwavering resolve. The message was clear: loyalty to the state above all, with any deviation met with uncompromising retaliation.

'Our goal,' Liu continued, undeterred, 'is to realign these lost sheep. They will be given a warning. Noncompliance is not an option.'

Over the next four hours, Liu issued his orders. His demands were nothing like the party officials had ever imagined. Secrecy was hammered into them, their futures threatened, family holidays canceled, and their loyalty under his grip.

A heavy silence overwhelmed the officials in the room. Each one understood the unspoken directive: failure was not a choice. Liu, with a final authoritative glance, confirmed the meeting's end. The path forward was clear, marked by unwavering allegiance and the harsh consequences of dissent. As the last stragglers left the room, Zhao Ming walked to the head of the table to shake hands with the General. 'Well played, General. Although, I hope they all keep in line. If word gets back to the President that you had a member of the Politburo removed from this meeting, he may start asking questions.'

Unfazed, Liu understood Zhao Ming, a diplomat adept in negotiation and international relations, known for his problem-solving acumen. Zhao Ming's key role was to guide the General through the international political landscape, especially in relation to espionage matters. 'Don't worry about that. Zhang Wei promises to take care of any nefarious behavior. His team is monitoring them closely.'

As Zhang Wei joined them, a brief smile crossed his face, quietly uniting them in their determination. The three men left together, focused on their mission. A renewed strength within hardened their minds. The conference room soon stood empty, only their strong words lingering in the air. On the streets of China, life moved on, oblivious to the shifting powers within the walls of the Ministry of State Security.

•   •   •

Mercer spent the morning indulging in local delicacies: fresh lobster, New England clam chowder, and mussels. The overnight drive from Langley to Bar Harbor, Maine, had been long and tiresome; now, he was ready to refuel and rest. The countless cups of gas station coffee he'd downed en route had left him jittery. To counteract this, he called the waiter and ordered a Black Bush Irish Whiskey to help him sleep.

Twenty minutes later, Mercer walked into a large house just off Old Farm Road. The classic New England cottage would provide some respite while the chaos in Washington, D.C. settled. His parents, having moved to Florida, had left him the old family home, which had sat empty for years. Mercer could never bring himself to sell it; instead, he spent his holidays visiting the town and restoring the property to its former glory.

The patio doors squeaked as Mercer opened them, letting fresh air into the living area. The view across Frenchman's Bay never failed to impress. He watched small fishing boats navigate the water. The cool, crisp air carried the scent of pine trees, mixing with the lingering aroma of Irish whiskey on his breath.

Mercer briefly considered the renovations he

could afford with the twenty million dollars Georg Wilhelm Schelling had offered him. The roof sagged, the porch and deck were rotting, and the private well needed to be rebuilt. As the list grew, he pushed it to the back of his mind, locked the rooms, and drew the curtains before undressing for bed.

When he plugged in his phone to charge, he noticed a missed call. Jeff Connor. Mercer sighed, knowing he couldn't ignore the man.

He cleared his throat and dialed. 'Jeff, what can I do for you?' Mercer asked.

'Mercer, I just got my face chewed off by Faulkner. I have no idea what you're wrapped up in, and that's messed up, considering it's my responsibility to oversee and understand every detail of your operations. I can't keep covering your tracks.'

Mercer sat down on the bed. His feet ached, and his eyes were heavy. 'I understand, Jeff. But I'm a one-man show. Don't worry about Faulkner. Dean Jameson gave both of us his word that our asses would be covered as long as we brought him the goods. You should have kept me on the Mong La operation. I would have bagged a few guys for you in the jungle.'

'The stuff you pull off in the jungle, we can hide. But that's nothing compared to the shitstorm you've caused in Washington, D.C. Honestly, keeping you in Asia would've been smarter. You're a loose cannon here, Mercer. Sure, you've got your high-powered allies in D.C.—Jameson included—shielding you. I haven't had a call from the White House yet, which is odd, since they're always up my ass.'

Mercer paused before responding. 'I have a few things to handle in Asia. Let me head over and investigate the factories producing these precursors. If we don't tackle the source, fentanyl and meth will keep crossing the border. It'll give me time to sort out some personal admin shit.'

'This isn't just personal admin, Mercer, goddamn it! It's a homicide investigation—Alexander West, and a double homicide that includes an FBI agent. Don't you get it? You're protected, but there's too much tying you to this. It's only a matter of time before someone calls in a favor bigger than your connections,' Connor replied.

Mercer looked around his sparse bedroom. Light filtered through the edges of the curtains, and the distant hum of outboard motors drifted in from the bay, punctuated by the sharp cries of seagulls. He thought about what Connor had said regarding his connections, a concern that lingered.

'Okay, I need to produce results—something to prove my actions are effective and that I'm an essential asset to the CIA. Give me a few days to gather solid intel, and we can discuss matters when I return.'

'Do you think you can avoid making headlines?' Connor sighed, frustration slipping through. 'Don't answer that. Get back to me by the end of the week, Mercer. But hear this—I'm warning you not to drag my name into anything immoral. You're a free agent, but you're still bound by the laws of the countries you operate in. If you get arrested, we will turn our backs on you.'

Mercer ended the call and lay down on his bed. The same narrative unfolded every time Connor felt the walls closing in. His mention of morality stirred something in Mercer—unease, or perhaps something deeper.

Does he know who I will be working for? A smile gradually spread across his face. *Fuck it, Que sera, sera.*

Shortly after, he drifted into a restless sleep, where familiar faces awaited—mistakes he couldn't forget and nightmares that never faded.

In the quiet of the Maine morning, with fog lifting off the bay, Mercer found himself at a crossroads not just in his career but in something deeper.

The veranda, its worn wooden floors creaking under his weight, had been the backdrop to many of his family's quiet moments. But today, it was the setting for a decision that could shift the balance of power.

The map before him, frayed at the edges and worn from years of use, was a testament to his time in the field. Indonesia, the epicenter of his current confusion, stretched beneath his fingertips—each line and symbol a fragment of the puzzle he was trying to piece together.

His motivation went beyond the simple binaries of right and wrong. For Mercer, this was personal. He had seen too many friends sacrificed on the altar of geopolitical games, too many innocents caught in the crossfire of clandestine operations. Each loss had left a scar, each betrayal a wound that never quite healed. It wasn't just about loyalty or the future of his country; it was about seeking justice in a world that seemed increasingly indifferent to it.

Mercer's mind flickered to a covert operation gone wrong in Surakarta, East Java, where a sudden government withdrawal had left his team exposed—and a local informant, promised safety, dead in the streets. The memory of fleeing under cover of darkness, the informant's pleading eyes still haunting him, was a sharp reminder of the cost of political games.

Revenge, however, was a double-edged sword.

It drove him forward, gave him purpose—but it also threatened to consume him. The line between fighting for justice and becoming what he despised was blurring.

This mission—this audacious plan—was perhaps his way of reclaiming control, of ensuring that his and his comrades' sacrifices meant something more than just another footnote in the annals of espionage.

As he punched in the number on a burner phone, part of him longed for another path. The solitude of Maine and the simplicity of life away from the demands of his profession were a quiet temptation. Yet he knew he couldn't turn back. Not yet.

With the message sent, Mercer stared out across the bay, its waters calm and unyielding. At that moment, he realized he couldn't do this alone. The Black Orchestra was too entrenched, its reach too widespread for a lone-wolf strike to be effective.

But who could he trust? Old allies may have turned. New acquaintances were untested. The decision weighed on him. Pulling in help meant exposing himself to potential betrayal, but going it alone was a guaranteed path to failure. His mind ran through the list of possible collaborators, each name bringing a flood of memories—assessments of loyalty, capability, and risk.

In the end, it boiled down to a simple truth: Mercer needed someone as disillusioned with the system as he was, yet not consumed by vengeance. Someone who still believed in the cause but had seen enough to question the means.

As the sun broke through the last of the fog, casting a golden light on the map, Mercer considered his decision. He would reach out to an old friend, a fellow operative who had left the field under a cloud of disillusionment. Together, they might just stand a chance.

The thought of reaching out to Charlie Halford brought a rare smile to Mercer's lips. Halford wasn't just another Tier One operator from the British SAS; he was the one person who had seen Mercer at his absolute worst and had never wavered.

A disastrously botched operation in Ciudad Juárez—where everything that could go wrong did—had nearly destroyed him. It was Halford's unflinching loyalty and understanding that pulled Mercer back from the edge. The memory of stumbling into an underground bunker, scanning the room through his night vision goggles, and seeing the lifeless bodies—women and children, horrifically decapitated—had pushed him past the brink.

Halford, a titan of a man from Wigan, England, with the build of a rugby player and the eyes of a sniper, had a way of keeping Mercer anchored when the horrors of their work threatened to consume him. His unwavering support and his silent strength in the face of unspeakable brutality reminded Mercer that there was still something left worth fighting for.

Halford's loyalty was ironclad, forged through years of special operations across the globe. They had moved through more conflict zones and fought in more close-quarters battles than Mercer cared to count. If anyone could steer through the treacherous waters ahead, it was Halford.

As Mercer folded the map, his eyes rested on the still waters of the bay, lost in thought. The past couldn't be ignored—it had led him to this moment.

Mercer had followed orders. West's name had been on The Langley Protocol list, flagged for elimination by the CIA's own AI. At the time, he hadn't questioned the directive. The program had been designed to identify threats within intelligence, defense, and government circles—men whose influence or allegiances put national security at risk. But despite the list's existence, the agency had stalled, its leadership unwilling or unable to act on the intelligence it had gathered.

Connor and Faulkner had buried the findings, either protecting their own interests or too cautious to move. The Langley Protocol remained unused, its flagged names locked away behind bureaucratic hesitation and political compromises. But someone in the White House had decided that waiting wasn't an option.

The names came from elsewhere now, through a quiet channel in the National Security Council. An NSC contact who saw him as a necessary instrument, bypassing agency politics to ensure The Langley Protocol's findings weren't ignored. The CIA wouldn't act, but Mercer would.

This next move would require a reliable ally.

'Time to make a call,' Mercer muttered to the rising sun, resolve settling like iron in his chest. Charlie Halford was the ally he needed—someone who understood the contract and didn't waste time on morality debates. Mercer had unfinished business. Halford didn't care about the politics or the bigger picture, but he never passed up the chance to put his skills to use. If Mercer had a target list and a plan, that was all the reason Halford needed.

TEN

Jakarta—Indonesia

The heavy humidity and noise, combined with the frenzied scramble at the cab rank, overwhelmed the small group of businessmen. The Qatar Airways flight had gone smoothly, touching down on time at Soekarno-Hatta International Airport in Jakarta and narrowly beating the onset of rush hour. A frantic dash from the airport to the taxi rank followed, with men ahead of Mercer eagerly attempting to bypass the queue. They wanted to grab the next black Mercedes limousine, which had just arrived. Others in the queue hurled protests and insults until the Soekarno-Hatta Airport Police intervened and quickly defused the tension.

Mercer caught the pungent aroma of food drifting from somewhere, slicing through the acrid smell of exhaust fumes. He ignored the grumble in his stomach for now. Joining the taxi line, he surveyed the area. Surrounding him were a mix of solo commuters, large families with trolleys piled high with luggage and cardboard boxes tied together with string, occasional backpackers, and small groups of men hanging around smoking clove-flavored cigarettes.

Despite the crowds and lack of assistance, everyone jostled through in their sweat-soaked clothes, finding clear routes out of the terminal. Mercer had noticed a few interesting travelers on his flight and a couple of heavily built men loitering around the arrivals hall. Such sights were not out of the ordinary for a major hub like this. The presence of intelligence agents posted in a crucial entry port to Indonesia seemed logical to Mercer as he stood there drenched in his own sweat.

A few minutes passed, and Mercer finally got his ride. He settled into the back of a spacious, air-conditioned taxi. The driver took off his white-colored Islamic head cap, placing it neatly on the passenger seat. He wiped his bald head with a napkin before putting the cap back on. A large gold ring with a bright red stone adorned his little finger, and a small tuft of hair on his chin added to his unique charm. Mercer liked his mannerisms and soft face; he was friendly and didn't ask too many questions.

Mercer discreetly checked the traffic behind,

careful not to appear suspicious. Because of the heavy traffic, it was impossible to determine if he was being followed. The driver changed lanes multiple times, using the horn and hand signals out the window instead of the turn indicators, which provided Mercer with some amusement. He marveled at the man's ability to find gaps in the traffic when there was nothing visible. From the airport to South Jakarta, the landscape changed quickly.

Huge office buildings, apartment blocks, and tower cranes dominated the horizon. Express roads snaked their way around the large buildings and over the encroaching flood waters and makeshift shanty houses built within narrow alleyways on the outskirts. In stark contrast, South Jakarta boasted luxury high-rises amid more elegant neighborhoods, complete with verdant gardens. The route still had traffic issues, although the driver knew all the side streets, which cut time off the journey. Soon after, he merged back onto the main road with ease. A short time later, the taxi pulled up without drama close to Mercer's hotel. He paid the man and provided a generous tip, then walked inside the huge Pacific Place mall to find the restroom.

The bustling mall teemed with shoppers. Men and women drifted from store to store, arms laden with bags of luxury items. Everyone around him exuded a sense of youth and vitality, with their well-groomed appearances and fit physiques. Shoppers and store workers who caught Mercer's eye offered friendly smiles and greetings. Signs in multiple languages beside the escalators provided information on each floor.

From the balcony, he could observe multiple levels, each one filled with locals and foreigners going about their day. Mercer scanned for the car park, food courts, and exit points, noting several security guards and individuals he suspected were undercover police engaged in purchasing coffee. The outline of a holstered firearm was distinctly visible against their waists. Their neat haircuts, clothing, vigilant eyes, and the confidence in their demeanor set them apart from the others.

There were emergency exit doors next to some shops and also private doors leading to staff quarters. Mercer proceeded to the restrooms, ducked into a cubicle to swiftly change his shirt, and donned a cap. Seconds later, he reemerged and headed toward the hotel. The same undercover police were standing next to the entrance of the hotel, sipping on their coffee. As one reached down to pick up a holdall at his feet, his loose shirt provided a glimpse of the weapon. A Taurus Model 82, the standard six-shot revolver used by the Indonesian National Police. The man caught

Mercer eyeing his firearm, and he quickly adjusted his shirt and gave a slight nod. Mercer did the same and hoped the police officer wouldn't have cause to use it any time soon.

Upon checking into his hotel, Mercer retreated to his room to take in the sprawling view of Jakarta. This city, familiar to him from numerous operations, sometimes as a collaborator with Badan Intelijen Negara, Indonesia's intelligence service, and at other times tracking foreigners exploiting the nation as a conduit. Jakarta's position, nestled in an archipelago, boasting vast coastlines, and serving as an aerial nexus between Asia and the South Pacific, rendered it a magnet for syndicates smuggling illicit goods and coordinating human trafficking. Yet, for Mercer, it also offered a gateway to serenity on the Eastern islands. There, he could meld into the laid-back essence of island life. He indulged in the vibrant taste of locally harvested mangoes, relished the smoky flavor of coral fish grilled over an open flame, and enjoyed the sweet, refreshing water of coconuts, freshly plucked, all while surrounded by the surf and under the shade of palm trees.

Mercer found solace in Lombok's legendary surfing spots, where the power and grace of the waves reminded him of the unpredictability inherent in both nature and his covert operations. Each session on the water not only challenged his physical limits but also connected him to the island's storied past, a welcome respite from his clandestine life.

The respite Mercer found in the Eastern islands served as a stark reminder of the life for which he fought. However, standing on the precipice of his next mission in Jakarta, he recognized the island's peace as merely a fleeting moment within the grand scope of his duties. This mission was unlike any he had undertaken before. The change of employer, a major concern, caused Mercer considerable anxiety. Although well accustomed to high risks, he could not dispel the sense of dread.

As he stripped down and readied himself for a shower, Mercer was acutely conscious of the intricacies of the situation he was about to confront. Given the prevalence of African and Middle Eastern gangs that went unnoticed in a city of over eleven million, there was a demand for men like Mercer. The Black Orchestra had business interests in the country that necessitated certain protections. Although these protections were not fully detailed to Mercer, it was clear his role involved eliminating potential problems before they emerged. It was a method for the newcomers to assert their power and intimidate their rivals. Mercer lived by a strict rule not to get involved in the host country's political issues or get drawn into the murky business of assassinations on behalf of lobbyists or other influenceable factions.

Mercer caught his reflection in the mirror. Looking back at him was a man marked by the job. Dark circles under his eyes and rugged stubble gave him a worn-out look, a face etched with betrayal. *Just one job. One hit, and I'm in the organization. Then I'll rip them apart,* Mercer thought silently as he splashed water on his face before smearing it with shaving cream. *Just one hit,* he echoed, knowing it was probably a lie. The thrill of the hunt was too addictive to give up.

An hour later, Mercer stepped onto the sidewalk with his backpack strapped tight. The broken and uneven ground reflected a city bursting at its seams. He moved through the crowd, observing faces etched with the hardships of life. Streets buzzed with motorcycles slicing through traffic, their engines harsh and persistent. Sidewalk vendors hawked their goods under ramshackle carts. The air carried the heavy aroma of street food, fried tempeh, charred satay meat, and simmering bakso mixed with the scent of clove cigarettes. Amid Jakarta's relentless hustle, a vendor, caught in the day's heat and chaos, paused to offer a Mercer a glass of iced tea, his smile a warm beacon of kindness.

This simple act, one among many throughout the city, reminded Mercer of the local generosity and resilience, illustrating how Indonesians navigate their world with a grace that softens the hard edges of daily life. He took the cool drink, thanked the man, ducked under the food cart, and seated himself on a plastic stool at the rear of the makeshift restaurant.

A large plastic tarp, covered with a list and drawings of the meals on offer inside, served as walls, shielding him from the sun's heat. This position allowed him to easily observe the passing pedestrians while remaining concealed from the brightness of the sidewalk. Mercer appreciated this vantage point for spotting any potential surveillance officers as much as he did the refreshing iced tea.

Suddenly, his attention was captured by four men who stood out from the crowd. The four were all neatly dressed in slacks and sneakers, well-built, and were constantly sector scanning, each concentrating on their specific arcs. They were spaced apart, yet close enough to communicate subtly. One man at the rear halted about thirty yards away to light a cigarette, while the other three pressed forward, eyes locked on the sidewalk ahead. The lead man accelerated his pace, passed the food cart, and vanished from Mercer's view, leaving the remaining two visibly frustrated.

From the corner of his eye, Mercer could see the old man observing the two men who were loitering around, likely waiting on instructions. Then he turned to face Mercer and rolled his eyes, exchanging a silent signal. With a nod of the head and a warm smile from Mercer, the old man sat down and lit a Djarum cigarette, lost in his thoughts of a crazy world. Mercer lingered for about twenty minutes, unsure if the men were tracking him or some local criminals. He ordered another glass of iced tea and a bowl of meatball soup, known as bakso, which helped pass the time and ease his hunger. The spicy broth provided enough time for the surveillance team to move on. After generously tipping the man, Mercer returned to the street and flagged down a taxi, realizing that this part of the city had proved to be off-limits. Settled in the back of the taxi, he considered the fact that those men could be from the National Central Bureau (NCB). *Kepolisian Negara Republik Indonesia. They have connections with Interpol. It's best I give them a wide berth,* thought Mercer.

Forty minutes later, the taxi dropped him off outside a motorbike distributor's office in Glodok, West Jakarta. Before entering, Mercer lit a cigarette and sat under a canopy so he could survey the area without looking too suspicious. Local workers busied themselves loading trucks, others stood by watching, and a man directed traffic. The alley was lined with rows of three-story buildings, each fronted by a roller door. Most were open for business. After a final check of the exits and the area's vibe, Mercer stood and entered the building. The reception was clean and cool, with the receptionist dressed more like an upmarket department store assistant than the laborer types seen in other stores.

'Good morning, sir. How may I help you?' The young lady stepped out from behind the desk and offered a handshake. Her uniform was bright orange with a white stripe around the waist, and a matching hat covered her hair, which was tucked up tightly underneath. Her makeup was a mixture of subtle earth tones that accentuated her features, bold eyeliner high-lighted her piercing gaze, and a hint of shimmer on her lips suggested sophistication without de-tracting from her professional demeanor. Her presence was a testament to the art of blending allure with authority, making her not just no-ticed but remembered. Mercer shook her hand and noticed the faint scent of spiced jasmine and sandalwood.

'My name is Tony Hoffmann; may I speak to Pak Rizky Pratama, please? He should be ex-pecting me.'

'Certainly, Mr. Hoffmann, please wait here.' The young woman then turned around and glanced toward the security camera positioned above the internal door to the back storage area before quickly retreating behind her desk to make a hushed phone call. 'Mr. Pratama will see you now. Please follow me.'

Without waiting for a response, she opened the door to the back and disappeared. Mercer quickly followed, trying to decipher what he was walking into. Georg Wilhelm Schelling provided little information about this operation on the night Mercer had planned to kill him. All he supplied was an address with a name, plus a reference number or some kind of coded message. Mercer wasn't sure what it was. Knowing his only protection was acute awareness and a capacity for violence if cornered offered slight reassurance. While within his expertise, Mercer preferred not to leave a trail leading back to the U.S. The decision to travel using a fake passport and credit cards under that identity eased his anxiety.

He refocused on the walk through the back of the store. His hand gripped the straps on his backpack and gently tightened them. Slowly, he reached back and undid the zipper of a pocket, where he could access a small knife swiftly. One side of his backpack contained a medical kit, and the other pocket had his knife, suitable for slicing a carotid artery or attacking the liver or other organs. The lady weaved past boxes containing gearboxes and brand-new engines, slowing only to caution Mercer about the low beams intersecting the gangway. At the store's rear, she showed the rusty iron steps leading up to a mezzanine-level office.

Mercer climbed the steps, knocked on the door, and entered without waiting for a reply.

'Ah, Mr. Hoffmann, I presume? That name suits you, doesn't it?' The portly man seated behind the desk smiled as he peered over his black-rimmed glasses.

Mercer looked around the sparse office, then crossed the threadbare carpet to shake the man's hand. 'Mr. Pratama. A pleasure to meet you.' *How much does this man know about me?* thought Mercer. *Pratama knew my name was bullshit, and I've only just arrived in Indonesia.*

Sensing his visitor's unease, Pratama waved dismissively. 'Don't worry, Mr. Mercer, you're safe here. Mr. Georg Wilhelm Schelling tasked me with looking after you during your stay. I only know what I need to know. Which is to provide you with a name and whatever you require to complete your job, yes? You understand? No problem, okay?'

Mercer didn't respond other than to take a seat and ease the straps on his backpack.

'Listen, I have been instructed to give you this,' Pratama said, opening a desk drawer to retrieve an envelope and sliding it across the table to Mercer. 'There is local currency and some U.S. dollars. Also, you will find the detail on our target, his home address and a work one in West Jakarta. He attends a tennis club and a karaoke bar. There are a few other places listed which he visits. Many places that you can easily find and kill him.' The last sentence rolled off Pratama's tongue easily.

Mercer caught the man's indifference as he spoke of murder with a casual, chilling detachment. This frankness, devoid of any qualms about taking a life, unsettled Mercer, revealing a cold, hard reality he was about to step into. In that moment, he saw the true face of Jakarta's power game, a world where human life was just another chip on the table, expendable and forgettable. Mercer gave away nothing as he picked up the envelope and removed the paperwork. His eyes skimmed the information before he asked, 'Who is this man? Why can't Georg or whoever is in charge here sit down and work out a deal? Why resort to such extreme measures?'

Pratama erupted into laughter. 'Yes, yes, imagine just sitting down for a chat!' His laughter subsided as he removed his glasses and rubbed his eyes. 'Apologies, Mr. Mercer, please excuse me. Those tactics simply aren't viable with the stakes we're dealing with. Our adversaries aren't known for their democratic principles. Negotiating with one demands negotiating with countless others, which we neither have time for nor the inclination to share our affairs widely. Such openness would only lead to police involvement, dragging us through endless legal battles. There are more effective strategies at our disposal.'

Pratama got up and moved over to the window where a small bar fridge was perched on a safe. He removed two bottles of Coke Zero and handed one to Mercer. He opened his bottle and tossed the cap into the trash can, turned up the air conditioning, and took his seat.

Mercer finished reading most of the documents, slid the envelope into an internal pocket of his shirt, and fastened it closed. 'This is where I come into the picture!' he said.

'Yes, this is where Mr. Mercer arrives and settles our dispute. Your target, a dangerous man named Hendrik, should provoke no guilt in you; he's rotten to the core. Like me, he was educated in the U.S. I attended Virginia Tech, by the way, majoring in mechanical engineering, before returning to Jakarta to start my business. In Jakarta, I enlist insiders to flip trade secrets on their company's technology. The cyber guys crack the rest, pulling data straight from their servers. This information, once abstracted, becomes a valuable commodity, sold to the highest bidder, bypassing the burdens of research and development.

'Now, Hendrik attempts to mirror my

strategy. We can't have that. I have cultivated my organization over many years, selling engineering designs to large companies in good faith. Then, from nowhere, he turns up, backed by the local mafia, having bribed politicians and police to target and drive me out of business. Fortunately, our good friend Georg has offered a solution. So, yes, that's where you come in. Eliminate Hendrik from the business, and Georg will take care of you.'

Mercer glanced around the office, searching for anything out of the ordinary. The space was clearly a façade for laundering money or doing business with unusual characters. As he settled his eyes back on Pratama, he formed the opinion that the Indonesian was well-connected and seemed out of place in such a neighborhood. His neatly pressed Italian shirt, expensive Swiss watch, gold rings, and impressive veneers suggested he relished the finer things in life.

'What timeframe are you looking at for this matter to be resolved, Mr. Pratama?' he asked.

Pratama took a sip, then removed a cigarette from a leather-bound case and offered one to Mercer. 'As soon as possible. But I understand how these operations go, Mr. Mercer. You'll want to conduct your own checks, I presume. We have laid as much groundwork as possible to assist you. Here, take this.' Pratama slid a cell phone across the table. 'There's an app on this phone connected to his and also a tracking device, which we placed under his car. You can use that to monitor his movements. Beyond the information in the envelope, we will leave the rest to you.'

Mercer fully grasped the consequences of relying on a complete stranger in a foreign country for the elimination of an unfamiliar target. Standing at the crossroads of trust and survival, Mercer knew that in Jakarta's merciless heat, every ally was a potential enemy in disguise. Infiltrating the Black Orchestra and unveiling their worldwide activities was his paramount aim. The possibility of arrest during the operation, risking decades in a squalid cell and labels of a double agent or rogue mercenary, loomed large. Speed and violence were his only options.

He finished his Coke and placed the bottle on the table, his mind reeling from the memory of the FBI agent he had killed in Washington, D.C. Mercer's goal to expose abuses of power could turn favorable, though U.S. intelligence laws presented challenges. Lacking clear legal backing for actions deemed for the *greater good*, the Intelligence Community's strict oversight was aimed at synchronizing security measures with legal standards. The framework of congressional and judicial oversight balanced stringent legal standards with the operational needs of espionage activities.

Mercer quietly questioned whether his actions, motivated by national interests, could align with these oversight guidelines. Yet, as he weighed the gravity of his actions against the potential for redemption, a gnawing doubt shadowed his resolve. *Can the outcome justify the methods, or will I cross a line of no return?* The moral compass that guided him through countless missions now spun erratically, leaving him to question not just his choices but the very essence of his duty.

After a brief pause, Mercer decided the risk was worth it. 'Right, leave it to me. But there's a minor issue to tackle. I need an untraceable weapon. Can you arrange that?'

Pratama nodded. 'Certainly, I've got what you need. Give it a thorough check, and then take your pick.' Pratama rose from behind the desk and strode across the room, peering out the window at the boxes stacked in the store below. 'Follow me.'

Mercer trailed Pratama down the stairs, his backpack securely positioned. With the threat level diminished, he discreetly zipped the pocket concealing his knife, feeling reassured. The store lay in shadows, illuminated by just a few functioning bulbs dangling from the ceiling. Pratama moved to the wall, flipping a switch for a recently installed security light. With the storage room lit, Mercer surveyed the area, attempting to deduce the contents of the boxes. Crates from China, Austria, Italy, Germany, and the United States filled the space. Many had been opened and resealed, others encased in clear plastic. Mercer watched Pratama closely as he positioned himself behind a row of smaller boxes, stacked neatly, ready for inspection.

'Your preference? Italy, Austria, Germany, or the U.S.?' Pratama asked as he lifted the lids off.

Mercer was taken aback by the array of new firearms. 'Choose what you need, Mr. Mercer. Our stock includes Beretta, Glock, Colt, SIG Sauer, Smith & Wesson. Attachments are included in those boxes on the floor. I believe you'll find the quality satisfactory. Don't be alarmed, okay? I am not the mafia. My business partners supply the Kopassus, which is our special forces, the Komando Pasukan Khusus. These warriors regularly train alongside American army special forces, the CIA and Australia's SAS regiment, and even Mossad, though we don't advertise that for various reasons.'

'I'm familiar with your Unit 81, the Gultor. I had the privilege of joining some of them in a training exercise at Fort Bragg a few years ago. They were quite impressive, Mr. Pratama.'

'Indeed. As Indonesians, we take pride in our

military. Given our geographical stance, it's crucial to possess the means and equipment to safeguard our interests. These weapons are surplus from the main order. Always handy to have spares, you know how it is, Mr. Mercer.'

Mercer, engrossed in thought, merely smiled. The row of boxes rested on large crates, their plastic torn away to expose labels detailing the contents. Mercer scanned the list of weapons in each crate, realizing the vast potential before him: HK 416D, M4 CQBR, Remington 870, MK 17, and SIG Sauer LVAW. With the arsenal before him, and assuming other crates held similar armaments, there was enough firepower to seize a small country. 'I should've brought a bigger bag,' he joked. Finally, he found what he was looking for: a suppressor compatible with a 9mm handgun.

Recognizing Mercer's intent, Pratama swiftly opened a box to reveal a Glock 19. Mercer inspected the weapon, tucked it into his waistband, and grabbed several boxes of 9mm ammunition. After securing the ammo deep inside his backpack, he turned and faced Pratama.

'If all goes as planned, you won't hear from me again. I trust your receptionist will keep my visit confidential?'

Pratama grinned. 'Don't worry, Mr. Mercer, she's fully briefed. You're not our first international visitor, nor likely the last. If you run into any problems, call me.' Pratama reached into his wallet and retrieved a business card, which he handed to Mercer. 'There'll be a private jet on standby at Soekarno-Hatta Airport, just in case. You will find a motorbike at the back exit, keys in the ignition. Grab a helmet from that shelf on your way out, and good luck.'

Mercer took the card, his grip firm as he shook Pratama's hand, a silent pact sealed with a nod. 'Thanks, much appreciated,' he said. After selecting a helmet, he hurried out to where a black Honda CB500F motorcycle was parked in the alleyway. Jakarta pulsed around him, its heat and humidity relentless, and the city's dust and smog assaulted his lungs. Sweat trailed down his face, mingling with the taste of salty dust laced with carbon monoxide. The mission's weight bore down on him as he brought the engine to life and went over his plan once again, recalibrating his strategy on the fly, a tactic that kept him alive many times before.

The ride into North-West Jakarta was meant to be quick, but it took an hour longer than required. Mercer's gut, honed from years in covert operations, told him he wasn't riding alone. He noticed too many coincidences: the same helmet in his mirror, turns mimicked almost perfectly, a glint of sunlight from a lens as he passed a car. He wasn't paranoid; he was trained. Taking unexpected routes became necessary, diving through less crowded streets, employing counter-surveillance maneuvers and testing his followers. Finally satisfied, he pulled into a parking lot, cut the engine, and removed his helmet.

Towering over him, on his right, was a huge office block, about seventy stories of glass and concrete, housing every sort of business imaginable. Somewhere within its vastness lurked his target, Hendrik, and possibly some form of security detail, as mentioned in Pratama's intelligence brief. Mercer didn't have time to go over all the details. What he needed was eyes-on, then he would act. One way or the other, he needed to take Hendrik out of the picture.

A variety of businesses lined the street opposite the office block, including restaurants, fabric stores, garages, and telecom kiosks. Mercer made his way to the smallest kiosk that sold cell phones and SIM cards, which had no customers, and sat down under its makeshift canopy to escape the scorching sun. The vendor was welcoming and immediately offered Mercer a chilled bottle of water from an ice-filled plastic box. Mercer took the bottle and placed it at his feet, then reached into his backpack to pull out the cell phone supplied by Pratama.

He flicked his thumb across the screen to check the applications stored on the device. Beyond the clock, settings, and weather app, only one application stood out. He moved his thumb to the red tile and pressed down on the screen. The app opened, and after a few seconds, it successfully loaded a map of the surrounding area. Unlike the detailed offerings from Google or Apple, this map lacked detail. It bore the hallmarks of a military-grade app, complete with a 3D option. Mercer selected the option, surprised to see a flashing red dot emerge amidst a mesh of fine green lines against a black background. By tilting the screen to avoid the sunlight, Mercer could clearly see the office block's outline, its levels marked by thinner green lines, each assigned a number. He zoomed out, then back in, finding the red dot had stabilized. The dot was on the forty-fifth floor. *Hendrik, who else?* Mercer guessed.

Apparently unsure what her new customer wanted, the vendor removed some SIM cards from a drawer and displayed them on the table in front of Mercer. He looked over the telecom brands and nodded. 'I'd like to buy a new cell phone, please,' he stated. Smiling broadly, she bent down and unlocked the cupboard. She carefully pulled out a box packed with new phones wrapped in clear plastic. Once the phones were laid out on the table, Mercer picked one up and handed it to her. 'This will do. Can I also get a prepaid SIM card?'

'Yes, of course, sir. I'll insert the card and activate it immediately.'

Mercer returned his focus to the phone's live feed, vigilant for movements of the red dot. A skilled individual had hacked Hendrik's phone, enabling real-time tracking. This tracking created an electronic trail, a potential evidence package for setting up Mercer if necessary. It was clear to Mercer that should he fail or become a liability, this evidence could end up with the Indonesian National Police, effectively ending his life. He sipped his water as the young woman keyed instructions into the new cell phone. Moments later, the device signaled its connection.

'All set, sir,' she announced, placing the phone on the table.

Hendrik's on the move, Mercer thought. The red dot oscillated between levels, marked forty-four, forty-three. *He's in the elevator*, he realized, pulling a wad of rupiah notes from his pocket. The vendor's eyes widened upon receiving the fresh banknotes, fully aware the sum was more than double, possibly triple, the phone's value. Mercer offered his thanks to the young girl and swiftly crossed the street toward the building's far side. After one final assessment of the exit points, he checked the map. The red dot descended to zero, then to minus one, minus two. *The parking garage, perfect,* Mercer realized, sensing he had Hendrik cornered.

He glanced around, ensuring there were no police patrols nearby, then raced down the ramp into the dimly lit parking garage. A faint hum from the extractor fans filled the concrete space, while Mercer navigated between parked cars, searching for the optimal vantage point. In the distance, the sound of car tires screeching on the smooth, polished concrete provided a reference point.

They're on the move, Mercer realized, knowing it was time to get in position. He backed up against a support column and attached the suppressor on his Glock 19, his breaths growing steady. Water dripping from a leaky pipe concealed the sound of his fabric rustling as he crouched, adjusting his stance. The sound of tires grew louder with each corner, signaling the vehicle's ascent from the lower levels. Mercer could almost visualize the men inside, oblivious to the ambush, Hendrik distracted with his phone, the guards at ease in the air-conditioned vehicle. He scanned his surroundings one last time. No security cameras, no guard. *Piece of cake,* he thought.

The squeal of tires on the ground floor signaled their arrival. Mercer advanced, using the vehicles as cover, employing tactics drilled into him during his special forces days. He kneeled and steadied his weapon, his focus narrowing on the ramp. The approaching vehicle's sound shattered the silence of the parking lot. A black Lexus SUV emerged, its license plate flashing briefly in the light as it approached the exit. At the barrier, the driver rolled down the tinted window and extended his arm to tap the electronic key against the receiver pad. The bodyguards couldn't react in time. Mercer stepped out and pressed the barrel of his weapon against the man's head.

Fuck, Hendrik wasn't in the vehicle.

'Where's Hendrik, your boss?' Mercer shouted as he moved the weapon to the center of the driver's forehead.

The driver fixed his gaze on Mercer, unfazed and fearless. A muffled shot sounded; the round found its mark. Mercer then aimed at the passenger. 'Your turn.'

Startled, the man's breathing became rapid and shallow. 'He never comes down here. We always pick him up at the lobby,' he stammered.

Mercer quickly pulled out his cell phone and tapped the app on the screen. Seconds later, the map updated, showing the red dot stationary at the front of the building. Another silenced shot broke the silence. Mercer swiftly secured his Glock inside his waistband, opened the doors, took the electronic key card, and dragged the two bodies out, dumping them next to the parked cars. He then got behind the wheel, activated the exit barrier, and drove the Lexus out of the parking garage. Within seconds, he rolled to a stop just outside the lobby. He scanned the exit points and monitored the storefronts across the street. The young woman at the telecom kiosk had another customer. Her innocent smile captivated Mercer. He got lost in a moment of serenity. Suddenly, the rear door opened behind him. Mercer twisted around in his seat; his eyes caught Hendrik's confused glare as the Indonesian businessman pulled the door shut.

'Who are you?' Hendrik questioned, his voice edged with fear.

Recognition was instantaneous for Mercer. The long, dark hair, designer glasses, and distinctive mustache matched his target perfectly. 'I'm here to deliver a message from Mr. Pratama,' Mercer replied, his finger sealing their fate as he pressed the lock button.

Panic flashed in Hendrik's eyes; survival instincts took over as he fumbled with the door handle.

A swift double tap, the silenced shots barely audible from the outside, ended the confrontation. Hendrik collapsed over the backseat. Blood, hair, and pieces of skull splattered over the car's rear window, unnoticeable from the outside. Mercer, undisturbed, drove the Lexus away from the lobby entrance, merging into the dense Jakarta traffic. His attention was divided by the rear-view mirror and the street ahead.

With the abandoned Honda motorcycle left in the parking lot and two dead bodies in the garage, time was closing in. It wouldn't be long before the Indonesian National Police started their search for the car. Aware of his cargo, Mercer exited the main highway, opting for the back streets once more. After thirty minutes of navigating winding roads, he spotted the ideal place to buy fuel. On the side of a dusty street, an old man sat hunched over a bowl of fried noodles. In front of him sat a rackety wooden stand containing petrol held in an assortment of bottles. This setup offered motorcycle riders a quick, affordable refueling alternative to the long lines at conventional gas stations.

Mercer purchased ten one-liter bottles of petrol and left the vendor a huge tip. Once back on the road, Mercer retrieved his new phone to make a single call to Mr. Pratama. Using his Gulfstream jet was his best option. After the call, Mercer rolled down the window, seeking relief from the overpowering stench of fuel that filled the car.

An hour later, the jet climbed and sharply banked, setting its course toward the destination. The sprawling city gradually receded into the distance. Landmarks emerged into view as trucks, cars and countless motorcycles navigated the streets, with Jakarta's smoky haze growing more distinct. Climbing another thousand feet, the Java Sea to the north glittered in the sunlight, dotted with container ships heading to port, while fishing boats maneuvered carefully around them. Mercer peered through the small window, identifying familiar landmarks like hotels, office towers, and stadiums. He quickly traced the main thoroughfares back to his earlier location. Amidst the dust, smog, and harsh sunlight breaking through the clouds, he finally located the site. A thin plume of black smoke ascended from the back of an abandoned furniture store. He could barely make out the faint blue and red lights blinking in the surrounding streets as the fire trucks closed in. *Too late.* Mercer knew that igniting the petrol would swiftly obliterate any DNA on the bodies, cell phones, and firearm.

As the jet pierced the clouds, erasing the city below, Mercer settled into his seat. His mind tangled with thoughts of Georg Wilhelm Schelling and the Black Orchestra. *How much money will I earn? How long can this double life continue? When will I gather enough evidence to go after them?* There were too many questions and possibilities to contend with. His mind drifted to the bodyguards he just eliminated. It wasn't a feeling of guilt, given their dossier, which highlighted their previous crimes: murder, torture, rape, and extortion. *They deserved it. Those that lived by the sword...* The thought trailed off; Mercer couldn't dismiss the nagging concern that his aggression bordered on psychotic.

The calm, authoritative voice of the captain flowed from the PA system, filling the cabin. *Sir, this is your captain speaking from the flight deck. We've reached our cruising altitude and are en route to Washington, D.C. Current speed is five hundred knots, cruising at forty-five thousand feet. The weather looks clear, and we expect a smooth flight ahead. Flight time, including refueling in Tokyo, is estimated at twenty-four hours. Should you need anything, please let me know.*

Mercer cracked open a bottle of whiskey, poured it over an ice-filled glass, and took a sip. He reclined his seat and instantly fell into a deep sleep as the jet made its way over the Java Sea, en route to a refueling stop in Haneda Airport. The aircraft's steady hum became a distant echo, as the nightmares of clandestine operations, the sharp recoil of his weapon in distant deserts, and the cold stare of adversaries in dimly lit rooms haunted his mind. Memories of narrow escapes from undercover operations in bustling marketplaces, the heavy silence after a successful extraction, and the weight of decisions that saved or sacrificed lives tormented his restless sleep.

ELEVEN

The ornate chandeliers of the Congressional Country Club in Washington, D.C., cast a warm glow over the rich mahogany paneling, their light reflecting softly off the collection of crystal glasses and polished silverware that adorned the tables. The setting spoke of power, legacy, and secrets whispered behind the velvet drapes of its historic rooms.

At a secluded table, away from the prying eyes of the private country club's elite clientele, the core members of the Black Orchestra convened. Their numbers were growing, serving as a testament to the organization's expanding influence and strength. Charles Clark, his balding head catching the light as he leaned in, was discussing logistics, his voice a low rumble that blended with the ambient noise of clinking cutlery and subdued conversation. Next to him, John Elder, his thin frame rigid as ever, listened intently, the gold ring on his finger glinting as he gestured for emphasis.

Kenneth Decker, whose hardened face bore the marks of his long service, was detailing a plan with a precision that reflected his military background. His eyes, accustomed to scanning horizons for threats, now scrutinized the faces of his compatriots for signs of dissent or fear. 'The stakes have never been higher,' he stated, his voice barely above a whisper. 'Mercer's work for us in Jakarta changes the game. We need to be sure of his allegiance or eliminate the risk he poses. We cannot afford to mess with this man; he is extremely volatile and aggressive. You've all seen how close his reach is by showing up at Schelling's house. The man is sharp and calculating. I acknowledge how valuable he can be, but listen carefully. We need to keep him on a tight leash and only share what he needs to know. Keep my name out of it; I can't afford to lose my position. Or my life, for that matter.'

His words spurred a quiet tension around the table. It was a stark reminder of the stakes involved, not just for the Black Orchestra but for each individual tethered to its success or downfall. The room fell silent. It was into this atmosphere that Senator Rick Sanderson, the last to join the meeting, arrived with his usual air of detached amusement. However, the gravity of the ongoing conversation quickly sobered his demeanor. His experience in the political games of Washington had taught him the art of survival, but the current predicament presented a challenge even he found daunting.

'Why the long faces? Is this about the new guy, Danny Mercer?' asked Sanderson.

Decker nodded toward an empty seat. Sanderson sat down before continuing. 'What is his story? What can he bring to the table?'

Decker cleared his throat, drawing the room's attention back to the pressing matter of Mercer.

'Gentlemen, while we deliberate our steps forward, let's not forget the caliber of individual we're attempting to craft. Mercer, a man whose career has been nothing short of a study in survival and strategy, poses a unique challenge,' he began, his tone underscoring the gravity of his words. 'I've crossed paths with Mercer in the field. His reputation within the Special Operations Group is legendary, not just for his tactical brilliance but for his ability to emerge unscathed where others falter. This is a man who, after leaving Delta Force, carved a niche for himself within the CIA's most secretive units.'

Decker's gaze swept across the faces of his compatriots as he prepared to delve deeper into the essence of Mercer's character—a man whose actions had once thrown the covert world into turmoil. 'To truly grasp the nature of the man we're dealing with, you need to understand the lengths he's willing to go to achieve his objectives. Mercer isn't just an operative; he's a force of nature, unpredictable and violent when cornered.'

He paused, ensuring he had the full attention of the room before adding. 'Take, for instance, an operation in Berlin. On a bustling afternoon on Friedrichstraße, Mercer commandeered a police vehicle right under the noses of the local authorities. What ensued was nothing short of chaos.'

Decker painted a vivid picture of the scene: Mercer, behind the wheel of the stolen cop car, his eyes fixed on a high-value target under surveillance. The streets were choked with traffic, but Mercer rammed his way through the congestion at an intersection, his determination bordering on crazy. Pedestrians scattered in panic as the sound of crunching metal and car alarms filled the air.

'He caught up with his target's vehicle, a black sedan, and without a moment's hesitation, smashed into it with such force that the car rolled several times before coming to a halt,' Decker recounted, his tone darkening. 'Before witnesses could even process the carnage, Mercer was out of the police car. Two shots rang out, and the target was dead, execution-style, in broad daylight. Hundreds of eyes on the street and in cars bore witness to this brazen act.'

Decker let the gravity of the story sink in before adding, 'Mercer then vanished into the crowds, leaving behind a scene of destruction and a city in shock. The German intelligence community, the Bundesnachrichtendienst, was in an uproar, pushed by their politicians for action. Yet, silently, they were relieved. The man Mercer eliminated had fueled a terror-led attitude in young radicals for years.'

He shifted in his chair and ran his finger along the inside of his shirt collar. 'Back in the States, the White House demanded answers from Langley. The name *Danny Mercer* was making the rounds in the halls of power, and just as quickly, the demands for accountability fell silent. Mercer's connections, his ability to walk the line between sanctioned and unsanctioned action, leave us all treading a fine line.'

Before Decker could further elaborate, Schelling raised a hand, signaling a pause in the conversation. The room fell silent, all eyes turning toward him. Schelling stood, his presence commanding immediate attention, his silver hair catching the dim light, giving him an almost regal aura.

'Gentlemen,' Schelling began, his voice steady and authoritative, breaking the momentary silence. 'While your concerns about

Mercer are valid, let us not forget the steps already taken to ensure his cooperation. You know, Mercer always prided himself on being a step ahead. Yet, it was we who managed to stay one move ahead of him.' A slight, knowing smile played at the corners of his mouth. 'By directing him to Jakarta, we didn't just remove a potential thorn from our side; we've intricately documented his actions.'

Around the table, murmurs of approval and nods of agreement rippled among the members, a collective acknowledgment of Schelling's tactical mind.

'We have him,' Schelling said, the confidence in his tone unmistakable. 'Every move, every decision he made in Jakarta, was under our surveillance. We possess enough evidence to lock Mercer away for decades. Not even the powers of the CIA or his connections within the White House could untangle him from this mess.'

The pride in their accomplishment was clear, echoing off the wood-paneled walls of the private room. But the smiles didn't quite reach their eyes. Charles Clark's previously furrowed brow smoothed into an expression of grudging admiration. He nodded slowly but deliberately, signaling his respect for the plan. John Elder, often reserved and stoic, allowed a rare and slight smile to crease his features, offering an unspoken acknowledgment of their strategic triumph. Sanderson, who had been swirling his whiskey, paused to slightly raise his glass toward Schelling in a silent toast to their ingenuity.

Decker, the most hard-nosed of the group, let out a low, appreciative chuckle, the closest he ever came to offering outright praise during these gatherings. 'Well, that is great news, although I want to warn everyone one last time.' Pausing to ensure his words sank in, Decker added, 'What truly sets Mercer apart is his adaptability. The same traits that make him invaluable to us also render him dangerous. His incursion into Schelling's home was a bold move, one that demonstrated not just his physical capabilities but his psychological acumen. Mercer doesn't just navigate threats; he manipulates them to his advantage. I've seen it in the field. He got away with so much simply because he delivers. The trail of destruction is a byproduct of his methods.'

Decker locked eyes with each of his colleagues in turn. 'While we possess substantial leverage over him following his operation in Jakarta, surveillance that indeed could imprison him for decades, we must tread cautiously. Push too hard, and we risk turning a potential asset into a formidable adversary.'

Sanderson, who had been following Decker's monologue with increasing interest, finally spoke up. 'So, you believe we can still bring him into the fold, make him one of us, despite the risks?'

Decker thought for a moment before nodding, 'Yes, but with conditions. We organize his missions with precision, divulging only what's necessary. As for my worries, they're not unfounded. Mercer's ability to tread the line between loyalty and betrayal will always be a concern. But remember, gentlemen, in this game, it's not just about holding the reins tightly; it's about ensuring our steed knows which way we want him to run.'

The room fell silent, processing Decker's assessment. It was clear that while the path forward with Mercer was fraught with peril, the rewards could very well outweigh the risks.

Everyone listened intently as Schelling detailed the intricacies of their operation in Jakarta, highlighting not just the surveillance but the psychological tactics employed to gauge Mercer's loyalty and potential as an ally. 'By providing him with just enough rope, we've seen how far he's willing to go. And let me assure you, gentlemen, Mercer has proven himself to be as valuable as he is dangerous.'

Schelling sat upright, picking up his glass as the ice clinked gently against the sides, creating a momentary pause that allowed his words to sink in. After a contemplative sip, he set the glass down and cleared his throat.

'Okay, moving on. Mercer presents us with a unique opportunity,' Schelling said. 'There are elements within the CIA—resistive fragments that do not align with our vision. Mercer, unknowingly, will become the instrument of their removal. The FBI is already in our pocket; we just need to maintain our links with them and focus on Langley.'

Schelling checked his watch, more out of habit than anything else. 'I have my strategy, but this organization thrives on the collective prowess of its members. I value your insights. Let us discuss our next steps. How can we further leverage Mercer's talents for our objectives?'

The invitation was simple. Schelling sought to cultivate a sense of inclusion, to remind each man of his importance to the Black Orchestra's machinations. It was a moment for them to contribute, to offer their intellect and expertise to the ongoing saga of their secretive empire.

As the group delved deeper into their strategy, a new mission was proposed, a test of loyalty for Mercer that would seal his fate with the Black Orchestra. 'Mercer's skills are undeniable, but so is his potential to unravel our plans, as Decker mentioned,' Clark noted, the weight of his shipping empire resting on the success of their covert operations.

Decker responded, 'We'll set the stage for his

next assignment carefully. An assassination that serves our interests and tests his commitment. If he succeeds, we solidify our hold on him. If not...' his voice trailed off, the implication clear to all present.

Outside the country club's prestigious grounds, the world of Washington, D.C., carried on, oblivious to the schemes being hatched within. Across the Potomac River, the analysts at Langley would be piecing together disparate threads of intelligence, sifting through encrypted communications, satellite imagery, and financial transactions with painstaking detail. But for those seated around the mahogany table, the decisions made in the hushed tones of their meeting would have far-reaching consequences, shaping the future of the Black Orchestra and sealing the fate of Danny Mercer.

The jet's engines wound down with a soothing whir. Mercer stepped out and was ushered through the airport via the VIP gate of Dulles International. He made a brief stop to buy some cigars before making it to the next hurdle. At the arrivals desk, he offered his passport, issued in the name of Tony Hoffmann, to the officer, who opened the photo page, glanced at Mercer, and then swiped it through a machine. A green light blinked on the officer's console, prompting him to tap a few buttons on his keyboard. The officer gave the passport another glance, for just a moment too long, before handing it back and welcoming Mr. Hoffmann to the USA with a nod that was as perfunctory as it was dismissive.

Mercer was acutely aware of the police presence, though he showed no outward sign of concern. Walking past a group of airport police huddled near the exits, some drinking coffee, others scrutinizing the faces of weary passengers, Mercer found his mind briefly revisiting his past actions. The elimination of the junkie in the drug house, seen as an obstacle in a dirty world, and the FBI agent, perceived as a direct threat, were decisions made out of cold necessity. And then there was Alexander West, whose end was a calculated removal. For Mercer, these weren't acts of violence but necessary actions to neutralize clear threats to national security. However, as he passed under the watchful gaze of the officers, a hint of unease stirred within him. This unease wasn't born from guilt but from questioning the simplicity with which he had labeled these lives as justifiable losses.

As he stepped through the airport's doors, this internal conflict seemed to momentarily fade, confronted by the immediate and tangible chill of the Washington, D.C. air, a sharp contrast to the climate-controlled interior he had just left. Armed officers patrolled the taxi ranks, quietly communicating over their radios as Mercer made his way through the crowd to a waiting vehicle. He approached a standard sedan, the type easily overlooked, where an attendant stood ready to hand over the keys.

The drive to his cheap motel on the Arlington Boulevard went smoothly despite the traffic. En route, Mercer made two brief stops, the first at Bayou Bakery for a sandwich and coffee, then at a cell phone store for two phones and SIM cards. Once checked in, Mercer quickly slotted a SIM card into a phone and powered it on. As soon as the phone linked to a cell tower, he locked his door and exited the motel. On the short walk to Hillside Park, Mercer scanned the streets, checking for any signs of surveillance. The park was small and contained little more than a few trees and picnic tables alongside a group of homeless individuals who were busy gathering their belongings before heading off to chase their first high of the day. Mercer chose a spot with a view of the entrances and unwrapped his roast beef sandwich. He had two important calls to make, both to contacts in England. *That's four hours ahead,* Mercer noted as he dialed the first number.

'Afternoon.'

'Hey, mate. It's your old brother from Ciudad Juárez. How are you?' Mercer said.

Charlie Halford, understanding the drill, steered clear of using Mercer's name over the line, as the mention of Ciudad Juárez was a hint to keep things low-key. 'All normal on my end. Been busy putting a few things together. Are we still doing this thing you mentioned earlier?' Halford said, straight to the point as usual.

'Yes. Expect a transaction later today. We've got a lot of ground to cover quickly. Have you reached out to our mutual friend? The man handy with keyboards?' Mercer's reference to Hobbs, his former SAS teammate turned MI6 operative, was clear to Halford. They often joked about Hobbs in this way, a light-hearted ribbing at the man who was once a fearful warrior, now in charge of facilitators assisting those in the field.

Halford let out a laugh. 'Mr. Keyboard was very helpful. He narrowed down your POIs to New York and has everything prepped for us. When and where will we link up? I am looking forward to having a couple of beers with you.' In Charlie Halford's world, *beers* was code for kill or capture missions.

'Excellent. Just hold tight, for now. I've got a situation to address here first. Then, I will be over in Bangkok. Give me forty-eight hours. Leave your movements and location with the keyboard so I can track you down.'

'Copy that. See you on the other side,' Halford said before the line went dead.

Mercer removed the SIM card and quickly torched it with his cigar lighter, then inserted a new one. He took another bite of his sandwich, washed it down with coffee, then tapped his thumb over the screen. Ready for another phone call, this one to Jeff Connor.

'Connor, it's Mercer.' His voice cut through the silence.

'Mercer. Fuck me, I was wondering when you were going to pop your head up. What's your status?' Connor asked.

'I'm back in D.C. Thought I'd check in. There are problems which I don't want to get in to, for opsec reasons. This Mong La task requires a more direct approach. So, I am building a team, and I'm running low on resources.' Mercer's statement was frank, revealing nothing more.

'Direct approach. What the hell does that mean? You are not invincible, Mercer, and you're certainly not above the law, despite what you may believe. A few days ago, I got a visit from Faulkner. He is on a warpath. The man thinks we're not being aggressive enough with Mong La. He even threatened to haul us in front of the Department of Justice's Criminal Division.' Connor's voice, though steady, betrayed a flicker of irritation and fear.

Angry at the thought of facing the DOJ, Mercer slammed his coffee cup to the ground.

'What the fuck is that man up to? I'm out here risking my neck, and he is playing politics.'

Connor didn't want to make Mercer any more reckless and attempted to steer him back on course. 'It's the game they play; they hold the hoop, and we jump through it. Just keep your head down, and damn it, use secure comms from now on. We can't risk leaks.'

Suddenly, Mercer noticed the same cop car again, turning into North Pierce Street. It slowed to a stop just past the intersection. The occupants stayed in the vehicle.

'I can't talk for long. Do you have anything on the FBI and the earlier problem?' Mercer asked, aware the agents would be out for his blood once they connected the dots.

'We are stalling at every opportunity. Any surveillance footage gathered was quickly destroyed, internal files went missing, and some higher-ups at the White House have put pressure on the FBI Director. But it won't hold forever.' Connor said.

While mulling over Connor's words, Mercer monitored the patrol car. The cops remained inside. Mercer knew if he walked off, it could attract their attention. 'I should have what you need in another week. Enough intelligence to show there is something sinister at play between the agencies. Which should ensure my previous dealings with the FBI resulted from their corruption and attempts to silence me.'

'I hope you're right. It's a tightrope, Mercer. Okay, one week. Get names and connections, and I mean concrete evidence. Financial records, surveillance footage, digital evidence, forensics, testimonies. Make sure it all lands on my desk first. We can't have the FBI involved.' Connor's tone sounded more like a warning.

Suddenly, the cop car's engine revved, and it tore down the street with sirens blaring and lights flashing until it vanished from Mercer's sight. His heartbeat spiked as he strained to hear the fading siren. As silence returned, he turned his attention back to the call. 'Right, you'll have it; just make sure the cash and everything else is ready.'

'You can pick it up at the usual place.'

'I'll be in touch.' With those last words, Mercer ended the call. Once again, the SIM card was removed and burned to a plastic blob. He flicked it off the picnic bench and remained seated for a moment. His eyes traced the park's sparse landscape. The place reminded him of a dilapidated park found on the outskirts of Moscow. Discarded syringes filled the garden beds, cigarette butts littered the footpath, and neglected hedges grew wild, their branches extending across the narrow paths. It was a scene of misery, only a stone's throw from the nation's power. Mercer let the silence sit with him, a rare companion in his line of work, where quiet moments were usually the calm before a storm. He knew there was no time to waste in D.C.—Connor hadn't asked to meet up, so there was no reason to hang around.

After a good night's sleep at the Red Lion hotel, he rose early, showered, and drove to the Pentagon City Mall. Among the early hustle of shopkeepers opening their shutters, he found a shop selling off-the-rack suits. Ten minutes later, he parked his car at the Union Station Garage on Massachusetts Ave. When Mercer stepped into the grand Beaux-Arts expanse of the bustling transportation hub, his sharp eyes swept across the soaring marble columns, intricate sculptures, and vaulted ceiling, taking in every detail. He noted the positions of surveillance cameras, exits, station police, and pickpockets, as well as street thieves looking for an opportunity to snatch a laptop or handbag.

He continued past a diverse throng of commuters: suited professionals tapping impatiently on their smartphones, tourists wide-eyed and hauling oversized luggage, and students plugged into their music, all weaving their own paths through the terminal. Mercer made a brief detour into a coffee shop to check the crowds more carefully. After a few minutes, he rose and made his way to the Amtrak counter to buy a one-way ticket to New York.

New York—USA

In the opulent confines of The Metropolitan Club, the legacy of New York's elite, from Vanderbilts to Roosevelts, whispered through the grand halls. Georg Schelling, Senator John McCarthy, and Arnold Becker from the DOJ convened in a secluded corner, steeped in the kind of quiet power that moved nations. Senator McCarthy, his black hair neatly combed back, showcased a weathered face marked by a life in the public eye. His eyes, sharp and calculating, scanned the room under thick, distinguished brows. A tailored suit clung to his lean frame, emphasizing a presence both polished and imposing. The club's rich history served as a fitting backdrop for their meeting, a reminder of the influence at their disposal.

'Senator McCarthy,' Schelling began. 'Your continued support is not just beneficial but essential to our collective objectives. The Black Orchestra has always valued discretion and effectiveness, qualities you've exemplified in your service to our cause.'

McCarthy, a man whose political acumen had been honed through years within the corridors of power, nodded, his expression one of unwavering commitment. 'Rest assured, Schelling, the resources and influence at my command remain at the Orchestra's disposal. The recent...complications,' he said, referencing Becker's failed operation in Geneva with a nod toward Becker, 'will not deter our course.'

Becker, seeking to redeem his earlier misstep, interjected with a carefully chosen assurance. 'The oversight in Geneva has only sharpened our focus. We're poised to adapt and advance with more precision.'

McCarthy dismissed the comment with a wave of his hand, then reached out and picked up a decanter. He poured a rich amber rye whiskey into crystal glasses, the liquid's smooth descent a silent testament to the riches surrounding them. 'The support from our end,' McCarthy said, setting the decanter aside with a soft clink, 'will continue to flow as freely as this whiskey, Schelling. But understand, our backers, both in the corridors of power and from Wall Street, crave results. They're intrigued by what our partnership with this new Chinese group can yield. Speaking of which, they are an unknown entity. This has caused some nervousness for my investors. I understand the sensitivity of this; however, I need to know who we are partnering up with.'

Schelling accepted his glass. 'Our friends

from the East,' he began, 'offer more than just additional funding and guaranteed returns. The stock markets, ripe for manipulation through insider investments, present a lucrative avenue. May it be New York, Shanghai, Tokyo, London, Saudi or Bombay's Stock Exchange. We will have our contacts inserted through this partnership. Moreover, the expansion into Chinese-controlled mines in Africa and their burgeoning industrial capabilities could revolutionize how we approach our... enterprises.'

McCarthy narrowed his eyes and took a slow sip. 'And what of the ethical boundaries, Schelling? Our backers are adventurous but cautious.'

Schelling smiled thinly. 'Senator, in our line of work, ethics are as flexible as the regulations we bend. Whether through industrial espionage that enables our new Chinese partners to replicate Western technology independently, or through less...conventional means, there's a spectrum of investment. The question is, how far along that spectrum are your backers willing to venture?'

The room fell into a momentary silence, broken only by the soft crackle of a cigar being lit. Becker, until now a silent observer, settled back in his chair. 'The stakes are high,' he added, 'but so are the rewards. We're not just talking about shifting the balance of power; we're re-shaping the future of global industry.'

McCarthy exhaled a cloud of smoke that drifted lazily toward the ceiling. 'And this new section of the Chinese government?' he finally asked. 'How do they fit into this grand vision of ours? My backers want assurances. They're ready to invest, but they need to know the ground they're building on is solid.'

Schelling nodded slowly. 'Our association with General Liu and his elite faction presents, shall we say, a complex but mutually beneficial arrangement. Liu, as you're aware from our operations, is a man of decisive action and bold vision. Our paths align significantly in both our goals and our methods, though, naturally, such relationships are not without their...teething problems.' He paused to let his words sink in, then continued:

'This is precisely why we engage in meetings like ours today, to navigate these complexities. Rest assured, Senator, the goals of this break-away group align closely with ours. Their interest in extending their investments into Western markets, their capabilities in industrial espionage, and their ambitions in Africa all serve as testament to this. Zhang Wei's arrival will solidify that foundation. The Chinese are not just participants; they're architects of this new world we're constructing. Their investment in our operations extends beyond mere financial contributions. We're offering them a stake in a new global order—one where their technology, produced through the secrets we provide, positions them at the pinnacle of economic and industrial dominance.'

A silence fell over the room, allowing the gravity of Schelling's words to resonate. After a moment, he added, 'And as for our Chinese friends, the advancements they can bring to our combined operations is one that we will have direct oversight on. Every move they make shall be watched, and the level of insider intelligence that we gain will be unparalleled. Something our intelligence community has failed to do.'

McCarthy crossed his legs, watching Schelling carefully before offering a brief nod.

'Very well, Schelling,' McCarthy concluded. 'Let's show our new friends from the East just how lucrative this partnership can be. But remember, our backers expect complete anonymity. And so do I.' As McCarthy emphasized anonymity, Becker shifted in his seat, a subtle sign of his discomfort, his gaze darting between the two men as he adjusted the cuff of his sleeve.

McCarthy checked his watch and glanced toward the restroom. He considered going to the toilet but dismissed the idea, knowing it might raise suspicion. Any movement, especially leaving the room, could be interpreted as hesitation or, worse, disloyalty. Despite being part of the organization, McCarthy couldn't shake the feeling of being an outsider, and he was determined not to give them any reason to doubt his influence.

'Zhang Wei will join us soon. He is, if I am not mistaken, the head of technical espionage and cyber intelligence at the Ministry of State Security. Therefore, he's in a prominent position to protect this partnership. It's vital the official party leadership in China doesn't catch wind of our plans. This could have global consequences.' The opulence of The Metropolitan Club, with its velvet and marble, suddenly felt suffocating. Becker's eyes darted to the grand windows, seeking a momentary escape, a silent admission of the tension gripping them.

'What are their plans for the current leadership of the CCP? A purge?' McCarthy asked. Schelling met this with a cool smile. This exchange did not go unnoticed by Becker, who was momentarily sidelined. He held his glass in a suspended motion.

Schelling glanced toward the entrance before locking eyes with McCarthy again. 'Trust me, John, this new faction led by General Liu Xiang, and backed by Zhang Wei, who we will meet soon, has everything in place to dismantle the current party. With heavyweights like

Zhao Ming and Liang Guang in their corner, who are among the most influential figures in the intelligence community, together they are unstoppable.

'What they're planning and how they execute those plans are not our concerns. We won't get involved in China's internal politics. Haven't our leaders made enough of a mess meddling in the governments of the developing world for decades? It is Liu's plan to overthrow the CCP, with significant backing by many others, including us. When he takes power, being ready to stand as partners will be advantageous for us. The White House had its chance. Regardless of who sits in the Oval Office, whether our President is a Democrat or Republican, it won't matter. It will be the Black Orchestra that controls the true power.'

A stern expression hardened McCarthy's face as he listened to Schelling's bold assertion of their impending power. This pause was punctuated by the soft clinks of cutlery and murmurs from influential lobbyists and politicians elsewhere in the club. Schelling and McCarthy, locked in a moment of silent appraisal, shared an understanding lof the high stakes, partners treading on a razor's edge.

McCarthy took a puff of his cigar before asking, 'Can you vouch for these men? Zhao Ming, Liang, Zhang, and the general? That's the crucial question. Your reputation, and perhaps life, depends on this.' McCarthy's question sounded more like a threat than a query. There was no way he would take the fall if this partnership failed.

'Can you vouch for our own President? For the other Senators that sit on the Senate Select Committee on Intelligence? They are tasked with overseeing intelligence activities, ensuring they align with our laws and the Constitution. Yet, here we are, contemplating a partnership that could redefine global power structures. Our endeavor could overshadow their official oversight, crafting a new reality beyond their conventional scope. Do you trust them to uphold their duties without interfering in our plans, or do we need to consider their potential as obstacles?'

McCarthy exhaled a cloud of smoke, his expression unchanging, the weight of decades in the political arena evident in his steady gaze. 'Schelling, in this town, trust is a currency few can afford, and even fewer can earn. As for those Senators, they play their part, as do we all. But make no mistake, I know how to navigate those waters. If this ship sinks, I'll make damn sure it's not my name they find in the wreckage. We're in this together, but your assurances need to hold more weight than just words. Your faction, Liu, and his plans are your domain. But the fallout, should things go south, won't be landing on my doorstep alone. We clear?'

Schelling's eyes narrowed slightly, but he maintained his composed exterior. Internally, he bristled at McCarthy's insinuation but chose his words with diplomatic precision, 'John, we navigate by the stars, not by the lights of each passing ship. Rest assured, our vessel is more than seaworthy.' Before he could further mask his irritation with politeness, a club staff member approached, guiding Zhang Wei toward their table, effectively shifting the atmosphere.

Schelling rose to his feet and offered his hand. 'Mr. Zhang, glad you could come.' As Schelling introduced Zhang to the others, he couldn't help but notice the displeasure in Zhang's eyes when he shook Becker's hand. The failure in Geneva was raw in everyone's mind.

Schelling nodded to the staff, who quickly left to retrieve another bottle and some food. 'Gentlemen, the recalibration of our alliance is not just necessary; it's critical. We stand at the precipice of reshaping the global power structure. Before we dive deeper, I should mention that I've just arrived from Washington. I had a productive session with the rest of the Black Orchestra, further aligning our strategies and ensuring our next steps are tightly controlled.'

Zhang ignored the statement and directed his

attention to McCarthy. 'Mr. McCarthy, I appreciate your time, and therefore, I will go straight to the point. The framework we're proposing involves strategic moves against the CCP's leadership. We will not only destabilize the leadership; we'll obliterate them. History will be rewritten. These moves that General Liu and our faction have planned are ready for execution. Our success translates into unparalleled opportunities for all of us. We are simply waiting for your side to show loyalty. We need to be satisfied with your capabilities.'

Over the next thirty minutes, Zhang aimed to instill confidence in McCarthy by detailing the operational framework for a series of covert actions against the CCP.

McCarthy knew that this rogue faction of the Chinese Communist Party came with faults. Their plan to seize control of the CCP and eliminate its current leadership was a risk—one that could implicate him. However, their access to cash from the global meth trade and other illicit industries gave them unlimited resources. With control over the shady mineral sector, crypto scams, and black-market operations stretching from Hong Kong to Zimbabwe, they were positioned to reshape the global underworld.

McCarthy understood the value of the black economy; it was where real money was made and influence wasn't tied to elections or public perception. Under Liu's leadership, China's dominance would force the world to accept the new order. With that shift, McCarthy's position in the West would be unshakable.

Within a couple of years, his goal of becoming CIA Director—then, in time, U.S. President—would be within reach. Controlling the agency meant controlling the flow of intelligence, deciding who was a threat, and ensuring no hidden scandals could derail his ambitions. The Senate had its power, but the CIA had reach—the kind that shaped governments, buried problems, and eliminated obstacles. With the backing of the Black Orchestra and the new CCP, he would clear the way, silence the doubters, and build the perfect narrative for his rise.

McCarthy's mind turned over the possibilities. He stared at his drink, considering how best to play his hand. After some thought, and with his skepticism barely masked, he responded dryly. 'And in exchange, you seek my influence within the Senate. A heavy ask, Zhang. What assurances do we have that Liu's faction won't turn the tables on us?'

Zhang's reply was swift. 'Because, Mr. McCarthy, our interests are aligned far beyond mere politics. This is about setting a new global standard, one where we both dictate the terms. Together with the contacts from the Black Orchestra and your intelligence from the committees, your power and influence, we can all benefit. We cannot do this alone. To ensure our global reach is secure and to combat any future challenges from Europe, it is imperative that we join forces. To achieve this symbiotic relationship, we need to trust each other, otherwise we all fail. I also assure you, Mr. McCarthy, that we too have concerns. It could be you who turns the tables. That is the risk we all take.'

McCarthy stretched out his legs and gave a simple nod before casually observing the other patrons of the club. He knew Zhang was right. He just needed a few moments to think.

Without a break, Zhang focused his attention toward Becker. His position within the Department of Justice and his connections gained over the years with the FBI were important. The man brought huge operational expertise to the group, despite the failings in Geneva. For now, Zhang would ignore Becker's past record and instead offer a mix of respect and strategic consideration.

'Mr. Becker,' he began, his voice carrying a tone of earnest acknowledgment. 'Your role within the United States Department of Justice is not just valuable; it's foundational to our collective endeavors. The breadth of your organization's influence, spanning legal authority, national security, and international law, is unparalleled. General Liu and our forthcoming government understand the significance of having a powerful ally within the DOJ. Your ability to navigate the legal and intelligence frameworks, both domestically and on the global stage, will be instrumental.'

Zhang's gaze hardened slightly. 'The operations we're planning within the U.S., while meticulously crafted, will undoubtedly encounter legal and political hurdles. Your expertise in counterterrorism, counterintelligence, and especially in managing the legal oversight of covert operations, will ensure we overcome these obstacles seamlessly.'

He leaned forward slightly, emphasizing his next point. 'The international legal environment is complex and fraught with challenges. With you, Mr. Becker, we have a direct line to someone capable of guiding us through extradition matters and international legal cooperation, ensuring our actions are shielded from unwarranted scrutiny.'

Zhang's tone softened as he concluded, 'General Liu places great trust in your capabilities. Your role is pivotal—not just as a facilitator but as a guardian of our mutual interests. We're embarking on a journey that will reshape the geopolitical landscape. And it's your guidance and influence within the legal and intelligence domains that will help secure our position on this new frontier.'

Becker cleared his throat, acknowledging Zhang's points with a nod, yet his expression carried a trace of professional annoyance. 'Mr. Zhang, while I appreciate the confidence placed in my role within the DOJ, let's not gloss over Geneva.' His voice was firm, betraying a hint of irritation beneath his composed exterior. 'The operation's failure wasn't because of a lack of planning or insight from our end. The counter-surveillance was your team's responsibility. A detail overlooked by your professionals.'

He held Zhang's piercing eyes without flinching before continuing. 'That said, the Justice Department, and indeed my connections within the FBI, afford us capabilities that extend far beyond mere legal maneuvering. We can provide a shield against domestic legal challenges, yes, but also a spear when it comes to intelligence gathering and operational execution.'

Becker's face tightened, showing his determination. 'Moving forward, my advice is straightforward: tighter coordination and a higher standard of professionalism, especially from those we rely on for field operations. We're playing in a realm where mistakes don't just cost us politically or financially; they can escalate to international incidents.'

He raised his chin slightly, his point made, yet offering a conciliatory note. 'Despite the setbacks, my dedication to our collective goal remains unwavering. With the resources and influence at my disposal, I assure you that the path we're carving will not only circumvent domestic and international legal hurdles but also lay the groundwork for our unprecedented ascendancy. Just ensure your side meets us with the same level of precision and commitment.'

Zhang absorbed Becker's critique with an unflinching demeanor, a testament to his experience in navigating the high stakes of espionage and international politics. After a brief moment, he offered a nod of acknowledgment, conceding the point with grace.

'You're right, Mr. Becker. The failure in Geneva highlighted weaknesses that were, frankly, inexcusable on our part,' Zhang admitted, his tone betraying no hint of defensiveness, only resolve. 'The debrief failed to address the hit team's lapse in counter-surveillance. A critical oversight that we've since rectified.'

He shifted slightly, signaling a transition in the conversation. 'On that note, I want to assure everyone at this table that we've taken comprehensive steps to overhaul our operational protocols. We have assembled a new team, highly skilled, rigorously vetted, and extensively trained for operations across Europe.'

Zhang's assurance was firm, aimed at reinstating confidence among his allies. 'This new team is ready to initiate the next phase of our plan, with a level of professionalism and precision that meets, if not exceeds, our collective standards. We've learned from our past. Moving forward, every operation will be a testament to our commitment to success and our ability to adapt and overcome.'

The earnestness in Zhang's voice was unmistakable, an open acknowledgment of past failures but, more importantly, a clear declaration of the strides taken to ensure they would not be repeated. His commitment to improvement and readiness to proceed with operations in Europe served not just as reassurance but as a rallying call for the collective endeavor they were all embroiled in.

Schelling kept silent during the exchange between Zhang and Becker, understanding the importance of letting the two men air their grievances and assurances. His thoughts, however, lingered on Zhang's commitment to a new, highly skilled team poised for operations in Europe. This shift toward professionalism sparked cautious optimism. This alliance, while promising immense power and influence, carried significant risks. The failure of any single operation could not only jeopardize their positions but could lead to international backlash or even war. Therefore, the meeting transcended mere dialogue. It was a commitment ceremony, binding these men together in their ambitious quest for power, with each one understanding the part they played and the immense risks they faced.

TWELVE
New York—USA

In a nondescript two-story CIA safe house, tucked away in the urban sprawl of Queens, Mercer began his preparations to meet Schelling. The location, chosen for its anonymity and strategic convenience, offered a stark contrast to the bustling energy of Union Station. Down in the quiet of the basement, Mercer's focus sharpened as he laid out his equipment on a worn rug: surveillance gear, bundles of cash, a Glock 19 9mm pistol, ammo, and a pair of surgical gloves. He slipped on the gloves, inserted fresh batteries into the cameras, and loaded a magazine into his Glock. Next, he powered up a cell phone and punched in a number.

'Keyboard man, glad you picked up. How's our mutual friend getting along? I hope you have been tracing his movements,' Mercer said as he paced the cold concrete floor.

'Good evening, sir,' Hobbs's voice came through, tinged with the crisp accent of British intelligence. 'Yes, great timing. We've just cracked a bit more intel into Schelling's inner circle. His operational security is top-notch; however, his personal staff and driver do not maintain those high standards. Our listening devices picked up some names and, after connecting the dots with flight manifestos, hotel bookings, credit cards, cell tower locations, metadata and so forth, we have built a pretty decent intelligence picture.'

'Great news. Is there anything actionable? I want to sit down with Schelling, and I know his private jet is in New York. So, I assume he is here, which is good for me as I'd rather be anywhere than D.C.'

'You assumed correctly; Schelling is in New York, staying in Manhattan. My advice is to stay out of D.C. because there is far too much ambiguity within your intel agencies. Let me explain. Over the past few years, we have compiled a list of high-profile individuals who invested in little-known companies on the stock market, both in the U.S. and abroad. Their investments returned huge profits, and it's the same people involved. From senators to high-ranking intelligence officers, attorneys to influential CEOs—all linked through their connections to Georg Schelling. Once we branched out, I noticed that your own boss, Jeff Connor, had irregular dealings with Senator Rick Sanderson. I am not saying that Connor is corrupt, although Sanderson is certainly rotten to the core. That's our assessment, anyway.'

Hobbs knew to remain silent. It was a lot of news for Mercer to process. His own boss being a potential fly in the ointment could cause huge consequences not just for the CIA but for America's national security.

'Understood. I'll deal with Connor later. Just get me what you have on Schelling and his cohorts,' Mercer said.

'There's chatter about a meeting with the Chinese arm of the Black Orchestra, or more specifically, a splinter group of the CCP. It sounds like they are brokering something big. It's all happening fast, Mercer. Schelling has been busy the past couple of days, rallying the troops for something big, I guess.'

The thought of this rogue faction of the CCP active in the U.S. angered Mercer. Dealing with hidden enemies within his own ranks was one thing, but having another element in the mix caused him concern. 'And in Europe, what is the reaction to this? Are we alone, or has this partnership caused your government problems?'

After a silent pause, Hobbs finally spoke, the flat tone of his voice unmistakable. He was spooked by something.

'The U.S. government is not alone, I assure you. After the assassination in Switzerland, both the French and Germans have remained silent. Behind the scenes, however, there's been significant movement by their intelligence agencies. The French DGSE has deployed their Action Division, the Germans have activated their Kommando Spezialkräfte, and our own E Squadron is also on the streets. They suspect the Chinese group might have more than one kill-or-capture team based in Europe. Their task is to find and eliminate them. As the motto of the French Action Division goes, *Nul ne verra, nul ne saura,* which translates to *None will see, none will know.*'

A smile flickered over Mercer's face as he remembered the professionalism of the Action Division. He had the honor of training with them during a course in Perpignan, France. 'That's what I like to hear; all good men. Okay, I don't have much time. Send me the details on Schelling and whatever else you have on this. Do it now before I destroy this SIM.'

'Will do, and best of luck.' The line went dead, leaving Mercer in the still silence of the safe house. He set the phone down and grabbed a second one, this time dialing François Rousseau. Mercer figured the French DGSE operative would have his finger on the pulse and could help embed him within the kill teams when required.

Rousseau answered on the third ring. '*Allô, qui est-ce, s'il vous plaît?*' he asked.

'It's Danny. Sorry to call you at home, but I have some information regarding our East Asian friends. I'd like to stop by sometime for coffee and go over some things with you.'

There was a slight pause before Rousseau replied. 'Sure thing, Danny. I don't want to mention anything over the phone, so we'll leave it until we meet. Same café as before. Just let me know when you're in town.'

A message alert appeared on Mercer's phone, momentarily distracting him. 'One second,' he said. He flicked his thumb over the screen and opened the message from Hobbs. As he read the details, he quickly scribbled down some notes before speaking to Rousseau. 'Gather up everything you know about Shenzhen, especially any recruitment and relocation plans of this breakaway group of the CCP. I will be there in a few days.'

'*Pas de problème;* consider it done,' Rousseau assured him.

'Thanks, François. I'll be in touch.' Mercer ended the call, broke down the phones, and destroyed the SIM card. He stashed the cash and equipment in a concealed floor compartment, then headed out to the streets of New York.

As he made his way to the designated meeting spot with Schelling, his mind replayed the conversation with Hobbs and Rousseau. The Chinese faction, the tech transfer, the growing boldness of these covert players—it was all leading to a convergence that could reshape the geopolitical landscape. Mercer knew he had to stay one step ahead, predict and maneuver, or risk being another casualty in a game where global dominance was the ultimate prize.

Mercer's alertness spiked as he entered the grand foyer of the Ritz-Carlton. No potential threats or suspicious glances came his way as he approached the counter. After a brief discussion about room options and views, he quickly paid and then headed for the elevators. Once in the room, Mercer pulled the surveillance equipment from his bag, checked the batteries again, and slid everything into his jacket. A slim electronic device hummed on the desk as he connected his key card and loaded an activation command.

Seconds later, his room key gained master control over all rooms. He slipped the cloned key card into his jacket pocket, removed a cell phone from a Faraday bag, and tucked his Glock into his pants. Before leaving, Mercer installed a magnetic door sensor linked to an app on his cell phone, set to alert him if anyone entered the room. This sensor, networked with miniature cameras and microphones, allowed remote access to live feeds.

When the elevator reached the correct floor, Mercer stepped out, casually scanned the hallway, and moved toward Schelling's room. He swiped the key card over the sensor and, once a green light illuminated, gently opened the door to enter. Inside, the large blinds were partially open, casting enough light for Mercer to install the devices.

Beyond a suitcase and a few neatly hung clothes, the room held nothing of interest. Schelling, seasoned and shrewd, wouldn't be careless enough to leave any incriminating evidence lying around. All the information he needed was securely memorized, his entire enterprise relying on a network of secretive meetings, discreet deals, and hidden financial transfers. *The man will not get his hands dirty,* Mercer thought as he surveyed the room before departing.

Descending in the elevator to the club lounge, Mercer was approached by a concierge adorned with a set of crossed gold keys on his lapels, a symbol of This membership in the prestigious *Les Clefs d'Or*. The concierge exuded professionalism as he led Mercer to a window-side table with views of Central Park. Mercer leaned back in his chair and gestured for the concierge to join him. After a brief exchange and a discreet handshake, Mercer passed ten one-hundred-dollar bills under the table. The concierge stood, nodded subtly, and discreetly moved away to issue orders to the staff. He then departed to carry out Mercer's instructions. Shortly thereafter, plates of food began arriving at the table, accompanied by whiskey and ice.

Hunched over the table, Mercer wolfed down rillettes, dates filled with goat cheese, and beluga caviar. A waiter arrived with another dish, set it on the table, and then disappeared. As Mercer lifted his head to inspect the food, he noticed a man being guided to his table. He didn't bother to stand and greet him.

'Mr. Mercer, I was surprised to get a message from reception that I had a guest waiting in the lounge. What brings you to New York?' Schelling's brow furrowed as he studied the potential addition to the Black Orchestra.

'Take a seat,' Mercer ordered. 'I've ordered enough for five men. It's been too long since I've had a decent meal.'

Schelling gave a faint, knowing smile as he considered his next words. 'Was the food in Jakarta not to your liking?'

Mercer ignored the question, grabbed a piece of pissaladière, and shoved it into his mouth.

'I have spoken to, how can I put it, investors and interested parties about your assistance in our international affairs,' Schelling said. 'There's plenty of work for a man of your talents. In saying that, I have a concern which I would like to address. I'm interested in your decision to work for us. I recognize that you're an intelligent man, Danny, and the wealth associated with your services will be monumental. Nevertheless, there's always an underlying motive deeper than wealth.'

Mercer swallowed the pissaladière and took a sip of whiskey before locking eyes with Schelling. 'Underlying motive! Interesting choice of words, Georg. I can ask that of every man you've ever dealt with, especially those in influential positions of power. I know some of the men you run with, men who have much more to lose than I do.'

Mercer leaned back in the leather chair, his fingers clasped around the glass of whiskey. 'Yes, I have some talents, but so do many others. However, your links to the FBI, CIA, DOJ, the White House are rarer and harder to cultivate. Any one of them could bring you and the entire operation to its knees. I have little to lose but much to gain. You, Georg, are an intelligent man and fully understand what an operator like me is worth to the government.

'I'm a disposable entity in any black operation. In my line of work, within the secretive unit I belong to, if I'm killed in a foreign country, there's no rescue mission. My body wouldn't be retrieved, and the government would disavow all knowledge of me. No ramp ceremony like the SEALs or what any other serviceman receives. I love my country, and I am proud of my service. But don't you fucking dare question my motives.' Mercer's expression darkened, and his jaw tightened as he stared down Schelling.

Schelling didn't know where to look. He swallowed hard, his body language betraying his desire to flee the tense exchange. Years of dealing with the darkest thoughts of the human mind had taken a toll. His face was etched with weary suspicion. Schelling turned and summoned the waiter, clearly hoping a glass of whiskey would ease his tension.

'I agree with everything you said, Danny.' His voice was smooth yet carried an undercurrent of trepidation. 'Every organization has its Achilles' heel, and I've mastered the art of finding those weaknesses over the years. We operate in the background, deeper than what some might call the deep state. Our members influence the world in ways most cannot even fathom. Only a handful of people know our real power, our connections, and our network. Your role in Jakarta was essentially an initiation. A lone operative like yourself is a valuable asset.

'A new Chinese political party has its own teams; Liang Guang oversees their operations. He's General Liu's enforcer. However, his professionalism is questionable. He lacks your level of expertise. And he'll never have your unique approach to missions. The Chinese Special Forces are rule-followers, adhering strictly to commands. These commands are passed down from high-ranking generals and other military leaders. Officers who bought their ranks rather than earning them. Quite frankly, I don't trust their competence. I'm willing to do business with them; that's no problem. But once they overthrow the current leaders of the Communist Party, we'll see a new China. Liu is an aggressive man, driven by a vision to forge a more competitive and dominant China. My goal isn't necessarily to help him achieve this, though it may appear so. Let's just say it's a complicated relationship. Your role would simply be to neutralize any mutineers or gatekeepers of information who might obstruct our success.'

Schelling glanced around the room, lowered his voice, and spoke again. 'Danny, you know as well as I do that bringing someone of your... particular skills into our operation isn't without its risks. You can find me anywhere, anytime, which puts me in a rather vulnerable position.'

Mercer smirked slightly, swirling the whiskey in his glass. 'That's true, Georg. But think of it this way: I'm not just your sword; I'm also your shield. You have a lot to lose, sure, but that's exactly why you need someone like me around. I have my own issues with the FBI, a matter that my own agency may decide to wash their hands of. After all my years of service, I will not be treated like a criminal. Therefore, I need some protection, which your connections could help with.'

'You're a wildcard, Danny, a fact I've come to understand well. Perhaps we could assist, though it would come at a cost.' Schelling's eyes narrowed slightly, his focus drifting out the window as he searched for an answer. 'I must consider this very carefully. My allies are few, my enemies numerous. Your presence could tip the scales, but I'm still deciding in which direction.'

Silence hung between them, punctuated by the light crackle of melting ice in Mercer's glass. Mercer nodded understandingly. 'And while you're deciding, I'll be doing what I do best by continuing to cover my ass and move my own pieces, Georg. This will have nothing to do with our future arrangements. However, until we reach a deal that secures my name being cleared of any wrongdoing, I'll keep operating for the agency.'

A *warning shot across the bow*, Schelling thought. It was obvious to Schelling that Mercer would rake havoc, cementing his loyalty to the CIA and American justice while waiting for Schelling to use his connections to rein in the FBI from pursuing his reckless killing of the agent in D.C. *He's doing what I would do.* Schelling took a sip of his whiskey, wiped his lips with a serviette, and smiled thinly. 'Right, let me get back to you. When I return to D.C., I will knock on a few doors and see where the FBI is in terms of their investigations. How can I contact you?'

'You can't. I will find you.' Mercer knocked back the rest of the whiskey and stood up. His muscular frame bulged slightly through the suit jacket as he towered over his slimmer, silver-haired opponent.

'I'm sure you will, Danny.' When Mercer walked off, Schelling stared out over Central Park. His mind was lost in potential scenarios. *I can't show weakness. Not after years of building something so powerful, a force larger than the White House. The balance of control must be corrected.*

Before leaving the Ritz-Carlton, Mercer met the concierge in a private room on the adjacent floor. The USB memory stick that changed hands contained surveillance footage of his meeting with Schelling. He inserted it into an encrypted drive and downloaded the contents. He also downloaded the audio from a recording device worn under his shirt. This recording captured the discussion between him and Schelling. He placed the encrypted drive in an electrostatic discharge bag, attached a tracking device to the package, and then slipped it inside a padded envelope. After successfully pairing the tracker with an app on his phone, he wrote an address for Albert Embankment, Vauxhall, London—home of MI6—before handing it back along with ten more one-hundred-dollar bills.

'Can you handle the customs declaration?' Mercer asked. The concierge took the package, nodded, turned, and left the room. Once alone, Mercer immediately contacted the flight desk of Thai Airways to confirm his booking was completed.

After returning to his hotel and gathering his belongings, an Uber whisked him away to JFK's departure terminal. Under the alias Tony Hoffmann, Mercer had altered his appearance slightly: a new hairstyle and a pair of non-prescription glasses helped obscure his familiar features. He carried a passport, and matching IDs securely tucked inside his jacket. Approaching the airport security checkpoint, he subtly avoided making eye contact with the smartly dressed men standing apart from the uniformed officers, who scrutinized the bustling crowd for any signs of suspicious activity.

Every step felt weighted, each glance from an officer a potential threat. *Just keep moving, Tony,* he reminded himself, reinforcing the persona he had adopted. The less Mercer showed, the safer Hoffmann would be.

Bangkok, Thailand

Bangkok greeted Mercer with its characteristic blend of sweltering heat and relentless energy. As he stepped off the plane and navigated through Suvarnabhumi Airport, he kept his interactions minimal, his appearance subtly altered to avoid recognition.

He exited the terminal and flagged down a taxi, immediately directing the driver to a lesser-known hotel in the Sukhumvit area. The ride through the city was a journey into relentless traffic and flickering neon signs that advertised everything from Thai massage to modern electronic gadgets, which Mercer observed with a detached interest.

Street vendors called out over the noise, highlighting their goods, grilled meat, cool drinks, amulets and exotic fruits. Further on, the streets in Bangkok's lesser-known quarters narrowed. The taxi weaved between food carts where locals huddled together on plastic stools, enjoying steaming bowls of Kuay Tiao Ruea. The silky dark broth, made with cow's blood, did nothing to spur Mercer's appetite. Seated in the back of the taxi, Mercer stayed focused, barely registering the packed sidewalks, neon signs, and street vendors. The noise, the movement—it was all background. He wasn't here for that.

His mind was preoccupied with the threats linked to the Black Orchestra, fueling his intuition to urge caution as he planned his next moves. Mercer's deep-seated distrust of the FBI and other agencies, fostered by past betrayals and dirty dealings witnessed in his previous operations, solidified his resolve. Hobbs' warning echoed in his mind, a stark reminder of the undercurrents within his own ranks.

'Connor's motives aren't as clean as they appear,' Hobbs had cautioned, hinting at a collection of interests that extended beyond mere bureaucratic power plays. Reflecting on his years under Jeff Connor's command, Mercer felt his mistrust deepen. Connor had always said, 'Play the game.' But to Mercer, these words hinted at something more sinister than mere rule-following—they suggested a compulsion to remain passive, to never question the motives underlying their operations. Every misstep, every faulty piece of intelligence that jeopardized his team, seemed too calculated to be mere incompetence. It felt organized as if a hidden hand was pushing him toward predetermined outcomes filled with betrayal.

How could he trust an agency that treated its agents as expendable? From Eastern Europe to Washington, D.C., each operation had taught him a harsh lesson: in espionage, trust was a liability. It could cost more than just a mission—it could cost lives. This constant danger had pushed Mercer to ally with the British for this operation.

When the taxi rolled to a stop at his destination, Mercer paid the driver, grabbed his bag, and stepped out into the humid night. He crossed the street, walking against the flow of traffic while subtly eyeing the occupants of the vehicles. At the end of the block, he turned left and increased his pace. At the next intersection, he hailed another taxi and, once inside, gave the driver directions to a quieter part of the city. Twenty minutes later, Mercer arrived a block away from a house rented by Charlie Halford. The use of a newly created Airbnb account for this meet-up added an essential layer of anonymity for the pair.

After sending the taxi driver on his way, Mercer strode along Phian Phin Alley until he reached the narrow street leading to Charlie's rental. He surveyed the street for followers before slipping into the laneway. The house, typical of the area, featured a brick ground floor and a wooden second floor. A high wall with a sliding steel gate provided security, while dogs barked and yelped in every yard he passed. Some homes boasted rolls of barbed wire along the top of their walls, while others had broken glass embedded in the concrete to shred the skin of potential burglars. Banana trees and other plants draped over the electrical power-lines, causing them to bow under the weight. Despite the haphazard construction and robust security measures, the area conveyed a surprising sense of safety.

Mercer arrived at the correct house and pressed the buzzer on the newly installed gate. A security camera, fixed on his position, allowed the occupants to monitor him. The sound of a magnet releasing the lock signaled their approval. He quickly slid the gate open, closed it behind him, and then stood for a couple of minutes, watching and listening to the street outside for one last surveillance check.

'Hey man, this is a safe neighborhood; you can trust your English brother,' Charlie Halford declared as Mercer finally entered the house. Mercer ignored the statement; instead, he surveyed the living area, inspected the kitchen and other rooms, and then the small area out the back.

Once satisfied with the security of the location, he returned to the living area and greeted

Halford with a hug. 'Sorry, brother. I trust you. Although these past few days I double check everything, otherwise I can't relax.'

Halford reached into the fridge, pulled out a couple of beers, and handed one to Mercer. 'No need to explain; Hobbs filled me in on the Black Orchestra and this new Chinese faction. Those guys are playing a dangerous game. Who the hell would attempt a coup against the CCP? How do those motherfuckers think they can purge the Communist Party and take over?'

Mercer popped off the bottle cap, took a swig of the Singha beer, and sat down on the worn-out leather couch. He kicked off his boots and shook his head, contemplating General Liu and his backers. 'This General must have a damn good plan. He's either got dirt on the Politburo Standing Committee—seven top dudes in the inner circle—or he's got a big set of kahunas. All I know is he has found partners in the States and across Europe. His money comes from many different investments, although a huge part of it is from the sale of drugs produced in Mong La. He also uses their casinos to launder some of it. That's the part I understand. For the other financial methods of moving their money, you'd need a forensic accountant to unravel them. Properties in Monaco, London, New York, and Zurich certainly don't come cheap.'

Halford pulled out a pack of cigarettes, lit one, and then settled into a chair at the dining table. The room was not well lit, except for a floor lamp and two wall lights. A ceiling fan spun overhead, and the fridge hummed in the kitchen. Beyond that, the house sat in silence. A large purple rug spanned the brown-tiled floor, and a portrait of the King of Thailand hung on the wall. At the center of the dining table, a Buddha statue sat next to a map of Myanmar. In front of Mercer, a large black towel covered the coffee table. On top was a collection of cleaning rods, jags, patches, brushes, a multi-tool, solvents, gun lubricant, and zip ties, all laid out in meticulous order.

He exhaled a cloud of smoke and took a sip of his beer before responding. 'We are such a small cog, Mercer. What makes you think that causing a disruption in Mong La will stop these actors from executing their plan? Don't get me wrong, I'm up for the task and fully support your decision; it just feels a bit optimistic.' One thing Mercer valued in Halford was his honesty. The man from Wigan sat in deep thought; his thick, dark curly hair and a nose twisted from too many rugby injuries added to his rugged looks.

'You're right. This task was originally assigned to the Special Activities Division, but they've been compromised, likely by a tip-off from someone inside the CIA. Those ground branch boys are the best; if Lin Mingxian, the head of Mong La, was tipped off as well, we're likely to face the same reception. Connor, my boss, is the only person who knows I am going back in. If we encounter resistance, it might just confirm his involvement with the Black Orchestra.'

Mercer took another sip of beer before noticing an orange and black striped cat dozing under the dining table. 'What are the rules of engagement once we cross the Thai border?' asked Halford.

'We are tourists until on target. Then, if they attack us, we shoot anything that moves,' Mercer explained, pointing to the coffee table. 'I see you're prepared. Now, we just need weapons, surveillance gear, and a good night's sleep. Who's your facilitator? Local crew?'

'Yes, and no. My contact is from MI6, and he's already in Myanmar. He oversees a team here that he personally vetted. Those local assets are crucial; without them, we'd be flying blind. I've arranged for our supplies to be dropped off at a secondary location,' Halford explained.

Mercer nodded, his mind rapidly processing the operational details. *We need to sort our gear, eat, then get some sleep,* he thought, his eyes drifting back to the sleeping cat. 'Let's prepare everything tonight. Tomorrow, we'll step off early.'

After receiving the encrypted message about the supplies, Halford stood up and left the house. Mercer organized their packs, found some food for the cat, secured the building, and laid clean sheets on the beds. The cat finished his meal, then leaped onto the lounge and groomed its paws while Mercer polished off his beer.

Ten minutes later, Halford returned, carrying a large holdall and a plastic bag filled with steaming hot food. Mercer seized the holdall and placed it on the dining table. He removed each weapon, checked their functionality and condition, and then laid them out for stripping and cleaning. Twenty minutes later, they washed gun oil from their hands and opened the containers of Tom Yum Goong, Khao Man Gai, and Massaman Curry. The men finished their meals in silence, absorbed in the flavors and their thoughts of tomorrow.

'As for tonight, we need to stay sharp. You sleep first; I'll take the first watch,' Mercer said. 'I'll wake you in a couple of hours.' Halford nodded. 'That sounds good. It's going to be a long day tomorrow. Don't forget to let the cat out before you lock up.' After double-checking their gear and reviewing their plan until every detail was committed to memory, Halford stood, stretched his weary muscles, and headed to the bedroom. The night passed without issues. Nothing notable occurred during their shift changes beyond a heavy downpour and the cat fussing at the back door, a huge black rat in its jaws.

As dawn broke, the early morning light filtered through the curtains, roosters crowed, and the buzz of the first scooters echoed from the laneway. By the time Mercer stepped out of the shower, Halford was already in the kitchen, studying a map spread across the table next to their hearty breakfast. The aroma of coffee mingled with the scent of tropical humidity that had seeped in from outside.

'All set?' Halford asked, eyes still fixed on the map. Mercer, tightening the straps on his boots, nodded.

'We just need to load up the jeep, then we can head off.' After enjoying a plate of eggs and Naem sausages, followed by a pot of coffee, the two men filled containers with fresh water and climbed into the jeep. Both wing mirrors scraped against the sides of the narrow laneway before they reached the main road. Mercer took the driver's seat first while Halford provided directions and monitored the traffic conditions ahead.

Mong La, Myanmar

They spent the better part of the day reaching the outskirts of Mong La, which included a twenty-minute stop at the border to pay a one-thousand-dollar *fee*. This fee secured them a safe passage into Myanmar via an unmarked, unofficial road, bypassing customs on both sides.

'Pull over here,' Mercer instructed. 'We'll park the car and walk the rest.' Many of the streets were unnamed, and those with street signs were in either Chinese or Burmese script. The two men jumped out; Mercer slung the holdall over his shoulder and quickly headed into the thick jungle, with Halford following close behind. Over four hours, they circled the main town of Mong La and positioned themselves just over the Chinese border near the Daluo Port. There, they installed surveillance cameras at the crossing before making their way back into Myanmar. Under the imposing Dwenagara Golden Pagoda, Mercer pointed out the warehouses he had previously surveilled. He described a Caucasian man he had seen liaising with local security forces and a contingent of Chinese officials.

After a few silent minutes watching the warehouses, Mercer signaled to move. Careful to avoid the route he used last time, he led Halford down to the murky river to find a clean entry point. Taking cover at the river's edge, Mercer dropped the holdall to the jungle floor and removed an AK-47, a Glock 9mm, and a hunting knife. He handed the AK to Halford.

'Cover me,' he instructed before sliding down the bank and slipping into the waist-deep water. The security lights from the warehouse cast silver reflections on the dark, slow-moving water. It took Mercer less than a minute to cross, carefully avoiding any splashes or unnatural sounds as he exited the river on the other side. Once in a covered area, he waited for Halford to make his way across.

Soon, the two men were positioned against the concrete walls of the warehouse, dripping wet, with their weapons ready. The sounds of forklifts and conversations pierced the night, boosting their confidence. Their arrival had been successful.

Mercer edged closer to the corner of the building, peeking around to gather intelligence on the location. After a few minutes, he signaled with his hand. Halford quickly moved up behind him, touched Mercer on the shoulder, and dropped into a firing position. At that moment, Mercer sprinted across an open area to the rear of a second warehouse. Halford aimed the AK into the open space between the warehouses, scanning for potential security threats. This was his domain; tasked with securing their exit route, he would hold his position for three minutes. If Mercer did not return within that time, it would mean failure.

Mercer moved stealthily, evading the

workers' attention. Forklifts zoomed past as he ducked behind pallets stacked with bags of chemical powder. He punctured one of the bags with his hunting knife, extracting a sample of white powder. After depositing the powder into a Ziplock bag, he advanced toward an office area.

Several men walked among the shipping containers, barking orders; one spoke into a telephone while another affixed labels to the pallets. However, another man caught Mercer's attention. This man, dressed in a green Myanmar police uniform, had numerous decorations adorning his neatly pressed jacket. He stood motionless, silent like a statue, his beady eyes closely watching the operations around him. The workers appeared flustered by his presence, perhaps because of a surprise visit or a special directive. Whatever the reason, it raised the stakes in Mercer's favor.

He pulled a set of binoculars with a built-in camera from his jacket, scanned the area, and, with a few soft taps on the button, quickly gathered intel. Inside the warehouse where the policeman stood, there was a small office; a monitor displayed shipping times, and a whiteboard was covered with scribbles. Mercer assessed that the electrical and plumbing systems must be relatively new, only a few years old, and more advanced than those in typical buildings throughout the area, which helped him to form a plan in his mind.

He stuffed the binoculars back into his jacket, retraced his steps outside, and circled to the back of the warehouse. He followed a narrow, dark path until he reached a small room housing the building's circuit breaker box. Using his hunting knife, he pried off some fuses and tossed them into the bushes. As he removed each fuse, the machinery sounds died; the area plunged into darkness, and voices grew louder.

Anticipating security protocols triggered by the power loss, Mercer acted quickly. He sprinted back to the warehouse entrance and weaved between the pallets until he spotted his target. Clearly visible in the shadows, the large police hat acted as a beacon in the night. The hunting knife met no resistance as Mercer plunged it into the man's throat; a sharp slash that allowed the blade to slice through the flesh like soft sushi. Mercer was gone before the man dropped to the blood-soaked concrete. There were no screams or cries, only the gurgling of warm blood and saliva as the man bled out silently.

Mercer and Halford made the journey through the jungle back across the Chinese border and quickly took up surveillance, aware that the barbaric act would provoke a reaction. The killing of a Myanmar cop was the best probe available to them. Intelligence collected on the operation at the warehouse would be complete when they found out which forces would respond, Chinese or Myanmar officials—or the mafia! Their night was just beginning, and the bugs were relentless; every piece of jungle moved around them.

'I hope this white dude appears. He is our primary target. I want a clear visual on him,' Mercer said as he set his binoculars on the ground beside him and casually wiped several ants off his face.

Halford donned a set of night vision goggles and offered another to Mercer, who refused. The men then lapsed into silence, tuning in and out of sounds as needed. The damp jungle floor kept moving, alive with ants and other stinging insects, attracted to their new heat sources. Trained to ignore the discomfort, the two men scanned the mayhem below.

Under the dark canopy of the dense foliage, Mercer quietly rummaged through his bag, his hand moving from item to item as the humid air of the Chinese jungle clung to his skin. His fingers skipped over the assorted gear to finally grasp the Mk12 SPR sniper rifle, its weight both familiar and reassuring against the oppressive environment.

Two workers rolled out an electrical cable and connected it to a diesel generator. A puff of black smoke signaled the generator's kick-off, quickly followed by emergency floodlights that illuminated the spaces between the warehouses.

Halford, lying a few feet away, removed his night vision goggles and selected a Vectronix rangefinder. The device was more than just a tool for measuring distance; it served as his eyes across the murky expanse, watching the dimly lit roads that snaked around the warehouse area. 'Distance at four hundred meters, steady,' he whispered, his voice barely above the hum of nocturnal insects.

Mercer nodded, acknowledging the distance with a slight adjustment on his rifle scope. Despite the jungle's relentless noise muffling other sounds, the soft clicks of the scope's dial remained crisp in his ears. He knew the capabilities of his weapon intimately and trusted his own judgment for such a small distance. Yet tonight, the precision of technology offered a solid reassurance. The strong scent of lubricant was pungent in the moist air, a crucial adaptation to maintain the rifle's smooth operation in the oppressive humidity.

Mercer positioned the rifle against his shoulder, the stock pressing gently into his flesh. No shot would be fired yet; the mission was solely to observe and gather intelligence, a test of the operation's professionalism and an attempt to draw out the organizers.

With his eye on the scope, he scanned the area, taking mental notes of the movements and patterns that unfolded in the warehouse's vicinity. Every detail, every slight anomaly, would be crucial for the mission's next phase. 'Check the surveillance cameras we set up,' Mercer ordered.

Halford immediately pulled out a small tablet, dimmed the screen's brightness, and launched the surveillance app. Seconds later, a visual of the main supply route from the Chinese border crossing into Myanmar appeared on the screen. Halford cycled through various cameras, adjusting the focus; the system was programmed to record when vehicles or people passed by. 'Just a couple of transport trucks by the looks of it. Non-military,' he said.

Mercer didn't acknowledge; his eyes were locked on the perimeter of the main warehouse where several men had appeared. He suddenly noticed they were armed and approaching the riverbank. He aligned the crosshairs of his scope on the lead man, who was shining a torch along the bank and across the river to the other side. Seconds later, four more men joined him. 'We've got guests.'

The excited barking of dogs alerted Halford to the problem. Improvisation was crucial for Mercer's success; amid the oppressive humidity of the jungle-clad terrain, he had to employ his escape and evasive tactics. 'Pack up your shit, and let's move deeper into Yunnan. I'm not sure if these men will cross the border. No matter what, we need to keep the advantage,' Mercer instructed, standing and slinging the bag over his shoulder before pushing through the dense vegetation. The two men moved swiftly, pausing briefly for Mercer to check his compass bearing. In the distance, the dogs' yelps could be heard, though they did not grow louder.

After two hours of navigating through the jungle, Mercer emerged onto wasteland. A main supply route ran east to west from Daluozhen to the Nanlan River, then connected to Mong Lah Road in Myanmar. New building projects were underway, with trucks, cars, and people busily working under floodlights, racing to construct factories, housing, and basic infrastructure in this remote part of Southwest China, another section of the new Belt and Road Initiative. One kilometer separated them from the border crossing back into Myanmar, where the jungle would keep them safe from the Chinese military.

Mercer paused again, kneeling to pull out his map and compass. 'They didn't cross the border, or else the jungle was too much for them,' he whispered.

Halford used the opportunity to check the surveillance cameras on his tablet. 'Mercer, black SUVs are crossing into Mong La. They just passed our cameras.'

'How many?'

'Five, with two motorbikes leading them.'

'Fuck. Right, change of plan.' Mercer refolded the map and carefully tucked it back into his jacket. He then stood up and sprinted into a parking lot filled with dozens of cars. He approached the nearest car and smashed the rear side window with his elbow and reached through to unlock the front door. He quickly jumped in and ripped off the plastic cover housing the electronics. Within seconds, the men were driving westbound toward Daluo Port. Once he found a quiet spot, they parked the car, jumped out, and set up an ambush. Halford checked his weapon again. Choosing the same weaponry as the local forces, Mercer swapped his Mk12 sniper rifle for an AK to obscure their team's foreign origins. This tactic aimed to ensure that any forensic evidence left behind would mislead investigators into suspecting local involvement, helping maintain deniability in their covert operations.

For five minutes, the men waited by the roadside. The rain started light and then built to a roar that masked the sounds of passing vehicles.

'Heads up; this is it. Wait for my lead,' Mercer announced, taking position behind a wall.

About five hundred meters away, the intense beam of headlights from the SUVs lit up the wet road as the convoy raced toward the border.

Let them get closer, four, three, two, one. Mercer opened fire on the lead vehicle, while Halford targeted the middle, then the two others. The first SUV swerved off the road, crashing into a brick wall of a new border inspection building. Mercer focused on the second, which dodged to avoid the attack. His rounds hit their mark, killing the driver and passengers instantly. Halford was wiping out the occupants of the fourth and fifth vehicles as Mercer approached the third SUV, which had rolled into the back of the second. Quickly changing a magazine, he fired more rounds into the third, then sprinted over and opened the back door. Inside, two men were slumped in the back seat, blood oozing from their necks and chests. The driver and front seat passengers were gruesomely disfigured, with parts of their heads missing. It took thirty seconds to confirm all in the convoy were dead before starting their search. They removed the driver's wallet and cell phone, before moving to the next person. Every one of them was checked thoroughly.

'Come here,' Halford shouted. 'I think we've found your friend.'

Halford unclipped the man's seatbelt, dragged him out of the SUV, and let the body fall to the ground. He rolled him over, and as the rain lashed down, washing blood from the face, it revealed an American man in his late fifties. 'Is this him?'

Mercer hurried over and kneeled down to get a better look. 'That's my guy. Quickly take a photo and grab anything interesting you can find from this vehicle. We need to take him with us.'

They dumped the other occupants of the SUV on the road, bundled the dead American in the back, and Halford took the wheel. Mercer, calculating their next move, chose to use the SUV as cover, betting on its military plates to avoid scrutiny at the border.

'There's no easy way to make this happen,' Mercer muttered, tension lining his voice as the vehicle hurtled toward the border crossing. As they approached, the border guards glanced at the imposing military insignia, then waved them through without a second thought. Searching the vehicle could mean risking their careers or, worse, their lives.

Once clear of the border and racing away from Mong La, Mercer cracked a rare smile and exchanged a fist bump with Halford. 'Let's see how Washington responds to this,' he remarked. 'The agency that comes after us will reveal the true players.' His gaze remained fixed on the road ahead, yet his mind was on the unknown American in the back, a wildcard with the potential to alter the game. This unexpected stratagem was poised to trigger a backlash that would resonate from the corridors of power, sweeping through every major intelligence agency and reaching as far as the White House. Or so he thought, at least.

THIRTEEN

The walls of General Liu Xiang's office, once symbols of formidable power and authority within the secluded confines of Zhongnanhai, now echoed with a tense and hurried silence. Around him, staffers quickly stuffed files into marked boxes, the remnants of a career being packed away in haste. The finality of each tape strip sealing cardboard felt like a verdict he hadn't been prepared to hear.

Liu, his face a grim mask of fury, snatched his cell phone from the desk and punched in a number, his fingers trembling slightly with barely controlled rage. The call connected, but instead of a voice, a sterile tone greeted him, followed by the automated message. *Your service has been disconnected.* The words, devoid of emotion, ignited a spark of raw anger in Liu. With a growl, he hurled the phone against the wall, where it shattered into pieces, its screen splintering, the battery sliding across the polished wooden floor.

At that moment, the door swung open. Zhang Wei and Zhao Ming stepped into the office, their eyes narrowed, displaying a mix of confusion and anger. Both men halted, taking in the scene of disarray, the tangible signs of their own precarious positions reflected in the dismantling of Liu's stronghold.

'General, the situation is deteriorating,' Zhang started, his voice tight with anxiety. He moved closer, lowering his voice despite the privacy the office offered. 'The assassination last night, within our own borders, will be used by the West as proof that we are involved in the manufacture of methamphetamine. What happens in Myanmar or elsewhere can be ignored, but these men killed our operational team in Daluozhen. Our control over Mong La is slipping. The United Wa State Army is the largest and best-equipped ethnic armed group in Myanmar, and now they will see weakness. If that happens, they could block the border and fully control the meth supply themselves. We need to hold a meeting and assure them we will not step back. The Americans—'

Zhao Ming interjected, his usual diplomatic tone frayed at the edges. 'Apologies for interrupting, Zhang, but this is urgent. I've just come from headquarters. The Director wants all intelligence on his desk by the afternoon. He has a meeting scheduled with the General Secretary. Our assets are under scrutiny, and there's talk of hauling in members of the Politburo Standing Committee as well. This situation is spiraling beyond our containment.'

Liu surveyed his two most trusted advisors, his mind racing through scenarios, each more disastrous than the last. He straightened his jacket and lifted his chin, the decision clear in his eyes. 'Order your staff to pack up everything. We are relocating operations,' he commanded. 'Maintain the highest level of operational security. Destroy all communication devices, switch to new encrypted cell phones, and contact all field operatives. Rebuild the Mong La network and heighten security measures. We are not withdrawing; we're tightening our grip. Showing weakness could embolden the Wa army to push us out and provoke the politburo into action against us. I will not allow that to happen.'

While speaking, Liu momentarily drifted into thoughts of the formidable armament of the United Wa State Army (UWSA). Each day, their presence in northern Myanmar grew stronger, bolstered by an arsenal that included missiles, armored vehicles, howitzers, and attack helicopters. This impressive military capacity enabled the proxy force to not only defend its territory but also sustain the production of narcotics. These operations, hidden deep within the jungle, crippled the West with addiction and channeled a steady stream of funds into Liu's covert activities. His advisors observed him intently, fully aware of the stakes involved. The unmistakable fear of the Wa army's growing power loomed as a constant threat throughout their discussions.

Zhang nodded, lines of worry etching deeper into his brow as he reached into his jacket and withdrew his cell phone to relay the orders. Zhao simply clenched his jaw and turned toward the window, gazing out over the buildings of power as he compiled a mental list of potential traitors.

When the last staffer departed, the door shut with a decisive click. Liu scanned his now empty office, viewing it as a strategic retreat from a battle he was not prepared to concede.

'Do not fear or falter, for we have long anticipated this day. We possess information mightier than any sword, details that have propelled us to our current position, and will elevate us further. The politburo is well aware of this. Today, I will impart a lesson, one that you must learn to gain the ultimate advantage.' Liu then marched to the office door, swung it open, and signaled for a man to enter.

'Allow me to present a true gentleman,' Liu

declared, pacing back and forth as he scrutinized the man at the center of the empty office. 'For years, our esteemed colleague, Mr. Gao, has dedicated himself tirelessly to protecting the integrity of the Communist Party. His strategic counsel to the Chairman and standing members of the Politburo will be recorded in history as the brightest tactical vision of the past fifty years. This eminent man has served the people of China with the utmost loyalty. His children, like him, received their education at respectable universities, and though his personal fortune remains modest, he stands before us as a symbol of modern China.'

'Your words are very kind, General. While it is my honor to serve the people, my ultimate goal is for China to stand tall, proud, yet humble within the global community, free from any accusations of criminal conduct or corruption.' As Gao finished speaking, a wave of pride swept over him. For years, he had dispatched the police to the homes of politicians embroiled in corruption and bribery. He was profoundly disgusted by the very act of stealing from the people of China. He removed his glasses, wiped them with a silk handkerchief, replaced them on his nose, and then tucked the handkerchief into his breast pocket.

Liu slipped his hands into his pockets and strode toward Zhao, who was absorbed in the view outside the window. 'There is a lesson in Mr. Gao's story: loyalty can shield you but also lead to your downfall.' The General then approached Gao and positioned himself directly in front of him. A thin smile briefly crossed Liu's lips. Without warning, Liu drew his knife and plunged it into Gao's abdomen. Gao screamed in agony and doubled over as Liu withdrew the knife, standing over Gao's collapsing form. He then bent down and slid the knife under Gao's throat. With a swift swipe, he sliced open Gao's neck, severing the carotid arteries and jugular veins. The gruesome act left a heavy silence hanging in the air, only broken by Zhao and Zhang's sharp gasps. Shocked and disbelieving, the directors of assassins had never witnessed such raw violence firsthand. Zhang recoiled, his hands covering his mouth. Zhao rushed to the door and slammed it shut. He couldn't bear to look at the scene unfolding in the middle of the room. Liu stood over Gao, his knife dripping with Gao's warm blood.

'This man was our adversary, actively leading an investigation into our activities. As the chief protector of the CCP, his relentless advocacy swayed all committee members against us. Executing him will temporarily halt their efforts. Should another member continue this investigation, we will respond swiftly and decisively. Confront further challenges with death; let this serve as a warning to his allies.' Liu turned to confront the two men. 'We must identify those behind this attack. Zhao, send a message to the Director. Threaten him, let him know we will target his family if he oversteps. He must tell the General Secretary that the investigation is ongoing and has yielded few clues so far. This will buy us some time.'

Liu turned his attention to Zhang, who remained still and composed despite his racing heart. 'Zhang, gather all information on the assassins and any support they received.' After checking his watch, Liu continued, 'We don't have much time. It's been a few hours; they could be anywhere by now. Zhang, determine their whereabouts. They've abducted our contact, a Westerner from the Drug Enforcement Administration. You need to get hold of the DEA-6, their internal report on active investigations. Once you get that '*six*,' forward it to me. This agent knows too much about our operations. It took considerable effort to turn him, and he has been a significant asset to us. Regrettably, we must assume he's been compromised. We only hope that he's already dead.'

Liu grabbed a black briefcase from his table and walked to the door. He glanced back at the body on the floor, then at Zhang. 'I am going to Chengdu to take care of business, then I will fly to the United States to fix this mess. Leave the body and get moving; do not disappoint me.' Liu left the office and made his way to his waiting limo, leaving the two men alone to organize their thoughts.

'Zhao, ensure the Director remains silent. Use whatever force is necessary; there's no turning back now.' Zhang exited the office, his focus laser-sharp on uncovering the American intelligence related to the killings on Chinese soil. Nearing the elevator, he noticed a group of men at the far end of the hallway. The low tones of their discussion in the poorly lit corridor sparked a flicker of suspicion. *Could they be police? State security?* he thought, his heart rate accelerating. He fought to suppress the rising wave of paranoia, reminding himself to stay alert and composed. The atmosphere was tense, and every slight movement seemed potentially threatening. Once in the quietness of the elevator, he retrieved his cell phone.

He needed to send one quick message before switching devices. Flicking open a new chat, Zhang searched the contact list for Liang Guang, his go-to operative based in Europe. For jobs that required kicking down doors and aggressive interrogations, the man was indispensable. With his calculated precision and strategic mind, Liang excelled at cutting through layers of secrecy to extract the intelligence he needed. Having sent the message, Zhang pocketed his phone and took a deep breath to center himself. As the elevator doors opened at ground level, he stepped out, ready to confront and neutralize any threats in his path.

Chengdu—China

By midday, General Liu had arrived at his luxurious home overlooking the Fuhe River in Chengdu's Jinjiang district. Liu entered his study, gazed out at the Fuhe River, then turned to his desk surrounded by the understated luxury of traditional Sichuan architecture. The floor-to-ceiling windows provided a panoramic view of the meandering river, shimmering under the afternoon sun. Beyond the river, the French Consulate General buzzed with activity, handling everything from trade and visas to employment and intelligence operations. However, Liu's actual concern lay with the latter.

His blatant assassination of Mr. Gao, the Communist Party's leading strategist, had violently stirred the hornet's nest. He was banking on his contact within the French DGSE to uncover the repercussions of this attack. Fear was still Liu's weapon of choice in negotiations.

Liu's gaze swept the study; though nothing piqued his interest, his thoughts raced at full speed. He walked to his drinks cabinet and poured a generous glass of baijiu. He needed a stiff shot to steady his nerves. His attack on the CCP aimed not only to send a message but also to deter anyone who would stand in his way. As the floral and fruity liquid settled in his stomach, a warm glow coursed through his veins, and a grin slowly crept across his face. He reached up to loosen his tie, then stroked his neatly trimmed mustache. Despite a few gray hairs, Liu's imposing build conveyed a threatening presence. He took another deliberate sip of baijiu, the strong flavor momentarily grounding him as he prepared to delve into the complexities of his work.

His attention then shifted across the study, a space where modern amenities melded seamlessly with traditional elements. The walls were adorned with intricate wood carvings, depicting scenes from Sichuan's rich cultural heritage, each stroke capturing the essence of a time-honored saga. Gray brick accents and a tiled roof with upturned eaves paid homage to the region's vernacular architecture. The room's centerpiece was a massive desk crafted from locally sourced timber, its surface polished to a warm, inviting sheen. Various documents and files were scattered across the desk, each one a piece of the intricate plot that Liu had been meticulously assembling. A state-of-the-art computer sat alongside an antique calligraphy set, symbolizing the delicate balance between tradition and modernity that permeates every aspect of this space.

As Liu settled into his chair, the soft rustling of the nearby bamboo grove outside his window provided a soothing backdrop to his thoughts. He took a moment to appreciate the tranquility of his surroundings, fully aware that this calm was merely a facade, concealing the storm brewing just beneath the surface. Taking a deep breath, he turned his attention to the task at hand, his mind already racing with the potential consequences of his next move.

He cleared his desk, then picked up the phone and dialed a number. After he entered his encryption key, the call connected immediately to Olivier Girard, the French intelligence officer from the DGSE based in Chengdu.

'Monsieur Girard, I appreciate your willingness to discuss matters of mutual concern today,' Liu said.

Deep within a building attached to the French consulate, Girard spoke softly, his nerves rising at the sudden call. 'General Liu, the pleasure is mine. I understand these are unstable times, and clarity between our nations is paramount.'

'Indeed. Monsieur Girard, the political currents in China are turbulent, as you're aware. I seek clarity on the assassination that disrupted our ranks at the border crossing into Mong La, Myanmar. This violent act has stirred much speculation and accusations of Chinese involvement. You are in the best position to understand the global ramifications of this. So, tell me, what is the French perspective on this matter?'

Girard paused, switching the call to a more secure, encrypted mode. 'General, the situation, as we observe, is fraught with what we might call 'market fluctuations'—our term for the current political instability. The French government monitors these fluctuations closely but remains committed to non-intervention. As of now, we have no direct evidence tying any specific factions within the CCP or any terror groups in China to the incident. However, the international community is quite troubled by the implications of such an event.'

'Monsieur Girard,' Liu interjected sharply. 'While the broader ramifications are indeed concerning, I need to focus on more pressing issues related to our recent border conflicts. Has the Black Orchestra been operating independently at the Mong La crossing? And crucially, is there any evidence that might link these incidents back to me or to unsanctioned operations?'

'General, our surveillance indicates that the Black Orchestra acts with significant autonomy. Currently, there's nothing concrete that connects them to the recent violence at Mong La or implicates you in any methamphetamine production. We are monitoring all intelligence feeds closely to maintain this status quo and manage any emerging threats discreetly,' Girard said, his voice a low murmur.

'That is somewhat reassuring,' Liu replied. 'Ensure that any emerging details that could change this understanding are intercepted and managed with utmost discretion. It's vital that the narrative remains uncontested, and any disruptive elements are quickly contained.'

'Absolutely, General. We prioritize the integrity of our operational security and the precision of our engagements. I'll personally oversee the intelligence filters to ensure nothing jeopardizes your position or our shared interests,' Girard affirmed.

'That is excellent. If a foreign nation meddles with Chinese domestic affairs, their relationship with us would immediately shatter, destroying trust and ongoing deals. I trust that any information suggesting Chinese rogue elements were involved will be handled discreetly by the DGSE? And more importantly, such information should be passed to me immediately,' Liu said.

'Of course, General,' Girard confirmed. 'France values its diplomatic relationship with China. We act within the boundaries of international law and respect national sovereignty. Now, if you don't mind, I want to discuss another pressing issue. The escalation of narcotics trafficking is a major concern for us, especially regarding European security. I want to know if you can help us with this matter.'

Girard hesitated, glancing at the secure phone on his desk. 'Let us consider, hypothetically, that certain discrepancies in maritime cargo records are not merely administrative errors but indicative of...deeper issues,' he murmured, his voice dropping to a near whisper.

Liu stood up and walked to the large window, his eyes narrowing as he looked across the river. 'Narcotics trafficking?'

'Yes, General. Our investigations have revealed an extensive network using major European ports to facilitate the importation of narcotics. The Ports of Rotterdam, Antwerp-Bruges, and Hamburg are significant entry points. We have identified Charles Clark, a shipping magnate, as a key figure in this network. His company, Sternenlicht Versand, allegedly manipulates logistics to allow containers filled with illegal substances into Europe.'

Liu sensed the evasion and began to pace the room, his voice low and controlled. 'Monsieur Girard, we have skirted around the truth of these matters for too long. I require concrete information, not insinuations.'

Girard shifted uncomfortably in his chair, his eyes flickering to his colleagues in his office. 'General, as you understand, the layers are complex, and my position does not allow me the liberty of complete transparency. I've heard through secondary channels—nothing I can verify—that the logistics executive might be more than just a businessman.'

'Well, nonetheless, I am not sure how I can help with European ports. The mafia will always find a way to provide drugs to their buyers, Monsieur Girard. How does French intelligence think China can help with your problems?' Liu asked.

Girard glanced across the room at his DGSE colleagues, who were busily working at their desks, before replying. 'It's delicate, General. While the DEA and CIA are the primary investigators, France is committed to combating international drug trafficking. However, there are challenges. For instance, there was a significant incident involving former DGSE agents Henri and Pierre-Marie, who were arrested and convicted for espionage on behalf of China. Cases like these have led to increased scrutiny and caution in our operations.'

Liu remembered them all too well. 'A regrettable incident that complicates matters. I hope these difficulties won't impede the necessary actions against this man Clark and his operations?'

Liu's mind raced. He had spent years carefully weaving alliances with the Black Orchestra, using their resources to secure cutting-edge technology and lure top Western scientists to China. The flow of meth money was the lifeblood of his plans to dominate the CCP. But now, their encroachment threatened his delicate balance. He couldn't afford for this violence to spill into China and disrupt his operations.

If necessary, he would send a clear message. Schelling and his cohorts needed to understand his reach and the price of crossing him. Any interference with his plans would be met with severe consequences. Liu's mind briefly entertained the violent possibilities. He had contingencies to sever ties and ensure obedience through fear. The Black Orchestra would learn the consequences of overstepping their bounds, ensuring his plans remained unchallenged.

'We are proceeding cautiously, General. The sensitivity of these operations, especially given past espionage scandals, requires us to act judiciously to protect our national interests without escalating tensions. Shared intelligence is crucial, especially if France receives it before the Americans, British, or Germans. We want to be on the front foot.'

Liu considered his words carefully. 'I see. It is in our mutual interest that these networks are dismantled, though my concern today is ensuring these actions do not unfairly implicate the Chinese state.'

'Of course, General. France has no interest in unjustly implicating any nation, least of all China, with who we share important economic and cultural ties. Our focus is strictly on criminal elements, irrespective of their national origins,' Girard said.

'Very well, Monsieur Girard. I am somewhat reassured by your stance. It is essential for China that any actions taken are balanced and just. We, too, are victims of the narcotics trade and its associated violence.'

'Understood, General. I assure you that our actions will continue to reflect our commitment to legality and fairness. We will continue our cooperation on these matters with the understanding that both our nations seek stability and justice.'

'One more question before I let you go. Philippe Dubois. I've heard he's leading your investigation into the narcotics flow through Mong La. Is this accurate?'

'Correct, General,' Girard replied, lowering his voice slightly. 'Mr. Dubois manages what we refer to as the 'complex logistics portfolio.' His nuanced understanding of these intricate networks positions him well to oversee their unraveling.' Girard glanced around to ensure he wasn't being overheard before continuing, choosing his next words carefully. 'He's been tracking the movements through European ports, uncovering how the Black Orchestra might be exploiting these routes.'

'That leads to my next point. The assassination that shook our ranks—is there any intelligence linking it to the European investigations? Could there be a connection we are overlooking?' Liu asked.

'It's possible,' Girard conceded. 'I've heard through third parties that Dubois is concerned the Black Orchestra's reach may extend further than we thought. He's cautious about sharing detailed intelligence because of recent leaks, but he believes the same networks involved in narcotics might also have ties to political disruptions within China.'

Liu's eyes narrowed; his grip tightened around the phone. *These Frenchmen are getting far too close. This man must be stopped.* Liu's mind flashed back to the reports from Geneva, when a Chinese kidnap team was ruthlessly murdered as they sat in their van. He understood that if the French tied the Black Orchestra to him and his plans of a coup, there would be calls for his execution.

'I need to understand the risks involved, Girard. If the Black Orchestra is indeed stirring chaos, it could jeopardize not just my position but also regional stability.' Liu's voice betrayed a hint of urgency. Assassinations were acceptable in Europe or in hotels in Washington, D.C., but bringing their mayhem to China was unforgivable.

'Philippe Dubois covers the European desk, as far as I know. His contacts and undercover operatives in international drug trafficking are legendary, having spent years in the UAE and various locations around Asia and South America. To be frank, General, if I start asking questions outside my wheelhouse, it could raise suspicions.'

'Yes, I guess it would. I appreciate your candor today, Monsieur Girard. Thank you.' Liu felt a deep annoyance with Girard as he returned to his seat. A frown creased his brow as he thought about Girard's cautious demeanor. *Years of nurturing trust with Girard, and still, he holds back, trapped by his own fears of reprisal.* It was becoming increasingly clear that Girard would never be the decisive asset Liu had hoped for. *The man is weak*, he thought as he ended the call.

Liu looked down at the name of Charles Clark and his company, Sternenlicht Versand, which he had scribbled on a notepad. *The French are cautious; it's time to bring them deeper into the conflict*, Liu thought, taking his last sip of baijiu.

He set the empty glass down and walked to his safe, hidden behind a classical oil painting. After entering the code, he opened the thick door and removed several thumb drives and a bundle of documents. The files contained dark secrets of his colleagues, collected over many years. These were a necessary shield against officers investigating Mr. Gao's murder in his Beijing office yesterday.

Killing Gao was a calculated move to instill fear and show his willingness to eliminate threats, ensuring that no one dared to investigate him. *Protected in China, for now,* he thought, staring out the window and reflecting on the past few days. His flight to Washington, D.C., was only a couple of hours away. *There will be many more murders before I take my seat at the head of this country.* A surge of energy coursed through him. His lips curled into a thin, menacing smile, and his eyes gleamed with cold determination as he switched off the light and strode out of the room.

Nice—France

Situated two blocks from the Nice-Ville Gare, the central train station in Nice, Liang Guang meticulously set up a safe house. The failed kidnapping attempt in Geneva haunted him. The memory of his men killed by Dubois' covert team sharpened his instincts and made him determined to control every detail of his operations. The apartment on Rue d'Autun was modest, located in a quiet neighborhood of locals and business travelers. Liang spent his days observing the neighborhood, noting the comings and goings of residents, understanding the access roads, and assessing local crime levels. He even timed the police response to a staged disturbance, noting their swift arrival within six minutes.

He checked his neighbors' backgrounds using online resources and discreet inquiries. The street had a mix of retirees, young professionals, and families. A local gang occasionally caused trouble, but they were low-level and posed no significant threat. To blend in, Liang knew he needed to adopt a low profile, limiting his movements and interactions.

For his operations, Liang required competent hitmen for delicate wet work. He handpicked a small team: a Moroccan expert in close-quarter combat, an Albanian marksman with a reputation for precision, and a French safecracker skilled in accessing secure locations. These men were experienced, ruthless, and, most importantly, loyal for the right price.

To procure clean weapons, he turned to a network of European criminals. First, he contacted an Albanian arms dealer known for reliability and discretion. Meeting in a secluded industrial area outside Nice, Liang carefully inspected the weapons—a selection of pistols, submachine guns, and sniper rifles—to ensure they were in pristine condition. He paid in a mix of currencies above the standard black-market rate, securing the dealer's silence. Next, he connected with a Polish ex-legionnaire turned mercenary. Through him, Liang sourced medical supplies and fake identifications. This man also introduced him to Murat Ozdemir, a leading Turkish gangster from Marseille. Ozdemir, the top boss of Marseille's drug flats, controlled gangs that sold millions of euros of narcotics across southern France, distributing kilos of product to other gangs in France, Spain, and Germany.

Inside various safe houses, Liang stored weapons, ammunition, cash, and medical supplies in hidden compartments. He created multiple layers of security, including alarm systems, hidden cameras, and reinforced doors. Fake identifications and escape routes were meticulously planned, ensuring he could access the houses, grab what was needed, and vanish at a moment's notice if necessary.

During lunch hours in Nice, Liang dined at Brasserie Le Gambetta, situated on Pl. du Général de Gaulle, a large roundabout that provided several escape routes if he was compromised. He used the Brasserie to meet business clients, and it provided the perfect vantage point to scan for surveillance. His pattern of life was beginning to be established as he built relationships with the staff, further facilitating his cover as a businessman.

Liang ensured there was a motive for his presence. General Liu provided enough funds for Liang to purchase commercial and residential property and hunt for startup companies. If the French Police ever questioned Liang, he could easily verify his credentials, from his new identity to meetings with high-profile realtors and business professionals. Liang began to enjoy his time in the Côte d'Azur, though he missed the real power he wielded in China, a power that only a handful of men could dream of.

He looked around the apartment, content with the furniture arrangement. Nothing would impede his movements in the darkness if intruders ever entered. Liang was paranoid enough to ensure every detail was perfect but not so paranoid as to cause hesitation. To ensure he could defend himself in an attack, Liang practiced maneuvering around the room with his eyes closed, darting around, pulling weapons from hidden compartments, avoiding obstacles, and dry-firing his way through the apartment.

The sound of pedestrians from the street

below pricked his ears, reminding him of today's meeting. He checked the time on his Patek Philippe wristwatch; it was almost lunchtime. Another chance to sit down with his Turkish contact. Liang had lingering concerns about working with Europeans; trust was an issue he hoped to solve with cash, lots of it.

At Brasserie Le Gambetta, Liang took his usual seat outside and ordered a bottle of wine and two glasses. Across the street, he watched as Murat Ozdemir got out of a black Mercedes. The heavily built Turk, dressed in jeans and a black leather jacket over a black T-shirt, strolled toward the Brasserie. A thick gold chain and matching bracelets glistened in the Mediterranean sun, as did his slick black hair. A veteran of the Özel Kuvvetler Komutanlığı, or Special Forces Command, he oozed confidence and flair. Liang didn't stand to greet or offer a handshake; instead, he gestured for the man to take a seat and pour his own glass. It was important for Liang to be in control. Intimidation tactics never unsettled the Chinese assassin; he needed to show a level of fear and respect, something that was hard to achieve with Ozdemir.

'Enjoy some wine, Mr. Ozdemir, then we can talk business,' Liang said.

Ozdemir gestured at the waiter and ordered a glass of Bière de Garde. 'I prefer beer, Liang. Now, before we get started, I want to remind you of my reach. If there are any problems with my merchandise, you tell me. If you are being followed or suspect you are, you tell me. If you bring other groups into your operations, you must tell me who they are. I don't want to deal with another cashed-up Asian who comes to France with money and thinks he can pay off all the gangs. I have to manage territories, allegiances, debts—these are all matters you wouldn't know anything about. If you fuck off back to China, I am left with gang wars and political pressures. Do you understand?'

Liang took a sip of his wine before pulling a cigarette from a gold-lined case. With a simple nod and a thin smile, he leaned toward Ozdemir and spoke quietly. 'I do not plan on leaving, Mr. Ozdemir, and of course, I will keep you updated. My business here will only help you. My business partners want to expand, not take over. We require local contacts, men we can trust. Together, we will make millions. What I offer is a high-quality product you cannot get in Europe.'

Liang offered a cigarette to Ozdemir, who refused, so he lit one for himself. He slipped an envelope containing one hundred thousand euros onto the table. 'One hundred grand, Mr. Ozdemir. A personal token of our friendship. Soon, you will understand my partner's commitment to Europe. We represent a new generation of Chinese, men who do not quiver at sanctions or Western intelligence agencies. Our power is unlimited; our reach extends to every city, town, and village globally.

'I understand the Direction Centrale de la Police Judiciaire has your name on file. So does Interpol. How did the French Navy, who worked with DNRED, seize cocaine from sailing vessels in the Gulf of Guinea? Their ongoing intelligence support from agencies like the DEA and NCA crippled your organizations, yes? Well, Mr. Ozdemir, these are matters beyond your level of influence. You are no Pablo Escobar. To professionalize your business procedures, you need me; otherwise, your time on the street is limited.'

Ozdemir eyed the envelope on the table, then glanced at the pedestrians walking past. The possibility of the French police suddenly appearing and arresting him was real. He always knew the DNRED would work hard to disrupt his activities. The Direction Nationale du Renseignement et des Enquêtes Douanières used surveillance, wiretaps, and undercover operatives to dismantle smuggling routes and carry out raids on gang leaders in Marseille and other cities in France. Ozdemir knew the risks; someday, they would come for him. His empire had potential, although his security budget was high. The money he paid his dealers to remain silent while they were banged up in prison was taking a huge hit to his profits. Ozdemir wanted to run his business empire from Dubai or Istanbul, yet he knew other gangs would take over if he were not in France to defend his territory.

'How can I be sure you have the power to control the French agencies? Or those from the United States?' Ozdemir asked.

A smile crept across Liang's face; he knew Ozdemir was buckling. 'Over the years, we have carefully bribed and blackmailed those with power in all American intelligence agencies. Those men hold incredible power and dictate to Europe which gangs to target and which to give a free pass. No questions asked. From the CIA, FBI, DEA, everyone you can think of, we have them like puppets on a string. We also have our own shipping lines, ports, and laboratories, producing the purest narcotics imaginable. All we need are distributors within Europe. That is where you come in. You can choose to work for us or not. Your decision, Mr. Ozdemir.'

The Turkish gang leader picked up the envelope and slipped it inside his leather jacket. He pulled out a cigar, clipped the end off, and rolled it between his fingers. As he watched pedestrians walk past the brasserie, he felt excited; the prospect of arrest no longer entered his mind. The Chinese man sitting next to him was not only offering protection from the

French agencies; this partnership meant Ozdemir could finally build the wealth required for his future plans.

'I can handle the distribution. That's not the problem, Liang. What I can see are problems from other gangs. To sell more, I need more territories, an expansion of my operations, and to hire more dealers. Or possibly take over other gangs and have them work for me.' Ozdemir was thinking of possibilities, restructuring his network. This was an exciting prospect for the special forces veteran, a man who specialized in war and control.

His concentration was broken as a waiter approached the table and laid out a plate of plats de mer, charcuterie platters, and moules frites. Liang wasted no time and began eating, allowing Ozdemir to come up with a plan.

'To make an omelet, we have to crack eggs, Liang. If I expand, there will be issues with some gangs. It's my opinion that not all of them will come on board. There will be blood on the streets,' Ozdemir said.

Liang washed down a piece of mussel with a swig of wine before replying, 'That's fine. I have a team established to take care of minor details. It includes a Pole, an Albanian, and a Moroccan, all special forces who will eliminate these problems. They will clean up and vanish; you'll keep your hands clean. All that's required are the details of those who oppose you. Provide their photos, names, and locations to any of these three men. I will handle the payments.' Liang slid a paper across the table containing the cell phone numbers of the men. 'I will be in touch with the shipping details. You can start work immediately. The first containers will arrive in a week. I trust you will be ready.'

The thought of having a network of assassins in France, ready to take out his rivals, caused a surge of enthusiasm in Ozdemir. 'You can leave it with me,' he said, taking the piece of paper, glancing at the cell phone numbers, and quickly securing it in his pocket. Ozdemir lifted his beer and finished it. 'I have a few calls to make, Liang,' he said, reaching over the table to shake hands before lighting his cigar and walking off into the sunshine.

Liang knew that the nightly headlines would be filled with gangland assassinations. Without emotion, the mastermind of Liu's plan to flood Europe with cheap drugs greedily tucked into his lunch when his phone buzzed on the table. He flipped the cover open and selected the message app. Liang's eyes narrowed as he studied the details. Dubois, the man responsible for the deaths of his operatives in Geneva, was now a confirmed target. He clenched his fist with grim satisfaction, his eyes wide with the anticipation of finally settling the score.

FOURTEEN

The dimly lit dive bar in Silver Spring, Maryland, was an unusual setting for two high-ranking CIA officials. It was a place where one could easily blend into the background, a crucial detail for Gregory Faulkner as he navigated to a secluded seat in the back. His appearance was markedly different from the last time he met Jeff Connor. Faulkner looked aged; his once sharp features were now marred by worry lines. Recent events had taken a visible toll on him. He wore a haggard expression, and his hand trembled slightly as he reached into his pocket for his heart medication.

Connor arrived shortly after, scanning the room with the precision of a trained operative. Spotting Faulkner, he made his way over, composed yet alert. He slid into the chair opposite Faulkner, noting the pallor of his complexion.

'Gregory,' Connor greeted flatly.

Faulkner nodded, taking a deep breath as he popped a pill into his mouth and washed it down with a gulp of Budweiser. He looked at Connor with a mix of frustration and desperation. 'Thanks for coming on such short notice,' he began, his voice betraying a hint of suppressed anxiety. 'We need to talk about Mercer.'

Connor's eyes narrowed slightly. 'What about him?'

'This has to be off the record, Jeff. Officially, we're not having this conversation.'

'Understood. What's the issue?'

Faulkner sighed heavily, running a hand through his graying hair. 'I have been watching Mercer's actions closely. His rampage through Asia is causing ripples with the Chinese we can't afford. The incidents in Myanmar, the connections with the Black Orchestra; it's too close to home. And what the hell did he think when he crossed over into China? We have an agreement with General Liu that borders will be respected. Mercer just shit all over that.'

Connor remained silent, waiting for Faulkner to continue.

Faulkner thought for a moment, his eyes drifting over the patrons at the bar. 'We're in a difficult position,' he continued. 'Supporting Mercer's mission could lead to international incidents we're not prepared to handle. But cutting him loose could be even more dangerous. He's unpredictable, and we both know what he's capable of. Why the hell can't he be like the rest of us—keep his head down and mouth shut? He wants to be some kind of hero.'

He waved his own question away and continued. 'We need to be smart about this. If we crack down too hard, we risk exposing our own ties. But if we don't make a show of reining in corruption, someone else will—and they might start looking in our direction.'

Connor rubbed his temple, frustrated. 'We know all too well that the Black Orchestra is growing in strength. Their influence is spreading rapidly, not just in D.C., but across the states and overseas. We've both made our decisions, and we need to keep covering our tracks. Our only real issue now is Mercer. It's pointless trying to persuade him not to go after men with power and influence, as that's his real targets.

'When Mercer left the Army, his hatred for top commanders and the politicians pulling strings was well documented by the agency. Yet we knew his talents were worth the gamble. He understands the power of lobbyists and politicians working for their own interests, not the country's. Any opportunity he gets to bring those men and women to their knees, he takes full advantage of. He knows far more than we give him credit for, and if what I hear is true, he holds classified files on important people. Even I don't know where he gets this from.'

Connor took a deep breath, his eyes drifting around the bar before continuing. 'If we bring in new operators, the risk of exposing our knowledge and sources is too high. We don't know who else is, or isn't, on the take for the Black Orchestra. Getting intel from them is difficult—you know how it works.'

He paused, something coming to mind. 'I found something odd, and I'm not sure what to make of it. I flagged suspicious offshore transactions linked to Mercer. At first, I assumed he was financing a team, but he knows how far he can push unconventional warfare. Maybe he's just building a retirement fund, though that's not like him. If he is, well, that's something I'll look into.'

Faulkner hesitated, his eyes flicking around the bar as if expecting someone to be listening in. 'Everyone finds some cream of their own. Just ensure nothing falls back on us, and this issue never comes up again. Our boss, Jameson, wants to debate our options internally to see if there's a way to send Mercer after these individuals without causing a full-blown crisis. I think that's crazy. I'm not so sure we can control him anymore. The more men he cuts down, the closer he gets to us.'

Connor's expression hardened. 'Mercer isn't someone you can control with a leash. We need to handle this delicately. If he gets wind that Jameson has given him the green light to eliminate U.S. citizens on home soil or wherever he tracks them down, he will go through them like a knife through butter. He isn't exactly a surgeon at this; the trail he leaves behind is getting harder to cover up. I will end up in prison, as he falls under my command. It's a balancing act.'

Faulkner's hands trembled slightly as he reached for his beer. 'I know. We're accountable for his actions, whether we like it or not. If he goes too far, we all take the fall. That's why I need your insight. You've worked with him closely. What do you think is the best course of action?'

Connor took a deep breath. 'We need to give Mercer enough freedom to do what he does best, but we also need to make sure he doesn't step on the wrong toes. I hate playing politics. This isn't what I signed up for when I came to the agency. But if we shut him down completely, we risk losing control of the situation. Until I come up with something better, I say we feed him selective intel—just enough to guide his actions while keeping him in the dark about who's really pulling the strings.'

Faulkner nodded slowly, the apprehension in his eyes not entirely alleviated. 'That could work, but we have to be careful. If he figures out we're manipulating him, he might start seeing us as part of the rot.'

'Then we need to be smart about this. Use trusted people only, keep communication channels secure, and make sure Mercer feels he's in control—and keep pushing Jameson, see if he slips up somewhere, as I think he is hiding something. It's a tightrope walk, but it's our best shot. I need to get access to this AI program and add a few names to it. When Mercer takes one of those out, I can erase the data. Then the assassination will simply be a murder by an unhinged operator,' Connor said.

Faulkner sighed, his shoulders sagging. 'Alright, Jeff. I trust your judgment on this. Just make sure we don't end up with an international incident on our hands. We cannot have the Chinese thinking we are employing assassins to carry out killings of our own people. Imagine the headlines. Their ambassador has requested meetings all this week with White House officials. I'm counting on you to steer Mercer. You remember how he treated Alexander West and the FBI surveillance agent?'

Faulkner didn't expect an answer. The very thought that Mercer could simply carry out a grisly attack in a crowded hall sent a shiver down his spine. One minor misinterpretation from Mercer, and Faulkner knew he could be next.

Connor nodded, rising from the booth. 'I'll do my best. But remember, Gregory, Mercer isn't the only risk we need to worry about. Every day, he's being fed more intel, and I need you to find out from who.'

Faulkner watched Connor walk away, their conversation pressing heavily on his mind. He knew they were playing a dangerous game, one that could easily spiral out of control.

Taking another sip of his beer, he couldn't shake the feeling that they were on the edge of a precipice. He removed his cell phone, looked at it, then placed it back in his pocket. *No comms*, he thought, deciding how to protect himself from his lingering fear of NSA surveillance. Another agency that would grab pieces of intel and form their own assessment, which could leave him exposed to criminal actions.

Slumped in his chair, Faulkner rubbed the back of his neck, thinking on his next move.

Out in the parking lot, Connor stood by his car and lit a Marlboro. The shift in Faulkner, and Mercer's actions in Mong La, concerned him. Faulkner had always been a capable officer, experienced and steady under pressure, but at the end of the day, he was still following orders. Connor had never seen him as an equal—he was a useful asset, not a leader. The man he had just spoken to wasn't even that. Faulkner looked and sounded paranoid, like someone struggling to keep control of a situation far beyond him.

He's the wrong man for such a high position within the CIA. His current state of mind is completely out of character, and if our enemies picked up on this, they'd send their operatives to exploit it.

Connor took another drag on his cigarette, trying to make sense of Mercer's next move and prioritize his own orders, when he noticed a white sedan parked along Bonifant Street. Two Hispanic men sat silently inside. Something wasn't right.

Years of surveillance work had taught Connor when to trust his instincts. Today was no different. He flicked his cigarette away, glanced at their license plate, then pulled out of the parking lot. As he headed south toward D.C., his eyes stayed on the rearview mirror. He made a few turns, adjusted his speed, then leveled out. Nothing to worry about. The road behind him was clear.

Paranoia is a bitch, he thought, picking up his phone and calling Mercer's encrypted voicemail. His message was brief—just a request to meet once Mercer was back in town. The thought crossed his mind that Mercer might have been detained by Myanmar or Thai authorities, who quietly approve interrogation methods that involve physical and psychological torture, though those methods wouldn't be enough to make Mercer talk.

He set his phone down on the passenger seat as he passed through Shepherd Park. There was nothing more he could do. Despite telling Faulkner he'd find a way to access the list and add names, he knew that was futile—it was well out of his reach, and digging around would only raise suspicion. *I'll let Faulkner try first, see if he gets burned in the process.*

Paris—France

The café Le Parc in Mairie de Clichy was a quaint, unassuming place, filled with locals sipping espresso and watching the world go by. François Rousseau sat at a corner table, engrossed in the daily edition of *Le Monde*. His years of experience had taught him the value of blending in, and today was no different.

As he sipped his coffee, a sense of unease settled over him. An article in the newspaper highlighted the growing drug wars in Europe, massive corruption within the political and legal sectors, and intelligence agencies' collusion with international criminal gangs. The journalist referred to an unnamed source within the agencies who handed over highly classified documents.

The information had been released over the past few days, causing riots and blockades across France. The officials named in the articles barricaded themselves in their high-security maisons in Paris and châteaux in the south of France. All questions were sent to legal representatives, as those named refused to face the media.

Rousseau worried about leaking this information but knew there was no other way to stop the corruption. He loved France; it was his birthplace, where he met his first love, raised a family, and as a child spent his summers in Provence with his grandparents. The smell of freshly baked baguettes and the sound of laughter echoing through their small kitchen felt like yesterday. His eyes would well up with tears as he listened to the national anthem at the beginning of rugby matches, the country coming together to sing La Marseillaise at the top of their voices. Those moments were etched in his heart, fueling his resolve to fight the corruption tainting his beloved country.

The honor he felt when he first joined the DGSE was enormous, and the oath he took that day many years ago was still fresh in his mind.

He folded the paper and set it aside just as his cell phone buzzed. He took another sip of coffee, then picked up the phone from the table.

The first numbers showed the international dialing code of Turkey; the second group of numbers contained the area code. The call was coming from the Anatolian side of Istanbul.

'*Allô? Qui est à l'appareil?*' asked Rousseau.

'François, glad I caught you. Guess you are still smoking those nasty Gauloises cigarettes? You know who this is, yes?' Mercer didn't want to provide his name over this connection.

'Still smoking them, and yes, I couldn't mistake your grumpy and refreshingly blunt voice,' Rousseau said with a laugh.

'Great, I hope you are doing well. Listen up, as I don't have much time. Our old friend is back in Paris. I need you to carry out surveillance on him again and let me know who he is meeting. There will be a small reward for your services.'

Rousseau immediately thought of Kenneth Decker. The SD card Mercer handed over on his last visit to Paris contained all the information required to build an intelligence picture of the man. Rousseau had felt troubled about carrying out surveillance on a high-profile figure from the Office of the Director of National Intelligence, although the twenty thousand dollars helped ease the concern.

'Leave it with me. When are you in town again?' asked Rousseau.

'I'll be in touch. But remember, François, this

man, despite the business suit and warm smile, is highly dangerous. Ensure you take all necessary precautions, okay?' Mercer ended the call.

When the line went dead, Rousseau set the phone on the table and looked outside. *Twenty grand, easy money. The Americans love to throw money around,* he thought with a smile.

London, England

Rain pounded the pavement as Edward Hobbs skipped over the puddles along the London streets, making his way back to his flat in Kensington. He lifted his parka hood just enough to check for the flashing green man on the traffic lights, allowing him to cross the street to make one last purchase at his girlfriend's favorite café.

A man in a green Volkswagen hatchback parked opposite the café watched Hobbs enter the small door, disappearing from view.

The warmth inside the café hit Hobbs in the face as he stood in line. Once he placed his order, he took a seat at the window and rummaged through his bag of groceries, searching for a packet of painkillers. His back was playing up again, aggravated by the cold wind blowing through the streets.

The young waitress delivered his black coffee,

and he immediately gulped down a couple of tablets, followed by a sip of coffee. The call from Mercer an hour ago had caused him to leave his desk at work and travel across the city and back to his home next to Holland Park in Kensington.

Over the years, Hobbs viewed Mercer as an equal, a man dedicated to solving the mysteries of the underworld, whether it be terrorism, drug smuggling, or espionage. He enjoyed working with the American and understood that British intelligence capabilities focused more on human intelligence gathering and covert operations, while the CIA had a stronger emphasis on technical intelligence and analysis.

Hobbs recognized the strengths of the two agencies, with Britain's colonial experience lending itself to a deep understanding of local cultures and languages. However, he also acknowledged the CIA's vast resources and global reach, which sometimes overshadowed the more discreet British approach.

Anything he could do to bridge the gap was welcomed by his bosses in Vauxhall. However, as Mercer had instructed, this particular operation was to be off the record. There was something in Mercer's voice that had worried Hobbs. As the rain lashed the window, the MI6 operative stared out at the pedestrians rushing past, their umbrellas struggling with the wind. Around him, the customers were busy in conversations or engrossed on their phones. Hobbs sat in silence, his hands cupped around the coffee mug, his mind flicking through names, networks, and threats.

He glanced at his watch, then took another sip of his coffee, reminding himself to buy his girlfriend's takeaway coffee before he left. Then it hit him: a plausible connection between Schelling and the rogue faction of this Chinese breakaway group. When he was at work, he noticed a commotion at the Chinese desk. The analysts had received intel from a hospital in Beijing. A member of the CCP, Mr. Gao, had been taken to the military hospital, pronounced dead from an illness. However, the diagnosis made by a surgeon described a stomach wound brought about by a sharp object. A cover-up was ongoing, although this link was too much of a coincidence. General Liu, Gao, Schelling— something was connecting them all.

Hobbs remembered a small detail from the intel, a sudden and unexplained change in Gao's death certificate. The initial report by the attending surgeon clearly stated a fatal stab wound, but within hours, the cause of death was altered to a generic illness. The timing of this change coincided with a visit from a high-ranking military official, rumored to be close to Liu. This kind of intervention indicated significant influence, suggesting Liu's involvement.

Hobbs stared into his coffee, the steam swirling like the thoughts in his mind. *Gao's murder wasn't just another hit; it was a calculated move by Liu, a man known for his ruthless precision. The alteration of the death certificate, the timing, the surgical strike, everything pointed to a cover-up. But why?* Gao had been a thorn in the side of many within the CCP, particularly those with secrets to hide.

Gao had built his reputation on exposing corruption and espionage, making enemies in powerful places. His work had led him across Europe and the U.S., collaborating with international agencies to dismantle smuggling rings and uncover illicit dealings linked to the Black Orchestra. His assassination was more than silencing a whistleblower; it was a message.

Hobbs could almost feel the weight of the implications pressing down on him. *Was Liu making a power play within the CCP? A symbolic assassination to assert dominance? Or was this part of a larger strategy, setting the stage for something more sinister?*

Hobbs considered his next move. *Should I contact Downing Street and brief them on the potential upheaval within the Chinese government? The ramifications of an internal power struggle could destabilize the region. Or perhaps keep my findings within MI6, to be handled with the utmost discretion. And what about Mercer? Should he be brought into the loop immediately, or would that only complicate matters further?*

The decisions weighed heavily on Hobbs. Each option carried significant geopolitical consequences. He took another sip of his coffee, his mind cycling through the possible scenarios. Contacting Downing Street could provide the leverage needed to offer covert support, but it also risked exposing their hand too early. Keeping the analysis within MI6 might maintain operational security but at the cost of broader strategic insight. And updating Mercer discreetly could strike a balance, ensuring that key actions could be taken without alerting their enemies prematurely.

Hobbs knew one thing for certain: the pieces were falling into place, and the connection between Liu and Gao's murder was the key. He had to tread carefully but decisively. The next move would set the course for their entire operation.

A flush of excitement coursed through Hobbs as he grabbed his things and exited the café. Out in the wet street, he didn't bother with the parka hood. The rain no longer bothered him, and the pain in his back had vanished, replaced by a sense of urgency. Crossing the street onto Stafford Terrace, he then remembered his girlfriend's coffee.

'Shit!' he muttered, halting abruptly. He

spun on his heel and started back toward the café. Cursing himself silently as he crossed the street, his eyes caught a fleeting glimpse of a lone figure in the reflection of a shop window. Suddenly, a realization dawned on him. Hobbs stepped out of the rain and took refuge in a doorway to the Stafford Court building.

He removed his cell phone and swiped his thumb over the screen. His breath fogged in the cold air as he dialed a number and held the phone to his ear. The man who sparked Hobbs's attention continued to walk north-bound, turning right and disappearing from view.

Breathe, man, breathe, he told himself before stepping out from cover and making his way to the café once again. He pocketed the phone, frustrated as his call went unanswered.

Five minutes later, Hobbs emerged from the café. Despite viewing himself as paranoid, he decided to wait a while to ensure the man never came back. The bad weather had intensified, and rain hammered down, turning the street into a flowing stream. However, there was work to do, and he couldn't do it hiding in a café like a child.

For the second time, he left the café and jogged as best he could, armed with a bag of groceries and a cappuccino, back to his flat.

The streets were busy as red double-decker

buses hurtled down Kensington High Street, Ubers ferried their passengers, and food delivery motorcycles collected their orders from the surrounding restaurants. The hood on his parka was pulled forward, protecting his face from the rain but restricting his view like blinkers on a racehorse.

He came to a halt at Stafford Terrace and spun around to check the traffic before darting across the road. Only a lone motorcycle approached, turning into the same street before continuing past the large four-level homes, most of which were renovated into apartments, or 'flats' as the Londoners called them.

Hobbs quickly crossed the road and made his way to his place. He bounded up the steps to the front door and removed the front door key from his pocket. As he opened the door, a familiar noise caused him to spin around to see who it was. The motorcycle rider had kicked his bike stand down and had begun removing the box of food from the back.

Noting that it was normal for residents of his building to have these delivery guys arriving at this time of day, Hobbs nodded toward the door to welcome the man inside. There was a strong possibility his girlfriend had ordered something.

'Which flat are you looking for?' asked Hobbs.

'Number four.'

'It's two flights up, mate.' Hobbs turned and crossed the small lobby toward his door. The thought of hot food caused his stomach to growl violently. It was typical for Hobbs to be so consumed by work that he would often forget to organize his own meals. He slowly shook his head as he inserted the key into the door lock.

Two muffled shots rang out. Blood splattered against the mahogany door as the delivery rider placed his weapon back into the food container. Hobbs stumbled forward, crashing against the door before sliding down onto the marble floor. Coffee mixed with blood seeped across the lobby, and the sharp scent of cordite filled the stairwell.

Another successful kill. The delivery rider quickly scanned the stairwell, ensuring no witnesses lingered. He bent down to retrieve the empty shell casings, then swiftly exited the building, his smile hidden behind the black visor.

FIFTEEN

Istanbul—Turkey

anny Mercer ended his call with François Rousseau, feeling a sense of satisfaction. Rousseau was now on alert and ready to provide crucial intel. As Mercer swapped out the SIM card for one that he used previously, his phone immediately buzzed with a notification—a missed call from Edward Hobbs.

A cold chill ran down his spine. *Hobbs wouldn't call without a good reason.* He quickly redialed, hoping to catch him. The phone rang twice before someone answered, but the voice on the other end wasn't Hobbs.

'This is Detective Inspector Williams with the Homicide and Major Crime Command of the Metropolitan Police. Who is this?'

Mercer felt his heart skip a beat. *Scotland Yard.* 'I'm a friend of Edward Hobbs. Is he alright?'

There was a brief pause before the detective replied. 'I'm sorry to inform you that Mr. Hobbs was involved in an unfortunate incident. I'm afraid I can't provide any more information at this time.'

Mercer's grip tightened around his phone. *Oh fuck. not Hobbs!*

After a moment, Mercer replied. 'Thank you, Detective.' He ended the call and took a deep breath, his mind racing. It didn't feel right. Hobbs had been onto something big, and now he was gone. The Black Orchestra was tying up loose ends, and Mercer knew he had to act fast before they came for him or anyone else.

Mercer removed the SIM card from his cell phone and tossed it into the water. *Hobbs' death is on me.* He tried to shake the thought out of his head, knowing he would deal with the emotional baggage later. Hobbs was yet another name on the list of fallen men.

From his position at Haydarpaşa Port, Mercer stared out across the Bosporus Strait toward the European side of Turkey. There was much work to be done, yet he felt powerless while waiting to make contact with a black-market supplier. Around him, trucks raced in and out of the port with trailers, loading and unloading their goods. Ships' horns blasted loudly, cranes worked quickly, dock workers shouted instructions, and the call to prayer could be heard from the Grand Selimiye Mosque to his east. Despite the chaos, everything ran smoothly, as it had for hundreds of years. Mercer checked his watch. Ten minutes before his contact was due to arrive.

He slotted a new SIM card into his phone and made another call. 'Jeff, it's Mercer. I'm letting you know I'll be back in D.C. soon.'

'Great to hear that. I have some new information for you. A list of names that will be of interest, and some intelligence that I picked up from our agency partners.'

Over the next five minutes, Connor updated Mercer with a curated list of men and their business dealings. Mercer didn't interrupt; instead, he dissected what he already knew and looked for holes in Connor's information. After a few questions, Mercer was satisfied and ended the call. Connor provided enough detail to work with and mentioned some names that could see him implicated in serious legal trouble.

His boss had taken a significant risk. If the truth came out, the Office of the Inspector General within the CIA would likely initiate an internal investigation, while the Department of Justice, led by its Public Integrity Section, could pursue criminal charges. The FBI would not hesitate to investigate obstruction of justice and conspiracy, especially if it involved undermining an investigation into national security threats. Congressional oversight committees, particularly the House and Senate Intelligence Committees, would demand answers. Potentially leading to public hearings and severe political fallout.

Mercer felt the weight of the situation, knowing that Connor's gamble had put them both in a precarious position, with powerful forces ready to hold them accountable. As Mercer considered the complexities of the situation, he couldn't escape his past, particularly the unresolved killing of an FBI agent that still loomed over him. This issue was a potential charge that could surface at any time and derail his every move.

He walked along the road toward the entrance to the port, where a few men had gathered to wait for their rides and smoke cigarettes. He stood off to one side and was soon picked up by a man he had dealt with once before. Neither of them spoke as they made their way to a cluster of old warehouses a hundred meters from the ferry wharf.

Once their car approached the grim-looking storage area, the driver rolled the car to a stop, and a couple of fierce-looking men in black leather jackets opened the door, signaling for Mercer to get out. With a cigarette hanging in his mouth, a large man quickly searched Mercer for a weapon before leading him into the warehouse.

The interior of the warehouse was dark, filled with a familiar greasy smell mixed with chemicals. Large lights hung from the metal rafters, and a fine net was fastened high above, spanning from wall to wall. A solution to stop birds from roosting if they found themselves inside the building. Along the wall sat stockpiles of chemicals, some in bags, others in barrels. Above each pile, a sign listed the contents: ammonium nitrate, sodium chlorate, nitrobenzene, and aluminum powder. As Mercer's eyes adjusted to the light, he took in the scene, evaluating the setup and resources to gauge how effectively this makeshift bomb factory could produce explosives.

Men dressed in white one-piece suits, similar to forensic officers, were busy crushing the ammonium nitrate fertilizer using cement mixers. They then set about milling it to ensure they had the perfect consistency for the next stage. Further along, one area was set up for removing moisture from the chemicals in large machines. A large area was cordoned off with huge tarps hanging from the ceiling, forming a crude curtain.

Through the gaps, Mercer could see pallets of icing sugar, a peculiar yet suitable incendiary booster. Next to that sat sacks of sawdust, soap powder, and linseed oil. Everything would be used in the manufacture of crude explosives.

The smell of diesel oil helped mask the thick, pungent stink of chemicals. Despite the fumes, Mercer hoped these men were sufficiently trained in bomb-making. If their calculations and handling were careless, it could lead to unstable mixtures. The end of the warehouse contained a locked storage cage that housed primers, detonation cords, and batches of Semtex and gelignite.

Fortunately, Mercer realized that the assembly of the timing and power units used for initiating the improvised explosive devices (IEDs) was being conducted in a different building. The same rule applied for the vehicles that would transport the finished IEDs to their intended targets.

A sick feeling crept into Mercer's stomach as he thought about some of the bombings that happened around the world. These men were selling their skills to the highest bidder. Many terror groups outsourced their bomb-making capabilities. Even some shadowy governments used these same IEDs for false flag attacks, giving them an excuse to launch counter-terror operations. Many innocent people would be killed at the hands of these men. *Heartless bastards,* Mercer thought as he approached a small office guarded by two heavily built men.

The office reeked of cigarettes and mold; the carpet had been pulled up and replaced with green plastic sheeting. All seats were stacked in the corner except for the one Movsar was seated in. Mercer stood in front of an old metal table, his eyes scanning the small office for anything unusual.

Movsar stood and shook Mercer's hand before directing one of his bodyguards to fetch a seat for Mercer.

'Your request is quite strange, Tony,' Movsar said.

Mercer felt comfortable reusing his alias, Tony Hoffmann. His reputation from the assassination in Jakarta gave him a level of acceptance in the underworld. Cold-blooded and professional killers were good profit earners for men like Movsar. The Chechen warlord liked *Tony*. A man like that might be useful, someone who could move freely between countries and carry out hits for hard cash.

'Ten IEDs, no more than ten kilos each. Delivered to Marseille by the end of the week. One hundred thousand euros. Couldn't be more straightforward, Movsar,' Mercer said.

Movsar nodded slowly as he tried to understand Mercer's intent. 'Of course, that is not a problem. I just don't want anything to come back to me. I run a decent business, dealing with many important clients. Would you be interested in doing business with me again?'

'The answer lies in the outcome of my

operation. If your IEDs work as expected and have the correct explosive density, then yes. I'll be back. My area of operations will expand significantly in a few months. If you can handle the logistics and meet my requirements on a tight schedule, then you can expect continued business.'

Movsar picked up his cigarette and took a deep drag before speaking. 'Where exactly is your area of operations?'

'The United States.'

Movsar immediately coughed up a lungful of smoke. The audacity of using bombs in America was not lost on the war-hardened veteran. He quickly composed himself and stared at Mercer for a moment.

'I do not think you are a madman. You have witnessed death; that much is clear. I will indeed let you have as many explosives as you want. Forgive my bias, Tony, but I do not like America. However, we both know that if you start setting off bombs there, you will be hunted down like a dog. They will come after you with the wrath of the heavens, as the angel of death pursues the wicked.'

Mercer smiled and nodded, relieved that the business meeting had passed the critical test. As he prepared to pay Movsar and leave, he kept his true intentions hidden behind a calm exterior. He had no plans to return for more business; instead, he was already plotting to ensure this factory, and its deadly operations, would be reduced to rubble.

This warehouse was a festering wound of evil, and when the time was right, Mercer would return to obliterate it in a blaze of fire and blood. He envisioned twisted metal and scorched earth, a fitting end for those who dealt in death. Mercer would make sure that no more innocents would be torn apart in markets or vaporized in hotels by the horrors concocted here.

London—England

Crime scene tape was being removed by uniformed police officers, while forensic officers packed up their equipment and loaded it into their vans. Mercer stood at the corner of Stafford Terrace and Phillimore Gardens alongside a number of residents who had gathered to watch and comment on the murder of the young man many of them had the pleasure of meeting. Most of the people around him were aghast at the shocking murder; some blamed immigration, others pointed the finger at the Russians, while some questioned the drug problems in England. For Mercer, it was frustrating to stand in the cold drizzle, listening to pointless accusations, unarmed and without a suspect.

The fight against the Black Orchestra had become more than a professional mission; it was a deeply personal crusade. He saw them as a representation of everything he despised: unchecked power, corruption, and the willingness to sacrifice innocent lives for profit and control. The loss of Hobbs crystallized this sentiment, making Mercer determined to bring down the entire network, even if it meant bending the rules and taking extreme measures. All his life, he detested powerful figures who were above the law.

As he fought in street battles with terrorists or cartels, these men in suits climbed the ladders of politics, shielding themselves with money and influence on each rung. After losing countless mates, his vows of vengeance had yet to bear fruit. Deep down, he felt the puppet masters were becoming stronger, while his grip was weakening. When men like Georg Schelling, Kenneth Decker, Rick Sanderson, Arnold Becker, and John Elder, names etched into his mind, began forming up with a rogue Chinese faction, Mercer knew he was losing this battle.

It was only a few weeks ago that he left the meeting with Jeff Connor at the CIA headquarters in Washington, D.C., with the mission brief fresh in his mind. Determined and aggressive, he killed the first obstacle in the drug house. The thought of killing the FBI agent that night caused Mercer's heart to skip a beat.

He pulled his parka hood tight around his head to keep out the cold wind blowing through the London street as he weighed up the consequences of that fateful night. *They were corrupt, and they got what they deserved,* thought Mercer. Only half-believing his own words, it was the best he could do to keep his mind from becoming scattered and worthless. *Focus on the next target, remember the mission brief,* he reminded himself as he watched the forensic officers drive off with their evidence.

The people around him began to drift away, shuffling back to their multimillion-pound homes to watch the BBC for further updates on the murder. Mercer thought about going straight to Georg Schelling and putting a bullet in his head, then, one by one, he could take out the rest. Although he knew that would scare the whole network and they would all go to ground, reappearing under a new form. Instead of mulling over wiping out every name on his list, he decided to walk around the block and piece together the planning of Hobbs' assassination.

From the street, he could work out how much information the shooter would have needed, and he could also assess whether there had been a well-organized team in place. He noted some recently rented flats, rental cars, and European license plates on a couple of vans. Further along Argyll Road, he spotted a black Audi with blacked-out windows on the rear passenger and driver's doors, and a fold-out solar charging panel placed on the dashboard with a cable running into the back seat. Mercer peered inside to check what the cable was attached to. Two small black boxes were attached to the driver's rear passenger window, with what appeared to be a camera mounted on top of a battery pack. Both had been attached to the inside window with rubber suction cups.

Mercer noted the car's license plate, the model, and a few other details, then discreetly left the area. He had the information he needed. The car was obviously used as a remote surveillance tool. Someone would return later to remove the car, and Mercer needed to provide this information to the homicide detectives, if they hadn't already picked up this piece of evidence for their ongoing investigation.

An hour later, Mercer was seated in an interview room deep within Scotland Yard on Victoria Embankment. Outside, the River Thames flowed peacefully under Westminster Bridge while tourists snapped photos of Big Ben and other famous London attractions, unaware of the hive of activity on both sides of the river. About a mile south on the east side of the river in Vauxhall, MI6, also known as the

Secret Intelligence Service, was busy investigating how one of their own was brutally gunned down on his doorstep.

Detective Inspector Williams, a veteran of the Homicide and Major Crime Command within the Metropolitan Police, was leading the investigation. He handed Mercer a cup of hot tea and took a seat opposite him. Williams was silent for a moment as he flicked through his notes, then he wrote something down, circled it, and looked at Mercer.

'You spoke to Hobbs just before he was shot?'

'I didn't speak to him; he tried to call me. When I saw the missed call, I redialed, and then you answered,' replied Mercer.

Williams didn't need to look at his notes. He already had the phone logs for Hobbs' cell phone. 'Why would he call you?'

'I had mentioned that I would be in London on business and was hoping to catch up with him. Hobbs was in the Army, like me, and we had the pleasure of working alongside each other in Afghanistan many years ago. We both liked the idea of grabbing a pint and talking about the old days.'

'Hobbs was in the Special Air Service, so it would be safe to assume you too were in the special forces.'

Mercer didn't confirm or deny. He lifted his

cup and took a sip of tea, signaling that he was not going to discuss his previous or current employment.

'Look, if there's anything you can tell me, then please do. We are both from different countries; however, we are all on the same team. The spooks were already in here this morning giving me the bum steer, and that's fine. I've figured Hobbs is one of their guys, and they're doing all they can to wrap things up in their own way. As long as this perpetrator is brought to justice, I don't care how it's done. But don't leave me hanging.'

Williams closed his notebook and stretched out his legs below the table, then relaxed his shoulders slightly, showing a less informal approach. 'I presume you haven't been across the river this morning with MI6. You made this your first and maybe only official visit. So, there must be something you want from me that you can't get from the spooks!'

A smile crossed Mercer's lips; he appreciated Williams's frankness, a trait not shared by British intelligence officers and the reason why Mercer didn't waste his time going down to Vauxhall.

Mercer set his cup down and slowly explained to Williams about the black Audi he spotted parked down the road from Hobbs' flat and the camera surveillance system set up inside it. He relayed his thoughts and concerns, including the potential for political pressures not to conduct a thorough investigation. Mercer was happy to lie. Whatever it took to get some information from the British, he would follow through, even to the extent of providing Williams with the number of his boss in Washington, Jeff Connor.

At the mention of the CIA, Williams immediately sat up, shoulders back, and reopened his notebook. He scribbled Connor's phone number down and a contact for Mercer, then looked up. 'What information do you need to know?' he asked.

'Detective Williams, I need access to all the evidence you've collected from Stafford Terrace—the shell casings, ballistic reports, DNA samples, fingerprints, and anything from Hobbs' electronic devices. I also want a copy of the CCTV footage and any forensic analysis you've conducted. Ensure you have a surveillance team watching that black Audi. Send all this information to Connor immediately. Timing is crucial, Detective, as there are others who could be targeted next.' Mercer's voice was as hard as steel, his true emotions breaking through his otherwise calm demeanor.

Mercer asked Detective Inspector Williams if he could exit from the rear of Scotland Yard to avoid the media gathering for the upcoming press conference at the front of the building. Williams obliged, leading Mercer through a network of corridors and past the forensic lab. As they walked by, Mercer caught a glimpse of the forensic team at work, utilizing advanced techniques to process evidence. He could see bottles of ninhydrin and cyanoacrylate on the lab benches, essential tools for lifting latent fingerprints from various surfaces.

Ninhydrin, a chemical reagent, is particularly effective for developing fingerprints on porous surfaces like paper and cardboard. When applied, it reacts with the amino acids present in the natural oils left by human skin, producing a deep purple compound known as Ruhemann's purple. This reaction enhances the visibility of the fingerprints, allowing investigators to photograph and analyze the unique patterns.

In contrast, cyanoacrylate, commonly known as superglue, is used for non-porous surfaces such as glass, metal, and plastic. The cyanoacrylate fuming process involves heating the glue, which then vaporizes and adheres to the moisture in the latent fingerprints. The resulting polymerized residue forms a white, raised print that can be further enhanced with fluorescent dyes or powders for better contrast.

Additionally, the lab was equipped with an array of fingerprint powders, each chosen based on the surface material and the environmental conditions in which the evidence was found. These powders, which can be metallic, magnetic, or fluorescent, adhere to the oils and sweat left in fingerprints, making them more visible under specific lighting conditions. The combination of these techniques allows the forensic team to meticulously reveal and preserve the fingerprints, providing crucial evidence that could link a suspect to a crime scene.

Amidst the bustle, Mercer couldn't help but reflect on the unique nature of this lab. Despite the widespread privatization of forensic services across the UK, Scotland Yard maintained a secret, in-house forensic facility. This specialized lab was designed to handle high-level homicide cases and sensitive investigations that required utmost confidentiality. It was a measure taken to ensure forensic integrity, free from the potential conflicts of interest and profit motives that plagued commercial providers. This clandestine facility was equipped with state-of-the-art technology for DNA sequencing and ballistic comparisons, serving as a bastion of independence and precision. For cases like Hobbs', where the stakes were extraordinarily high, this lab provided a crucial safeguard against miscarriages of justice, allowing the Metropolitan Police to conduct thorough and secure forensic examinations away from prying eyes.

As they exited through the back, Mercer felt

a grim satisfaction knowing that, within these walls, the pursuit of justice was still a carefully guarded endeavor.

SIXTEEN

Washington, D.C.—USA

Parked next to Schelling's Rolls-Royce Phantom was a line of limousines, all neatly reversed. Their fronts faced the large fountain in the center of the circular driveway. The drivers, familiar with the facilities provided by Georg Schelling's staff, chose to remain outside as the warm sun on their faces was a welcome change from the air-conditioned cars, and they could speak more freely.

They noticed newly installed security cameras and a few additional guards patrolling the vast property, but it was nothing to be concerned about, one driver noted. It wasn't uncommon to see heightened security now and then. The men often joked that the level of security matched their bosses' egos. Smoking cigarettes under the shade of a large oak tree, they were served coffee, freshly made croissants, and cinnamon rolls by the kitchen staff. As usual, their hushed conversations focused on traffic, sports, and their irritation with the increasing frequency of short-notice trips. One driver returned to the table, followed closely by a security guard.

'If you need to use the toilet, there's a bathroom next to the rear entry, beside the kitchens,' the guard barked.

The guard was clearly annoyed that the driver had chosen to relieve himself in a newly planted garden bed behind the oak trees. The others laughed and joked at the driver, who had quite literally been caught with his pants down, as he shuffled off toward the bathroom.

The mood inside Schelling's house was far less jovial. The men had gathered in the library to discuss their operations and Kenneth Decker's current trip to France. All afternoon, Schelling had been trying to convince Arnold Becker, Charles Clark, and Senator Rick Sanderson that his contacts in the FBI were not conducting any investigations into their operations. John Elder, the attorney seated to Schelling's left, nodded slowly, confirming Schelling's information. Elder generally remained silent unless challenged or when he found an irregularity in the details presented by the group.

With his expertise in uncovering the dirty secrets of those in law enforcement and political circles, he was armed with crucial intelligence. Elder's additional support gave Schelling the confidence to proceed with his well-crafted plans.

Becker from the DOJ and Sanderson were convinced and accepted Schelling's plans. This approval didn't come easily; it took lengthy debates, with their questions eventually answered directly by Elder. Despite the convoluted legal language in some of his responses, the men found Elder's arguments watertight.

Satisfied and somewhat exhausted, Sanderson opened the glass door of a large humidor perched next to a drinks cabinet and began to select a cigar. Becker waved a hand toward Sanderson, signaling that he was also in the mood for a smoke.

Charles Clark waved away the offer of a cigar. Instead, he leaned forward awkwardly and cleared his throat, signaling that he had more pressing matters to address. The shipping magnate and owner of Sternenlicht Versand was grappling with a strategic setback he believed Schelling was deliberately avoiding. 'As you all know, the French authorities have revoked docking rights for several of my ships at the Port of Marseille,' Clark began. His eyes narrowed as he considered the implications.

The loss of Marseille wasn't just a logistical inconvenience; it threatened to disrupt key supply lines that fed into the heart of Europe. Marseille had been a linchpin in his operations, offering not only a gateway for goods but also a strategic foothold in the Mediterranean. Without it, Clark faced delays and increased costs as his ships would need to reroute to less efficient ports. Worse still, losing access to Marseille could weaken his leverage in the region, allowing competitors, particularly those backed by foreign powers, to gain ground. This wasn't just about business; it was about maintaining control and influence over one of the most critical shipping lanes in the world.

Faced with silence, Clark reached into his jacket pocket and retrieved a letter from his chief legal counsel. He unfolded it carefully and began to read aloud. 'Mr. Clark, the French customs authorities have exercised their right to revoke docking privileges for Sternenlicht Versand under the French Maritime Code. This regulation allows for immediate suspension or revocation of docking rights if a shipping company is found to be involved in contraband cases. Unfortunately, the discovery of illegal arms and narcotics in several of our shipments over the past six months has provided them with ample justification.'

Schelling listened carefully as Clark read, then turned to Elder and gave a slight nod.

Elder took the hint and spoke in his usual

calm tone. 'Charles, I understand your frustration, but the pattern of discoveries, combined with the repeated fines and warnings, has made it difficult to defend your case. The French authorities are taking a hard line on organized crime, especially in Marseille, which is under intense international scrutiny. Even if you could prove third-party involvement, the damage to your reputation has been significant.'

'What about the dockworkers? I've been paying them for over twenty years to organize my containers. There should be mediation on my company's behalf; the union should be held to their word. This needs to be rectified, and it needs to be handled quickly,' Clark demanded.

'It appears the dockworkers' union is no longer cooperating with you. Sources suggest they've been influenced by other interests, potentially linked to your Chinese competitors. One name that has surfaced is Liang Guang, General Liu's man in Europe. We know how the unions are controlled by mafia groups, and it seems they've been directed to make your operations as difficult as possible. Their pressure on the authorities to scrutinize your shipments more closely has resulted in these problems. It appears Liu is positioning himself to take over the Mediterranean routes.'

Elder took a moment to study Clark's reaction before continuing. 'You can challenge the revocation in court, but it would be a lengthy process, and the damage to your reputation and shareholders may be irreversible by then.'

Clark looked over at Sanderson and Becker for some support, but the two men were busy mumbling to each other as they passed cigars back and forth. He leaned back in his chair and gazed at the letter in his hands. It was immediately apparent that his attempts to leverage the Black Orchestra's power were futile.

While Clark saw the loss as a stain on his reputation and a threat to shareholder confidence, Schelling understood that their true goals lay far beyond the logistics of shipping routes or the profitability of Clark's company. The Black Orchestra was not built to manage petty concerns; its overarching goal was to establish control over key geopolitical events using a combination of espionage, political manipulation, and economic sabotage. Schelling's focus was on steering global outcomes in their favor, whether through orchestrating coups, destabilizing regions to create power vacuums, or manipulating international markets for strategic advantage.

Clark is obsessed with Marseille, while I have entire continents to consider, Schelling thought. To shift the focus, Schelling moved onto the topic of Danny Mercer and his potential.

Schelling had always understood the value of

control, maintaining a firm grasp on every element within his orbit. But Mercer was different. Mercer operated beyond conventional limits of morality and order, guided not by the rules governing most operatives but by an internal code that was as ruthless as it was unpredictable. Mercer was like a wild animal, feral and untamed, moving through the world with a lethal precision that left little room for compromise.

He had risen through the ranks of the CIA not by following orders but by achieving results others could only dream of, often by circumventing the very rules meant to restrain him. This made Mercer one of the CIA's most effective operatives but also a significant threat. His ability to operate without the usual guardrails was precisely why Schelling found him both fascinating and dangerous. Schelling knew that a man like Mercer, if left unchecked, could dismantle everything he had built with the Black Orchestra. But Schelling also understood a fundamental truth from the teachings of psychological warfare and the wisdom of ancient strategists: keep your friends close but your enemies closer.

Schelling recognized that Mercer, with his volatile nature and penchant for violence, could never be tamed. But that wasn't Schelling's goal. Instead, Schelling sought to guide Mercer's destructive potential, to harness it and direct it toward the enemies of the Black Orchestra. By bringing Mercer further into the fold, Schelling believed he could channel that raw power and unpredictability into something useful. It was a calculated risk, one that required constant vigilance, but the alternative, allowing Mercer to remain a rogue element, free to act against them, was far more dangerous.

The sound of Mercer's name caught the attention of the men, most notably Charles Clark, who raised his head and then placed his letter neatly back into his breast pocket. The four men settled in and watched Schelling intently.

Schelling stood, walked to his bookshelf, and pulled out a well-thumbed copy of *On War* by Carl von Clausewitz. It was a book he often turned to, finding its insights into the nature of conflict as relevant today as when it was first written. He flicked through the pages, his eyes settling on a passage that guided many of his most critical decisions. After reading a few lines, he carefully returned the book to its place and turned to face the men.

'In war, understanding your enemy is crucial,' Schelling began, his voice calm and authoritative, 'but mastering them is paramount. I know you all have doubts about Mercer, but allow me to explain...'

He paused, letting his words resonate in the silence that followed.

'Mercer is unlike any other operative. He doesn't follow the rules that restrain others. He's guided by his own code, one that's as ruthless as it is effective. This makes him incredibly valuable but also incredibly dangerous. He's a man who operates in what Clausewitz might describe as the *fog of war*, where uncertainty and the unpredictable nature of human actions reign. This is why he's been so successful for the CIA, and why he could be a threat to us if left unchecked.'

Schelling's gaze swept across the room, taking in the expressions of the men as they digested his words. It was Elder who broke the silence.

'I understand that Mercer is indeed a unique character. It is apparent that the CIA has a hard time keeping him on a leash. His friends in the White House and the old boys within the agencies use him when they believe diplomacy is no longer an option. However, Georg, if I may be so bold, I sometimes worry that Mercer is the nut you cannot crack. You spent your best years influencing powerful figures, and when Mercer crossed your path, you perhaps found him to be more of a challenge. He's a man who can solve many of your problems yet could crush everything you've built. My counsel to you would be to ensure your judgment isn't clouded and to tread carefully.'

Schelling moved across the room in silence,

his expression remaining resolute, the embodiment of calculated strategy. He patted Elder on the shoulder and took his seat.

'That's what I appreciate about you, John. You keep a level head, and at the same time, you keep us all in check. But this is precisely why we must keep Mercer close. Clausewitz teaches that war is an extension of politics, a means to achieve greater ends. Mercer's unpredictability can be our greatest asset if we direct it properly. By integrating him into our operations and giving him a sense of purpose aligned with our goals, we can guide that lethal force to work in our favor. By having the CIA's main hitman on our side, we protect ourselves from legal prosecution. The U.S. government cannot come after us if we can prove that our end goals, and the resources we use to achieve them, are no different than theirs. If we go down, the whole leadership of the CIA goes down with us.'

The room remained silent as the weight of Schelling's words sank in. The men around him, though still wary, began to see the logic in his approach. Mercer was a risk, yes, but in Schelling's hands, he could become the decisive factor in their success.

Sanderson had finally lit his cigar, taking a few slow puffs as he watched the smoke curl and drift upwards, dissipating into the dim light of the room. He was in deep thought, trying to piece together the fragments of Schelling's plan for Mercer, but something didn't sit right. The man was a wild card, and Sanderson couldn't see the full picture of how Schelling intended to keep him in line.

'I agree with your plan,' Sanderson said finally, his voice thick with doubt. 'However, I don't know what it would look like in practice. What steps do you have to protect us if things go wrong?'

Schelling leaned back, his eyes narrowing slightly as he thought about his response. 'We already know Mercer has a knack for eliminating problems. Take his work in Jakarta, for instance. It was a surgical operation, took out a high-value target, destabilized a network, and he walked away with a healthy payday. We've got all of that on record, so if Mercer decides to get clever and walk away, we can use it as leverage.'

Sanderson frowned, still not entirely convinced. Schelling continued, his tone calculated. 'And let's not forget, Mercer's on a warpath after the assassination of a British intelligence officer. This wasn't just any agent; this man worked closely with Mercer. They had history. His death is a festering wound, and it's driving Mercer to seek out whoever's responsible. That kind of rage can be a powerful motivator. It's also why he'll be inclined to partner with us—to use our resources to find the people who took out his ally.'

Becker, who had been quietly observing, finally spoke up. 'Do you know anything about the murder?' His tone was direct, probing.

Schelling's jaw tightened almost imperceptibly. He hated such questions, especially when they came from Arnold Becker. The man's track record had been tarnished ever since Geneva, since that disastrous attempt to recruit Philippe Dubois, the DGSE officer. Becker had fumbled the operation, turning what should have been a smooth acquisition into a botched affair that nearly blew their cover. And then there was the failed abduction attempt that followed. Schelling's trust in Becker had been eroding ever since. Now, every question from him felt like an unwanted challenge.

Schelling exhaled slowly, his irritation barely masked. 'What I know is that Mercer's grief is real, and it's raw. He's not going to rest until he finds the people responsible, and that makes him useful to us. But make no mistake, Arnold,' Schelling's voice dropped to a near whisper, 'if you continue to stumble like you did in Geneva, I'll make sure you're not around to ask these questions anymore.'

The room seemed to grow colder, the weight of Schelling's words pressing down on everyone. Sanderson shifted uncomfortably in his seat, while Becker held Schelling's gaze, his expression unreadable. They all knew the stakes. Mercer was a risk, yes, but if Schelling's gamble paid off, Mercer could be the weapon that secured their power, and their survival.

Schelling shifted in his chair, his eyes locking onto each man in turn. 'Now, let's discuss Kenneth Decker's current mission in France. As you're all aware, Decker is one of our most reliable assets—a man who operates with absolute focus and delivers results without compromise. His current assignment is critical to our broader strategy.'

Sanderson tapped the cigar, letting the ash fall into the tray. 'Who's he targeting?'

'François Rousseau,' Schelling replied, his voice as cold as steel. 'Rousseau has been a significant player in European intelligence circles for years, with connections that run deep, connections that include Mercer. Decker's mission is simple: find Rousseau and eliminate him. This will send a clear message to anyone thinking of aligning with Mercer.'

Sanderson frowned, his eyes narrowing in concern. 'Rousseau is a high-profile target. Why take such a huge risk? If something goes wrong, it could bring unwanted attention on all of us. Decker's good, but this could spiral out of control quickly.'

Schelling allowed a small, tight smile to cross

his face. 'Decker isn't there to pull the trigger himself. His role is to ensure that the operation runs smoothly, no fuck-ups like in Geneva. He's there to oversee the hit, to make sure everything goes according to plan. We've lined up local assets to do the actual job, men who know how to make it look clean, like an accident or an internal settling of scores.'

He paused, his gaze shifting deliberately toward Becker, who sat quietly at the edge of the table. The silence grew heavy as Schelling's eyes bore into him. 'This time, there will be no mistakes.'

Becker stiffened slightly, feeling the weight of Schelling's unspoken accusation. The Geneva fiasco still hung over him like a dark cloud, a failure that had nearly compromised the entire operation. Schelling's words were a clear reminder of that failure and a warning that there wouldn't be another chance.

Elder, sensing the tension, broke the silence. 'Taking out Rousseau won't just cut off one of Mercer's allies; it will weaken Mercer's global network. Rousseau has been the linchpin in Mercer's European operations. Without him, Mercer's ability to operate on the continent would be severely compromised. Furthermore, gentlemen, I am sure you have all seen the news related to the French riots. Someone leaked information to the media regarding collusion between the French intelligence agencies and the criminal groups based all over Europe. The snowball effect of such disturbances is increased scrutiny of the intelligence agencies and their power. The French police are under immense pressure to eradicate bad actors and shine a spotlight into dark corners. So, I ask, who leaked such material to the press? Well, allow me. I have made some inquiries to our contacts within the Direction générale de la Sécurité intérieure, and they believe it was our friend Rousseau.'

Schelling nodded, his attention returning to the group. 'Exactly. There is no doubt Rousseau's death is a priority. Not only will it cut off leaks, but it will also isolate Mercer, leaving him vulnerable and more likely to seek out an alliance with us. If we control the only remaining paths available to him, he'll have no choice but to cooperate.'

Sanderson tapped his cigar against the ashtray, finally understanding the full scope of the plan. 'So, this isn't just about revenge. It's about narrowing Mercer's options, forcing him into a corner.'

'That's part of it,' Schelling said, pausing as he considered how much to reveal about Decker's situation in France. 'Decker isn't just dealing with Rousseau; he's navigating a delicate balance between multiple intelligence agencies. He's already had a meeting with one of our contacts in Paris, but he wasn't alone. The French DGSE and Chinese MSS both had eyes on him.'

Sanderson frowned, his concern deepening. 'And he's still supposed to carry out the hit with that much attention on him?'

Schelling nodded, his expression unreadable. 'Yes. That's precisely why Decker is the right man for this job. He's aware of the eyes on him, and he's playing them against each other. The French are convinced they're monitoring a Chinese operation, while the Chinese believe the French are after one of their own assets. Decker is operating in the middle of this, using their focus on each other to move undetected. His presence is acknowledged, but his true purpose remains hidden. This is how he'll get close to Rousseau without raising alarms.'

Elder leaned forward, his tone cautious. 'The French have always had a particular sensitivity about foreign operatives on their soil, especially someone with Decker's reputation. Decker is walking a tightrope. I hope he has a Plan B if there are any loose ends.'

'Decker is fully aware of the stakes. His primary objective is to review the plans made by our local assets, execute the hit on Rousseau, and shake off any tails. He will oversee the operation and ensure that neither the French nor the Chinese interfere. If the situation escalates, Decker has contingency plans in place. He's not new to this game. Don't let his current role fool you,' Schelling said.

The room was silent as Schelling's words settled in. The men knew the risks, but they also understood the necessity of the plan. Decker's mission in Paris wasn't just another kill; it was a calculated move in a dirty game.

'I will keep you all updated on Decker's progress,' Schelling said, his sharp tone suggesting the conversation had come to an end. 'The sooner Rousseau is eliminated, the sooner we can bring Mercer into the fold, on our terms.'

SEVENTEEN

New York—USA

Once the aircraft taxied into position, the sky corridor was swiftly attached for the passengers to disembark while the pilots performed their post-flight checks. Flight attendants stood at the exit, ensuring passengers from flight BA115 stepped off safely.

'Excuse me, sir, we've landed in New York,' said the perfectly groomed flight attendant as she gently squeezed Mercer's shoulder.

Mercer opened his eyes, took a deep breath, and thanked the flight attendant, who, despite her smile, seemed eager to finish her duties and get into the city. The British Airways crew had a one-night layover before flying back to London the next day. Judging by how quickly she ushered the passengers off, she wanted to make the most of her time.

Mercer reached under the seat and grabbed

his flight bag—which contained nothing more than a shaving kit, toiletries, a couple of burner phones, and a charger—and quickly exited the aircraft. With his pack slung over his shoulder, he turned right and walked along the carpeted sky corridor. He ran his fingers through his thick black hair, brushing it into place, then rubbed his face, feeling the coarse stubble that had formed overnight.

Despite being one of the last off the aircraft, he noticed a few men in suits lingering at the end of the sky corridor. The grogginess from the flight quickly gave way to focus as he weighed up the situation. Mercer glanced behind to check for anyone important. Maybe he had over-looked a foreign dignitary, or someone being es-corted by marshals. His mood dipped when he saw only the technicians and flight crew.

It's definitely me they're after, he thought. Mercer considered the possibility that Jeff Connor had sent a team to escort him to Washington, D.C., or to obtain a quick debrief before he went to a hotel to freshen up. Connor wasn't one to waste time. He was a man whose day was divided into minutes, not hours.

As Mercer got closer, the men turned to face him. He sized them up and decided they weren't from Langley. There was excitement in their eyes, a hint of adrenaline, and their suits were too flashy. Some had a bulge at their ankles, revealing backup weapons. The CIA wouldn't draw that much attention. If it was a well-trained agent, they'd approach more casually, blending in with the crowd. With this quick assessment, Mercer's senses heightened as he approached.

'Mr. Daniel Mercer, my name is Special Agent John Hayes with the Federal Bureau of Investigation. You are under arrest for the murder of an FBI Special Agent in Washington, D.C. You have the right to remain silent. Anything you say can and will be used against you in a court of law. You have the right to an attorney. If you cannot afford an attorney, one will be appointed for you. Do you understand these rights as I have read them to you?'

'I understand,' Mercer said.

One man stepped forward and took Mercer's backpack. Another took his jacket, while a fourth man patted Mercer down. 'Please turn around and place your hands behind your back,' Bayes said.

Mercer didn't argue when the cuffs went on. He kept his cool and evaluated the face of Special Agent Bayes. The man gave nothing away; he was all business, making sure nothing was thrown or dropped from Mercer's clothing before leading him out of the terminal through a series of corridors.

Bypassing passport control and customs, Mercer was taken to an underground garage, where he saw more FBI agents standing by their vehicles. A door slid open on a black unmarked van, and he felt a hand on his back pushing him toward the darkened interior. He stepped up into the van, took a seat, then an agent removed the handcuffs. From what Mercer could see in the gloomy interior, the van had a crudely welded cage installed, inside which was his chair. An air vent blew stale air, and an infrared camera was directed right at him. Once the van door slammed shut and the customized locks clicked into position, he was truly imprisoned.

Flanked by several SUVs, the convoy raced out of the airport and into New York traffic. The journey to the Metropolitan Detention Center (MDC) in Brooklyn via the Belt Parkway took less than thirty minutes. When the van stopped abruptly, the driver quickly applied the parking brake and killed the engine. Suddenly, the doors slid open, and two large agents stepped in and unlocked the cage. Mercer was forcefully hauled out of the van. He stumbled slightly on the step but corrected himself before the agents readjusted their grip on his arms. Their attitudes were a stark contrast to before. Mercer was now in their territory, out of view of the civilian staff at JFK. He was no longer treated as a suspect, innocent until proven guilty, but rather as a worthless, dirty rat, undeserving of any humanity.

The two burly men frog-marched Mercer as they walked beside the vast concrete and steel walls of the MDC, twisting his wrists. The handcuffs bit into Mercer's skin, causing extreme pain. Blood started to run down his hands, into his palms, and between his fingers. Mercer ignored the pain, refusing to show anger or give in to their games. Over the years, he had been held in captivity and endured violent interrogations, not just during Delta selection but in real-world missions.

They can't kill me, just suck up the pain, he repeated to himself. Even though his breathing was relaxed, his mind raced with possible scenarios surrounding his arrest.

'This is nothing compared to what's coming. Once your cellmates know they're bunking with a spook, they'll fuck you up,' one agent whispered in Mercer's ear. The other agent smirked and winked at his teammates gathered at the entrance to the detention center. They all wanted a glimpse of the man who had shot and killed one of their own.

The FBI agent's words cut deep into Mercer's soul. *The death of that FBI agent was a line I hadn't wanted to cross. It wasn't supposed to go down like that. But now...now it's too late for regrets. And anyway, why was I being followed? What did you all expect? It was his fault, your fault, all of you... His life or mine, and he lost.*

Mercer's mind was spinning, angered by the dead agent's actions that night and by the FBI command. Now, here he was, being led through steel doors, enduring the jeers and taunts of the FBI escort team, walking the same path as criminals. The heavy stench of bleach stuck in his throat as he tried to clear his head and make sense of the situation.

The fluorescent lights inside the MDC buzzed overhead, casting a harsh, sterile glow on the faces of the FBI agents watching. The walls were a dull gray with grime built up over the years. Dirty black streaks marked the walls, caused by detained inmates' shoes kicking out as they used the wall for leverage in fights with the guards.

Mercer was shoved toward a desk manned by a surly-looking man in his fifties with a thick mustache.

'Special Agent Hayes, FBI. We're processing a high-value detainee: Mercer, Danny Mercer. AKA Tony Hoffmann.'

Mercer's heart pounded in his chest. *Tony Hoffmann. Bastards. Who tipped them off?* Mercer could feel Hayes' breath on his neck when the agent leaned in close.

'We know everything about you, Mercer.

Your colleagues have abandoned you; welcome to hell.'

Mercer ignored the man, trying instead to contain the rage building inside him, the kind of rage he felt after puncturing a man's neck multiple times on the outskirts of Vladivostok, Russia. Mercer's mind drifted back to the parking lot where the man had opened the trunk of his car to reveal bags filled with copper and steel pipes. The weapons smuggler had merely attempted to double-cross him during the trade. *Whoever ratted me out to the FBI will learn their fate, no matter where they're hiding*, he thought.

The man at the desk punched some information into a keyboard, then motioned for Mercer to step through the metal detector. The cuffs were swiftly removed, then a push on his back sent him on his way. One guard pulled a pair of gloves out of his pocket and snapped them on while his partner moved in close to begin a thorough search. When ordered to strip naked and drop his clothes in a tray, Mercer obeyed. His gaze was ice-cold defiance, but his movements were relaxed.

'Squat,' growled one of the guards. 'Cough. Cough once more. Stand up. Get dressed. Leave your shoes in the tray. Take a pair of slippers, and once you're done, walk over to the wall and wait for your mugshot.'

Mercer followed all the commands; he knew

it was pointless to try to escape or talk his way out of this. He could only hope that somewhere in the CIA building, a phone would ring, and his arrest would reach CIA Director Dean Jameson. The Harvard man had high-level connections and was an expert in damage control. His thoughts then shifted to Connor. *Are you the one playing games? Are you working with Schelling, or does General Liu have something on you?*

For now, Mercer placed Jeff Connor at the top of his list of suspects. Despite having his back through multiple black operations, Connor was too ambitious and strategic. That always worried Mercer; ladder climbers in Langley were distrustful in his eyes. *Once you swap your weapon for a pen, your loyalty ends,* he would often tell his closest friends.

After a few more minutes of paperwork, FBI Agent Hayes signed the last form, then he and his team left.

The MDC guards reapplied the handcuffs before leading Mercer deeper into the facility. He counted nine solid steel doors that had to be unlocked and locked before the next one could be opened. Surveillance cameras monitored his movements from every corner, while the screams and shouts of inmates grew louder with each step.

A door opened up on his right. It was stark

and freshly painted, with a metal table and bench both bolted to the floor. There was a camera in the corner, which appeared to be disconnected. A pitcher of water and a stack of cardboard cups sat on the table. The guards worked quickly, their motions fluid and emotionless.

A guard gestured to the bench. 'Sit.'

Mercer complied. His handcuffs were rearranged. He was now cuffed to a small chain link welded to the metal table. It allowed him just enough movement to drink water and sign documents, nothing more. A guard poured a cup of water, placed it in front of Mercer, and then left without a word. Mercer quickly gulped down the water and tried to reach the pitcher to refill his cup, but the chain pulled tight. A thin smile swept across his face. *Trapped like an animal*, he thought as he eyed the camera. *Whoever is behind this, they're the real masterminds, the puppet masters who control both sides of government and all the agencies. It can only be the Black Orchestra:* Schelling, General Liu, Decker, Liang, the list was growing. Then there was Connor. *What's his position?* Mercer grappled with the question.

His thoughts were interrupted when a guard returned with a phone. The guard placed it on the table within reach and plugged it into the wall socket. 'You've got one call,' he said before stepping back to watch.

Mercer hesitated for a moment, his instincts screaming to call Jameson, but he needed answers. He dialed Connor's phone instead. The phone rang, each tone dragging out longer than the last. No answer. His heart rate quickened as he tried Connor's mobile. More ringing. Nothing. He hung up, his eyes narrowing as he stared at the phone. Connor's silence was the only answer he needed.

Paris, France

Kenneth Decker shook hands with the Director of the Coordination Nationale du Renseignement et de la Lutte Contre le Terrorisme (CNRLT) and then looked for the exit. The meeting lasted most of the day and involved intricate discussions on comparative legal frameworks for signals intelligence collection, methodologies for inter-agency data fusion, protocols for classified information exchange under multilateral agreements, and analytical approaches to identifying low-probability, high-impact geopolitical events.

Those were topics in which Decker was well-versed, and despite his enthusiasm, this wasn't his true reason for scheduling the meeting. He wanted to use his time with the Director to forge a closer friendship, and over time, he would build on this trust. Decker would lever-age the Director's ambitions for closer EU-U.S. cooperation, enticing him with promises of exclusive intelligence and enhanced access to the ODNI's analytic exchange program, all of which could advance the Director's career while serving U.S. interests. It was a simple matter of planting a seed in yet another fertile mind.

With the last of the pleasantries exchanged, Decker stifled a yawn and took his overcoat from Jason, his assistant and the newest member of staff, then made his way to the parking lot. *Different types of discussions, same goals*, he thought as he slipped on his overcoat. These talks had drained his energy and his patience, but he knew the real work was about to begin. With his mind on the night ahead, Decker walked with purpose while Jason followed close behind. The fresh graduate was rambling about key points of the meetings and potential opportunities. Decker was sick of listening to the young man. The sight of his crimson and white-striped Harvard tie, which he wore to official meetings, pissed Decker off.

He crossed the street while scanning the traffic. The wind had picked up, and despite running his fingers through his thinning black hair, he couldn't keep it in place. *How many more meetings will it take before I earn my place in the White House? That is the real power,* he thought.

Years earlier, when Decker switched from the CIA to the Office of the DNI, he reminded himself to play the long game, the game of a strategic thinker: cunning and decisive. Today was part of that cover story, one that would ensure his presence in Paris was credible, albeit impromptu. A rare but defensible requirement.

Decker had a tough time moving through the Army before being picked up by the CIA, and then to the ODNI. Each step of the way, he watched men and women around him move into handpicked positions, most of which appeared to him to be custom-built for their qualifications, not their experience. This infuriated Decker. Apart from his few years at West Point, where he completed his officer training, he had no other network of influence. Not like his peers at the ODNI or CIA, who came through Ivy League schools and had been groomed from a young age in the most prestigious private academies. They attended elite summer programs in international relations and participated in exclusive internships with influential political figures. All the while, they built connections that paved their way to powerful positions in government and intelligence, often benefiting from preferential treatment during recruitment.

Decker couldn't help but scorn those who flaunted their alumni ties at functions, a constant reminder of their privileged backgrounds. They had been handed opportunities on a silver platter, while he had to fight for every inch, knowing that their elite connections often overshadowed merit when it came to recruitment in the intelligence community. *They flaunted those ties like badges of honor, reminders of their privileged pasts.* And right now, one was close on his heels.

He clenched his jaw as Jason kept yapping on about data standardization and aggregation; the young assistant's enthusiasm was nauseating.

'Enough, Jason. Listen, take the rest of the evening off. The time is your own. Tomorrow, you can head back to D.C.; I no longer require your involvement. Ensure you have a report on my desk upon my return.'

Without waiting for a reply, Decker left Jason and climbed into his limousine, leaving him to find his own way back to the hotel.

The trip back to his hotel on Rue Boissy d'Anglas took little more than thirty minutes. Decker knew he would be followed. There was no need to turn around and check; he could almost feel every move the DGSE surveillance officers made as his limo weaved its way through the late evening traffic. Following his instructions, his driver stopped at the intersection leading to Rue Boissy d'Anglas and blocked the traffic for a few moments. Decker jumped out of the car, quickly crossed the street, and got into a waiting black panel van. Then his limo driver proceeded down Rue du Faubourg Saint-Honoré toward the center of Paris. Decker waited a moment in the back of the van, peering through the blacked-out rear windows until he spotted the surveillance team. 'Good lads, chase that rabbit,' he muttered to himself.

The driver of the van started the engine and weaved his way through the streets until they reached a safe house in Mairie de Clichy. The premises had a ground-level parking garage secured with an iron gate, allowing the van to be parked off the street and ensuring a high level of privacy. Decker climbed out of the back of the van and entered a corridor through an internal door. An old marble staircase led him up to the apartment. Once inside, he made a quick sweep of the rooms and found everything to his liking.

The hit team had followed their instructions well, he noted. The four men assembled in the kitchen said nothing to Decker when he finally entered and took a seat at the table. Apart from the cigarette smoke and the strong smell of spices, there wasn't anything unusual.

Decker nodded at the huge pot of garlic, liver, and tripe curry simmering on the stovetop.

The pungent smell wafted around the apartment, out into the common area, and into the street. The pot of curry was used to mask the smell of the chemical mixture sitting on the kitchen table.

The men had spent most of the day putting the finishing touches on the IED, which was set inside a large plastic box. A soldering iron sat next to a cell phone, its back cover removed to expose the internal components, including the vibration motor. Decker leaned over the table to inspect the device. The vibration in a cell phone is caused by a small DC motor with an offset weight that spins to make the phone vibrate when it rings.

Decker put on a pair of surgical gloves and picked up the phone's circuit board. He checked the contacts that supplied power to the vibration motor with a multimeter and traced the circuit to identify the positive and negative terminals. Small-gauge wires had been soldered onto the vibration motor's power contacts. These wires carried the signal from the vibration circuit to the IEDs triggering mechanism.

Next, Decker checked the low-current relay, which would serve as the bridge between the phone and the detonator circuit. A battery pack was already taped in place inside the plastic box. Next to it, a block of C-4 plastic explosive was secured, with an M112 detonator carefully embedded into the material and connected to the relay. Decker checked the wires running from this battery to the detonator circuit and those connected to the relay. He made some adjustments and disconnected the battery from the actual detonator to ensure the system was perfectly calibrated. He inserted a SIM card into the cell phone, then punched in the number and hit the dial button. Within a couple of seconds, the connection was made, and the phone sent power to the vibration motor. The modified circuit directed power to the relay, closing the circuit that would connect the battery pack to the detonator and trigger the explosion.

'Okay, good. Insulate these exposed wires to prevent accidental shorts, and take it down to the van,' Decker instructed.

While one man sat down in front of the IED and carefully got to work with electrical tape and heat shrink tubing, Decker opened a map of the local urban plan of Saint-Denis, which had been obtained from the municipal council. Various pieces of information were added to the map by the hit team, such as the route their car was to take, one-way streets, areas of high traffic congestion, and the parking locations of secondary getaway vehicles.

Decker asked Pierre, the leader of the gang, a huge Frenchman with a thick beard, to describe in detail each stage of the operation. Then he questioned each of them about their roles to ensure complete understanding, even probing them on potential failures to check if they had covered all aspects. He traced the roads on the map with his finger as they spoke, looking for flaws in their plan. Once he was satisfied, he instructed the men to destroy the map and handed out new SIM cards.

'How much do you expect the bank to be holding?' asked Pierre.

Decker smiled briefly at the innocence of the question. 'There is no money to be made from this. Tonight, you are not breaking into the bank vault in Saint-Denis. Instead, the job is to kill a traitor, a piece of vermin. The payment is the same: five million euros.'

'What the fuck do you mean? We have prepared for this. It was all arranged. We have the tools for the job and cars in place. You can't change the plan,' argued Pierre. The rest of the men rose from their seats, their anger evident to Decker.

'Relax, guys. This job is much better for you. It is less risky. It was for operational security reasons that we discussed and planned for blowing the vault. If the police compromised our communication channels, they would be expecting us in the north of the city, at that bank. Instead, we will be here, in Mairie de Clichy, doing our thing.'

'You do not trust us, American?' asked Pierre.

'I trust you. I'll tell you why. Over the years, I got to know the Chinese man, Liang, very well. He is a complete professional. When he told me that this French team is highly regarded in the underworld, I was convinced you were the right team for the job. This is how I operate: I was brought into France because I know how the intelligence agencies work, and I know they are positioned all over the country. I needed to cause a distraction. It would be impossible for them not to know what is going down in Paris tonight.

'Their expertise in penetrating signal intelligence is second to none. Now we have them distracted. I apologize, but this was a necessary step. Liang has provided a secondary plan. Now, if you all agree, we will go over this operation with the same attention to detail as the bank job.'

Decker knew how to handle professionals. Honesty was the easiest and quickest method.

Pierre looked at his men and nodded for them to take their seats, then turned back to Decker. 'Six million euros. An extra million; otherwise, we step aside. Think of it as a change of contract charge.'

Decker couldn't care less about an extra million; it wasn't his money, and he had anticipated such an increase. 'Agreed.'

Over the next couple of hours, the men were brought up to speed on the plan that Liang had created. Decker drilled every detail into their heads until they could explain it verbatim without looking at the map he had brought. Decker leaned back in the chair, rubbed his face, then stretched his back. The thought of traveling down to the south of France and swimming in the Mediterranean was very appealing right now. He couldn't wait to be done with this operation. *One more nail in Mercer's coffin,* he thought before he turned his attention back to the IED.

'The explosive strength of this bomb is exactly what we need for this operation. Once our target is eliminated, I need this bomb placed inside the café before you drive off. Use this cell phone number to set it off.' Decker read out a number, and Pierre punched it into his phone.

It took about five minutes for everyone to suit up and decontaminate the area. Forensic gloves were snapped on, hair nets applied, boiler suits pulled on, and respirators covered their mouths to prevent breath and saliva traces. A fresh change of clothes had been placed into a sports bag. Duct tape was then applied on the cuffs of their sleeves and ankles to prevent any DNA from falling from their skin. Then they sprayed themselves and the area with a chemical that destroyed any biological evidence. Finally, they collected their drink glasses, ashtrays, and the waste from the bin before leaving the apartment.

Downstairs, the men climbed into their van, stolen earlier and fitted with fake license plates. With each man in his correct position, weapons were removed from under a seat and handed to the two shooters. Each man had his own job: the driver, a man riding shotgun providing directions, two gunmen, each armed with Heckler & Koch assault rifles and 9mm handguns, and the last man, Pierre, in charge of the IED. Decker was to ride behind the van on a black Yamaha motorcycle, his earpiece and mic connected at all times to the driver. Decker would follow at a distance and check for surveillance. He would also serve as a backup in case the shooters failed. Armed with a well-maintained Glock 17, Decker would deliver the kill shot if required.

'Okay, let's roll,' Decker ordered into the mic as the Yamaha roared to life.

Within minutes of driving through the narrow streets of Mairie de Clichy, the van stopped at Rue Henri Barbusse to await instructions while Decker got into position on Rue Georges Soret.

The two shooters in the back of the van used their time to take another look at the photograph—supplied by Decker—of their target, the man they had to assassinate. He was of average height, lean and good-looking, with dark graying hair neatly combed back. There was no name given to their target. All that mattered was the six million euros, split between the five of them. Identities at that price didn't matter. This was a payday beyond anything they could ever imagine. For years, they were recruited by various gangs involved in turf wars to eliminate rivals, from pimps to drug dealers, even politicians, prosecutors, and homicide detectives. No one was off-limits. Tonight's job was fairly simple: a soft target, unarmed, with no bodyguards.

Within a couple of hours, the van would be burned out in a back street. Stolen cars, which had been stashed in various locations, would be their secondary getaway vehicles. These would also be burned once they reached their next location. Finally, each man would take another vehicle, fitted with legal license plates and registered in fake names. These would be used to cross either into Belgium, the north of France, or travel east toward Germany.

With limited street lighting making its way into the back of the van, the two gunmen used a small flashlight to illuminate a photograph. Other snapshots that Liang had provided showed the exact location where the van was to pull up. This position was directly next to a zebra crossing adjacent to the café entrance. The men would then slide the door open and jump out, masked, with weapons at the high ready.

The next photo showed a small two-inch step from the sidewalk up into the café, a minor detail but critical, as Liang wanted to ensure the men didn't trip in their haste to shoot their target. Liang also highlighted on the photograph which side the café door was hinged on, what kind of handle was fitted, and the type of floor covering in the café.

The first man out of the van would open the door of the café, allowing the shooter to enter with both hands firmly on his weapon. Pierre would follow closely behind with the IED, placing it on the bar before retreating to the van.

The last photograph showed the layout of the café and the usual table where their target sat every evening. This spot was where the shooter would aim his weapon once he navigated around the tables. Once the target was eliminated, the shooter would backtrack out of the café and get into the van, quickly followed by the first man. Once the van door was slid shut, the driver would take off. Pierre would then dial the cell phone to trigger the IED, blowing the café to pieces.

When the two men were done looking at the photographs, they discarded them into a waste bag and rechecked their weapons. They were both armed with Heckler & Koch G36C rifles, the shorter 9-inch barrel suited for close-quarter battles. The German-made assault rifles were fitted with thirty-round magazines, and 9mm Glock 17s attached to their thigh holsters provided them with a reliable backup weapon.

The photograph of Rousseau that the two shooters had been studying was taken only a few nights before, at the exact same café where he was about to be slaughtered. Liang had surveilled the place on a quick trip from his current operation in Marseille, in the south of France. Once Liang provided his plan to Decker on how the assassination should happen, Decker advised him to plan a dummy bank robbery. Between the two of them, they kept the freelance assassins in the dark until the last moment.

Decker steered his Yamaha into Rue George Soret and leaned the bike onto its kickstand, then stepped onto the sidewalk. They now had the café covered on both sides. He kept his helmet on and lifted his visor, then whispered into the mic, 'I am in position; wait for my signal.' Decker needed to get eyes on Rousseau before giving the order for the kill team to move in.

The van driver on Rue Henri Barbusse kept his eyes on the side mirrors, watching for signs of a police operation. His hands were sweaty, and he could feel his heart rate rising. No matter how many jobs he had been on, the adrenaline rush was always the same. He craved this feeling. The thrill of being on a kill team was better than any drug. He adjusted his earpiece and increased the volume slightly. The device was so clear that he could make out Decker's breathing and his footsteps as he walked toward the café. *Any moment now*, he thought.

'Confirmed. Target is in position; engage,' commanded Decker.

'Copy that. Engaging.' He turned his head and peered into the darkness of the van, catching Pierre staring back at him. Both men nodded. Pierre picked up the IED and held it on his lap. He pressed a recessed button on the side of the device and carefully removed a small safety pin, engaging the internal arming mechanism. He was ready.

The driver moved out into traffic and flipped his right-turn blinker on at the roundabout; the van was less than forty meters from the café as it crept slowly toward the zebra crossing.

Decker's gaze darted between the café entrance and the van's progress, every second stretching into an eternity as he anticipated the brutal killing of the DGSE agent, who for too long was a cancer to his plans.

Pierre motioned for the first gunman to get into position at the sliding door of the van, ready to burst out. Then, for a brief second, a ringtone broke the silence within the van.

A blinding white light, followed by a deafening boom that shook the ground. The windows in the surrounding streets shattered, cars rolled into each other, and pedestrians ducked and ran for their lives as rubble fell from the buildings. Fire raged through the van, the flames fanning out, scorching the brickwork of the surrounding structures.

Pierre and his men were blown to bits. Seconds later, the heat from the inferno ignited the ammunition inside the van, causing a cook-off that resulted in rounds discharging within the vehicle.

Decker couldn't believe his eyes. As the van exploded, his mind reeled. He felt a pang of shock, not for the loss of his men, but for the sheer chaos unraveling his meticulously laid plans. The Black Orchestra didn't tolerate failure. He had to act quickly. The motorbike helmet protected his head from falling debris. Static in his earpiece continued to drown out the screams of the injured, and he was temporarily blinded.

He quickly turned and made his way toward the Yamaha. His knees felt shaky, and by rapidly blinking his eyes, he tried to force his vision back to normal. He could almost taste the burned skin of human flesh. Thoughts of black operations he conducted in Africa flooded back into his mind. He removed the bike key from his jacket and went to swing his leg over the back of the seat when he was grabbed and roughly dragged into a waiting SUV. His body convulsed, then went limp when a Taser was fired into the back of his neck, and everything went dark.

Through the dust and shouts from inside the café, Rousseau appeared at the entrance. He stepped out onto the sidewalk, crossed the street, and got into a waiting car.

'That was a close shave,' Rousseau said to the man sitting in the passenger seat.

Philippe Dubois glanced at the shaken Rousseau in the rearview mirror. He had spent days meticulously surveilling the gang's safe house, planting wiretaps, and listening in on every conversation. When he overheard Decker providing the phone number to Pierre, the number that would later trigger the bomb, he took a huge risk. Using this crucial piece of information, Dubois had been able to set off the IED prematurely, turning Decker's own plan against him.

Dubois couldn't help but feel a surge of satisfaction. This wasn't the first time he had outmaneuvered them; his quick thinking had also thwarted their plans in Geneva. Twice now, he had turned Liang's meticulous

schemes to ashes, a fact that would surely infu-
riate Decker.

'You will live,' he remarked with a smile.
'Let's drive; it's going to be a long night.'

EIGHTEEN
New York—USA

Mercer awoke to the sound of two guards knocking sharply on the cell door. They ordered him to step toward the door, turn around, and place his hands behind his back. The guards entered, quickly cuffed him, then, without a word, marched him through a maze of sterile corridors to a waiting area. A light flickered on above a door leading to an interview room before the guards opened it and ushered Mercer inside. The guards sat Mercer on a cold steel bench, locking his cuffs to the table before quickly leaving and slamming the door shut.

The room was cold and eerily silent; the only sound was the faint hum of the overhead lights. Mercer noted the complete absence of noise—nothing from the corridors, adjacent holding cells, or interview rooms. *Whoever is coming has cleared the entire wing of the facility.* A smile tugged at the corner of his mouth. *It's the CIA. They haven't abandoned me.*

The first thing Mercer planned to do upon his release was head to the CIA safe house in Queens for a long, hot shower, followed by a massive ribeye at one of the nearby steakhouses. Afterward, he would take the trip up to Langley to ensure his name was cleared of any lingering issues before resuming his mission to dismantle the Black Orchestra. At Langley, he planned to sit down with Jeff Connor and Dean Jameson, the CIA Director. *Have the meeting and put everything on the table, so there are no misunderstandings about Connor's loyalty,* he thought. Mercer began to feel optimistic despite the humiliation of being arrested and detained at the Metropolitan Detention Center.

Time dragged on. Mercer estimated it had been about four hours since he'd been awakened. As he sat there shivering and tense, his foot tapping on the floor, he compiled a list of questions that needed answers. The men he needed to shake down and how much violence would be necessary to get those answers.

His mind shifted to the IEDs being manufactured in Turkey by Movsar, the Chechen warlord. Mercer made a mental note to contact him and ensure everything was on track and that the delivery date would be met. Then his thoughts turned to Alexander West, the young AI entrepreneur who had been selling secrets to the rogue Chinese faction on behalf of the Black Orchestra. *Slicing his neck in a packed hall might have been unnecessary. I'll need that investigation wiped,* Mercer thought.

Even the killing of Hendrik in Jakarta for Georg Schelling, despite being carried out on foreign soil, could still be used against him. Like a forensic investigator, Mercer carefully considered the details he'd need to bury to ensure Langley could cover his tracks.

Suddenly, he heard the faint squeak of footsteps in the corridor outside. They were getting closer. His thoughts halted as he turned and stared at the heavy metal door.

The door creaked open, and a well-dressed man ducked his head inside. After spotting Mercer cuffed securely to the table, the visitor stepped inside with an air of confidence. He closed the door, scanned the room for recording equipment, then took a seat. The man placed his black leather briefcase on the polished floor and pulled a cigar case from his pocket.

'Good morning, Mr. Mercer. I assume you know who I am. Mind if I smoke?' he asked.

'It's illegal to smoke in a federal facility. You could get a fine or be asked to leave,' Mercer remarked with hostility.

Senator Sanderson smiled, placing the cigar

between his teeth. After lighting it, he blew gently on the glowing tip before turning his attention to Mercer.

'You're probably wondering why I'm here instead of your agency colleagues,' Sanderson remarked. 'It's quite simple. I'm here to present you with an opportunity. Take a good look, Danny. This is a signed document from Mike Gelder, the Deputy Attorney General, and this one's from the man who put you here, Special Agent John Bayes. It's a request for your release, due to key evidence being deemed inadmissible because of procedural errors and conflicting witness testimonies. All I need to do is make one call, submit this paperwork, and you're walking out of here within the hour. The choice is yours.'

Sanderson slid the documents across the table. 'We do this my way, or you can wait for your buddies at Langley to put their reputation on the line and admit fault. But tell me, Danny, which one of your bosses will step up to protect you? The CIA admitting one of their own killed a U.S. citizen, on U.S. soil, and a federal agent, no less! You know how Langley operates. I don't need to spell it out for you.'

Mercer knew Sanderson was right. *There was no way in hell the CIA would take the fall for this. Even my contacts in the White House would disown me.* The writing on the wall was clear to

Mercer. Whatever orders the FBI was following that night in Washington, D.C., when the two agents tried to kill me, would've been long covered up. And those involved would have destroyed all the files. Everything is against me. The political ramifications of this shitstorm are unimaginable, he thought. Mercer leaned back in his chair and stared into Sanderson's eyes, taking a moment to weigh this information.

'I know you're a smart man, Danny. You know how this works. The FBI doesn't reverse decisions like this every day. What you're holding isn't just pieces of paper—it's a testament to the power and reach of the people I represent. The same people who can either make your life a living hell or set you free. The choice is yours. Make no mistake about that.'

Something didn't feel right. Mercer barely glanced at the letters, but he knew he wasn't in a position to negotiate.

'Time's running out, Danny. You can take the chance I'm offering or wait for a rescue that's never coming. But consider carefully: if you refuse, these letters go right back into my briefcase, and you'll face the full force of the law. Think about that before you decide.'

Mercer's eyes narrowed. He understood the gravity of the situation but sensed the manipulation. Accepting Sanderson's terms would make him indebted to the Black Orchestra.

'I'm not interested in your games, Sanderson. What's this really about? There's no way your Black Orchestra would risk exposing themselves like this. So why are you here instead of an attorney?'

Sanderson leaned forward, mindful of the chain attached to Mercer's cuffs. 'It's about your British friend, Edward Hobbs. I know how close you were. His murder in London caught us by surprise. I mean, there's a connection we didn't foresee.'

Mercer's expression darkened. The mention of Hobbs' death hit him hard. For a moment, the room seemed to tilt. The words echoed in his skull, like the delayed shock of a bullet hitting bone. Hobbs. Dead. The man had pulled him out of more than one impossible situation. Now, he was gone, and the reminder brought a wave of guilt. He bit down hard on the inside of his cheek, tasting blood, using the pain to block out the rising anger.

Sanderson remained calm, but Mercer noticed the manipulation in his eyes—a slight twitch of satisfaction at the power the news held over him. He couldn't let him win. Not like this.

He clenched his fists, trying to control his rage. 'Tell me, then, who was behind his murder? Hobbs had no interest in the Black Orchestra. The man was a desk jockey, a low-level civil servant.' Mercer lied. He knew how vital Hobbs had been in exposing the men behind the Black Orchestra and the Chinese faction seeking to overthrow the Chinese Communist Party.

Sanderson smiled briefly at Mercer's lie. 'Hobbs, ex-SAS Tier One operator, later recruited by MI6. Your British friend was much more than a paper shuffler. He was working on your behalf, tracking the Chinese faction of the Black Orchestra. More specifically, he was following a trail that started in the jungles of Mong La, leading to the murder of a Chinese official, Mr. Gao, and straight to the covert power struggle within the CCP. A struggle involving General Liu and his secret ties to the Black Orchestra.

'Hobbs was smart—too smart. Once he uncovered Gao's assassination, he connected the dots between General Liu, Schelling, and the Black Orchestra. Gao wasn't just some bureaucrat; he was a reformer who exposed corruption and had deep ties to Western intelligence, including MI6. His murder was a message, a move to consolidate power within the CCP and silence anyone who knew too much.'

Sanderson paused, letting his words soak in. He took a puff of his cigar, studying Mercer as he pieced the information together. Sanderson wanted to pull Liang's name deeper into the conversation.

Blowing smoke into the air, Sanderson spoke again. 'The Chinese faction feared Hobbs would become a whistleblower. General Liu then sent word to his enforcer, Liang, who was operating between Nice and Marseille. Hobbs was the biggest threat, one that had to be eliminated immediately. Liang decided to take him out to protect the network. As the saying goes, *A single thread can unravel the strongest fabric.*'

Mercer scrutinized Sanderson, trying to gauge the man's intentions. 'So, Liang killed Hobbs to cover up their power play. And you expect me to believe the Black Orchestra knew nothing about it? Bullshit. You're here because you need something from me. So, what the hell do you want?'

Sanderson waved a hand dismissively. 'Look, Danny, I'm telling you this because you deserve to know why your friend is dead. You helped us with our Jakarta issue, and honestly, I don't want any blowback from you or anyone else gunning for revenge. I'm here to be upfront, for you and whoever else you work with. We can get you out of here.

'Like I said, Liang acted without the Black Orchestra's approval, which means he doesn't fear us. If he keeps cutting down whoever gets in his way, he'll expose us all. I'm giving it to you straight, Danny. If you deal with Liang and let go of any personal vendetta against the Black

Orchestra, the FBI will drop everything. We'll make sure your name disappears from any FBI investigations on U.S. soil. And remember, this isn't about loyalty or patriotism anymore. It's about your future. Right now, I'm the only one standing between you and a prison cell. Hell, you might even find a way to flip the tables on the FBI regarding their attempt to kill you. But that only happens if you're out there, not stuck behind bars.'

Mercer glanced at the door, then down at his wrists, red and swollen from the cuffs. *Langley's damage control group appears significantly weaker compared to the Black Orchestra's influence. How much pull do these men really have? If Sanderson's playing both sides, who else is pulling strings behind the curtain?* As Mercer considered the agencies they'd penetrated, the lies Sanderson had spun, and what Liang's death would mean for the Senator, one thing was clear: he had to get out of the Metropolitan Detention Center, secure his freedom, and contact Jameson. *The CIA Director needs to provide real insurance for me against these traitors.*

Mercer mentally compiled a list of actions before turning back to Sanderson and giving a curt nod. His decision was made.

Sanderson smiled awkwardly, gathered his things, and stood to leave. 'I'll go ahead and get this paperwork sorted. Here are your copies.'

He laid the papers in front of Mercer, then paused to check his cell phone.

He flicked open a message and sat down, his eyes scanning the words on the screen. 'Shit. Another one.'

'What is it?' Mercer asked.

'An assassination in Paris. A DGSE agent, François Rousseau, was killed last night. The café he was in was blown up.' Sanderson glanced up at Mercer. 'A friend of yours, I guess.'

Mercer froze for a moment, in shock. 'Tell me, was it Liang?' he finally asked.

Sanderson scrolled down, reading the rest of the message from Georg Schelling. 'Liang,' he confirmed, keeping his expression impassive, though beneath the surface, satisfaction simmered. Now Mercer had two powerful reasons to take Liang out, and Sanderson needed that. The Senator's real concern, however, lay far from geopolitics or the fate of the Black Orchestra. It was the logistics company, Sternenlicht Versand, poised to resume operations once again in Marseille. A legal business agreement between him and Charles Clark that would funnel a steady flow of cash into one of his shell companies. With Liang gone, Marseille's ports would open up again, and the shipping empire would be free to expand.

But he couldn't reveal that, yet.

Sanderson leaned back, crossing his arms. 'As I said, Danny, Liang doesn't fear anyone. He'll take out anyone who threatens his plans. And believe me, his vision goes beyond simple espionage or technical gains. The drugs he's pushing into European ports. They're not just about money. Liang and the faction he represents have something far more insidious in mind. They're playing the long game. Flooding Europe with cheap narcotics will weaken entire communities, eroding stability from the inside. It's warfare, Danny. Economic, social, and generational warfare. The drugs are a weapon. His real target? Europe's future, the same way it's happening in the U.S.'

Mercer could feel the muscles in his jaw tightening. 'Go and get that fucking paperwork sorted, Sanderson,' Mercer barked. His mind was already racing. He knew there were others out there who Liang could target. Mercer needed to be free, armed, and ready to hunt. Once out, he would deal with things his way.

Washington, D.C.—USA

General Liu had arrived at Georg Schelling's large, stately mansion on the banks of the Potomac River and was greeted by a courteous staff member who led him into the library.

Schelling unscrewed the lid of a bottle of whiskey and poured a measure into two glasses. He passed one to Liu, then reclined in his chair, his attention split between Liu and the documents on the table. 'Liu, I understand your ambition and the resources you need to fuel your plan, but I'm still unclear on one point. How do you propose to carry out a coup in a country as vast and complex as China? The Party's grip on power is formidable. The military alone is massive, spread out across the country's many regions and cities. Even with your influence, how do you plan to organize and implement something on this scale without drawing attention early?'

Liu set his drink on the table. He had anticipated this question. The answer was one he had been refining for years. 'It starts from within,' he began. 'The political system in China may seem monolithic, but it's a system built on personal loyalty, ambition, and opportunism. These are weaknesses I've been exploiting for years. The Central Committee of the Communist Party and the various governing bodies are not as united as they appear.'

Liu sat forward, preparing to break down the complexities for Schelling. 'The Chinese Communist Party is at the top of this structure. It's not just a political party; it's the backbone of the entire system, controlling every aspect of the state and society. The Party's leadership is concentrated in a few bodies: the Politburo, the Politburo Standing Committee (PSC), and the Central Committee. The Central Committee, which consists of about two hundred full members, is responsible for making key decisions about party policies and leadership. However, true power rests with the Politburo—twenty-five members—and even more so, the Politburo Standing Committee, which is the highest decision-making body, made up of just seven members, all handpicked by Secretary-General Li Yucheng.'

He paused, assessing the look of interest on Schelling's face before continuing. 'Li Yucheng has solidified his control through the 20th Party Congress, filling the PSC with his loyalists. But loyalty in the Party is a fragile thing. Many of the military leaders I've worked with—men with power over entire military districts—are dissatisfied with Li's centralization of authority. He's sidelined the Central Military Commission, which oversees the People's Liberation Army. The CMC is technically the top military body, and while it is chaired by Li, I have connections within the ranks, generals who feel marginalized and see an opportunity to restore the military's autonomy.'

Schelling raised an eyebrow. 'You're telling me the military is ready to turn on Li?'

Liu gave a small, cold smile. 'Not all of them, but enough. You see, the military is loyal to the Party, not just Li. Many generals and officers remember the days before his reign, when power was more distributed. They've witnessed how key leaders were removed under the guise of anti-corruption campaigns, but in reality, it was about consolidating power at the top. The CCP Central Commission for Discipline Inspection, which is responsible for investigating corruption, is one of the most feared bodies in China. It answers directly to Li. But here's the thing. When the time comes, the fear of being purged might drive some of these military officials to act. They'll back me because they want to survive. I've been quietly building a coalition within the ranks of the PLA, especially in regions critical to military logistics and operations.'

Liu pulled out a handkerchief and wiped a bead of sweat from his brow. 'The Central Military Commission may officially oversee the PLA, but in reality, many of the district commanders, the men in charge of the vast military regions like Beijing, Nanjing, and Guangzhou, are more concerned with their own power and security. These are the men I've been working with. When the time is right, they'll mobilize their forces, but not as a unified coup. It'll be a strategic takeover, city by city, district by district.'

Schelling picked up the remote control, lowered the room's temperature with a click, and turned back to Liu. 'That explains the military. But what about the civilian government? The National People's Congress, the Standing Committee, the Chinese People's Political Consultative Conference. These are powerful institutions,' he said.

Liu chuckled softly. 'The NPC and Standing Committee appear powerful, but they're ceremonial bodies, rubber-stamping whatever the Party wants. They don't control the military, and they don't have any real power without the Party's backing. What concerns me more are the CCP Party Secretaries, the men who control the provinces and municipalities. They wield real power at the local level, overseeing the military garrisons in their regions, and enforcing party discipline. If they remain loyal to Li, they could disrupt my plans.'

He paused, his face hardening. 'But loyalty, Georg, is bought. Many of these Party Secretaries are opportunists. With enough leverage, such as financial incentives and promises of power after the coup, or even threats, I can ensure their cooperation. They've seen how rivals like Hu Jiancheng and other prominent figures were removed from power. They know they could be next. I'll exploit their fear, their ambition, and their desire for survival. And let's not forget, I have the support of Olivier Girard, my contact in the French DGSE. His intelligence on key Party figures, who's vulnerable, who's plotting, who's hiding their own corruption, gives me a distinct advantage.'

Schelling thought for a moment. 'Fear and greed...classic motivators. But even with the military and Party officials, Li has built his power on loyalty. How do you ensure the PLA won't fracture during the coup?'

Liu replied quickly. 'Because I've made it clear to them, the Party isn't the enemy. Li Yucheng is. When we move, it will be swift, targeted, and controlled. Li's men in the Politburo and the Politburo Standing Committee will be neutralized. I've already identified key figures like Zhao Lian, the new head of the National People's Congress, and Wang Jinhai, Li's propaganda chief. They are obstacles, yes, but they are not untouchable. We'll make them disappear quietly, one by one, replaced by men loyal to the new regime.'

He paused, giving Schelling time to process the plan. 'This isn't just a coup, Georg. It's a surgical operation. Li has built his empire on fear and control, but once those at the top see that he's vulnerable, they'll fall in line. The Politburo will collapse into infighting, and by the time they realize what's happening, it'll be too late. The Party will still stand, but it will be my party.'

Schelling nodded, impressed by the precision of Liu's vision. But one final matter lingered. 'And the military? Once Li is gone, what's stopping the PLA from turning on you?'

'I'll be the one holding the purse strings. The Central Military Commission might claim to control the army, but money talks. With revenue from the narcotics trade and the support of the Black Orchestra, I'll make sure every officer, every general, is compensated. Their loyalty will be bought and paid for, just like everything else in China.' Liu said.

Schelling raised his glass in a toast, eyes gleaming with approval. 'To your success, General. May your takeover be swift, and may we both profit from the downfall of Li Yucheng.'

Liu held up his glass, but Schelling noticed something was bothering him. He reached for the humidor on his desk. The glass lid opened with a soft click, revealing a tray of cigars. Schelling selected two cigars and used a cutter to snip the foot off one before handing it to Liu. 'What's worrying you, Liu? I've been negotiating for decades, and I can tell when something needs smoothing out. So, let's hear it.'

Liu lit the cigar and puffed slowly, choosing his next words carefully. There was much to discuss, but he wasn't ready to show his hand. He found it difficult to negotiate with fewer chips on the table than Schelling. The American clearly had more cards up his sleeve than Liu could ever imagine. The fortunes he could promise from the takeover of the Chinese government might interest Schelling, but Liu knew that power was what they were both after.

'As you know, Mr. Schelling, there's much to be gained once I have full control of China. You'll be in a powerful position, well let's say, my top powerbroker from the West. That's not in dispute. Over the years, we've worked well together, cultivating alliances and swiftly eliminating any threats.'

Liu took another puff of his cigar before speaking. 'There's something that could work in all our favor. With the way technology is evolving—and considering how much we've all invested—I've come across some interesting changes at the CIA. They're using AI for targeting and interrogation now. This is really something. What do you know about this?'

The question carried more significance than mere curiosity. The Langley AI breakthrough was a golden egg for the agency, replacing years of surveillance and intelligence work on U.S. threats.

Schelling's mind raced, trying to piece together how Liu had managed to learn about something so closely guarded. He turned to the window, buying himself a moment. Despite their relationship, the CIA's AI research was still off-limits to the Chinese. But if he wanted to keep Liu onside, he needed to bring him closer, even if only a step. He offered Mercer as a pawn.

'What the CIA has developed over the years is nothing short of revolutionary. As far as I know, only one person fully understands how it's being used, because he's the end user of the intelligence products. That man is Danny Mercer.'

Liu's eyebrows lifted. 'Mercer again. His name seems to surface everywhere. Tell me more, Georg.'

Schelling smoothed nonexistent wrinkles from his shirt, buying more time. 'Well, my sources in the FBI said Mercer holds documents which explain how the CIA utilizes AI to identify and eliminate perceived threats. The AI targeting system was designed for counterterrorism, but got repurposed for domestic operations. This angered some people, who then came to us.'

He paused, gauging Liu's reaction before continuing. 'The program, which functioned with minimal human oversight, was effective at identifying legitimate threats. However, it was not infallible. The system occasionally produced false positives, categorizing U.S. dissidents, including activists and whistleblowers, as foreign-led operatives due to biased or incomplete data. The CIA knew about the errors but saw them as acceptable collateral, prioritizing results over ethics. Instead of fixing the errors, the CIA pursued and neutralized anyone flagged by the system, trusting it was accurate enough. They made those decisions coldly, trusting the AI to deliver actionable intel, no matter the human cost.'

Schelling lowered his voice. 'Mercer's job was to eliminate those threats. He passed intel to contractors and hit teams to ensure anyone seen as a threat to American interests was neutralized. No questions asked.'

Liu let the silence hang, taking a slow sip of whiskey. Setting the glass down, he glanced at the door, a flicker of annoyance crossing his face. 'And this AI system…just operates on its own?'

Schelling crossed his legs and set his cigar in the ashtray. 'The CIA's AI targeting system was built to neutralize foreign threats. But the FBI uncovered it had been repurposed for domestic use, hidden under the guise of national security. Fueled by surveillance data and behavioral algorithms, the system determined threat levels autonomously. But flawed inputs led to countless misidentifications.'

Liu's brow furrowed slightly. Schelling picked up on it and explained further.

'The FBI tried to catch Mercer with

documents linked to the AI system, but one of their agents was shot dead. The AI didn't just mark foreign operatives but also American citizens—journalists, whistleblowers, activists critical of government overreach. Misidentified as threats, they were added to the elimination list. This violated the CIA's mandate, which prohibits domestic law enforcement.'

Liu set his glass down. 'And the FBI...?'

'Investigating these suspicious deaths, they suspected the CIA was using national security as a cover for these eliminations, sparking direct conflict between the two agencies.' Schelling answered.

He picked up his cigar again, holding it between two fingers as he continued. 'The documents also revealed that the AI's algorithms, built on surveillance, communications data, and behavioral analysis, became increasingly independent in determining threats. Its self-learning protocols compounded errors, flagging domestic dissidents as foreign operatives. With little human oversight, these miscalculations went unchecked, leading to wrongful deaths that drew the FBI's attention. The documents also exposed an AI-enhanced interrogation system created to replace traditional questioning methods. This AI, designed to read real-time physiological and psychological responses, adapted its techniques to maximize pressure, extracting information more efficiently than human interrogators.'

'But...?' Liu raised an eyebrow, sensing where it was headed.

'But the system quickly overstepped ethical boundaries.' Schelling confirmed. 'Its techniques pushed interrogation limits, often causing extreme psychological distress. Flawed algorithms led to its use on Americans misidentified as terrorists, resulting in wrongful detentions and coercive methods used against innocent people.'

'Quite remarkable. I would guess that the collateral damage, as you mentioned, would be worth the loss. Having access to such technology would be beneficial to us.'

Schelling gave a slight nod. 'I've wondered if my name, or any of my associates, is on that list. You can see why gaining access is imperative. My attempts to bring Mercer into the fold haven't yielded much. The man is headstrong, maybe even unhinged.'

'How so?' Liu asked.

'After surviving the FBI's attempt on his life, Mercer kept moving with a mission on U.S. soil, unfazed. One of the AI's high-priority targets was Alexander West, a young entrepreneur on the verge of an AI breakthrough. West had ties to Chinese groups, you know the kind. The CIA's AI flagged him as a national security threat because it predicted he was likely to share sensitive tech with those foreign groups. And unlike past mistakes, West represented a legitimate threat. His links to China, paired with his tech advancements, made him a serious threat to U.S. intelligence. Mercer eliminated West, following the AI's directive, but it was more than that. Maybe it was personal; after killing that FBI agent, he had to maintain his own integrity.'

'Interesting. We need access to that system. If you're on the list, then so am I. Surely there's some leverage to bring Mercer over to our side. If money won't do it, what about family?' Liu asked.

'He might bend for money. He already did a job for me in Indonesia; could've been to get inside knowledge of our organization, or maybe it was about money. He's hard to read. Honestly, I don't know if I trust him. As for family, he's a ghost. There's no relatives on record. Changed his name multiple times. Apart from a house in Maine, which he rarely visits. Mercer just vanishes and then shows up out of nowhere.'

Liu's jaw tightened; another flash of irritation crossed his face. 'A man like that, free to roam, while you're still chasing shadows? This is not a game, Georg. When was the last time you spoke to him? And where do you think he is now?' Liu asked.

'A few days ago, in here. As I said, he just

turned up. Now, he's being held in the Metropolitan Detention Center in Brooklyn.'

Liu's eyes lit up. 'He's in prison?'

'Detention, for now. The CIA lawyers will get him out soon, unless the media get hold of the incriminating details surrounding their involvement in the FBI agent's death. I pulled strings with the FBI to arrest him when he landed back in the States. Then I sent Senator Rick Sanderson to offer him a way out. The deal is simple: he works for me.'

'So, it's an open and shut case. What's the problem? Have him bring the AI architecture here and get us that list of names. We'll replicate the system ourselves,' Liu said.

'Easier said than done. We're moving fast because Mercer won't be held for long. The legal complications and agency politics make it tricky. The FBI is stuck between exposing the CIA's overreach and admitting West's elimination might've been justified. Mercer's role in executing West has become a key point in the FBI's investigation, worsening the tensions between them and the CIA. It's only a matter of time before the President decides what to do with Mercer. In my opinion, Mercer will be a free man within hours. That's why Sanderson reached him first.'

Liu clenched his fist under the table, his patience thinning. 'And what if Sanderson fails?

Can you afford to lose Mercer? He is becoming more vital by the minute.'

Schelling took a slow breath, choosing his words carefully. 'Look, Liu, if Sanderson gets Mercer out, the CIA and the President won't push the FBI for answers. They'll sweep the whole thing under the rug.'

Liu raised an eyebrow, waiting for more.

'It's all about plausible deniability. If Mercer walks free, they'll deny any knowledge of the AI program, and the operations. No hearings, no investigations. The CIA doesn't want the public or Congress poking around, asking questions about domestic hit lists or rogue algorithms. If Mercer disappears quietly, so does the whole mess.'

Schelling puffed on his cigar again, letting the smoke curl lazily toward the ceiling. 'The FBI already botched their chance. One of their agents is dead, and they've got no solid case to stand on. By letting Mercer slip through their fingers, they're practically giving the CIA a gift, an out. And you know how it works in Washington. Once they get their man back, the agency will claim they had no involvement, no knowledge of his actions. Everything buried in bureaucratic fog.'

Liu leaned forward, intrigued. 'So, they'll just abandon the case? Which means Mercer can continue to hunt down those on the list.'

'To answer your first point, yes. They can't afford to dig into it. If the CIA acknowledges why the FBI arrested Mercer, then they have to admit the existence of the AI system. And that's something the agency can't allow. National security, legal coverups, all of it; if Sanderson pulls this off, the President will quietly order everyone to back off, and the FBI will have to close the investigation. No more questions, no more leaks.'

Schelling hesitated, then pressed on. 'Mercer might be free to act, but not without restrictions. And that's where Sanderson becomes key. He's got a signed document from Mercer and the FBI, plus a secret recording of their meeting. That should be enough to convince Mercer to work with us. Sanderson never moves without an exit plan. Leverage on Mercer is part of it.'

He is bullshitting me, taking my power for granted. What do I need him for if he can't handle major problems? Liu's thoughts went into overdrive as he crushed his cigar into the ashtray with a sudden, forceful twist. His voice simmered with barely contained anger. 'What are the odds Mercer actually comes to us and delivers what we need? I'm not here for games, Georg. I need that AI information before anything about me reaches the CCP. You should've been on top of this, not sitting here gorging on ribeye and red wine. You need to access that list—scrub our names from every CIA record and bury this whole mess. But, instead, you're relying on a signed piece of paper. You just admitted Mercer could vanish at any moment. So, tell me, can you fix this? Or are you wasting my time and putting us at risk?'

Schelling's face flushed red as his pulse quickened. No one had ever dared speak to him like this, and it stoked his anger. *Twice now, in this very room. First Mercer, with a gun aimed at my head. And now this unstable General. Something has derailed him,* Schelling thought.

He needed to lay down the law. 'Liu, over the years, I have always delivered. I have granted you access to our top research, our universities, and companies' boards. This situation with Langley and their AI program is one more area in which my years of back-room negotiations can unearth what you request. Please do not question my abilities. And I'll say this only once.'

Schelling stabbed the table with his finger. 'This is not China. You have no authority here. You do not come into my house, in my country, and raise your voice to me. Do you understand?'

Schelling spoke with fury, spit flying from his mouth and landing on the table. He could feel his neck swelling against his Italian shirt collar.

He stood and walked over to the large window, taking a moment to collect himself.

Liu remained perfectly still, his face impassive. His eyes tracked Schelling's every movement, but there was no rush in his body language. There was no need for him to react to this tantrum. Schelling's authority had already crumbled; it was only a matter of time before the man realized it.

'Georg, I am sorry for overstepping my mark,' Liu said. 'I apologize. We have done great things together. We have accomplished so much.' He slipped his hand inside his jacket, resting it calmly on the weapon hidden there. Liu's apology was a courtesy, nothing more. Schelling had outlived his usefulness, and Liu knew the risks of keeping him around. There was no room for sentiment in this business.

'My insistence on meeting you face to face today was not simply to discuss matters related to American interests. As you know, my business affairs in Mong La in Shan State, Myanmar, relate to methamphetamine production, which in turn finances a great deal of my plans. What I have been finding out from Zhang Wei, my right-hand man within the Ministry of State Security, is worrying.

Schelling kept his back turned, his jaw tightening as he listened. Liu's calm tone only heightened his unease. He was losing control of the conversation.

'Zhang Wei has been doing a lot of work on technical espionage and cyber intelligence. Over the past few weeks, he has had numerous meetings with Sanderson, John McCarthy, plus a few other...interesting men.'

Schelling's heart pounded in his chest. 'And?'

'For myself, I am dealing with two problems. The first one is the United Wa State Army in Mong La. It has been brought to my attention that this ethnic armed group is being funded by a private donor. Who might that be?'

Schelling turned from the window, glaring at Liu. He thought of the payments made from one of his shell companies *This is dangerous territory.*

Liu continued. 'Now I have found out your friend Charles Clark was using his company, Sternenlicht Versand, to undermine my operations. Liang Guang is putting a stop to that once and for all. Clark is lucky I still have use for him.'

'Charles Clark is a fine gentleman, I assure you. These allegations you are making of him are no more than slander. All men who work under me were vetted by myself; each one brings unique qualities to our business affairs. You have lost all sense of reality; you seriously need to calm down.' Schelling moved over to the liquor cabinet, his hand trembling slightly as he fixed the drinks. His mind raced as he thought of his connections with the United Wa State Army. *How can this all be traced back to me?*

Schelling poured the whiskey into the fresh glasses, the tremble in his hand causing some to spill. He missed the faint sound of metal scraping against metal.

Liu's voice remained steady. 'Clark is being managed. That is one rabbit we will put back in the box. Although it still leaves me with one major problem. Insubordination.'

Schelling froze. 'Insubordination?' The word cut through the air like a blade, an accusation, a slur against him. He turned to Liu, his eyes burning with fury, fresh glasses of whiskey gripped tightly in his hands. When he locked eyes onto Liu's, his jaw dropped.

Liu stood slowly. 'It was a great plan, Georg. I must say the Black Orchestra is a highly intelligent and well-organized group. But you've been playing both sides of the field, haven't you? In the event my coup fails, you can take over the meth production in Mong La, using the Wa army you've been secretly funding. Furthermore, you can claim, through your connections in the American agencies, that our dealings were simply to gather intelligence, highlighting failures in both the CIA and FBI. You had meetings with Jeff Connor, Mercer's boss, and William Baxter, the FBI's Counterterrorism Division Director. Georg, you are—how can I say this?—the Epstein of the intelligence world. And as such, your time has run out as others have filled your shoes.'

Schelling shook his head vigorously. He could feel walls closing in. He was caught, but perhaps, just maybe, he could talk his way out. 'Listen to me Liu. Please lower your weapon. You don't understand. I mean, we can do so much together. Let me explain...'

Liu squeezed the trigger. The round struck Schelling in the stomach, knocking the air from his lungs. The whiskey glasses crashed to the floor as Schelling fell to his knees, blood soaking into his expensive Italian suit.

Liu took a step forward, calm, deliberate. He aimed the 9mm at Schelling's chest and emptied the rest of the magazine into him.

'Long live the king,' Liu said sarcastically as he unscrewed the silencer from his pistol and slipped it into his jacket pocket. Liu stared at Schelling's lifeless body. The man had once been an asset, a necessary ally, but now he was a liability. His influence had dwindled, and worse, his loose ties to the law made him a threat. Liu couldn't risk being exposed by someone who no longer had control over his own fate. Cutting ties was no longer a choice—it was a necessity.

NINETEEN
Washington, D.C.—USA

Mercer marched into the conference room on the third floor of the New Headquarters Building, located in the West Wing. Known internally as the Analysis Hub, the room was part of the Directorate of Analysis. Director Dean Jameson and Jeff Connor had chosen it for its shielded walls, designed to resist electronic eavesdropping. The two men arrived early, exchanging small talk as they waited for Mercer. Both men felt guilty. Their failure to help Mercer after his arrest at JFK still weighed heavily on them.

They rose quickly, extending their hands to greet Mercer.

'Thanks for bailing me out, you lazy bastards,' Mercer growled, brushing past them and ignoring the outstretched hands.

He began pacing as they took their seats. Mercer pulled a crumpled piece of paper from his pocket and tossed it on the table. 'My release was organized by Senator Rick Sanderson. The same Senator working openly for the Black Orchestra, who seems to have more influence than the CIA.'

Connor picked up the paper and smoothed it flat.

'We were doing everything we could, Mercer. Approval was a matter of time. I apologize for the delay in getting a judge to sign the paperwork. It's not unusual for legal procedures like this to drag on. You know how government bureaucracy works.' Jameson said.

Mercer waved a hand dismissively and walked to the table, which was laden with freshly prepared sandwiches, coffee, and water. 'When did you know I was coming to D.C.?'

'Well, you called this morning. A couple of hours ago,' Connor replied.

'Long enough to have sandwiches ready. I sat in detention in Brooklyn for hours, and not one of you got in touch.'

'We get it, Mercer. What's done is done. You're out, and Faulkner's making sure your name is cleared at his level. The man's on a warpath. We already got blasted by him last night for not acting quicker. I think he is looking to replace me as the new Director; either that or he's got something under his skin. I let him rant, as you know, as when he blows off steam and settles down, he can make good decisions. He'll be with us shortly,' Jameson said.

Mercer grabbed a few sandwiches and took a seat at the head of the table. Twelve seats circled the large, featureless table, no whiteboards, no electrical sockets, no ports. A windowless room for off-the-record discussions. He was a free man, the sandwiches were good, the coffee hot. Mercer knew there was no point in sulking.

Just then, the door cracked open, and an aide peeked in before stepping back. Seconds later, Gregory Faulkner entered, nodded at Mercer, and took the seat beside Jameson.

'Good to see you out, Danny. Now, back to business.' Faulkner wasn't in the mood to discuss the FBI arrest of his top man or the difficult call he had with the Vice President. He opened a manila folder and slid out an envelope.

'As luck would have it, Danny, the VP had more pressing matters than to listen to me explain why one of our CIA blue badgers was arrested for the murder of an FBI agent. You could call it friendly fire, a communication failure, or jurisdictional overlap. Take your pick. The VP was satisfied this is all yesterday's news.'

Mercer gave a thumbs-up and continued eating.

Faulkner looked down at the envelope and

pulled out a confidential document, marked *Top Secret*. 'My discussion with the VP shifted to an urgent development with China. A request, actually. Not really our problem, but something we can assist with, and it'll score us some diplomatic points with our friends in Asia. This open invitation also lets us put our boots on the throats of an international criminal organization, and, of course, gather intelligence. After all, we're not here to play peacekeepers.'

'This is the real reason we've been summoned to this wing.' Connor remarked.

Faulkner ignored the comment and scanned the document, his lips moving as he read in silence. 'Right, this is a request for direct action from Beijing,' Faulkner said, shifting his gaze to Connor to gauge his reaction.

Connor raised an eyebrow. 'What kind of action?'

'China is asking that certain men within their government, more specifically, rogue factions, be *handled discreetly*. The wording's vague, but I'm interpreting it as tacit approval to...clean things up. Quietly.'

Mercer set his sandwich down and wiped his hands on a napkin. 'And by, *clean things up*, you mean...' He raised a finger to his head and mimed pulling a trigger.

Faulkner rolled his eyes but couldn't suppress a slight smile. 'Pursue your leads. Take action where necessary. The expectation is that we don't create a spectacle that would escalate tensions with Beijing or draw attention to their internal issues. It's an informal green light to proceed, with certain restraints.'

'So, I guess we're talking about General Liu, Liang, and his support staff, but we avoid any direct blowback that could strain U.S.-China relations?' Mercer asked as he poured himself a coffee.

'Removing any bad actors against the CCP would be seen as an internal matter by Beijing, not something that would impact official diplomatic channels. So yes, if the Chinese are desperate to keep this quiet, they'll be more concerned with silencing any leaks than retaliating.' Faulkner read over the document once more before passing it to Jameson.

Connor looked at Mercer. 'The Chinese need this handled as much as we do. They wouldn't have reached out if they didn't think we could manage the situation discreetly. We proceed carefully, take out Liu and Liang, and then close up shop.'

Faulkner phrased his next question carefully. 'What's your take on this, Connor? You seem very comfortable with how things are playing out.'

'I trust our team can handle it. We've been through worse, Faulkner. We stick to Liu and

Liang, and we keep this quiet. That's what matters.'

Faulkner didn't respond immediately. He looked at Jameson, who was reading the document, then back at Connor. Something still wasn't right.

As the conversation unfolded, Faulkner's mind drifted back to that unsettling meeting in Silver Spring, Maryland. It felt like weeks ago, but the image of the white sedan parked on Bonifant Street still lingered. Two men, watching. Waiting. Connor had brushed it off, and no reports of a suspected surveillance operation had been filed, despite Connor's years of operational experience. But something in Faulkner's gut unsettled him as he watched Jameson causally flick through the paperwork.

Why didn't I investigate that?

He glanced at Connor, seated across the table, as calm and composed as ever. But Faulkner couldn't shake the feeling that they'd been watched, surveilled by the Black Orchestra, or, worse, their own agency, under the watchful eye of Jameson. *Had we already been compromised back then?* Faulkner knew the Black Orchestra was everywhere, infiltrating the deepest corners of the intelligence world and searching for potential additions to their group. Pulling strings, manipulating alliances.

The fact that Connor had so easily dismissed

those men gnawed at Faulkner. *What if this whole time, they had been keeping tabs on both of us? The Black Orchestra had already shown they could eliminate obstacles with ease, much like the CIA. Is it only a matter of time before someone decides to eliminate me, too?*

Faulkner stood; he needed to rethink this in private. He gathered his folder, signaling an end to the meeting. As far as he was concerned, the sooner Mercer got back on the streets and thinned out the herd, the better. He needed a warrior, someone who would strike without fear of political fallout.

'Okay, that's enough. Let's wrap this up. Mercer, thank you for attending.' Faulkner walked over to Mercer and offered his hand. 'I'll pass a message to the Vice President that we'll consider the Chinese request and resolve matters with the utmost discretion. Gentlemen.'

Faulkner left the room as quickly as he had entered. The brief silence was broken by the sound of Mercer putting on his jacket, grabbing a couple of sandwiches for the road, and picking up his cell phone from the table.

'Looks like I have my orders from the top,' Mercer said.

'Yes. Friends in high places. But remember, Danny: discretion. Faulkner had his meeting with the VP, but I had my own sit down with our President. He gave a promise to the Chinese President that we would take out any threats to them on our soil. This will lay groundwork for future business dealings with them on trade issues.

'The two leaders want to stabilize relationships with China instead of playing political games. We need to be mindful of our role on the world stage; the Europeans are watching us, as are Russia and Iran. Our President wants to get out of the Cold War mentality and forge a new path. However, our office in Berlin has reported heightened activity at the Russian, French, British, and Iranian embassies due to leaked threats against high-profile individuals. Our AI system has identified unusual suspects for, well, you know what I mean. Let's be frank, Danny; we need to be smooth and professional. As I said: discretion, slow and calculated.' Jameson stepped forward and shook Mercer's hand. Jameson sighed slightly when Mercer turned for the door as he caught sight of him smiling.

'Discretion. Yes, sir,' Mercer repeated as he walked out of the office.

Marseille—France

The salty Mediterranean breeze slipped through the narrow alleys of Marseille, carrying with it the muted sounds of the port, a blend of waves crashing against the harbor and the distant hum of cargo ships. Mercer sat perched on the balcony, overlooking the bustling streets below. He'd spent the past week here, running surveillance with his old friend Halford, an operation that had grown increasingly tense. Down below, Marseille was a city of contrasts, its charm underscored by an ever-present current of danger.

Halford leaned against the doorframe of their rented apartment, a cigarette dangling from his lips. 'How much longer do you reckon we've got before he snaps?' he asked.

'Another hour, maybe two at most,' Mercer replied, his gaze still fixed on the street.

The muffled screams drifted out from the other room. Halford stepped out onto the balcony and closed the door tightly behind him. 'Decker's one tough son of a bitch,' he muttered. 'You said you worked with him in Tangier, back when he was in Special Forces.'

'I did,' Mercer said. 'Last time we spoke was at Le Faubourg Café in Paris, a few weeks back. He was with Connor, my boss, along with Nathan Harrow and William Baxter, both FBI.'

Halford took a seat on the balcony, his brow furrowed. 'Big players. So, why would Decker get his hands dirty trying to kill Rousseau?'

'That's what we want to find out,' Mercer

said. 'Dubois was one step ahead, though. When I found out Hobbs was killed, I knew the Black Orchestra had powerful friends. What's worrying is if they've infiltrated our intel agencies. Have they gotten inside yours? MI6 is good, but they still couldn't protect Hobbs.'

Halford flicked the cigarette over the balcony, watching the ash spiral toward the street below. 'There's only one way to find out. And Decker's the key. Break him, and we pull the rest of the pieces together.'

Mercer nodded, already thinking ahead. Decker, once a trusted colleague, was now in the hands of the DGSE. The French kidnapped him off the street, whisking him away after François Rousseau was removed from the café in Paris—just moments before the explosion that the Black Orchestra assumed had killed him. It was a well-played move that allowed the French intelligence service to manipulate the Black Orchestra into believing their attack had succeeded. Now, with Decker in their hands, they finally had the chance to extract some answers.

Mercer rose from the balcony, stretching out the tension that had settled into his muscles after a week of sleepless nights. 'It's time,' he said. 'Let's pay Decker a visit and give Rousseau a break.'

The streets of Marseille were starting to fill with the early morning crowd. Mercer sat at a small café along the Quai du Port, his eyes scanning the people moving past, though his focus was elsewhere.

His phone buzzed in his pocket as he caught sight of Movsar on a motorbike weaving through the crowd. The bike slowed near Mercer, just long enough for Movsar to drop a set of keys on the table. Then he was gone, back into the traffic.

Mercer slid the keys across the table to Halford. 'Get to the garage in La Castellane and start prepping the explosives,' he said.

Halford nodded, pocketed the keys, and headed off toward his rental car parked nearby.

Mercer's cell phone buzzed again. He took a sip of his espresso, then picked up the phone and glanced at the message: *Decker sent the details about the next hit. Liang is taking the bait.*

The night had gone as planned. Worn down by hours of pressure, Decker had finally cracked under Mercer's interrogation techniques. He agreed to cooperate with the DGSE by sending a message to Liang's secure phone. Liang, still believing Rousseau was dead, thought the DGSE officer had been blown up along with the hit team overseen by Decker.

Now, Liang would prepare for the next stage in eliminating threats to their takeover of the European drug market, starting with Marseille.

The message from Decker to Liang was brief: *Philippe Dubois. There can be no mistakes. Handle this yourself, no outsiders.*

Mercer smiled to himself. Everything was falling into place. The tension from his arrest in New York and his doubts about Connor lingered, but he had made it clear to Jameson and Faulkner that this operation was his. No interference.

News of Georg Wilhelm Schelling's death had started circulating on U.S. networks. Commentators speculated wildly, but Mercer knew the truth. Security footage showed a man in his late fifties, Asian, black hair, trimmed mustache, entering and leaving Schelling's mansion near the Potomac and again at a service station on the way to New York.

General Liu, thinning out the herd, Mercer thought. He took another sip of his espresso, contemplating Liu's ruthless efficiency. *The General had drained Schelling of every advantage, like a parasite, then dispatched him in cold blood when he was no longer useful.*

Mercer turned his thoughts to Dubois. Just days ago, Dubois had dangled Rousseau in front of Liang and Decker's hit team in Mairie de Clichy. Now, Dubois was in the crosshairs.

Like Rousseau, he agreed to play bait, exposing himself to draw out Liang. He was relying on Mercer to act first. Mercer knew the pressure all too well.

He finished his espresso, tucked five euros under the cup, and made his way to Marseille Saint-Charles station to catch the train to Paris. As he moved through the back streets, Mercer kept a wary eye on his surroundings, ensuring he wasn't being tailed. He made a call to Pak Rizky Pratama in Jakarta. Pratama could get him a jet. Mercer quickly informed him that Schelling had been gunned down and that he was going after those responsible.

'That is terrible news, Mr. Hoffmann. If there is anything I can assist with, let me know. And I'd appreciate it if my name never came up in any investigation of his past,' Pratama said, using Mercer's alias.

'I'll make sure everything stays quiet,' Mercer replied, mixing truth with lies.

Pratama agreed to help. A Bombardier Global 8000 jet would be fueled and ready at Paris-Le Bourget Airport within a few hours.

Mercer thanked Pratama, ended the call, and checked the platform for his train. He bought a ticket in cash and quickly boarded the carriage.

•   •   •

Liang was both pissed and pleased with the recent developments. Decker's order to take control in Paris meant traveling back up from Marseille, enduring the heavy traffic. But the chance to kill Dubois, the man who foiled the Geneva job, was a welcome reward.

The job in Mairie de Clichy, where he had orchestrated the assassination of Rousseau, had been a disaster. His local French team botched the bombing, blowing themselves to pieces along with the café. Losing that team was an inconvenience, though replaceable. The Parisian criminal underworld had no shortage of men, but Liang was intent on solidifying his control. The important thing was that the DGSE was down one agent. *Rousseau won't be bothering us any longer,* he thought.

Liang changed lanes, taking the off-ramp for Paris. Traffic was building up as the sun dipped over the horizon. His thoughts shifted to the call from General Liu earlier that week. Liu had informed him that Schelling was eliminated, and that Sanderson would likely be the next in line to take over. The Senator had valuable contacts that Liu wanted to exploit, not least Senator John McCarthy, who Liu admitted to him, had more to offer. But Liang had no interest in building further alliances with Western powers. He was driven by revenge and control. Despite the change in the Black Orchestra leadership,

Liu's cold efficiency sent a shiver down Liang's spine. He'd never trusted Schelling or the others, and Schelling's death meant nothing to him. What unsettled him was Liu's audacity, a reminder of the General's true nature.

Liang never forgot that even he could be outsmarted and eliminated if he outlived his usefulness. Checking his rearview mirror, he made a ten-minute detour, looping through roundabouts and back streets before settling back on course toward the northwest of Paris. He knew it was time to prove his worthiness.

Marseille, France

Halford parked a block away from the lockup garage in La Castellane and approached on foot. The grimy concrete blocks of La Castellane stretched across the Marseille suburb, their weathered exteriors and laundry-filled balconies reminiscent of the toughest projects in the Bronx or South Chicago. On the ground floor, metal shutters covered the shop windows. A few lights glowed behind curtains, but most windows were dark. The walls bore layers of spray paint, graffiti tags in looping Arabic script overlapped with French slogans. A moped engine revved in the distance, then faded. Young lookouts perched on walls at the entrances to La

Castellane, scanning for police vehicles, formed the first line of defense for the drug networks that had turned the estate into their fortress.

He reached the garage and checked the garage shutter. The number plate matched his key ring. With a quick glance over his shoulder, Halford unlocked the shutter, slipped under it, and pulled it down behind him. The stale air hit him first: oil, rust, and the faint odor of diesel. He flipped on a small LED light, revealing the packages tucked under a tarp in the corner.

Halford pulled back the tarp, exposing the blocks of C-4 and other bomb-making equipment. The material was familiar: light gray, malleable, and deadly. He picked up a block, weighed it in his hand, and then set to work. He hadn't sourced the material himself and couldn't rely on a Chechen warlord, no matter his experience. Halford needed to run his own test. He pulled out a small plastic vial from his kit, an Explo-Test designed to verify the potency of the C-4. He cut into the block with a utility knife and sliced off a small sample. After checking the texture and consistency, he placed the piece on a steel surface and added a few drops from the reagent vial.

Halford watched closely as the liquid seeped into the C-4. Within seconds, the sample turned a deep blue, indicating the presence of RDX, the primary explosive component of C-4.

The color's intensity told him what he needed to know: high-grade material, potent and ready for use. Satisfied, he moved on to the next step.

He selected a detonation cord, a slim, flexible wire that would carry the explosive shock from the blasting cap to the C-4. For this operation, he chose a pressure switch as the trigger mechanism. Simple, reliable, and effective. He wired the pressure switch to the blasting cap, the critical link in the assembly. Next, he carefully inserted the blasting cap into the C-4. When the pressure switch was activated, it would trigger the blasting cap, setting off the C-4.

He paused, considering the placement. Vehicles? Sure. Shipping containers? Maybe. But his mind kept circling back to the docks, where a single well-placed device could cripple Clark's entire operation. The pressure switch would trigger with the slightest shift in weight, a container lifted by a crane, a car door opening, or a footstep on a ship's deck. The possibilities were endless, and so was the damage.

He repacked the explosives and detonators, methodically tucking everything into a duffel bag. There were ten blocks in total, and each one had a purpose. Some would stay in Marseille, ready to take out Clark's key assets. The rest would be shipped to the U.S., where Mercer had his own plans for the Black Orchestra.

Halford locked the garage behind him and

took a circuitous route back to his car, avoiding the youths lingering at the steps to the apartment buildings. The duffel bag was secure on his shoulder. Satisfied that he wasn't being followed, Halford reached his vehicle. He placed the duffel bag in the backseat, then slid into the driver's seat. With one last scan of his surroundings, he started the engine and drove off, heading to a nearby safe house where he would switch vehicles and wait for nightfall to make his move.

Paris—France

Liang eased the black Citroën to a stop a few blocks from Rue de la Villette. He cut the engine, letting the silence settle around him. In the distance, a car horn blared, but here, only muted conversations from a nearby café broke the peace. His first pass revealed little about Dubois's home, and it was too risky to attempt another. The narrow, one-way streets in this neighborhood had little traffic, and strangers like him would stand out.

He checked the message on his cell phone once again: *Dubois. Depart: DGSE HQ 18:00. Arrive: Rue de la Villette 18:10. Red Peugeot 508— License: BW-739-GP.*

Exiting the vehicle, Liang locked it with a

physical key, avoiding the telltale beep of an electronic lock. He pocketed the key, scanning his surroundings as he stepped into the street. A woman walking her dog gave him a quick glance before she dropped her eyes disapprovingly and continued along the street.

As he walked, Liang's eyes took in every detail without lingering. The old woman pulling her shopping trolley, the young couple kissing on a doorstep, the cat darting under a parked car. Each was noted and mentally filed away. He was trained to recognize patterns of life, to spot anything out of place, and nothing here suggested he was being watched or followed. The MSS had drilled into him the importance of observation without making it obvious. In Paris, as in Beijing, the art of surveillance was about blending in while seeing everything.

He took his time, walking past Dubois's building without slowing his pace. The rental was nondescript, a typical Parisian apartment with nothing to distinguish it from its neighbors. The curtains were open, and there was no movement inside, just as expected. Dubois was likely still at the DGSE headquarters or perhaps making his usual stop at the Monoprix grocery store. Liang kept moving, continuing down the street as if it were a normal evening stroll.

His thoughts turned to China, to the security and power he commanded there. Operating in

Europe left him exposed. To him, it was a continent rife with dangers, leaving him vulnerable to risks he wouldn't face at home. His mission here was progressing, but the sooner General Liu's plan unfolded, the better. Once the methamphetamines from Mong La flooded Europe, the continent would be gripped by a drug crisis that would strain law enforcement, destabilize economies, and cause social unrest. Governments would be weakened, distracted by internal pressures, unable to counter external threats effectively, and China's influence would quietly expand in the vacuum.

Liang's anger simmered. Cleaning up the Black Orchestra's recklessness wasn't his mission. *I'm not here to do their dirty work,* he thought, yet circumstances had pushed him into this role. His mind flashed back to Nice, where every detail had been meticulously planned, every move calculated. He had built a network there, a foundation for what was supposed to be a swift and precise operation. Now, it felt like he was constantly playing catch-up, dealing with problems that shouldn't have existed in the first place. The Black Orchestra's failures were a distraction, dragging him away from his true objectives.

Liang clenched his jaw, suppressing the frustration that threatened to surface. He needed to stay focused. The mission was too important to let emotions cloud his judgment. Europe was just a stepping stone, a means to an end. Soon, he would return to China, where his true power lay, and Europe would be left to crumble under the weight of its own decay.

At the corner, he paused to check his watch, the simple action concealing a quick glance back at the way he'd come. No one appeared to be following him. Satisfied, Liang crossed the street and entered a small bakery. The more he blended into the mundane, the less likely he would be remembered. He purchased a single baguette to eat during his stakeout. With the breadstick in hand, he walked a few blocks in the opposite direction before circling back, this time passing the building on the other side of the street.

His car was still where he'd left it, untouched and unnoticed. Liang retrieved it and drove a few blocks closer to Dubois's building, positioning the car for a swift escape. He made sure it was positioned for a quick exit, front-facing the direction he'd need to go. Again, he opted for a side street, avoiding the main thoroughfares that might have more traffic or surveillance cameras.

It was nearly 6:00 p.m. now. He'd watched the area for nearly an hour, and nothing had set off any alarms. Still, Liang knew better than to rush. He'd wait until well after nightfall, giving

Dubois time to settle in, maybe even to feel a false sense of security.

He adjusted his rearview mirror to keep an eye on the entrance to Rue de la Villette while he reviewed his plan. The MSS taught a methodical approach: careful, patient, precise. He wasn't in a hurry; rushing was how mistakes were made. When the time was right, he would make his move. The blade tucked into his coat wasn't just for the kill; it was for confirmation. Up close, he would ensure it was Dubois and not some decoy.

As the minutes ticked by, Liang sat quietly in his car, tearing pieces off the baguette and chewing methodically. Around him, the city continued its evening routines. He'd already scouted the route to the house on foot, noted the position of the streetlights, the placement of parked cars, the proximity of Metro stations, and the distance to the nearest police station. He gently removed the interior light bulb above his head, dropped down the visor to offer a little privacy, then checked his equipment: a suppressed 9mm pistol, house-breaking tools, a steel knife, and latex gloves, all within easy reach. Everything was prepared.

Darkness came slowly in the street, which was quiet save for the occasional pedestrian or car passing by. Suddenly, Liang's attention snapped to the lights of an approaching vehicle. The familiar red Peugeot 508 came into view, its headlights lighting up the narrow street as it rolled into Rue de la Villette. Liang's eyes narrowed, tracking the car's every movement.

The Peugeot slowed, its blinker flashing as it pulled up to the curb directly in front of Dubois's building. The engine idled for a moment, then cut off. Liang watched as the driver's side door opened and a man stepped out. Even in the fading light, Liang could see the unmistakable outline of Dubois, tall, athletic, with the confident stride of someone accustomed to control.

Dubois glanced around the street, his eyes briefly scanning the surroundings before he unlocked the garage door and headed back to his car. Liang remained still, his hand resting on the pistol grip.

He waited, watching as Dubois drove the car into the garage. The sound of the garage door closing echoed faintly, and then the street fell silent once more.

Liang took a deep breath, his mind sharpening as he prepared to move. The time for observation was over. Now, it was time to act.

'You took your time. Tell me you avoided eye contact with Liang,' Mercer said as Dubois entered the kitchen.

'It's important that I appear normal. He might have had someone tailing me from HQ, but no, I did as you said. I looked relaxed but slightly cautious,' Dubois replied as he set the Monoprix bag down on the table.

'Careful,' Mercer said as he moved some of his photographic equipment off the table.

Dubois didn't bother removing the food from the bag; it only served the purpose of maintaining a normal routine. 'How long has he been sitting there?'

'About forty-five minutes. He walked around for a bit, checking escape routes, one-way streets, and dead ends. I couldn't see any long guns, so no sniper shots. I expect him to come in here during the small hours of the morning to try and kill you,' Mercer said calmly.

Dubois thought for a moment as the reality hit him. 'Right. I'll need to update my team, let them know I'm in position, and have backup ready.'

'No comms,' Mercer snapped. 'We don't know what hardware he has. I don't want this job compromised. I'm so close I can see his chest rise and fall through this lens. We can't afford to let him slip away.'

Dubois stepped forward, peering into a small screen Mercer had placed on the kitchen table. A wire ran from the device along the floor and into a bedroom facing the street. Dubois traced the wire to a wardrobe where a camera was taped inside. Mercer had drilled a small pinhole through the wood and covered it with a cloth to deflect the light from the lens. Through this hole, Mercer had a view of Liang seated in his car. Despite the grainy picture, he could see the assassin eating his baguette and occasionally adjusting his mirrors to check the street behind him.

'Why don't you take a shot from here?' Dubois asked.

'Your field ops support unit didn't provide me with a rifle. Something about paperwork. Different here than in the States, I guess.'

Dubois's dismay turned to anger. 'My life is at risk, and our bosses are worried about regulations,' Dubois fumed.

Mercer ran his fingers over the touchscreen, adjusting the zoom and brightness. 'It's your bosses. Mine are fine with it.' Mercer squinted as the screen flared brightly. 'Each time a car passes in the street, their bloody headlights distort my view,' he said.

Mercer looked up at Dubois, who had just turned on the television. He could see the anger in his eyes. 'Don't worry, Philippe. I have a better strategy to deal with this swiftly than to wait for clearance.'

'Okay, what's your plan?'

'The best plan is to act on instinct,' Mercer replied as he stood up and grabbed a black jacket.

Mercer slipped out the rear exit and scaled the six-foot wall in one fluid motion. He landed quietly, tugging his baseball cap lower to avoid the street cameras.

The street was nearly empty, only a few cars drifting by. Distant footsteps echoed briefly before fading into silence.

Mercer jogged around the block, circling to the street where Liang's car waited. Rounding the corner, he spotted Liang's car, still in place.

Mercer stepped into a liquor store doorway, observing a man in a dark suit murmur into his phone as he passed. A dog barked from a balcony above, but by the time Mercer stepped out, the street was empty again.

He unzipped his jacket and crossed to the other side of the street. Staying in the car's blind spot, Mercer covered the final twenty meters and dashed behind the vehicle. Coming alongside the driver's side, he yanked the handle, swung the door open, and, with a swift thrust, buried his knife in Liang's neck, severing vital arteries.

Finally, he thought, his heart pounding.

Mercer rifled through Liang's jacket, searching for a wallet or weapon, when something caught his eye. The man wore glasses. Mercer hauled the man halfway out of the car, tilting his head into the streetlight.

Fuck. Even as the man choked on his own

blood, eyes dimming, Mercer realized he'd been tricked.

This isn't Liang!

Mercer ducked, scanning the street, and quickly swapped the knife for Dubois's 9mm Glock. With one knee on the sidewalk, he raised the Glock and took aim up the street.

The sharp crack of a gunshot echoed through the narrow Parisian street, the round shattering the window of the car Mercer had been kneeling beside. Glass rained down on him as he whipped around, catching sight of Liang already sprinting away. Mercer didn't hesitate. He vaulted over the hood of the car, feet pounding the pavement as he closed in on his target.

Liang reached the entrance of Place des Fêtes metro station, his eyes scanning for threats. He knew Mercer would be on his tail. Liang grabbed a passing woman by the arm, yanking her toward him. In a fluid motion, he spun her around, her body now a shield as he waited for Mercer to come into view. Liang walked backward slowly, his hand clamped over her mouth to muffle her screams. Once he spotted Mercer, he fired another shot. The round whizzed past Mercer's ear, slamming into a nearby lamppost.

'Stay back!' Liang snarled, tightening his grip on the hostage.

Mercer's whole body buzzed with adrenaline,

but his mind was clear. He couldn't take the shot without risking the woman's life. In the split second of hesitation, Liang shoved the woman aside, sending her stumbling to the ground, and bolted down the steps into the metro. Mercer was right on his heels, the chase driving them deeper underground.

The dimly lit stairwell amplified the sound of their footfalls, the echoes bouncing off the tiled walls. As they descended into the depths of Place des Fêtes, one of the deepest stations in the Paris metro, Liang knew he could disappear easily in the vast city once he reached the train network. His years of training had taught him how to blend in. All he needed was to lose Mercer, then change stations and alter his appearance to avoid the police.

He bumped his way past the pedestrians walking down the steps, then crashed through the crowd at the platform, shoving people aside with brutal force. A man stumbled and fell, his bag spilling across the floor, while a woman shrieked as she was pushed into the path of another commuter.

Mercer didn't pause. He leaped over the fallen passengers, his eyes locked on Liang's retreating figure. Just as he reached the platform, a train pulled in, the brakes screeching loudly, metal grinding against metal. He caught a glimpse of Liang glancing back, his face twisted in a mixture of anger and determination, before ducking inside one of the train cars, lowering himself from view.

Mercer scanned the platform, weighing his options. *Fuck*, he thought. *If I jump into the train, Liang will jump out and leave the station.* But something told him Liang wasn't looking to hang around here. Mercer waited, watching as people boarded the train, biding his time, preparing his next move. His eyes narrowed, and at the last second before the doors closed, he slipped inside the train.

The car was packed with passengers, the usual late-night crowd, their faces reflecting a weariness that came from the grind of the day. But beneath the surface, unease rippled through the crowd, the anger of those who had been manhandled evident in their loud discussions. Mercer ignored them all. He moved quickly, his Glock drawn but held low, hidden from sight as he navigated through the cramped aisles. His eyes fixed ahead, moving from face to face, searching for the telltale sign of his prey.

Suddenly, a series of shots rang out. The noise was deafening in the confined space, and the muzzle flashes were bright in the dimly lit car. A passenger to Mercer's right crumpled to the floor, blood splattering over those around him. Screams erupted, panic spreading like wildfire as people scrambled to get away.

Mercer ducked, using the passengers as cover as he edged closer to the source of the gunfire. His breath was steady, his grip on the Glock firm. He peered over a man's shoulder and spotted Liang at the far end of the carriage, a terrified little girl clutched to his chest. The assassin's wild eyes scanned the crowd for any sign of Mercer, but the madness worked to Mercer's advantage.

The train slowed near the next station—Pré-Saint-Gervais—the screech of brakes cutting through the silence. Mercer knew he had only seconds before Liang made his move. He steadied his aim, his heart hammering in his chest. The train doors hissed open, and in that instant, Mercer squeezed the trigger. The shot was perfect, catching Liang in the left shoulder just as he rose to flee.

Liang let out a strangled cry, his grip on the child loosening. The little girl fell to the floor, her cries piercing the air as she crawled away. Blood flowed freely from Liang's wound, but he didn't stop. With grim determination, he staggered off the train and onto the platform, leaving a trail of blood in his wake. Some passengers on the platform, oblivious to the threat to their own safety, began recording and live streaming on their cell phones.

Mercer pushed through the crowd, emerging onto the platform just in time to see Liang disappearing up the steps toward Boulevard Sérurier. Mercer pulled his cap down and sprinted past those on the platform.

The streets above were eerily quiet, the usual buzz of the city subdued in the late hour. Liang was losing strength, his pace slowing as he clutched at his bleeding shoulder, but he wasn't finished yet. He pulled his pistol up, ready to take out any threats around him.

Mercer saw his chance. 'Liang!' he shouted, his voice cutting through the night. Liang turned his head for just a second, and Mercer took the shot.

The first round went wide, smashing into the brick wall of a nearby building. But the second shot was true. It caught Liang in the back, the force of it driving him to his knees just outside a Franprix supermarket. He slumped forward, blood pooling around him, his breathing ragged.

Mercer approached cautiously, Glock raised, eyes scanning the surroundings for any signs of backup. But there was no one; Liang was alone. Mercer kicked the gun from Liang's hand and rolled him over with his foot. The assassin stared up at him, his eyes glazed with pain, but there was something else there, too. A strange sense of peace. A look that Mercer had seen in his own men over the years before they took their last breath.

'We meet at last,' Liang gasped, blood bubbling at the corners of his mouth.

Mercer looked down at him, his face betraying no emotion. He gave a single, slow nod, his eyes never leaving Liang's.

Liang's mouth moved as if to speak again, but no words came. Only a gurgling of blood could be heard. The bullet wound in his neck bled out the last of his life. In one swift motion, Mercer raised the Glock and fired a single shot into Liang's forehead. The assassin's body jerked once, then went still.

Mercer took a step back, his eyes sweeping the empty street. Despite the few locals who had taken cover, the danger was over, at least for now. He held his Glock close to his body, not yet ready to holster it. He glanced around one last time, ensuring no threats remained, before turning away. He headed around the corner, then quickened his pace, disappearing into the night.

TWENTY

Paris—France

Mercer stood in the kitchen of the safe house, drinking a glass of water. His breathing had steadied, though his body still buzzed with adrenaline from the shootout with Liang. He wiped sweat from his brow. This wasn't the first operation to go sideways, and it wouldn't be the last.

The door to the apartment creaked open as Rousseau slipped inside, a bag slung over his shoulder. He looked across the room at Mercer. 'You mentioned Paris-Le Bourget. I'll drive you. You'll be on that plane to the States in an hour.'

Mercer nodded, stripped, and stepped into the shower. The cold water barely registered as he scrubbed at his skin with D-Lead soap, methodically erasing every microscopic trace of gunpowder residue. Two minutes later, he stepped out and pulled clean clothes over his damp body.

As he dressed, he glanced at Rousseau stuffing gear into the bag. 'Who was the man in the car?' Mercer asked.

'A Chinese diplomatic staffer. Liang probably used him as bait,' Rousseau replied.

Mercer grimaced and peered through the curtain. The first police cars were arriving, blue and red lights flickering off the buildings. 'They'll lock down the street soon. We need to move.'

Dubois crossed the room, grabbed a burner phone from the table, and tossed it to Mercer. 'I'll take care of your clothes and wipe down this place,' he said, adjusting his earpiece as more intel came in. 'There's another issue. Bombs just went off in Marseille. Ports and highways are shutting down. French security services are on high alert. Getting you out won't be easy.'

Mercer pocketed the phone. 'We need to move, then,' he said, glancing at Rousseau.

They left the apartment and made their way to the garage. Rousseau eased the vehicle onto the street, driving toward the intersection where an undercover cop in a black leather jacket with an orange armband waved them down at the roadblock.

Rousseau flashed his credentials and exchanged a few words in French. The officer shone his flashlight at Mercer, then at the black sports bag in the back seat, before waving them through.

As they drove on, Rousseau's earpiece crackled. 'New update,' he said. 'A murder outside Pré-Saint-Gervais station. They're broadcasting your description across Paris.'

Mercer grunted as he processed the news. He reached for the radio and switched to the news. As they neared the airport, the news anchor's voice came through: explosions had rocked Marseille, with reports of a ship sinking in the harbor, a port office obliterated, and multiple cranes destroyed.

Mercer smiled. *Nice work, Halford.*

Rousseau looked at him but didn't say anything. After a moment, he asked, 'How does this end, Mercer?'

'When Liu's dead and buried, and the rest are locked up.'

'I mean for you. What are you going to do? You're pretty much compromised now.'

Mercer didn't answer, his focus fixed on the road ahead. 'Pull up here,' he said, motioning toward a hangar in the distance.

The lights of the Bombardier jet glowed ahead as the pilot completed final pre-flight checks. When the car stopped, Mercer unbuckled his seatbelt and stepped out.

He grabbed his bag from the backseat and shook Rousseau's hand. 'It's been a pleasure,

François. Do yourself a favor, cut back on those Gauloises and get some sun. And keep an eye on Olivier Girard at your consulate in Chengdu. He's flagged in our intel program. The sneaky bastard's been feeding Liu information.'

Rousseau's eyes narrowed. 'I'll look into it.'

Mercer turned and climbed the steps to the jet. Inside, he fastened his seatbelt as the engines powered up.

'Washington, D.C.,' he told the pilot, his mind already racing ahead to what awaited him in the States.

Langley, Virginia—USA

Dean Jameson sat at the head of a large table while the junior staff sat at the back of the conference room. His gaze rested on the scattered collection of reports, a cup of cold coffee beside him. Gregory Faulkner was seated to his right, his fingers clasped around a glass of whiskey, the third glass this evening. Jameson waited until everyone else filed in and took their seats.

'Sir, we need to be more aggressive.' Faulkner's voice had an edge, the kind that annoyed Jameson. Faulkner was enraged; within the room of about fifteen people, some were from the FBI and possibly the NSA. Something wasn't right. He ran his finger around his shirt collar, then removed a pen from his shirt pocket and placed it back again. 'Connor's late, and this whole operation is spinning out of your control. You can't afford to make decisions without internal discussions and agreements. There are many outstanding issues we need to resolve here in-house.'

'Settle down, Gregory. You are giving me a headache. Remember who is in charge here.'

'With respect, sir, your caution might have worked when we were dealing with the Soviets or Arabs, but times have changed. How we operate is more gray; the Bureau is black and white, and you know that's not how the intelligence game works. Let's discuss things in private.'

Jameson stared down Faulkner. The man was a shadow of his former self, yet here he was pushing the boss, his bullish behavior a constant reminder of his ambitions. Faulkner held Jameson's gaze; he made no secret of his thoughts. He believed himself better suited for Jameson's seat at the top. The subtle digs and the frustration with Jameson's methods were just part of it, and Jameson was about to detonate on him.

Before Jameson could unload, the door creaked open, and Jeff Connor entered.

Connor nodded and placed a number of files on the table. He removed his suit jacket and sat down. Faulkner avoided looking at Connor;

instead, he took a sip of whiskey and waited for Jameson to begin.

Connor looked around the room, taking in the regular faces. Then, a shot of panic coursed through his veins when he caught sight of the strangers seated amongst them. *Crisp suits, combed hair, briefcases, FBI bastards!*

Once everyone was finished fidgeting, Jameson addressed the room. 'Good evening, everyone. Thank you for assembling on such short notice. I've called this meeting to address a matter of utmost importance to our agency and national security. We are investigating a significant leak of classified information, and it's clear that this breach originated from within our intelligence agencies.

'Following my meeting at the White House, I requested an emergency meeting with the National Security Council. It has become evident that the repercussions of this leak extend beyond internal damage. It has compromised a foreign ally's military operations and strained key international relationships.

'Documents containing highly sensitive details have been shared with members of the media and, as such, have been posted on unauthorized platforms, forcing our ally to delay critical operations. The gravity of this situation cannot be overstated. The President expects decisive action, and so do I.'

'What documents are you referring to?' Connor asked.

Jameson held up his hand. 'Sorry, before we dig deeper, I forgot to introduce our partners from the Bureau. Gentlemen, this is Special Agent Mat Donovan, Agent Sam Sullivan, Nathan Harrow, and William Baxter.'

The men dressed in fine suits nodded to those around them. Baxter moved forward and shook Jeff Connor's hand. 'It's been a while since our meeting in Le Faubourg Café. Nice to see you again. Pity Decker couldn't join us here today. He is otherwise engaged, I believe.'

Connor's face drained quickly at the sound of Decker's name; he forced a smile before replying. 'Good to see you boys on another trip out of the office. Hopefully, you all can learn a thing or two.'

Jameson waited a moment until Baxter took his seat and for the testosterone levels to drop before continuing.

'Agent Sullivan has been running surveillance on the Black Orchestra and possible connections with our own agency and that of the Bureau. Sam's Area of Responsibility, or AOR, encompasses Silver Spring and its surrounds. It's a critical zone, just north of D.C., straddling the Maryland-District line. Sam's been the Bureau's eyes and ears there for the past eighteen months, monitoring any suspicious activity that might impact national security.' The CIA Director paused, his gaze sweeping across the room. He caught Faulkner briefly looking across the room at Connor before returning his attention to the whiskey.

'Now, I don't need to remind you of Silver Spring's strategic importance. It's not just some suburban outpost. We've got major hotels that are used by federal agencies there, including NOAA and the FDA. Plus, it's a stone's throw from our counterparts at Fort Meade. Sam's work in this AOR is crucial. He's the Bureau's frontline in detecting any potential threats or foreign intelligence activities in that sector. Remember, in our line of work, every neighborhood, every office park, every metro station could be a goldmine of intelligence or a hotbed of espionage. That's why the FBI send their best people, like Sam, to watch over these key areas. Silver Spring might not make the headlines, but in our world, it's prime real estate.'

Jameson then removed a number of photographs from a manila folder and passed one to Faulkner. 'That is a photograph taken a few weeks ago, which shows an Iranian conducting surveillance outside Walter Reed National Military Medical Center; the next one shows a woman sitting in McGinty's Irish bar. She is also a known foreign agent, Russian.' He passes another to Faulkner. 'These photos show a group of special forces guys from Fort Meade, being entertained by women, who are on the payroll of a man linked to a Chechnya warlord.'

Faulkner passed the photos around, and slowly, they made their way to William Baxter, who paid little attention to them. He simply passed them to Harrow, who then offloaded them to the junior CIA staffers at the back of the room.

Jameson looked over at Connor briefly before removing the last photo. He held it up and turned it around. 'This photo taken only a few days ago on Bonifant Street, downtown Silver Springs, shows Jeff Connor leaving a dive bar; Gregory Faulkner then exits the same venue shortly after.' Jameson passed another photograph to Faulkner, who refused to look at it. He sank his whiskey and slammed the glass on the table, then turned to Jameson and shook his finger in his face.

'You fool. What the hell do you think you are doing? So, what! Jeff and I had a meal together; there's nothing illegal about that. You're fucking paranoid, jumping at shadows. I always knew you haven't got the bottle for your position.' Faulkner pushed his chair back and rose to his feet while Connor remained silent. Then Connor's eyes shifted to Jameson, who pulled something from his shirt pocket.

Jameson tossed a USB flash drive onto the

table. 'A full recording of your meeting. The audio and video surveillance taken from inside the bar.'

FBI Agent Sam Sullivan stood up, his expression grim as he slid a folded document across the polished desk in front of Faulkner. 'Gregory Faulkner, this is an arrest warrant issued by the United States District Court. You're being charged under the Espionage Act for unauthorized disclosure of classified information.' Sullivan paused, his voice lowering slightly. 'I never thought I'd be serving one of these to a colleague from Langley. But here we are. You have the right to remain silent. Anything you say can and will be used against you in a court of law.' He then turned to Connor. 'Jeff Connor...'

Connor nodded and stood patiently, his eyes fixed on the CIA emblem on the wall behind Jameson. The others in the room sat in silence as more agents and police officers entered the conference room before leading the two men out in handcuffs. William Baxter winked at Jameson as he left, followed by the remaining FBI agents. Once the door closed, Jameson took a moment to gather his thoughts, then he told the junior CIA staffers to gather round.

'Today marks a somber moment for our agency. While the accused are entitled to due process, the evidence against them is substantial. If found guilty, they face the prospect of lengthy incarceration at the Federal Correctional Institution in Terre Haute, Indiana. I've gathered you here not only to inform but to serve as a stark reminder of the severe consequences for those who betray our nation's trust. It is essential that we build a new team, one that remains vigilant against the pitfalls of manipulation and unethical behavior.'

The fresh-faced officers, recent Ivy League graduates, sat upright and began murmuring among themselves about establishing HUMINT networks, implementing SIGINT collection strategies, and coordinating interagency task forces. Jameson noted their enthusiasm but knew they'd need seasoned guidance to tackle the complexities ahead.

His thoughts drifted to more pressing matters. The transcript of Decker's confession lay before him, and Mercer's audacious plan both reassured and unsettled him. Two critical tasks demanded his immediate attention: crafting a carefully worded press statement and confronting the most significant threat of his career. Jameson's jaw clenched as he contemplated the gravity of what lay ahead. Locating General Liu was paramount; however, the devastation Mercer could unleash was a double-edged sword, and impossible to fully control. Jameson knew that once set in motion, there would be no turning back.

Washington, D.C.—USA

The meeting room, located deep within the Embassy of the People's Republic of China, was an exemplar of counterintelligence engineering. Its triple-layered walls, embedded with copper mesh and radar-absorbing materials, effectively blocked electronic surveillance. Lined with sound-dampening reindeer moss, the room ensured natural acoustic isolation. The minimalist design was free of visible technology—no cameras, microphones, or digital devices to compromise security. Electromagnetic shielding prevented external signal penetration, and the structure featured multiple fail-safe entry points equipped with biometric and multi-factor authentication systems. A curved table made of non-reflective material dominated the center, its surface engineered to deter any covert listening devices. The air circulation was isolated, preventing sound leakage through the ventilation. Entry to this impenetrable space was strictly monitored, with a rigorous security protocol allowing only thoroughly vetted personnel access.

General Liu stood at the head of the table, facing four senior MSS officers seated across from him. These men were chosen specifically by Liu. Their unwavering loyalty to the CPP was second to the prospect of prosperity. While in the U.S., their children enrolled in schools, and the gated communities where they lived were safe and friendly. However, this was nothing compared to what could be. A high-ranking officer with links to the top men in the politburo in China would bring wealth and power they could only dream of.

Despite being highly trained intelligence professionals, their information had been strictly controlled over the years to the extent they were shielded from the truth. The sitting power was doing well, both in domestic and international politics. However, the intelligence and tasks set to them by Zhao Ming slowly made a chink in their armor. Now, Liu was about to bring them into the fold and set them loose with a new mission.

A secure video link on the wall-mounted screen displayed Zhang Wei and Zhao Ming, both in eastern China. Their locations were secure but undisclosed, and the encrypted feed ensured no external monitoring could compromise their conversation.

'There are traitors in Beijing,' Liu barked. 'They have undermined the sovereignty of the People's Republic, placing their personal gain above national duty. These individuals have betrayed the trust of the Party and jeopardized our unity. This is not loyalty; it is a violation of their responsibility to our nation, and their actions risk dismantling everything we have worked to secure. They must be held accountable.'

The MSS officers exchanged brief glances. One adjusted his posture slightly, his fingers brushing an unseen speck of dust from the table, while another's gaze lingered momentarily on Liu, betraying the faintest hint of skepticism. As Liu took a sip of water to let his words sink in, one officer raised a question.

'General Liu, your concern for the Party's unity is understood. May we ask if this intelligence has been reviewed at the highest levels, or are we to act directly under your directive?'

Liu held his hand up and continued speaking without addressing the man. 'The clandestine world of international cooperation has shifted. In a calculated move, the United States and the People's Republic have extended their Science and Technology Agreement, forging pathways for joint research in frontier fields. Simultaneously, a covert war against the fentanyl trade is underway, with intelligence shared between our nations to dismantle precursor chemical shipments. Military communication channels, once dormant, were revived following the Biden-Xi summit, reducing the risk of dangerous miscalculations.

'In the digital arena, our diplomats and their technology firms convene in secrecy, drafting principles for artificial intelligence governance. Meanwhile, a surge in cultural exchanges and academic programs served as a convenient pretext for operatives to build networks and gather intelligence under the guise of higher learning.'

Liu flipped open his notebook and quickly skimmed over his notes. He hesitated slightly before continuing. 'This is the new geopolitical battlefield: cooperation mixed with competition, and conflicting interests. They have allowed the Americans to exploit us, weakening our position internationally while manipulating us domestically. This level of treachery cannot be ignored, and it cannot be forgiven. It is a rot undermining our leadership, and it must be excised. Their betrayal will be revealed, and they will be punished in the same way they deal with anyone who challenges them: with death.'

One of the officers broke the silence. 'General Liu, your analysis of the geopolitical shifts is clear, and your dedication to the Party is unquestionable. May we ask if the Chairman has personally sanctioned the measures you are proposing?'

Another officer added cautiously, 'It is imperative that our actions align fully with the Party's broader strategy. Clarity on this point will ensure our success.'

Liu held his temper. There was clear skepticism

at their readiness to act without question. 'Corruption, disloyalty to the Party, and treachery have taken root,' Liu said. 'This mission to preserve the People's Republic's sovereignty comes from the highest responsibility; that's all you need to know. You were chosen because you have the skills and connections to follow through on what must be done.'

He thought for a moment before adding, 'In the garden of power, weeds grow faster than flowers. We must become the gardeners our nation needs.'

The general slid open the drawer, removed his standard-issue sidearm, the QSZ-92, and racked the slide to put a round in the chamber. He placed the weapon on the desk, its polished surface reflecting the overhead lights. His eyes narrowed as he scanned the faces of his officers, who shifted uneasily in their seats. The general drummed his fingers on the desk near the pistol. The room fell silent, save for the muffled sounds of the air conditioner. One of the younger officers shifted uncomfortably, his throat tightening. The general let out a small grunt, assured his message was clear.

He then gestured to the screen, which showed both Zhang Wei and Zhao Ming sitting patiently. Liu nodded into the camera, 'Zhang Wei, please begin.'

Zhang smiled slightly, thanked the General,

and updated the officers on his plans to take down the government. His voice came through the encrypted line clearly.

'The files I have constructed include logs of covert payments routed through offshore accounts and fabricated surveillance orders. They've been planted in secure servers tied to key figures in Beijing. Once retrieved, they will appear authentic.'

Liu then turned his attention to Zhao. 'Good. Now, Zhao Ming, what is the status of dissemination?'

Zhao Ming spoke. 'The files will be sent through whistleblower platforms and anonymous leaks to journalists and intelligence analysts. They've been timed for maximum visibility. The origin will be untraceable.'

The screen shifted to display the forged financial transfers as Zhang Wei continued. 'These documents show direct communication between the President's office and rogue CIA operatives. The evidence includes secret financial deals and surveillance directives targeting dissidents and foreign officials. This is all they need to prove treason.'

'When this data is released, those responsible for this treachery will face exposure,' Liu said. 'Their deceit will not withstand scrutiny, and the Party will take swift and decisive action to restore discipline.'

One of the officers asked, 'What if the Americans investigate and find inconsistencies?'

'They won't,' Liu said. 'By the time they even begin, their intelligence agencies will be in disarray. Congress will demand answers, their media will fuel the fire, and their own officials will be too busy defending themselves to focus on anything else.'

He turned back to the screen. 'The cyber-attacks?'

'Ready to launch,' Zhang replied. 'The targets include energy grids, transportation hubs, and financial systems. The attacks will disrupt but not destroy. Evidence has been prepared to tie the actions to the President's administration, as though they are covering up their collusion with the CIA.'

'Deploy them when I give the command,' Liu said. He turned to Zhao Ming. 'And the embassy operatives?'

'They are prepared,' Zhao replied. 'The false-flag attack will proceed, and all evidence will lead directly to the President's inner circle. This will begin his downfall.'

Liu turned to the MSS officers in the room. 'The Americans will be mired in disarray, while Beijing will confront the betrayal within. At the appropriate moment, we will act to restore order and reinforce the People's Republic's strength. This is where your years of working in the U.S. come into play. Your undercover operatives need to be on the front foot and comply with directions. From now on, take orders directly from Zhao and follow them without question. There will be bloodshed and ongoing confusion stemming from the media, but do not falter. You all have diplomatic immunity, so act aggressively and do not take a step back.'

One of the officers raised his hand. 'General, we keep hearing about a man called Mercer. Was it he who shot Liang? If so, give the order. Liang trained us well. We will hunt him down; it will be our honor.'

'By all means, I want that dog ripped apart,' the General said coldly. 'We are using every available resource to locate him, and you will do the same. If any of you catch even a trace of him, report it immediately. If you see him anywhere, no matter the location—airport, on the street, a hospital or in a church—kill him without hesitation. Is that clear?'

The elder of the four, a man with scarring on his face and an oversized gold ring on his little finger, chuckled softly. 'General, that's what we needed to hear.'

Liu looked across the table at the men; for a moment, he felt sorry that their futures in the intelligence agency were coming to an end. These men would be dangled like prey to distract the wolf. 'Do not underestimate him.

Mercer is a cunning enemy, and he will strike first if you hesitate for a moment. Failure is not an option.'

He reached into his desk once again and retrieved four cell phones and their chargers, which he slid across the table. 'Take these, keep them charged, and do not make any calls other than what is programmed in them. Only use those certified cables for charging.' Next, he produced four canvas bags, each containing pistols identical to his own, along with several loaded magazines.

The officers retrieved the weapons, each inspecting the firearm briefly for functionality. They inserted fresh magazines, checked their chambers, and holstered the pistols beneath their jackets without a word.

'That is all from me. You are dismissed.'

The officers stood, collected their phones and chargers, and left the room. Liu listened as he heard the doors outside the room clinking shut as the men passed through the security passages, then Liu turned his attention to the screen once again.

'Keep a close eye on them and ensure timeframes are well managed. Now listen carefully. Our mission is critical to the future of our nation. Effective immediately, implement the following directives: Operation Golden Root: Manipulate key economic indicators and falsify reports to the Central Committee. Target GDP growth rates, manufacturing output, and foreign exchange reserves. Ensure all data aligns with our narrative of economic instability.'

Liu studied his notebook once again, then read out his next direction. 'Operation Red Dawn: Identify and exploit existing factions within the People's Liberation Army. Focus on the Eastern and Southern Theater Commands. Spread disinformation to key personnel, emphasizing ideological differences and resource allocation disputes.'

He turned a page and skimmed over the words before speaking. 'Operation Silent Mist: Intensify covert activities along our borders, particularly in the South China Sea and near the Line of Actual Control. Increase frequency of *accidental* airspace violations and naval incursions. Provoke responses from neighboring forces without direct engagement. Remember, absolute secrecy is paramount. Any leak will result in severe consequences. Select members within the Joint Operations Command Center operate under my direct authority; leave them to me. Maintain communication silence except through our designated encrypted channels.'

The screen then went dark as Zhang Wei and Zhao Ming ended the call to initiate the coup. Liu remained seated, his eyes fixed on the screen displaying global stock prices alongside the times for Beijing, London, and Washington, D.C. He knew the two men would bypass normal procedures, issuing the orders directly to the heads of the Central Military Commission and the Central Political and Legal Affairs Commission. Any opposition to these directives would be killed immediately by Liu's comrades in JOCC, the operatives he had meticulously groomed over the years for this precise moment.

It's done, he thought. *The Party's future depends on all these years of loyalty and deception. Hesitation will only embolden my enemies.* Liu picked up his pistol, turning it over in his hands. It wasn't just a weapon, it was a symbol, a reminder of the choices he had made and the sacrifices he was willing to make. If everything failed, it would serve its final purpose.

TWENTY-ONE

Washington, D.C.—U.S.A.

Dean Jameson stood beside Mercer, watching the breaking news on the television. Over the past two days, Europol, assisted by the DEA and FBI, had arrested scores of suspects across Europe. Jameson lowered his hood and removed his cap, revealing his bald head. Mercer noted the sharp blue eyes and neatly trimmed white beard-features that once lent Jameson an air of vigor-but now only emphasized how much older he appeared with each passing day. His face was marked by deepening wrinkles, but it was the tension hidden in his eyes that revealed the sleepless nights and silent burdens he carried.

'You need to take a holiday after all this is over,' said Mercer.

'Over. It's never over. You know that as well as anyone, Mercer. Look at Europe. You can only imagine how many drug lords are already planning their next moves to take over the networks. Every few years we take them down, and like rats in a flooded sewer, they all come back in again when things settle down.'

'That's someone else's problem. We will deal with things on our side. The Mong La situation is back running at full production. No one cares about stopping the heroin and meth flooding out of the jungle, Dean. So why should we?'

Jameson didn't reply. He knew Mercer was right. Despite the surveillance and intelligence collection, there was no appetite to clamp down on those involved. 'I don't know, Danny. I am out of answers.' The CIA Director looked down at the table. His eyes shifted from item to item before his attention returned to the TV again.

'What's the latest on Connor and Faulkner? Did the arrests hold?'

Jameson, seated in a worn armchair, exhaled deeply, rubbing his temples as though the weight of the agency's troubles rested solely on him. 'They've been released on bail,' he said flatly. 'Protecting the CIA's reputation has become the priority. Both men are working closely with investigators, trying to hammer out plea deals.'

'Plea deals? fuck me.' Mercer shook his head. 'Remember Alexander Yuk Ching Ma? A former CIA officer caught spying for China. He still got ten years even after cooperating with prosecutors.'

'We are looking into it, Danny. We still don't know what their involvement was, but believe me, their life is over in terms of their career in the agency. They will be lucky to get a job flipping burgers after this.'

'You know what, Dean? I'm more disgusted with our own government than with these bastards. They're out on bail, probably sipping Cognac...'

'Look, here we go.' Jameson pointed the remote at the TV and turned the volume up. The two men were silent as the cameras captured both the U.S. President and Chinese President walking along the West Terrace of the White House, where they came to a stop at a podium. Waiting media stood patiently for the two men to give their pre-written speeches before a few hand-selected journalists could ask their questions. The Rose Garden, usually a picturesque backdrop, was now shrouded in a light drizzle as both the U.S. and Chinese Presidents stood side by side at their respective podiums. Despite the drizzle, both leaders maintained their composure, their words calibrated to calm growing international panic.

The U.S. President leaned into his microphone, his voice steady and reassuring. 'Let me be absolutely clear: the United States, including our intelligence agencies, has no involvement in China's internal matters. We respect China's sovereignty and support a peaceful resolution to their domestic situation.' He paused slightly as he considered his next words. 'Our friendship with China remains strong, and we are committed to maintaining stability in the global markets.' The Chinese President nodded in agreement, then addressed the gathered press. 'China appreciates the support of our American friends during this challenging time. I want to assure the world that the situation in Beijing is under control. The rumors of CIA involvement are completely unfounded and are being spread by those who wish to destabilize our great nation. We are handling this matter internally, and I call on all nations to respect our process.'

As the two men began responding to questions, the light rain got heavier. Dark clouds rolled across the skyline as the media huddled under umbrellas. Jameson shook his head and turned the TV off.

'Pass me the remote,' Mercer said as he checked his watch.

'Remember to wipe this place down. I'll have a team come in later tonight to remove what you don't need.' Jameson caught Mercer's eye. 'Thank you again, Danny. We both know you don't have to do this.'

'Wrong. We both know if I don't do this, our global reputation will never recover. If the cyber capabilities of what we have created fall into the wrong hands, we will be the first target of every government in the world. Our agency created this AI tool, which could easily be turned into a monster. We have ruthless enemies from inside and a suspicious Europe. If the Chinese leadership is overthrown by a bunch of Liu's henchmen, that alone could spark an all-out war. It's me and you who will be blamed. Our own people will be lining up to take us out.'

Jameson thought for a moment before putting on his baseball cap. 'You're right. It's a fucked-up situation. Damn bastards.' He then moved to the door and pulled his hood over-head. Jameson clicked on his earpiece, and a burst of static came through. He then turned to face Mercer.

Mercer pulled on a pair of surgical gloves and nodded at Jameson as he left the house. Then he quickly disassembled the TV remote, revealing its internal components. Mercer carefully removed the circuit board, which housed the key elements: an integrated circuit (IC) chip, an infrared LED, a transistor, resistors, and capacitors. He replaced the standard IC with a custom microcontroller, reprogramming it to emit a specific coded signal. The infrared LED was swapped for a more powerful radio frequency

(RF) transmitter, capable of sending encrypted signals over a greater distance. He added a small, inconspicuous switch as a safety mechanism and disguised a secondary trigger button as a volume control.

Next, Mercer prepared the receiver unit. He modified a small RF receiver module to act as the detonator's trigger, ensuring it would only respond to the remote's specific coded signal. He carefully connected the blasting cap into the plastic explosive, ensuring a secure fit. Then, he soldered the blasting cap's wires to a small circuit board containing a transistor switch. This transistor would act as the bridge between the low-current signal from the receiver and the higher current needed to trigger the blasting cap.

Mercer integrated a Bluetooth module as a secondary triggering method. He employed a frequency-hopping spread spectrum (FHSS) to resist jamming. To power the system, he installed a compact, high-capacity lithium polymer battery, chosen for its long life and small size. He added a voltage regulator and capacitors to ensure a stable operation across all components.

After reassembly, the modified remote appeared completely ordinary. Mercer tested the safety mechanism and secondary trigger, confirming their functionality without activating the device. Satisfied with the device, Mercer stood and opened the kitchen cupboards. He pulled out a round biscuit tin, its faded label still visible. He popped off the lid, emptied the last few cookies into the trash can, and wiped away the crumbs. Inside, he carefully arranged the receiver module, circuit board, battery, and the small block of plastic explosive with its blasting cap, securing everything with anti-static foam padding to prevent movement.

He drilled a small hole in the container's side for the receiver's antenna, carefully threading it through and sealing it with a dab of epoxy. Mercer attached a powerful neodymium magnet to the container's bottom with industrial-strength adhesive, ensuring electrical isolation from the internal components. After a final check, he sealed the lid tightly, confirming it was watertight. He gave it a quick once-over, verifying it still resembled an ordinary, slightly battered biscuit tin. He slipped the modified remote into his pocket, keeping it separate from the main device. The IED now rested innocuously on the table, ready to be quickly attached under a vehicle.

That's the first one, Mercer thought as he took a swig from a bottle of water before beginning the assembly on the next IED. Outside, the streetlights flickered to life, illuminating the streets and casting shadows from the cars parked along the sidewalk. When he leaned back to stretch, he could feel his back muscles ripping and joints creaking. The house was cold, almost freezing. He pulled on a parka jacket and placed a black cap snugly on his head. Satisfied with his electrical work, which was neatly laid out in front of him, he turned his attention to the weapons.

Mercer disassembled the CIA-issued Glock and, using a fine-toothed file, carefully removed each serial number on the frame, barrel, and slide. Slowly, the engravings disappeared before his eyes. After filing, he wiped down each part with a damp cloth of acetone, removing the metal filings and residue. A thin coat of gun oil, which contained corrosion inhibitors to protect the exposed metal, was applied before the weapon was reassembled. Mercer cycled the action a few times, checking for smoothness. The once-registered firearm was now a ghost, suitable for his needs. Last of all was a couple of hunting knives, holstered tightly. One against his body, the other strapped to his ankle. He stood up, squatted down on his haunches, then back up to check if his weapon placement needed to be adjusted.

Mercer's main prep was finally complete. His last task was to remove any DNA traces in the safe house. Mercer checked each room, packing what he needed into a rucksack while going over his plan. A plan he knew would likely evolve multiple times. Before leaving, Mercer moved methodically through the safe house. With a respirator covering his mouth, he sprayed a mixture of sodium hypochlorite solution and TriGene, misting every surface, from the bedding and floors to doorknobs and light switches. Jameson would have a crew of support officers swing by later, but Mercer took no chances.

Closing the back door behind him, Mercer stepped into the dark night, his bag slung over his shoulder. He walked down the driveway, pausing at the curb to glance up and down the quiet residential street. Satisfied it was clear, he made his way to the car parked a few houses down. He opened the door, placed his bag on the passenger seat, and started the engine. After a quick check of the rearview mirror, he shifted into gear and eased onto Warren Street.

The rain fell heavily, streaking the windshield as he drove through the empty streets of Van Ness. As he headed toward his objective, Mercer varied his speed, avoided predictable routes, and made a series of turns designed to expose any surveillance operators tailing him. Once Mercer was satisfied that he was alone, he merged onto a busier street, the rain hammering against the windshield as he drove toward his target.

As Mercer drove through Washington, D.C., he thought about the men and women the President would summon to his office. Motorcades would tear through the streets, ferrying the Vice President, Secretary of Homeland Security, Secretary of State, Chief of Staff, and other advisors, depending on the fallout.

Mercer instinctively recalled which streets to avoid as he changed lanes, heading toward the intersection. In his rearview mirror, he caught a flash of red and blue lights. Moments later, patrol cars sped past, trailed by a fleet of ambulances and blacked-out vans.

Washington, D.C. is alive to the threats, Mercer thought, knowing these vehicles were positioning themselves across the city, preparing for who knew what.

The roads grew quieter the farther Mercer drove from the city. This made it harder for surveillance teams to ply their trade, giving Mercer a measure of safety. The rain distorted his view through the side windows, so he rolled them down a few inches to get a clearer look at the street.

House numbers passed one by one as he neared the entrance to Kedleston Court. He pulled in a few houses down on Turkey Run Road, parking beneath a massive scarlet oak.

This operation stretched into days, each new command more challenging than the last. With every passing hour, the stakes continued to climb higher. Domestic operations always came with risks. No matter the outcome, there was always a trail of dread. Mercer had little time to process how he had ended up here.

It had started as a reconnaissance task in Mong La, adding a few names to a target list, then cozying up to Georg Schelling under the pretext of joining the Black Orchestra. Sloppy attempts to earn their confidence and gain deeper insight into the group led Mercer to assassinate Alexander West in D.C. and Hendrik in Jakarta, alongside his two bodyguards.

Mercer recalled the night Halford joined him in Myanmar. What began as a plan to cause a disturbance and gather intelligence ended in the execution of a Myanmar policeman in Mong La and the assassination of Chinese officials in a Yunnan border town. A dead American who had been with the Chinese was dumped. More recently, his boss and the Director, Faulkner, had been arrested.

Connor's arrest didn't faze him, but Faulkner's weighed on his mind. *What the hell was Faulkner playing at?*

News of their quick release didn't add up, politics or corruption, whatever the cause, there wasn't much he could do. *My job isn't politics. It's to clean up their mistakes. And for what? My good mate Edward Hobbs gunned down at home.*

Liang had paid the price for that, but Sanderson...*Rick Sanderson*. Mercer held the name in his mind, replaying the conversation he had with the Senator at New York's Metropolitan Detention Center a few days ago.

He needs to go. Otherwise, the judicial system will be played like a puppet. Mercer's hand was already on the bag, the other on the door handle. He knew there was no other way to end this.

Jagged lines of cocaine streaked across Sanderson's mahogany desk. A bottle of top-shelf Scotch stood beside a box of flash drives, while a stack of documents lay on the floor, ready to burn.

Sanderson paced between his safe and a leather satchel, pulling what he needed and sorting confidential documents for destruction. Between barking orders and muttering to himself, he was visibly paranoid. He paused to snort another line, chased it with a swig of Scotch, then returned to the safe.

Arnold Becker, who had arrived first, watched in silence, weighing his own predicament.

'Tell me again what you heard,' Becker said.

'Didn't you read my message, Arnold? It's all

falling apart. General Liu has launched his coup; he's activated all his sleeper cells.'

Becker eyed the cocaine on the table, the half-empty bottle of Scotch, and the unstable Senator pacing the office.

'Why should that concern us? We have mitigating avenues to distance ourselves from any connections. What Liu does in his country doesn't fall on us,' he said, shrugging off his overcoat.

'Aren't you forgetting our good friend Kenneth Decker? He's been in DGSE custody for days now. He rolled on us, Faulkner, and Connor too. The FBI picked them up,' said Sanderson.

Becker pointed toward the window. 'Faulkner and Connor have been released. Their roles were minor. Lucrative for them, but minor nonetheless. As you know, those two were tough nuts to crack, but we were making progress.' He exuded confidence as he turned his back on Sanderson, then settled into a leather armchair by the window. His mind shifted as he watched the heavy rain lash the glass.

'As for Decker, well, there won't be a trial. I'll make sure of that. The media will ask too many questions. The French will take a deal one way or another. His interrogation and whatever he's admitted won't hold. Decker will spend the rest of his life running, barely scraping by in Saharan Africa or Southeast Asia. If he ever sets foot on U.S. soil, there's only one place for him—federal maximum security.'

Sanderson glared at Becker. 'I'm not worried about Decker, you fool,' he shouted. 'It's the reach of the FBI and CIA. We haven't protected ourselves properly. Will Baxter, Nathan Harrow, none of them are answering my calls. I helped those men in their careers, just like I helped you climb the ladder in the DOJ.'

Becker kept his anger in check. He knew Sanderson was right. The Senator had helped many men reach top positions within the U.S. government, from the ODNI to the NSA and even the Federal Reserve. Sanderson had the best connections in D.C.

'So, what's the gameplay now, Rick?'

Sanderson took a few seconds to gather his thoughts. He walked to the window, stared out for a moment, then returned to his desk. The cocaine looked tempting, but he'd had enough. As he scraped the remaining lines into a small box, he explained what needed to be done.

'Those in the White House need to protect themselves from political fallout. With the elections coming up, there's no appetite for a geopolitical scandal, especially with the Chinese. Their President is asking ours to handle everything discreetly. If this gets out, they'll look weak. For a lot of them, it would be political suicide. Their weakness is our only advantage, and that is what we will use.'

'Behind the scenes, the White House is trying to make amends with China and our European partners. It's like a football game: too many fouls, but the referee has to keep the game going,' Becker said.

Sanderson shook his head. 'We don't have international partners. Not really. It's all political strategy. One day, they're allies; the next, they're enemies. It's like a tight-knit family. All we need to do is deny, degrade, and disrupt. Stick to the three Ds, and we'll move past this.'

'And the stack of files?' Becker asked, nodding toward the pile across the room.

'Intelligence files, payment transactions, and contacts of those involved in scientific discoveries, space programs, AI, and emerging technologies. I helped General Liu and his men establish relationships with these companies, setting up a program to streamline partnerships. If this ever got out, my career would be over.'

Becker stiffened. He shifted uncomfortably in his seat, then leaned forward to take a look. 'Whose names are mentioned in these papers, Rick?'

'Everyone you can think of. It's a mix of personal protection and leverage.' Sanderson could see the worry on Becker's face. 'Don't fret, Arnold. I'm burning them all.'

Both men turned at the sound of the office door creaking open. John Elder stood in the doorway, clutching a briefcase tightly against his chest. The thin attorney, dressed in his standard black suit, wore a gold ring encasing a single diamond that sparkled under the light. His thinning black hair was losing its battle to cover his narrow head.

A staff member ushered Elder into the office, closing the door behind him. Once inside, Elder removed his gold-rimmed glasses, rubbed his temples, and walked across the hardwood floor. Elder scanned the room. His face sagged, and the dark bags under his beady eyes matched his mood. Without a word, he opened his case and pulled out a handful of documents.

'These are all the files you asked for, Rick,' he said.

'Place them on the floor with the others,' Sanderson ordered. 'I have a fire going in the living room. These will be thrown in soon.'

Elder emptied the briefcase, placing the documents face down in the pile before taking a seat.

'I've just been going over our situation with Arnold. There's nothing to be concerned about, John. I know you would have kept tight security regarding these documents, and I trust you haven't kept any copies,' Sanderson said, pointing to the stack of papers.

'Of course not. Why would I be so foolish? You must destroy them properly. These papers contain all the evidence of corporate contracts, financial records, client-attorney communications with Chinese officials...'

'Yeah, that's great, John,' Sanderson said abruptly. 'I don't have time to go through them. Just be prepared for the FBI's counterintelligence division to start crawling up your ass, looking for classified documents. I sincerely hope you've cleaned up your office, and I sure as hell hope you don't have anything at home.'

Elder shot a glance at Becker, who was on his knees studying the files on the floor. The DOJ official leafed through the paperwork, searching for anything that had his name or office attached.

A wave of irritation filled the room. The walls seemed to be closing in. Sanderson grabbed three glasses, opened a fresh bottle of Scotch, and filled them. After passing the drinks around, he dropped into his chair and stared at the men. Becker kept sifting through the documents while Elder watched the rain streak down the windowpane.

Sanderson took a sip of Scotch and let out a quiet chuckle.

'What's so funny?' Elder asked.

'This situation. We're sitting here fretting like children. Scared. Scared of what, exactly? There's nothing to be afraid of. The rot in the government can never be cured. Our influence runs deep in every department and every city. We are untouchable. We are the government,' he said before breaking into laughter.

Elder thought for a moment about Sanderson's simple assessment before forcing a smile. More for Sanderson's benefit than his own.

Becker rejoined the men, sinking into a leather armchair next to Elder. He drained a mouthful of Scotch and stretched his legs. 'We may be untouchable, but I won't rest until Connor and Faulkner put this to bed. I don't want any nasty surprises from them. Liu needs to be removed from the country. His presence is a risk to all of us, and we have no idea what he's planning.'

'He can't do anything without our help, Arnold, so relax. Liu will go back to China when his men have toppled their leader. Which has nothing to do with us. Let's not waste time chasing our tails. Faulkner and Connor were arrested. If the FBI had anything on us, we would have been picked up long before them.'

The two men nodded, a quiet confirmation of Sanderson's assessment. The FBI would need solid intelligence before moving on high-profile individuals from two different agencies.

Becker loosened his tie slightly, a faint smile forming on his face.

'Good call, Rick. Let's drink to that. To the FBI,' he joked, lifting his glass. Despite the shift in mood, Becker couldn't shake the dread of what was coming.

Rain pounded relentlessly on the asphalt of Kedleston Court, a quiet cul-de-sac in the prestigious Langley area of McLean, Virginia. Mercer trudged through the soaked grass, his Salomon hiking boots gripping the ground as he neared the Georgian-style estate. Massive trees dotted the garden, while thick ferns lined the border between the road and neighboring properties.

Mercer found a gap in the ferns and slipped through, sprinting across the manicured English garden. He reached a set of steps leading to a terrace lined with limestone balustrades. The rain muffled his footsteps on the slick flagstones as he hurried to the large windows and dropped to his knees.

From his position, Mercer spotted several security cameras along the roof's edge, with two more overlooking the swimming pool beside a bronze fountain. Water spilled over from the downpour, splashing onto the stone base and masking the sound of Mercer rummaging through his bag for a small box. He strapped the bag securely to his back, then crept along the terrace toward the windows.

Light spilled from the house in all directions, making it difficult to stay hidden. The thought of private security patrolling the streets and spotting his car, or worse, a guard dog picking up his scent weighed on his mind.

I have three minutes to get the hell out of here. Speed beats security, he thought. A quick glance at his watch. A check for any dog bowls. Then back to the windows.

Move. Keep moving, he mumbled as rain streamed down his face and into his thick beard.

At the farthest window, he spotted a dim glow flickering against the wet glass. Peering inside, he saw a marble fireplace with a wood-burning fire, its flames curling around thick logs. A brass screen enclosed it, catching any stray embers.

Then, a figure stepped into the room.

Senator Sanderson... *You bastard.*

Mercer dropped low, waited a few seconds, and then inched closer to the window. Sanderson was an imposing figure—not tall, but he carried a commanding presence, especially to those who didn't know him. His short, black curly hair framed a face weighed down by thick, drooping cheeks that tugged at his eyelids. His portly frame was dressed in a meticulously tailored white shirt and dark pants, a charcoal gray wool cardigan adding an extra layer against the cold night.

Mercer watched as Sanderson removed the fireguard, then prodded the logs with a poker to improve circulation. Satisfied, he stepped out of the room and turned left down the hallway, disappearing from view.

'Change of plan,' Mercer murmured.

He set the box down, then reached into his jacket pocket and pulled out a small jimmy bar. He checked the old Georgian window frame for a security alarm. Relieved to find nothing, he quickly wedged his tool between the frame and the window, then carefully pressed down with all his weight. The wood crunched and cracked, followed by the sharp pop of the window latch breaking.

Mercer slid the old sash window halfway up, grabbed his box, then turned and raced to the other windows along the terrace. Satisfied that Sanderson was alone, he wanted to move fast and get the job done cleanly.

At the far end of the terrace, Mercer took a knee again. This time, when he peered through the window, he saw two men sitting in armchairs next to the glass, with Sanderson leaning back behind a large desk. Despite the rain streaking down the glass, distorting their faces, Mercer recognized them immediately.

John Elder, the attorney. Arnold Baxter, DOJ.

Those sons of bitches. This was unplanned. Fuck.

Mercer slumped onto the wet flagstones and thought about the implications of what he was about to do. Seconds ticked by as rain pelted his face. Exposed to the elements, he weighed up his options, then suddenly remembered the un-official motto of the CIA: 'And *ye shall know the truth, and the truth shall make you free.*' A smile crossed his face as he braced a palm against the slick stone, dragging his knees beneath him until he rose into a crouch. Cold seeped through his trousers as he steadied himself and stole another glance inside the room.

Elder and Baxter were in his zone. As for Sanderson...*let's see.*

Mercer set the box on the windowsill, an-gling it so the back faced the two men. He slid back a piece of plastic, exposing the safety switch. With a flick of his thumb, the device was armed.

After a final check of the room to ensure no one else had entered, Mercer sprinted to the other window and climbed into the living room. He pulled out the remote control, flicked the safety switch, then reached out the window and aimed at the box.

Mercer tapped the key to fire the IED.

Nothing. He tapped again. And again. Silence. The device wasn't responding. He pulled his arm in and gave the remote a quick once-over. It was soaked. Then he remembered the secondary trigger: *Bluetooth. Volume button.*

With a single tap on the key, a sharp crack split the night, followed by a deep thump that rippled over McLean. Seconds later, shattered glass hit the ground, followed by chunks of masonry knocked loose by the blast. Mercer immediately drew his Glock 9mm and rushed toward the hallway. He made a quick half-sweep to the left, then a fast head-check down the hallway's far end. Muffled moans and faint cries for help drifted from a door farther down the hallway.

Mercer gripped the handle and raised his weapon. He shoved the door open and stepped back, taking cover behind the wall. He inched toward the doorframe, sweeping his angles, scanning for arms or movement. A quick glance confirmed what he already envisioned. The blast had torn Elder and Baxter apart, and left Sanderson dazed and on the brink. Glass and brick fragments had shredded their bodies.

Stepping inside, Mercer instinctively cleared the room, more out of habit than necessity. Holstering his Glock, he surveyed the damage. Elder and Baxter had taken the full force of the blast. The shockwave had slammed into their bodies, inflicting blunt trauma to the chest and abdomen. Elder had shards of glass embedded in his face. Baxter was covered in deep lacerations. Blood streamed from both their ears. Their lungs were failing, their torsos riddled with puncture wounds. They had seconds left.

Then Mercer turned to Sanderson, the source of the pathetic cries for help. Blood streamed down Sanderson's face. His vision blurred, his speech slurred into incoherence. Files and sheets of paper, receipts, invoices, all evidence of corruption and deceit, lay scattered across the floor. None of it mattered to Mercer. He wasn't here to investigate.

Without a word, he grabbed Sanderson by his short, curly hair and yanked his head back. Sanderson coughed and spluttered, blinking rapidly, but his vision remained murky, the blood and dust congealing into a grimy film over his eyes. He rubbed at them but only made it worse.

'Water,' he croaked. 'Help me.'

'You think I'm here to help?' Mercer shouted, knowing Sanderson's ears were likely still useless.

From the corridor, Mercer could hear the sounds of approaching footsteps.

'Senator! Senator, are you okay?' A staff member was about to walk into the room.

'Rick Sanderson. This is Danny Mercer. I come with a message from Hobbs,' Mercer shouted into Sanderson's bloody ear.

Despite the damage and the repeated blinking that slowly brought a glimmer of light back into his eyes, Sanderson suddenly went quiet. He twisted his head toward the voice standing above him.

'*Mercer*,' he mouthed.

'Mercer, yes, and this is from Hobbs.'

Without another word, Mercer reached into his jacket and pulled out his hunting knife. With one sweeping motion, he slit the Senator's throat, then pulled him forward and plunged it deep into his back.

A staffer appeared in the doorway and gasped in horror at the sight before her. The screams would come, and they did, just after the man, clad in black, climbed out the window and disappeared into the darkness.

TWENTY-TWO

The Key Bridge Boathouse, tucked along the Potomac River in Georgetown, gave Mercer a brief refuge from the downpour and a moment to gather his thoughts. He stepped out of his car and watched the river swell, its currents rising higher up the banks, pushing toward Chesapeake Bay.

He reached into his jacket for a cigarette, then remembered he'd smoked the last one earlier. Wind whipped between the concrete pillars, scattering leaves, crushed beer cans, and plastic bags across the wet asphalt. The stench of river mud and rotting vegetation, laced with boat fuel, hung in the air. Light reflected off the puddles as the bridge creaked softly. To Mercer, it was a familiar sound, reminiscent of freezing nights huddled inside observation posts, watching the enemy.

Discomfort, boredom, and the fear of nodding

off during long, cold nights and sweltering days—hidden in vegetation, rubbish heaps, or perched on rooftops—were etched into his mind. Back then, the filth he operated in masked his scent from guard dogs. The taste clung to his throat, and nothing he did could erase it. Those memories churned his stomach. Cigarettes had helped then, a small tool to distract the mind.

Mercer pushed the memories aside and checked his watch. A crunch of gravel snapped his focus back. He turned, eyes scanning the darkness. His hand went to his weapon as a figure emerged. The silhouette sharpened, becoming more distinct.

'It's me, Dean,' Jameson said, stepping into view.

Mercer let go of his pistol and straightened his jacket. 'You're late again,' he said, more as an acknowledgment than a greeting.

'Yeah, well. I stopped at the gas station. Here, you want one?' Jameson pulled a cigarette from a fresh pack and flicked open his lighter, the flame casting an orange glow on Mercer's face.

They smoked in silence for a moment before Jameson spoke. 'Patrol cars are racing toward McLean. Reports of an explosion and gunshots. I presume it's done.'

'It's done,' Mercer said flatly. 'He had guests, which was something I didn't expect. Elder and Becker... They're out of the picture too.'

Jameson shot him a look over his cigarette before taking a slow drag. The CIA Director fell silent, lost in thought.

'I don't know how the President will handle this. That wasn't part of the plan, Mercer.'

'You're confusing me with someone who gives a fuck.'

Jameson turned sharply, his face red with anger. 'This is the U.S., not South America. You don't have the authority to run around wiping people out, Mercer. How the hell can I keep covering these deaths up, for Christ's sake.'

'Two fewer people to worry about, Dean. And besides, you called me to clean up this mess. This is what I do.'

Dean didn't reply. Mercer was right. Deep down, he and the President were more than happy to see these enemies taken off the board.

Mercer's eyes stayed on the fast-moving river ahead. He took a final drag from his cigarette and flicked the butt into the water. 'So, what now?'

'General Liu is holed up in the Chinese Embassy. We have eyes on him. Charles Clark is en route. We assume he's linking up with Liu. Clark's operational security has tightened. All we have is physical surveillance. The White House is in contact with the Chinese President. Our orders are to wait for his decision—intercept and kill, or capture.'

Mercer tilted his head, weighing the options. 'If we capture him, he'll be sent back to China. He's got a diplomatic passport. Best option is to kill him and be done with it.'

'No. That defeats the purpose of intelligence work. We need intel. This time, we stay in our lane. It's now a joint operation with the Chinese, albeit at a higher level, or should I say more trusting. And there are more agencies involved than just us.' Jameson flicked his cigarette into the river, then scanned the entrance road. After a few seconds, he spoke again. 'Zhao Ming and Zhang Wei were picked up in Beijing. Their Minister of State Security passed on his thanks to U.S. intelligence. The MSS will be turning the screws on those two. Despite the headaches they caused, their fate lies with the Chinese. The arrests must have spooked General Liu. He's running out of options unless he gets back to his cronies. His last move here was activating sleeper cells under his control. The FBI, Homeland Security, and NSA are handling that. Our hands are tied right now. It's a waiting game, Mercer. All we have is Clark and his movements with Liu.'

'Liu will step back, lick his wounds, and regroup with all his men before making another attempt at power,' Mercer replied. 'Next time, he'll be better prepared. We don't know how deep his contacts and influences go. This is our chance to wipe him out. You know that. Just give the order.' Mercer stared at Jameson.

'Fuck, Mercer. I wish you'd let intelligence operatives do their job for once...' Jameson held up a finger, listening to his earpiece. He shook his head and walked toward a black Mustang, Mercer following.

'What's happening?'

'Clark has been pulled over northbound at Cleveland Park. The FBI is handling it, and our guys are with them.' Jameson said. He held up his hand to silence Mercer as he listened to the chatter in his earpiece. 'They're searching him now. The FBI received orders to intercept Clark and find out about Liu's plans,' he said, opening his car door and sliding behind the wheel.

Jameson retrieved another earpiece and radio, its wires tangled, and handed it to Mercer. 'Frequency. November one-six-seven, Delta zero-five.'

Jameson clicked his microphone and spoke calmly to his CIA contact at the scene. 'Get the FBI to offer Clark an ultimatum. I don't care how you do it; just make sure they cooperate and let him meet Liu. Don't let him out of your sight.'

Mercer pressed the earbud into place, tuned the radio to the FBI's special operations channel, and tucked it into his jacket. 'Tell the men to gather all intel on Clark's movements and send it to me.'

Jameson nodded as he checked a message on his phone. 'Interesting. It's Faulkner. He wants to meet up.'

'What do you think he wants?' Mercer asked.

'Maybe to cut a plea deal, or maybe to expose something bigger.' Jameson checked his watch before speaking again.

'He's at the Watergate Hotel. That's only a mile from here.'

Jameson scratched his chin, thinking of his next move. 'This is good. He might have something we can use. Okay, Mercer, stay put. I don't want Faulkner spooked. Keep an ear on the comms and step in only if necessary. Let the FBI do their job. Our guys are only observing and advising; we don't have the authority to make arrests on U.S. soil.'

Mercer gave nothing away. He smirked, but it didn't show in his eyes. Jameson studied him for a second, then offered a slight wave before driving off, his red taillights fading into the darkness.

With nothing to do but wait, Mercer walked along the river, processing the night. For a few minutes, static bursts came and went, followed by short updates between the CIA officer and Jameson. It was clear that Clark panicked and agreed without hesitation to work with the FBI. The threats and lies worked perfectly.

Mercer jotted down details on a pad as he

listened to Clark sobbing through the comms, pleading with the FBI. The men weren't playing games. They quickly silenced Clark, made sure he pulled himself together, then ordered him to follow through with the original plan to meet Liu at the embassy.

Mercer made his way back to his car and got inside when a burst of static came through once more. Mike six was trying to contact Jameson.

X-Ray, this is Mike six, Target Bravo is mobile, over.

Jameson didn't reply.

X-Ray, Mike six. I say again, Target Bravo is mobile. Do you copy? Over.

Mercer froze, waiting for Jameson's reply. A few seconds passed before Mercer double-tapped his mic button, sending two bursts of static—hoping the noise would alert Jameson and force a response.

Still nothing. He started the car and thought for a moment. A sickness soon filled his stomach.

It's a trap. Fuck. Mercer cursed himself. It was clear in his mind. Jameson was set up.

I should have followed him, he mumbled, starting the ignition and racing out from under the bridge. A minute later, he turned off Virginia Avenue and pulled into the underground parking lot. The tires screeched as he took the ramp, shattering the flimsy boom gate as he sped into the garage. His eyes adjusted to the dim lighting, scanning the parked cars.

He reached the far end and circled around, his tires leaving streaks on the concrete. Then he spotted Jameson's mustang, neatly backed into its space. Mercer jumped out, drew his weapon, and ran toward it. He gripped the handle and ripped open the door. The interior light flicked on.

'Dean! Dean! It's me!' he shouted.

Jameson's head was resting on the steering wheel. Mercer tugged at his shoulder. No response. He pulled him back against the seat.

'No fucking way!' Mercer shouted.

Jameson's body was lifeless—two entry wounds to the face. Shot at point-blank range. The exit wounds had blown out a chunk of his skull.

Mercer swung around, aiming his weapon at every potential hiding spot, ready for another attack. After a quick sweep, he turned back to Jameson. There was nothing Mercer could do except check if anything had been taken. A quick search found Jameson still had his firearm, cell phone, and ID.

His radio and earpiece are missing. Fuck. He gently closed the door and walked back to his car. *The operation is well and truly screwed now.* Mercer knew the value of intelligence operations; however, this one wasn't only compromised—it was a complete failure.

In a few hours, someone would be knocking on Jameson's door to deliver the news that their husband and father wouldn't be coming home. Mercer shook his head and pushed the thought aside. There would be plenty of time to grieve. For Hobbs, and many others lost in operations over the years. The list kept growing.

With the engine still running, Mercer shifted into gear and drove out of the parking lot into the rain-soaked streets of Georgetown. His mind was in overdrive. Whoever killed Jameson had known he was in the area, and that Clark was under surveillance. The only thing Mercer wanted now was revenge. It was the only solution.

A surge of anger flowed through him, some toward himself, and some toward Jameson and his hands-on approach to the past few weeks. Despite being a CIA Director, Jameson, in Mercer's opinion, had no place in ground operations. He was acting like a young hotshot operator. That made him a target. Someone had been able to draw him out, and kill him.

Mercer's grip tightened around the wheel as he tried to dissect what had just happened and what was coming next. Driving around Washington, D.C., gave him time to think. His mind worked better when he was on the move. Turning left onto Constitution Avenue, he settled into a steady focus.

As he drove past the White House, he noticed how it was all lit up. *So many lights on, all hands on deck*, he thought, cranking up the heater. The streets were quiet, with traffic relatively light for the evening. A police car passed by, followed within seconds by half a dozen cars and then an ambulance. Everything seemed normal for this time of night.

Mercer didn't like normal. It never added up. High-ranking CIA officers weren't supposed to be arrested for treason—then walk free hours later. Something about Faulkner wasn't sitting right. *Was it really him? Or did the killer get to Faulkner first? Why would Liu need Clark at the embassy?*

'Distractions,' Mercer muttered. *Liu is planning his escape.*

Mercer checked the rearview mirror, then slammed the brakes and spun the car into a full one-eighty.

Ronald Reagan Airport, located on the other side of the Potomac River, was only a few minutes away. The traffic leading into the airport was light, apart from several taxis and limousines. Mercer overtook them all, raced the next two hundred yards, then pulled in abruptly, skidding to a halt beside the VIP area.

Before leaving his vehicle, he grabbed his bag and slung it over his shoulder. Ignoring the curious glances from bystanders, he sprinted toward the private jet service desk, scanning for a uniform.

At the departure gate, he spotted two Customs and Border Protection officers reviewing a traveler's paperwork. Mercer approached, made eye contact with one of the officers, and gave a slight nod. The CBP agent said something to his partner and walked over to Mercer.

'Can I help you with something, sir?'

'You certainly can, but I'm light on details and even lighter on time. I'll keep this brief. I need immediate contact with the FBI's Washington Field Office, specifically Special Agent Mat Donovan or Agent Sam Sullivan.'

The officer hesitated before turning his head to catch his colleague's eye.

Mercer shot a glance at the departure boards. 'I need access to the Advance Passenger Information System to confirm flight details of a high-value target wanted for the murder of a federal agent.'

This caught the Border Protection officer's attention. He pulled a notepad from his jacket pocket. 'FBI Agent Sam Sullivan, and who else did you say?'

Mercer provided the details as required and was told to take a seat while the CBP officer made some inquiries.

He made his way to the coffee machine, dropped in a few coins, and watched as a cardboard cup slid into place. Seconds later, steaming liquid filled the cup. As he reached for the cup, he noticed a pair of legs beside him.

'Mercer, Special Agent Donovan is on his way. He verified you and asked us to assist in any way we can.'

'That was quick. Good work.' Mercer took a sip of his coffee before setting it down. 'Now, get me to the hangar.'

The officer gestured toward a crew door and started walking. 'We can also reach out to the Federal Aviation Administration or the Department of Homeland Security if needed.'

Mercer kept his focus 'No, don't do that. What I need is access to the jet. I don't want this guy spooked. Keep everything normal. Make sure Agent Donovan doesn't come rushing in here wearing his FBI jacket and flashing his badge to everyone. I need to be subtle. I'll deal with the arrest, have the agent hang back in the car lot.'

The officers exchanged a brief glance before one nodded. 'Understood. I'll make the call.'

A small office sat beside the hangar that serviced private jets. A sign on the door read: Federal Employees Only. Once inside, the officer sat behind a computer and tapped a few keys.

'Sir, the passenger information system confirms your target's flight details. He's using a jet leased to the Chinese Embassy. The flight manifest shows it departing D.C. for Moscow, with a stopover in Greenland.'

Mercer nodded, piecing it together. *Russia, then back to China.*

'How long before the flight leaves?'

'The slot is confirmed for...' The officer glanced back at the screen. 'In thirty minutes.'

Mercer rotated the bezel on his watch, aligning the zero marker with the minute hand. 'Right, I need you to clear the hangar. Engineers, flight crew, everyone. Tell them there's a gas leak, or run a random drug and alcohol test—whatever it takes to get them out without suspicion. I need access to the plane to install surveillance equipment. Can you do that?'

'Give us five minutes.'

'Nice. Now step out of the office, please. I need to get a few things in order.'

Once the officers left, Mercer locked the door and set his bag on a chair. He reached in and removed a few items, placing them carefully on the desk—a slim laptop, no bigger than a tablet, a small box, a handful of tiny wireless transmitters, and finally, a compact device disguised as a standard power bank.

Mercer powered up the laptop, fingers moving swiftly across the keyboard as he launched a custom script. Strings of code flickered across the screen as his program tunneled into the jet's onboard Wi-Fi. Once airborne, the system would establish a covert access point, allowing him to monitor digital communications in real time.

Next, he focused on the transmitters, each no larger than a cufflink and designed to blend seamlessly into the cabin's interior. Once positioned, they would intercept every conversation, turning the aircraft into a surveillance hub.

The device disguised as a power bank was more than just camouflage. It functioned as a signal amplifier, boosting and encrypting transmissions from the bugs before relaying them to a secure server halfway across the world.

Mercer finished the setup and ran a final check.

Soon, he would be listening in on his target, gathering intelligence. Not that it matered much. Nothing would bring Hobbs and Jameson back.

A knock at the door signaled it was time to move. He packed his bag, slung it over his shoulder, and left the office.

The hangar was empty; its massive doors had been slid shut, and the hum of machinery and power tools had faded. As Mercer approached the Bombardier jet, he double-checked the tail number, then pulled on the door handle to lower the steps. Before stepping inside, he turned to the Border Protection officer.

'When the guests arrive, let them enter the hangar as usual. This jet needs to take off on time. It's being tracked, and we can't afford to tip them off to the arrest. Understood?'

'Copy that, sir,' he said.

Mercer nodded, grabbed the handrails, and yanked them sharply to disengage the gust locks before pulling the cabin door inward.

The cockpit was eerily quiet, aside from the soft hum of the aircraft's internal components. Beyond the pilot's seat, beneath a removable floor panel, lay the forward avionics bay.

He crouched, fished a small pry tool from his pocket, and popped the latches. Inside, a tangle of circuit breakers, relays, and flight control modules fed into the jet's electrical bus, a web of connectors routing power to critical systems. Bundles of precisely arranged wiring snaked along the avionics racks, feeding power to the fly-by-wire units, autopilot, and navigation computers. The air carried the scent of warm circuitry and hydraulic fluid.

He retrieved a custom-built IED: a slim block of Semtex wired to a modified Russian UPT-100 detonator. The device was wrapped in Mylar shielding to block radio interference and evade security sweeps. Small enough to avoid suspicion, powerful enough to turn the avionics bay into shrapnel. Mercer didn't need to blow the jet apart—just kill its brain. A well-placed charge in the avionics bay would sever the jet's flight control, leaving the pilots wrestling dead weight at 40,000 feet, a death spiral inevitable once they lost the ability to adjust pitch, yaw, and roll.

Mercer moved fast. He found the landing gear safety relay—a small switch that pulsed with 28 volts the moment the wheels locked into the fuselage. It was buried in a thick harness of insulated cables, but he'd planned for that. He pulled a multitool from his pocket and stripped a fine-gauge wire to expose a section of the relay's output line.

He uncoiled a thin copper wire and clipped a T-tap splice to piggyback onto the circuit. He tested the connection with a multimeter—no faults, no grounding issues. When the landing gear retracted, the system would send its routine voltage spike. That pulse would trip the detonator's activation circuit, starting a precise fifty-minute countdown. No beeps. No signals. Nothing detectable. Just a silent trigger, waiting for altitude.

He adjusted the delay fuse—fifty minutes. Just enough time to get the jet over the Atlantic before detonation.

Mercer wedged the IED inside the avionics bay, tucking it between a flight data processor and a cable conduit. Locking it in place with industrial adhesive, he pressed a strip of matte-black duct tape over it to kill any reflection from a maintenance flashlight.

Satisfied, he wiped the panel's edges clean, snapped it shut, and smoothed the carpeting back into place. A quick check of his gloves confirmed no fibers or residue. Nothing. With no trace left behind, he slipped out of the jet and headed back to the federal employee's office.

Moments later, the ground crew returned to the hangar, their voices breaking the silence. The aircraft staff followed soon after. From a small window, Mercer watched as the pilot completed his final walk-around, checking the landing gear, control surfaces, engine inlets, and fuselage before boarding.

At the entrance, a flurry of activity erupted. A door swung open, and two heavyset men stepped into the hangar, sweeping the area before boarding the jet. A minute passed before one reappeared and spoke into a radio.

Liu arrived, flanked by four military officers. His posture was rigid, his shoulders tight with tension, and anger hardened his gaze. It wasn't a look of defeat but one of controlled violence. His jaw was clenched. He had a briefcase in one hand and a cell phone in the other. Liu barked orders to his men, who quickly disembarked from the jet. Then he handed the phone to one of the men and motioned for him to step aside.

Mercer checked his watch. Four minutes until takeoff.

A flight attendant ushered Liu aboard while his security detail remained outside. The stairs retracted, the hatch sealed, and the ground crew moved clear. Moments later, the jet's taxi lights blinked on.

The sleek white jet eased out of the hangar. With the coast clear, Mercer left the office. He retraced his steps, slipping through an unmarked side door and merging with the flow of passengers near the private departures lounge. A plainclothes CBP officer approached, identified himself, and gave Mercer a rundown on the operation unfolding in the parking lot.

'A man named Charles Clark has been taken into custody, Mr. Mercer. Special Agent Donovan told me you would...' The officer paused, stumbling over his words. He glanced around the lounge, frowning. 'I was told you were arresting a Chinese General!' It wasn't a question.

Mercer kept walking. 'Yes. It's an ongoing operation. I have it under control.' To his right, a glass wall overlooked the tarmac. The jet taxied toward the runway. Mercer checked his watch. One minute. He sat on a bench near the window, eyes fixed on the aircraft. The Rolls-Royce Pearl turbofans spooled up, their distinct whine barely audible through the thick airport glass. The jet rolled forward, lining up on the active runway.

The CBP officer fiddled with his radio, pulled out a notepad, read something, checked his watch, then stuffed the pad back into his pocket—clearly annoyed.

His fidgeting started to grate on Mercer's nerves. Once Liu was in the air, it was over. *The job is done*, he thought.

The CBP officer stepped closer, his patience wearing thin. 'Listen, Mr. Mercer. We operate under Title 19 of the U.S. Code. It's our job to protect the nation's borders. The Homeland Security Act...'

'You're interrupting an undercover operation,' Mercer growled. 'There's no nice way to say this, so just fuck off somewhere for five minutes.' His voice trailed off as the jet raced down the runway and lifted off.

Mercer didn't even notice when the CBP officer stormed off. He stood, left the departure lounge, and made his way to the taxi rank, knowing his car would have been impounded and the parking lot was crawling with FBI.

A quick glance behind was enough.

About a dozen SUVs took up positions, blocking the exits. A news crew pulled cameras from their van while onlookers gathered, craning for a glimpse of the man in handcuffs.

The FBI had revised its plan. Someone had

overruled the earlier decision to use him as an informer. They needed arrests—someone to parade before the nation, proof that the intelligence agencies were in control.

Mercer shook his head. *Who better to use as an insider?* he thought as the taxi pulled up.

Once in the back seat, and with directions given, he checked his watch again before his mind flashed to all the men who had paid the ultimate sacrifice. Revenge didn't take away the hurt—it was simply the right thing to do.

Sussex, England

Large black ravens squawked as they fought for space in the centuries-old oak trees overlooking the graveyard. Thick, leafy branches provided some cover from the steady rain. The wind had died down somewhat but still threatened to return.

Mercer and his old friend Charlie Halford stood in silence. Fresh flowers added a touch of color against the black granite tombstone.

Fifty yards away, near the church, three black SUVs pulled up—a rare sight in the English countryside. Their engines went silent, and all doors opened in unison.

As men poured out, one man split away, making his way up to the graves. He was perfectly dressed for the occasion. A long, waterproof black coat was buttoned tightly, a thick scarf covered his neck and lower face, and a fedora was pulled down snugly, shielding his eyes from the rain. The rim obscured his face.

Mercer nudged Halford. 'Friend of yours?' he asked.

'Nope. He's all yours.'

The man followed the well-worn path, zigzagging through the graves. The damp earth carried the smell of decay. When he reached Mercer's side, he paused, staring at the grave. After a few awkward seconds, he made a sharp sign of the cross, then pivoted to face Mercer.

'Senator John McCarthy. Sorry, hard to get used to that...I'm no longer a Senator. John is fine. I'm sorry to meet you, Danny, under these circumstances.' He extended his hand.

Mercer narrowed his eyes as he put the name to the face.

He ignored the handshake. 'McCarthy...another Black Orchestra traitor. So tell me, why hasn't the FBI arrested you yet? Or have you walked free, just like the rest of them?'

Halford turned slightly to get a better look at the man. 'Want me to take care of him, Mercer?'

McCarthy ignored him.

'I'm trying to think of a good reason not to snap your neck, McCarthy,' Mercer said.

'Maybe it's because of the men I have back there?' he replied.

'No, it's because we're standing on sacred ground. This man at our feet, Edward Hobbs, died because of the group you work with.'

McCarthy glanced over his shoulder at the men but didn't signal. He turned back to Mercer. 'Past tense, Danny. Yes, I was part of some operations, but nothing related to killings. I don't expect you to believe me, so I won't waste our time trying to convince you. It's a murky world. Maybe you can relate to that.'

Neither man moved. A gust stirred the damp leaves at their feet, but they didn't break eye contact. The silence was broken only by the rustling wind through the aged trees.

'Danny, I needed to meet you face to face in case you disappear again—which seems to be a habit when you murder civilians.'

'Fuck you,' Mercer said, stepping closer, fists clenched.

'Sorry. That came out wrong.' McCarthy lifted a hand to his chest. 'Just hear me out. I'm sure you're aware of the jet explosion a couple of days ago, which...' McCarthy hesitated. 'Well, it nearly wiped out a village in northeast Canada.'

Mercer froze, realizing the flight path would have crossed that region. *Fifty minutes was too short. Bad mistake*, he thought.

Halford listened in silence, his gaze sweeping

the fields and the stone walls bordering the church grounds. He didn't know who the good guys were or what the American's intentions were. If he had to escape or fight his way out, he needed to be ready.

'The Canadian government is calling it an act of terrorism. Our government is providing as much assistance as necessary—allegedly. And the Chinese? Well, they issued a statement claiming no Chinese citizens were on board.'

McCarthy pulled a cigarette from a leather case, letting his words sink in. 'We both know who was supposed to be on that flight,' he added, testing Mercer.

McCarthy's insinuation put Mercer on edge. *I watched Liu board with my own eyes*, Mercer thought, trying to picture the jet taxiing from the hangar before he left the office. His eyes lifted to the gray clouds. 'Why come all the way to England to tell me this? What do you want?'

'Didn't your office tell you? I'm your new boss. I've been appointed Director of the CIA.' McCarthy looked over the green fields as he placed the cigarette between his lips.

Mercer glanced at Halford, who returned a blank look, then turned back to McCarthy. 'How the hell did you manage that?'

McCarthy didn't reply. He lit the cigarette and smoked in silence.

Over his shoulder, the security detail spread

out around the church, blocking the roads leading into the grounds. A couple of men scanned the fields with binoculars while another operated a drone. They all carried themselves with military precision—confident, alert, and ready to engage at a moment's notice.

'Can I have one of those?' Mercer asked, nodding toward the cigarette. He needed time to think.

More ravens settled in the trees above. The clouds darkened, the rain intensified, and the wind howled through the branches—yet no one seemed to notice.

The CIA followed a structured process. Mercer took a drag on his cigarette, trying to find the missing link—a gap in their intel cycle, or an outsourced operation. To whom? He thought about mission planning, intelligence collection, processing, analysis, and intel production.

Any challenge deemed unsolvable by the policymakers was forwarded to the Special Activities Center. The Director of SAC would consider all available options. Occasionally, if a crisis was too hot to handle, it landed on Mercer's desk.

He exhaled a stream of smoke that vanished into the wind. The game had shifted too fast. He tried to track the moves, but the board itself had flipped, and the pieces—his pieces—were gone. He had played a role, but whose?

Mercer dissected the moment, stripping away the illusions. The CIA hadn't just been compromised; it had become the Black Orchestra. The architects of chaos now sat in the Director's chair.

Smart move. No better man than McCarthy to hold the position—he had all the secrets.

Mercer took another drag, letting the burn settle. *So, what does that make me? A patriot? A pawn? Or just a weapon left on the battlefield, abandoned now that the war has changed?*

I killed without hesitation. No reports. No oversight. Just the mission. I served my country. But whose orders was I really following?

And now? What the hell am I supposed to do?

The wind cut through the graveyard, biting at his skin. He didn't show his discomfort. The church bells rang out. McCarthy checked his watch—not to confirm the time but as a signal. Somewhere, another agent was waiting. This meeting needed to be wrapped up on his terms.

Mercer ignored McCarthy's action. He exhaled slowly, watching the faint mist of his breath being shredded by the wind.

McCarthy broke Mercer's thoughts when he handed him a folded piece of paper. 'Call me when you're back stateside. There's a lot of work to do. If not, well...' He shrugged. 'Remember Alexander West, Senator Sanderson, Elder, Becker, the jet bombing—someone needs to go down for that. Homegrown terrorist. CIA agent gone rogue. Doesn't sound great, does it, Danny?'

McCarthy glanced at his men, gave a slight nod, then turned back. 'Best to stay on the inside. That way, you can find someone else to take the fall. You're good at what you do. I'm sure you'll make the right decision.'

Without another word, McCarthy walked back toward the waiting SUVs. The doors shut in unison, and the convoy rolled out, leaving behind the quiet rustle of the wind and the distant caw of ravens in the trees.

Halford let out a slow breath. 'What now, Danny?'

McCarthy's words cut deeper than the cold, sinking into Mercer like the damp seeping through his leather shoes. The sodden grass sucked at his soles, heavy with rain. He pulled up his collar, a grim smile forming as the chill settled in his bones.

'You heard the man. It's business as usual, Charlie. I am who I am.'

Halford exhaled, shaking his head slowly. 'Just like that, huh? Something tells me this is going to get messy.'

Mercer gave a slight shrug, trying not to pressure him. 'Are you in?'

Halford let the question hang. His eyes lingered on the tombstone, tracing the name etched deep into the granite, followed by the simple words: For King and Country.

Rain streamed down his face as he looked up at the dark clouds. 'You already know the answer to that, Danny.' A muscle twitched in Halford's cheek. He blinked away the raindrops and finally faced Mercer. 'This ends only one way—with them in the ground.'